The Ignatius 7

The House of Phoenix Chronicles Book III

The Ignatius 7

The House of Phoenix Chronicles
Book III

by
Kurt W. Oster

All Genders Press

an imprint of
Perceptions Press
Victoria, BC
Canada

2023

The Ignatius 7
The House of Phoenix Chronicles Book III

Copyright © Kurt W. Oster 2022 2023

All rights reserved. No part of this publication may be reprinted, reproduced, stored in a retrieval system, or transmitted in any form or by any means, electronic, mechanical, photocopying and recording, or otherwise, now known or hereafter invented without the express prior written permission of the author, except for brief passages quoted by a reviewer in a newspaper or magazine. To perform any of the above is an infringement of copyright law.

No AI training. Without in any way limiting the author's [and publisher's] exclusive rights under copyright, any use of this publication to "train" generative artificial intelligence (AI) technologies to generate text is expressly prohibited. The author reserves all rights to license uses of this work for generative AI training and development of machine learning language models.

This is a work of fiction. Names, characters, places, events, locales, and incidents are either the products of the author's imagination or used in a fictitious manner. Any resemblance to actual persons, living or dead, or actual events is purely coincidental.

Revised version published in paperback in 2023
First published in paperback in 2022 Wilhelm P. Ostir

Cover Image and Design: Margot Wilson (Midjourney)
Illustrations: Kurt W. Oster (Canva Pro)

ISBN: 978-1-998924-77-6 (paperback)
ISBN: 978-1-998924-78-3 (Kindle-book)

Published in Canada by
All Genders Press
www.allgenderspress.ca

an imprint of
Perceptions Press
www.percpetionspress.ca
Victoria BC
Canada

Contents

Heroines, LGBTQIA+, and Neurodivergence

The House of Phoenix Chronicles series continues to be an extraordinary journey throughout time and the world of fantasy. Early on, I realized that the journey in The House of Phoenix Chronicles, Volume I, *Rise of the Magical Three,* was just the beginning. With the growing success of Volume I, I understood that I had to keep things going, and ten months after the release of Volume I, it gave me great pleasure to share with all my readers, Volume II, *Secrets Echoed,* of this epic and fantastic series. Now, in the third installment, *The Ignatius 7* continues the remarkable story throughout the Arcane fantasy world and time travel.

For me, the most significant challenge growing up was reading. Although I grew up in a family of readers and academic scholars, I was not fond of books as a young person. It was not until my high school years that I began to enjoy reading and became engrossed in fantasy fiction. Then, in college, I discovered that I am dyslexic, a severe reading disability. Once I had that under control, I thrived in my college education far beyond what I could ever have expected. When I was young, my dyslexia created a significant barrier and an absolute disdain for reading. Today, I embrace my dyslexia, remember its challenges, and use it to my advantage in order to write a book that is, hopefully, friendly to readers.

As the late Ruth Bader Ginsburg said:

> Reading is the key to many good things in life. Reading shaped my dreams and reading helped make my dreams come true.

In developing the House of Phoenix Chronicles, I live by Ginsburg's words. My goal as an author is to write a series that helps open doors to many good things in life: enjoyment, happiness, amusement, a sense of awe, adventure, and an overall love for reading. At first, reading was my enemy. Coming to love reading opened the doors for many opportunities in my life, opportunities that I hope others will experience through my writing.

For me, as an author, the first question that comes up is, where does one begin? My love and passion for fantasy literature have been the driving force behind the development of the House of Phoenix Chronicles. This truly remarkable series pushes the bounds of the literary community and presents twists and turns at every step of the way. Perhaps the title of Volume IV, *Things are Never What They Seem*, best summarizes the series and my writing. I laugh about it on a daily basis because things never are what they seem in the series.

Whenever I am asked to summarize the series, I say this. As a writer, the journey of developing the storyline, the sophisticated characters, and their everyday and complex lives becomes an art form in itself. For me, telling the story was simple: share what I love, but do it with a twist. Accordingly, my love of fantasy and science fiction has allowed me to develop this exciting story where you, the reader, meet some unique characters, who are relatable, fun and serious by turns, and a storyline that is easy to follow but, at the same time, leaves mystery and questions with each page you turn.

By now, as the reader—especially if you have read other volumes in the series—you will have discovered that, throughout this series, I have changed or challenged specific traditional literary themes. In short, I wrote the series as an experiment in creating new precedents in the fantasy literature genre. Fantasy fiction allows the reader to immerse themselves in mystical worlds and unique storylines and to meet an incredible lineup of characters. As a writer, I am inspired by the world around me, by our rich history, cultures, and literature that tell of folktales, faraway lands, and incredible journeys. And, although much of the vast body of fantasy literature is grounded in the *Hero's Journey*, nevertheless, fantasy fiction is bound by some unspoken rules and traditions.

The first of these rules addresses the ways in which the *Hero's Journey* is told. The *Hero's Journey* is consistently set around themes of good versus evil, nature versus machine, bravery versus cowardice, parent versus child, and so forth. And that, unfortunately, routinely requires that female characters be cast as "damsels in distress," who are saved by colorful and daring companions, almost always men. As a gay man and the father of a teenage woman, I feel strongly that there are not enough stories with female heroines in the literary world. Thus, the House of Phoenix Chronicles series steps out of literary tradition and begins with the adventures of a young heroine and her two brothers. Their struggles with coming of age, good versus evil, love, and power shape their destinies and the destinies of their children and grandchildren to come.

As I noted in the Afterword of Volumes I and II, my writing is greatly influenced by my social sciences career. My experience working in mental health, life coaching, education, and helping the LGBTQIA+ community, combined with my love of history, have influenced my story themes, characters, and relationships portrayed in the House of Phoenix Chronicles. Volume III of the series, the one you are about to read, was actually the first book that I wrote back in 2012. I wrote this part of the series as an epic journey of characters, struggling with their identity, their family relationships, and who they were yet to become.

While these themes are echoed throughout the series, I found that, as an author, I was not satisfied to start the story in the middle, like many other sci-fi or fantasy stories in either literature or film do. Hence, I took some time over the years since writing *The Ignatius 7*, stepped back from this particular story, and created the expansive House of Phoenix Chronicles series, beginning with the *Rise of the Magical Three* (Volume I), followed by *Secrets Echoed* (Volume II). In these two books, the reader meets a truly remarkable heroine, who, along with her two brothers, navigate issues of coming of age, sibling and family relationships including the complexity and conflict of family, and the complexities of growing up in a magical family. While developing the first two books, my intention was to create a coming-of-age, modern-day hero's journey but with a female protagonist at the heart of the story. Beyond that, I also wanted to tell the story with a twist.

As readers and consumers of visual and literary genres, we have become accustomed to certain traditions in literature. One of those traditions is that the male protagonist stands at the heart of the series, usually with two extraordinary sidekicks, typically one male and one female. However, when I began developing the House of Phoenix Chronicles, I decided that although I wanted to retain the theme of the *Hero's Journey*, I wanted to do so with a twist. Instead of our hero being male, I created a heroine. Thus, the House of Phoenix Chronicles becomes the extraordinary story of the heroine Roslynn's journey. Her two brothers accompany her as her sidekicks as they discover their roots and learn about a dark family secret. I wrote the character of Rose as the second major character in the series, the first of which is Noel who is central to *The Ignatius 7* volume.

I remember reading to my daughter when she was younger, and every story was based on some form of the *Hero's Journey*, and the female characters were always portrayed as secondary and inevitably in need of rescuing. I wanted to change this image for my daughter. Thus, it was that

I created Rose as the heroine of the story, a strong female character who, by *The Ignatius 7* volume, has transitioned to become the wise elder and guide for the next hero on their journey. Initially, I envisioned her as the great sage who would guide Noel throughout his journey. But in establishing her character as the "sage," it occurred to me that it was only right to go back and write her story first. Thus, I parked *The Ignatius 7* and took the opportunity to tell Rose's "heroine's journey" story in the *Rise of the Magical Three*. Now, by Volume III, Rose has come into her own and she remains a driving force in the stories that follow. Not only that, but I developed a number of other female characters within her immediate circle who are essential to the storyline and stand as examples of what strong women can accomplish.

In another twist, that makes the House of Phoenix Chronicles different from many other fantasy novels is that it pushes the boundaries of the themes, styles, and literary traditions that characterize fantasy fiction. Actually, I was unaware that I had done this initially until it was pointed out to me in discussion (cf. The Outsider's Perspective: The Big Questions with Kurt W. Oster https://www.youtube.com/watch?v=inKzllYrlRk,) that I had undertaken two important and unique innovations that set this book series apart from other fantasy literature. First, I've been asked many times whether I realized that I had written a fantasy sci-fi fiction novel. The answer to this is yes and no. As a reader and as a writer, I always thought that science fiction and fantasy were intertwined, just set in two different environments. However, fantasy fiction is typically characterized by complex magical systems, good vs. evil, sophisticated mystical characters, a strict hierarchy of power, and high-flying action. By comparison, science fiction is generally characterized by different themes, such as time travel, psychic abilities, alternate dimensions, and advanced technologies. I transcended these expectations in the House of Phoenix Chronicles by combining the characteristics of both genres. Thus, the House of Phoenix Chronicles is a fantasy series, set in modern times, that brings together the power of magic, time travel, psychic abilities, and technology. The sophisticated characters, each with their own complex back story, have access to technology (in particular, nanotechnology) but they also have access to a complex system of magic that is interwoven with several of them having psychic abilities and/or the ability to time travel.

In fantasy, stories are routinely set in mystical times, however, throughout these stories, the characters and the storyline are set in modern times. As I developed the story, I wanted the characters to be as authentic as possible for a modern setting but also tied to a rich, complex, magical history. Throughout the series, conflicts arise between different sibling groups and/or within the family units. However, conflict is not the only thing that arises. The story touches on relationships and what those relationships mean for individuals, the challenges of expressing those relationships to others, and the journey of each individual within that relationship. The characters all have distinct identities, yet they all intermix. Within the story, themes emerge around same-sex relationships, the struggles of coming out and creating authentic LGBTQIA+ identities, and what that means within families, as well as parenting challenges for same-sex couples. These issues are addressed in subtle and respectful ways.

The third unique aspect of this series that lies at the heart of the storyline is a focus on culture and identity. Traditionally, in fantasy fiction, the main characters represent a heterosexual norm. This is also true for a few of the primary characters in the House of Phoenix Chronicles. However, in addition to LGBTQIA+ characters, I have also written characters with differing abilities, older characters, and characters from all walks of life and experience into the narrative. As an individual who identifies as a member of the LGBTQIA+ community and also someone with a disability (dyslexia), my intent is to present characters in a way that demonstrates the essential part they play in the storyline and legitimates alternative ways of being in the world that subtly differ from many currently held community values and perspectives on these issues.

Finally, the other aspect that emerges as a critical theme in the House of Phoenix Chronicles is the issue of disabilities. While I consciously wrote one particular character with varying exceptionalities, there is a second one, whose difference only came to light after I began working on the edits for Volume III. That is, the development of the character of Noel as neurodivergent was, for me, entirely subconscious. "Noel," short for Noble Elder, is one (along with Rose) of the two main protagonists in the series. Noel is the main character at the heart of *The Ignatius 7* story. Clearly, the influences of my years growing up with neurodivergent family members and my work, outside of my writing, with individuals who are neurodivergent, have had an unconscious impact on my writing. Like the heroine who is, traditionally, not at the center of *Hero's Journey* stories, neither are individuals with varying exceptionalities. But in the House of Phoenix Chronicles, Rusty, the father of Noel, is the first character in the storyline who demonstrates varying exceptionality. Rusty's character is visually impaired, and, although he cannot see, he utilizes his magic and other senses to interact successfully in the world around him. I enjoyed developing Rusty's character, and, like the character of Roslynn, he serves as one of several "sages" throughout the series who provide advice and guidance in their later years. Although Rusty is visually impaired, in the story, he does not let that stop him from becoming a pivotal force in the story arc.

By contrast, Noel presents with challenges of socialization and basically wants to be left alone. Through Noel's character, the reader experiences the struggles neurodivergent individuals often have in order to fit in, to get along, and to be who they truly are. Noel looks at the world around him differently. He doesn't enjoy socializing, and he prefers to live a solitary life that doesn't require interacting with others, particularly those he sees as less intelligent or, in some cases, not worthy of his attention. Readers will find that Noel prefers to keep a close circle of a very few individuals around him.

There is still much more to come from the House of Phoenix Chronicles. It is my sincere hope that this series inspires the next generation with a love for reading, for our fellow humans, and for the values that redefine relationships with, and acceptance of, all people.

Kurt W. Oster

Currently Available

Rise of the Magical Three (2021) **Secrets Echoed** (2022)
The Ignatius 7 (2022) **Mystical Way of Time** (2023)
Available in Hardcover, Paperback, and E-book
(www.allgenderpress.ca)

Upcoming Publications

Things are Not What They Seem (2023)
The Curpendulums (2024) **The Two Princes** (2025) **Holidays at
the Mystical Way of Time** (2024)
(www.allgenderspress.ca)

Preface

The old priory lay quiet, the rain hitting the ceramic roof tiles, bouncing off as the sound of water could be heard—drip, drip, drip. A pop breaks the stillness, and a figure appears as the pipe organ begins to play enchanted mystical music. The ruined parts of the priory reassemble as stones fly around the space. The figure watches as the stones fly around them, running their hand over the surface of the stones as each takes its designated place.

As the figure walks down the long center aisle of the priory, the stone columns rise toward the enchanted ceiling. Looking as if they are ascending into the sky, they are only lit by the glow of candlelight. Stopping and observing the place, the figure lowers their hood, revealing their distinguished elvish features and flips one of the pews as if it was as light as a feather into the others, causing them to domino.

The figure falls to their knees, screaming, as streams of magic spin around them. Their cries echo through the space as spirits materialize around the figure, observing and chattering among themselves as two comfort the figure.

Eventually, the figure nods. Standing, they wipe their face. They spin their hands in a clockwise motion, catching the magic flying around them and controlling it as it levitates them into the air. Then, they watch as the magic dances through their fingers, spinning in their hands. Finally, as the magic gains speed, flying around their hand, the elf raises their hand, projecting the magic away from them.

With the magic spinning throughout the old priory, every remaining candle explodes as everything in the space comes to life, and music begins to echo over the space from the glowing pipes of the organ. Then, closing their eyes and raising their arms, the figure allows the magic to continue to fly around them.

The water of the baptism font flies down the center aisle as fire from the candles circle the figure. The maple and birch doors of the priory fly open as leaves fly down the aisle, spinning in the wind. The wind, water, and fire encircle the figure as they tilt their head, looking down the grand aisle, as the stone floor turns to grass as flowers blossom.

Raising their hand, everything stops moving, and the priory falls silent, nothing moving, no sound. The figure spins around, observing the space as they raise their hands over their head, making a star appear that begins flying above the figure. A moment later, another star appears, flying in the opposite direction of its counterpart. Then, a giant clock appears, the stars serving as the tips of the hands. The elf spins their hands over their head as the clock flies around them and lifts them back into the air. The elf's wardrobe changes to black trousers, a white tunic and majestic purple, silver, and white cloak as the spirits bow.

Waking from his dream, a young man sits straight up in his bed as he examines his clock.

Definitions

Arcane: known or knowable only to a few people, secret, mysterious, obscure, esoteric, magical, an enigmatic mystical force in the world, heavenly or spiritual, arcane magic entails forces or phenomena that somehow transcend the natural laws that govern the world by directly manipulating unknown energies that bend the fabric of reality to create a desired effect.

Arcane of Mystical Experience: an individual of secret, mysterious and mystical force in the world that may not necessarily be magical but still transcends the natural laws that govern the world by directly manipulating unknown energies that bend the fabric of reality to create a desired effect. May include: dwarfs, vampires, centaurs, animagus, and mystical creatures. Individuals may be seen as having only a percentage of magical or mystical heritage.

Arcane of Mundane Experience: an individual known or knowable only to a few people, secret, mysterious, obscure, esoteric, a magical force in the world of arcane magic (or non-magic), entails forces or phenomena that are of this earthly world, relating to, belonging to, or characteristic of the earth, earthly, in relation to the immediate concerns and activities of human beings, resides among humans and is part of their daily life. May include: particular houses in which individuals may have grown up in the Mundane world, known to have, or having, magical powers. Includes members of the Houses of Phoenix and Pendragon. Individuals may be seen as having only a percentage of magical or mystical heritage.

Arcane of Magical Heritage: an individual known or knowable only to a few people, secret, mysterious, obscure, esoteric, a magical force in the world of Arcane magic. May include fairies, elves, and certain wizards and witches. Includes the Houses of Ignatius, Drake, Phoenix, and Knight. Individuals may be seen as having only a percentage of magical or mystical heritage.

High Arcane: an individual known or knowable only to a few people, a magical force in the world, heavenly or spiritual, Arcane magic entails forces or phenomena that somehow transcend the natural laws that govern the world by directly manipulating unknown energies that bend the fabric of reality to create a desired effect, considered to be immortal. Includes The Nobles.

Elders: an individual of High Arcane or an Arcane of Magical or Mystical Experience considered to be an ancient being through birth or lived experience, considered to be "immortal" with high levels of magic. An Elder can be a Noble, or elf of exceptional age.

Covens: a group of individuals with a shared interest of Arcane of magical experience or mystical experience. Covens live among both Arcane and Mundane.

Mundane: of this earthly world, relating to, belonging to, or characteristic of the earth, earthly, in relation to the immediate concerns and activities of human beings.

Prologue
A Unique Story

A single moment of time contained in an orb zipping around me, buzzing as it flies and then, nothing, just quietness.

Disgusting, why does the darkness always insist on attacking? Clearly, they have not learned.

Kneeling down, I place my hand over the forehead of

the dark creature, searching its mind, trying to discover its leader's next move. Lost in confusion, the creature's mind races in and out of its jumbled thoughts. Then, suddenly, I stop and open my eyes. They glow white, allowing me to retrieve the information I am searching for.

Got it. What are you up to, Merlin?

Rising, I walk across the field and start ascending invisible stairs into the sky. Walking across the stars, I peer down, watching and listening to everything, the cars bustling by below, people running, walking, shopping, everything the Mundane do, animals moving about the earth, and magic streaming through everything, giving it life but also death. Watching, I am always amazed at what I observe and, to think, I was about to give this all up.

As I stand on a star, leaning on my staff a scream echoes from the earth below. I raise an orb and it flies in front of me, lighting, revealing image after image of the darkness attacking the earth.

Tsk-tsk. This will never do. Hmm. Why is it I cannot get one evening of peace and quiet?

With that, I spin my staff, causing a grimoire to appear, the pages flipping and sand blowing out of the pages as it begins to spin around me. The star grows bright under me as it flattens into a light circle under my feet, and I disappear from the sky. In my deep casting voice, I say,

Patet.

Clear.

Stepping out of the sand cyclone, I look around as I drop the grimoire on the ground. The darkness looks up, snarling as I raise my right hand over the book and the pages fly open again, rapidly flipping and causing armies of elves, dwarves, centaurs, and vampires to emerge. The darkness screams and begins to charge, then silence falls over the land as the armies disappear back into the pages, leaving the army of the dark lying dead on the ground.

As I walk past the grimoire, it flies into the air, slamming shut and the clasp seals as it floats behind me as I step over the darkness. Kneeling for the second time, I place my hand over the forehead of another dark creature, closing my eyes, listening. A flash of light occurs as a dark creature freezes and falls to the ground, shaking. Then, the creature screams as it explodes.

Opening my eyes, I look around. Then, after examining the space, I sit quietly on a rock, looking down the cliff's edge over the sprawling urban city.

Such a fascinating place, it is a lot more active than the academy. I raise an orb that circles around, flashing, and a story begins playing, images of figures emerging from it, dancing across the sky.

Shall we see where the orb drops us? By the way, do not get used to magic. If you remember, magic is still boring, bound by rules that make no sense and limiting to one's true magical potential, but, then again, as always, it also has its moments.

❧

Let's see. Where to begin? Surely you remember our story, a unique one at that which began long, long ago. Okay, wait, more like centuries ago! To know my family, the great houses of Phoenix, Drake, Knight, Pendragon, Noble, and Ignatius is to know the story of time and magic. You see, to have any knowledge of the story I am about to share with you, you will need to know about a concept that is so strong that it has unraveled the very essence of the story I am about to tell you. To know about time is to know my family's story, but, then again, to know about magic is also to understand our story.

You see, to understand the story of time and, ultimately, of magic, you need to know about a simple but very complex word, "family." Over time, and it has been centuries, my family has fought to save the Arcane and Mundane alike. As a result, my family has been tasked with the critical, but straightforward, job of serving as the epic guardians and keepers of time and magic. Being charged with those responsibilities is a big task, which some in my family have embraced, while others, well… have not gotten the hang of it yet. I am one of the ones who has not gotten the hang of it yet, and I hope I never do.

There are certain beliefs in my family and among the Arcane. Many believe the Magical Three—or as the younger generation in our family calls them, grandmama and great uncles—were fated or, as some would say, were foretold to be the ones who would save the world and magic. However, it would *not* be until many years later that the true story would emerge and would alter that perception.

It was a story so powerful that it was hidden away and kept a secret in order to protect one child, an extraordinary child as the legends foretold. The story was so dangerous that, if revealed, it would unravel the very foundation of magical belief. But you are probably asking yourself, "How could one child unravel everything and, at the same time, need to be protected?"

Actually, it is rather simple. You see, a child who is that powerful would frighten Merlin. This particular child is not just a child. Their power is unlike any ever witnessed. This child's magic is considered unstoppable, they do not need a wand or a staff to cast magic, but to deceive enemies, they still utilize one, if not both.

Their magic is considered "unnatural." They are telepathic and telekinetic, and their magic is freakishly weird. They are a sorcerer who controls the elements and bends them to their will. While many elemental wizards and witches exist, none of them can stand against this extraordinary sorcerer. Any magic they cast against the child, or others, the child can twist and turn around against them. Magic is limitless for this child.

Take a simple spell, for example. Let's think? Hmm. Oh yes. The spell of the shining star. A simple, but effective, spell. You see when one is in a dark space, all one has to do is cast the spell, and it launches bright shining stars into the air to light the area. Simple, right? No!

You see if the child was to cast,

Lux Lumen.

Shine Star.

It would create the stars the way they are meant to be, but they would be altered, becoming exploding stars, trapping the darkness and eliminating it instantly.

That is just a mild example. So, you see the child's power is so strong that they frighten even the very Nobles and Celestials themselves. Yes, the same Celestials who are immortal and gave magic to earth by way of the Nobles.

Legends explain that the child is of Arcane blood, but, then again, they become Mundane, and yet, it is unclear, in any of the foretelling of the story to date, if the child would ever become Arcane again. However, when you have witnessed the changes of seasons and time as I have, you learn a thing or two.

This must remain a secret between us, but they do become Arcane again, and when they do, they become extraordinary. They become the way of life for all magic, and you could say that they become unstoppable.

Captivated yet? I am, like you, curious about the story of this child.

Are you here, like me, to take the journey and find out?

Ok. Where shall we begin? Excuse me for a minute. I know it is here somewhere, but where? Oh, that's right. Now, I remember.

Raising my hands, the wind begins to spin around me as I whistle.

"Fintan, old buddy, where are you?"

Quiet! Shh! Listen!

Indeed, this is truly a remarkable beast, Fintan can carry weights ten times his own, and, somehow, they always find the proper grimoire to help facilitate any story, moving it along.

܅

Hmm, this grimoire holds many unique stories but to find the right one, the point in time to reengage the story…

Oh yes, let's go back to the child's life growing up. For you see, the child grew up with great wealth, never needing or wanting for anything. Anything he needed was provided for him, but still, the child did want something. Something so powerful that money could not buy it. That something was "love."

Although he was considered rather odd, a child of the books, he was an empathetic child, who loved all things, was gentle and nurturing, and cared for his siblings even when they did not return the favor. Now, the child was so unique that the moment in time, when everything changed and the child gave up their magic and stopped being a magical Arcane, they, without realizing, became destined to be the very Mundane who would save both the Mundane and Arcane.

But, first, we have to learn about this powerful child of magic, born into an extraordinarily gifted and magical family. A boy, he is so powerful that he would rather sacrifice his own magic to live a rather ordinary life every day. But why give up his magic, you ask? Why cease to be Arcane and become Mundane instead? To date, the truth behind why he chose to give up his magic has never been revealed or understood.

But before we speak of that story, let's jump back to the very beginning. Our journey begins long ago in the English countryside. Why, you ask, would you begin the story at a time not focused on the child? Because our story is complex. All events leading up to the birth of the child, and his destiny to change the Arcane and Mundane forever, were written amongst the stars and shape the man this child will become.

❧

A great castle rises over the landscape. The towers reach for the sky and the palace grounds are beautifully kept. Outside the walls of the castle stands a small village. The villagers bustle about here and there. The lives and the times of the people prove to be exciting, and amongst the great turmoil and chaos, a king and queen come to power. The king is much loved by his people and advised by a wizard. Now, the wizard thirsted for power and became hellbent on world domination. For years, the king suspects, that his wizard friend needs to be watched closely. Concerned about the wizard Merlin's actions, King Arthur seeks guidance from the Lady of the Lake and others of Arcane blood. Arthur works in secret to ensure Merlin will never fully gain the power that he so desires.

At the direct orders of Arthur, and behind Merlin's back, Arthur's knights hunt everywhere for the Curpendulums. If found, Arthur orders that they be destroyed.

Throughout the years, whenever Merlin gets sneaky, Arthur and others close to him seek out Noble Elder for guidance. The most significant challenge comes when the great Noble Elder is, suddenly, nowhere to be found. One day, he is there and then, the next, he is gone. He simply vanishes. What complicates the situation is that no Arcane can explain where Noble Elder has gone or how to find him. Unknown to the Arcane Council, Noble Elder has a plan, one that will require incredible feats of magic to accomplish.

For you see, Noble Elder is jumping through time, ensuring the safety of the Curpendulums. Much like his best friend, Elder Yule, whenever Merlin gets close to a Curpendulum, Noble Elder, twists time in order to stop him, thus ensuring the safety of each Curpendulum throughout the many timelines.

Over the years, Merlin grows in magical strength. Many Arcane become concerned that Merlin, consumed by the need for power, will inflict immediate repercussions on those who stand against him. However, in a mere moment, everything changes when the Lady of White, the great Lady Elder herself, the mother of the Great Lady Mora, on her deathbed, foretells of a prophecy. This one prophecy will set the wheels in motion for Merlin to launch a greater rift between the Mundane and Arcane communities. Hearing the prophecy foretold by his daughter-in-law, Noble Elder leaves, jumping through time and arriving at a cave.

&

Walking into the cave, the torches explode into flames as Noble Elder approaches the great stone circle in the middle of the room. Standing at the bottom of the steps, he closes his eyes, listening. Voices speak through the wind, the chatter of the great stories of the past, present, and future. Listening closely, Noble Elder hears one name echo among the voices, all of them in unison saying, "Noel." Taking a deep breath, Noble Elder opens his eyes, then climbs four steps to a platform at the back of the cave. Turning, he examines the space. Then, walking to the pedestal, he picks up a stick and waves his hand over it, causing the tip to spark. Smoke rises into the air. Looking around, he walks to the middle of the room where he sits down, crosses his legs, closes his eyes, and levitates into the air in meditation. Continuing to listen, Noble Elder opens his eyes as five beings appear, each one made of a different element.

"Noble Elder, you come seeking answers?"

"Lady Terra Nova, my dear Lords and Ladies, I do. My daughter-in-law foretold of a prophecy."

"Ah, yes. The Grand ArchSorcerer, his name has echoed over the winds for days, the one known to be so powerful magically, that he will be able to tear the very fabric of magic apart. We know of him, great Noble Elder," the five state in unison as they sit back on their thrones made from the same elements they represent.

"He is the one, isn't he?"

"The one what, Noble Elder?" the elemental spirit, Lord O'Ryan, inquires.

"The one for whom we have been waiting. The one whose story has been foretold among the stars and planets, the one known as the Master of the Curpendulums and my successor?" Noble Elder replies.

The five elements grow quiet, regarding each other cautiously.

Finally, O'Ryan speaks. "He is the one. His magic will have no bounds. His magic will be endless. But heed this warning, Noble Elder. Merlin will push him to the point that he could bring about the complete destruction of the Arcane and Mundane worlds."

"The Lord O'Ryan is correct. However, if pushed, he is the one who could destroy magic and, thus, destroy the earth," the Lady Terra Nova notes.

"But, Noble Elder, a journey will take place, and something changes. This person will not destroy the power, instead, he will change fate with his actions," O'Ryan explains holding up an orb as the other four tap their fingertips together.

"You see, his path is unclear. Someone, or something, has messed with the very fabric of time. One path shows him saving the Arcane. The other path shows the total destruction of everything. The one common thread, in all of this, is his magic. In both paths, the magic is unlike anything ever seen or known," the five explain in unison.

"I understand. Can the destruction of magic be stopped?"

"Yes, Noble Elder. But, if pushed, Noel's actions will come at a great cost. Our old friend, you must promise us that you will protect him, watch over him, and guide him. Besides, as you noted, Noel is slated to become the Magister Elementorum (the Master of the Curpendulums)."

"My Lords and Ladies, did Elder Yule know about him?"

"Yes, of course, he did, our old friend. He knew. That is why he protected the Curpendulums. The Grand ArchSorcerer is the one true Master of the Curpendulums, not Merlin, but, as you know, the battle for light and dark has just begun."

"If he is the Master of the Curpendulums, then he truly should have the power to stop Merlin," Lady Terra Nova responds as the other four nod in agreement.

"My Lady, Elder Yule saw his magic, and Noel has the power to control them, to make them do things that not even the Celestials imagined," Noble Elder states as the Elementals begin to fade.

Lowering himself to the ground, Noble Elder rises to his feet, examines the cave as he raises his hand. A clock appears, causing the five elements to return.

"No, Noble Elder, time must not be messed with," the five elementals note, looking concerned.

"But time has been altered. I do not dare to mess with it. Even with my power, I would be afraid of shattering it further," Noble Elder notes, disappearing and returning to the park in the dead of night. It is the night, the very moment in time when Ambrose gives up his power.

෨

Sorry about that. Holding visions of Noble Elder is very difficult to manage. Where were we? Oh yes, discussing the events leading up to discovering what caused the twist to the story that no one foresaw. When Ambrose gave up his power, he altered everyone's memories. Except for his grandparents and two great uncles, everyone, including his parents and siblings, forgot that he had been born of any magical power. It would not be until four years later that it would be revealed and all of them would learn about what truly happened.

So, in that moment of sacrifice, Ambrose altered the timeline in ways no one knew or could imagine. The burden of the great hunt for the Curpendulums no longer rested on his shoulders but on the shoulders of the Magical Three, or so, everyone thought.

For, you see, no one knew that time was working overtime, changing the story repeatedly. A twist would occur. No one was aware, until after the fact, that a single individual, a wizard, would set in motion a fate so powerful that when Merlin returned and tried to stop the Arcane, he would meet a sorcerer so powerful it would shatter the fabric of all time. You see, a nifty relic exists. This relic is not just any old relic, and despite what you may think, it is not a pocket watch. We all know the watch is nifty. The new artifact that I am referencing, is something quite ordinary. Still, to a particular group of the Arcane, it is not ordinary at all. Rather, a simple snow globe holds the very essence of Ambrose's magic.

Our story begins on a cold Christmas Eve night, a fight breaks out amongst siblings. Then, one ran away, and, when he did, he chose to give up his power. Something he longs for in his life is to be "normal." Although he gave up his magic, he did not give up the knowledge he possessed.

❦

In the moment of sacrifice, Ambrose no longer exists, and he assumes his birth name of Russell, or RJ, for short, as he likes to be referred to these days. So, RJ grows up in the Arcane School of Magical Teaching; he learns everything he can of magic but can no longer wield it. He knows every spell and, to his grandparent's frustration, rejects ever taking his magic back. Countless nights pass in his teenage years, while he lives in his grandparents' household, during which he and his grandmother would have arguments about magic and its benefits or, in RJ's opinion, the lack thereof.

Although they argue, he never commits to returning to the Arcane lifestyle. So, watching from afar, his grandparents, the High King Alezander and High Queen Rose, keep him safe and teach him everything they know, so he can defend himself, even without magical powers. They hope only for the best for him. In secret, they guard and watch over the snow globe that contains Ambrose's power until on one particular evening, when time, in its ever-bizarre behavior, sets the wheels in motion to alter the story.

It is an evening that changes everything. A crash rings throughout the Ignatius manor of Zander and Rose. The suits of armor that stand quietly around the grand estate come to life, pulling their weapons as Cedric materializes in the study. Examining the room, he prepares to leave when broken glass crunches under his boot. Lifting his foot, he examines the crushed pieces of glass. They begin to glow revealing image after image playing out, then, suddenly, go out.

"Extraordinary," Cedric remarks, reaching down and picking up a broken piece of glass, examining it, observing an image, there one minute then gone the next. Then, he looks up at the fireplace mantel.

"Oh dear, this is not good. The protective charms have been shattered," Cedric says, raising his hand and reaching toward the mantel. Suddenly, realizing something is really not right, Cedric pulls his hand back and magic flies around him and throws him across the room and into the door. The protective charms in the space are activated as magic spins in the space.

Getting up, Cedric grabs an orb off the shelf next to him and drops it on the floor as two figures begin to materialize. Stepping out of the beams of light, Rose and Willow appear.

"Cedric, are you okay?" asks Willow.

Cedric nods and points at the mantel.

"My Lady, the magic the protective charms, have activated," Cedric notes, tripping over his words as Rose spins her wand, revealing an illusion mirror spell. Her eyes narrow as she points her wand at the illusion mirror field, and it explodes. The mirrors dissolve into dust as Rose examines the area.

"Gone!" she notes.

"What was that all about?" Willow asks as Rose turns and regards the two of them.

"Willow, summon your parents immediately. Cedric, summon my brothers and their spouses," Rose declares, holding up an orb as Willow and Cedric disappear. When Rose throws the orb into the air, Esther materializes.

"Good evening, Grandma. You summoned?" she inquires.

"The mantel, what do you notice?" Rose asks, pointing at the empty spot.

"The globe of dear cousin is missing," Esther replies, pulling a reflector magnifying hand glass from her pocket and examining every inch of the mantel. Then, a pop echoes through the study.

"You summoned, sis? Cedric said it was urgent," Ethan says, hugging his sister as Sebastian follows.

"Good evening. I will explain in a minute when the others arrive," Rose replies as the flames in the fireplace begin to change color and Matthew appears. At the same time, a knock on the old cupboard sounds through the room as Rusty and his wife, Meredith Ignatius, arrive.

Matthew hugs his dads as Rusty and Meredith acknowledge Rusty's mother. Then, several more pops occur, indicating the arrival of Oliver, Olivia, Ari, Amber, Hope, Theo, and Zander.

"Where is Vivian?" Rose inquires, tapping her foot. The flames in the fireplace change color and then explode, causing Esther to jump back as Vivian slides across the floor on her back, holding up her arm blades.

"Vivian?" Zander says, helping her up, her clothes charred.

Brushing herself off, Vivian says, "Thank you, Father. We have trouble on the horizon."

"What has happened?" Hope inquires, wiping her glasses and placing them back on her nose as Vivian points to the mantel, and the group freezes.

"Vivian, do you know where the globe is?" asks Rose, concern in her voice.

"I do, mother," Vivian replies, stowing her arm blades, pulling her wand, and spinning it as her clothes are immediately clean.

"Stolen. Some cloaked figure with a bad attitude, on some sort of power trip, or they just have a death wish in trying to steal that orb," she remarks, looking displeased and revealing an orb.

"You caught them?" Matthew chuckles.

"Dear cousin, while I am one of the top elf huntresses? No! But I think everyone will want to see this," she says as she holds up the orb, and it flies into the air, circling the ceiling.

Sand spins around the group and muffled sounds can be heard as they land in the middle of a street. A thick fog circles them as lights can be seen in the distance. Waving her hand, Rose dismisses the fog, and the group finds itself standing in the middle of a busy city street. As Rose walks through one of the cars that are zipping by, a hotdog stand flies by her and crashes into a car.

"What the…?" Zander turns, watching, as a cloaked figure projects various objects at the dark creatures around them, all while protecting a second cloaked figure.

"There are too many of them," the female figure notes as they point their wands at a bench, which begins to vibrate and the bolts holding it down spin rapidly and the bench flies into the advancing sea of dark creatures rushing toward them. The second figure examines the area and then, holds up the snow globe as the light flashes, then dissolves the darkness.

"Remarkable. What an interesting power," the figure remarks when Vivian appears, arm blades drawn.

"Give me that artifact. It belongs to the Queen of the Elves," Vivian demands as her blades clash with the blade of the first figure.

"Sir, I have her. Get out of here. Protect that thing at all cost," the cloaked woman declares as she flies into the air, her cloak falling to the ground, and she is transformed into a golden eagle. Stowing her arm blades, Vivian takes off after the other figure who runs into a park. The chase through the park begins as Vivian slides over the hoods of cars and enters the park, where she runs across the pond's water. Retrieving her bow and arrow from her back, she nocks an arrow and shoots it at the figure. The arrow explodes and a net appears, hurling toward the figure, which raises their wand and the net dissolves. Pulling her sword, Vivian reaches the figure. Dodging magic, Vivian flies backward as the man spins his hands, causing a field to appear and the image freezes.

જ

The group notices Rose walking across the space, the park dematerializing around them until all that remains is the cloaked figure.

"Mom?" Rusty inquires when Rose raises her hand, motioning for him to stop.

"Steal from me and an artifact of that power?" Rose remarks, her eyes narrowing on the bracelet that the man is wearing.

Zander walks up and circles the man, examining every aspect of him. Then, he too stops and notices the bracelet.

"Rose, is that what I think it is?" Zander inquires, pointing the tip of his wand at the bracelet.

"Vivian?"

"Yes, Mom?"

"How did you know about the artifact being taken?"

"Bridget saw it happen. She froze during dinner. When she finally came too and told me what had happened, I went after the man."

"Rose, do you care to explain what is going on? As the President of the Arcane, do I need to worry?" Oliver asks, placing his glasses on his nose and examining the figure.

"It appears we have a normal, run-of-the-mill, cloaked figure," Sebastian notes.

"Yes, but his cloak is made of satin and silk in the colors of white and purple, representing the light, and what is even more interesting is it appears to have gold inlay," Oliver explains, placing his monocle over his left eye while holding up the fabric and examining it closely.

"He wears the bracelet of the Elders," Ethan notes, crossing his arms and tapping his foot.

"But why at this point in time? Why now? Why steal the globe?" Rusty inquires, encircling the man.

"Zander, love, would you call your mother, please?" inquires Rose.

Zander turns and snaps his fingers and Cedric and Mora appear.

"You rang?" Mora inquires, laughing.

Then, she stops abruptly, peering past Zander, then, pushing past him. Gliding across the floor, Mora lowers herself down in front of the cloaked figure.

"Fascinating. He is dressed identically to my grandfather, the Noble Elder. But he is not Noble Elder. Far from it," Mora declares, snapping her fan shut.

"If he is not Noble Elder, then who is he?" Ari and Theo ask simultaneously.

"That, Ari and Theo, is the mystery," their grandmother explains.

"Rose, dear, unfreeze the image, please?" inquires Mora as Rose spins her hands, causing the image to come back to life. The figure backs up and looks at Mora.

Mora holds out her hand, "The globe, Noble Elder, if you would not mind?"

The figure holds the globe in their hands and raises it into the air as they start to flicker.

"He is trying to get away," Ethan and Oliver remark as the figure suddenly flies backward.

"I told you not to tamper with time, old friend," a voice says as the group stops and looks around.

"How can this be? You are dead," the cloaked figure remarks as a young man materializes out of thin air. A top hat rests on his head and a monocle is perched over his right eye.

"Tsk-tsk. I am not dead. Just ascended, and, at the request of the Celestials, back," the young man replies, smiling and holding out his hand. The young man acknowledges the group, then approaches the Lady Meredith, bows, and then rises, looking at the cloaked figure.

The young man bows for the second time as fireballs begin to fly around them and time freezes. The man is completely frozen.

"Vivian, you appeared with burn marks on your clothes? Did he attack you?" Rose asks, looking at Vivian, who nods.

Rose walks past her daughter, looking at the young man who has appeared, and turns, looking back at the cloaked figure.

"Thoughts?" Rose asks.

"He knows something that none of us know," the young man explains, now leaning on his cane, which has a giant Phoenix head on it, the eyes glowing purple.

"You are Lord Yule?" Hope inquires as Zander, Oliver, and Ethan give each other side looks.

"Indeed, My Lady," the young man acknowledges, tipping his hat. His monocle disappears as he starts walking toward the figure.

"What is your angle? The Elders are not allowed to intervene. Why now and why that globe?" Lord Yule asks, circling the figure until suddenly he stops.

"Lord Yule?" inquires Rose as she places a hand on his shoulder.

"Where is Ambrose?" Lord Yule inquires.

"Not here," Rusty responds.

Lord Yule turns, pops his cane up into his hand, and, using it, tilts his hat at the group members.

"If Ambrose is not here, then let the figure go," Lord Yule declares.

"Let him go?" Vivian inquires, confused.

"The wheels that have been set in motion cannot be stopped. Now is not the time to intervene. Let him have the globe. He would not dare use it," Lord Yule explains.

As Mora prepares to speak, Lord Yule disappears.

Spinning her hands, Mora causes the vision to spin while sand appears to encircle the group until they land back in the study.

"It appears time has the situation under control," Rose remarks, her hands behind her back, tapping her wand.

"Under control? Sis, what is going on? Is this going to be an issue of which the parliament needs to be aware?" inquires Oliver.

"Ollie, I do not know. I doubt it, but this is Lord Yule we are talking about. We know there will be trouble wherever he is," Rose explains as Mora nods.

"Mom, I cannot believe you are okay with that globe being out there," Theo remarks.

"Okay? Who says I am okay with it? But, Theo, if there is one thing your father, uncles, and I have learned over the years, it is never to challenge an Elder, particularly the Master of Time himself," Rose replies.

"I agree with your mother. However, all of you be on the lookout for that globe. Olivia, would you mind notifying your and Oliver's daughters about the missing globe. Matthew and Sebastian, get the magical investigation teams involved. I want to know everything we can learn. Report back to Rose and me. Mom, I know you're retired, but I think we may need you at the school."

"My children, not a word of this to anyone, not a word. Esther, go to the nexus. Anything, and I mean anything, weird, immediately let us know. Oliver, do what you have to keep the parliament at bay. If they do not mention anything, repeat not a word of what you saw here this evening," Zander orders as members of the group start disappearing.

∾

Ah, there you are. Interesting, is it not? Here comes the more important question in all of this, What is to happen next? Ambrose has given up his power, a mighty orb is missing, and I have always said the worst thing to do is steal from the Queen. I should know, I have done it multiple times, and, always, it did not end well.

You see, to steal from the Queen is like stealing from a bank. You don't do it, particularly if you value your magic, your life, and your sanity. But, on the other hand, the Queen does have these nasty artifacts laying around, protecting magical items and, if touched or activated, they can do some damage. One of my favorite parts of the story that I just told you illustrates why magic is a weapon, that is, when Vivian appears to be burned.

So, magic is always unpredictable. At least with time, we know that it is broken. It does not work. But magic works in odd and bizarre ways when it does work. Knowing how time works is excellent, but you become unstoppable if you can control magic and time together. Right now, there is only one who has that power. But you did not come here to hear about him, the great Noel, the successor of Noble Elder and the one who will forever shape magic and time. Unfortunately, you cannot escape him, and he is in every aspect of the story.

Knowing our story means that time, magic, and the Curpendulums are interwoven. They all interact with each other, but they also mess up the timeline. The globe taken from the Queen was the pivotal balance that keeps the timeline under control. If it is not bad enough to search for those blasted Curpendulums, now a globe with the magic of the most powerful Arcane ever is also out there.

To understand this story, we must take a journey, a simple hop, skip, and jump across time to that moment. A moment where, indeed, the story, as always, both begins and ends. Oh yes, as always, when we pick up at one spot in the story, you may remember from past stories that time is not easy to control, except with much practice. Finally, however, I have now come to understand what time is capable of doing.

Now, where to begin the story? No, no, no. You have already heard the stories of time, of the Curpendulums, of the great Magical Three. No, we need something new, something different, an incredible story. Ah, I know, the story of seven siblings.

A rather unique, but odd, group of siblings. The Ignatius 7 are an exciting piece of the story, one that is very different than many expected, but one that finished in a way not known to any. You see, the story with them is just beginning. As we begin, the seven are adults, who are going about, living their everyday lives. But we start at the part of the story that sheds light on these particular moments and events in the timeline. For you see, the seven are the future and the unique bearers of magic.

Chapter 1
The Masters of the Curpendulums and Time

Spinning rapidly in the air is a simple but unique magical artifact. A watch. Observing the space, the witch notes.

I will not be able to hold time still much longer. Keep it together, Luciana, keep it together. I have to buy them time. It is the only way to help stop the darkness. Now that I know the truth, I have to stop this madness. Time, magic, ancestors, hear me, my family's fate hangs in the balance. I need your help. I am the daughter of Time and the Master of the Curpendulums. My fathers are the greatest guardians of time and of the Curpendulums.

The hands of the pocket watch begin to slow when Luciana spins it.

No, you cannot stop. I will not let you. Timekeeper, you have played your games for years, but not this time. Magic has rules, but my family does not follow those rules. So, this time, I am in charge.

Raising her hand, Luciana spins magic around her in the Sanctuary as the hands of the watch begin spinning rapidly.

I will use every ounce of magic I possess to keep you from stopping this time. The story will play out, and you, Timekeeper, will no longer act bizarrely. My Papa and my Dad must succeed, they must stop Merlin, and you, Timekeeper, are the barrier.

Floating in the air, circling the Timekeeper Luciana begins to glow as the clocks in the Sanctuary all came to life, ticking.

Tick, Tick, Tick, Tick.

Extraordinary! Luciana thinks looking around to observe all of the clocks. With each tick, more streams of magic appear, spinning and keeping the Timekeeper under control. Suddenly, the streams explode as the Timekeeper stops and Luciana slides across the floor, spinning her hands as the clocks in the space all separate into thousands of pieces, floating in the air.

How is it that this watch is too powerful for enchantment? I have thrown every spell in the fifteen Curpendulums at it, Hmm. What am I missing? Think Luciana, think. How is it that such a simple pocket watch is the cause of the story's bizarre behaviors?

Frustrated, I circle the Timekeeper again. Then stopping, I pull my wand and speak,

Oblitero.

Obliterate.

As always, nothing, one of the most potent offensive spells around, and it does not even leave a mark. Unfortunately, this watch has become more of a headache than it is truly worth. Staring at the watch, I stop, walk over to the bookshelf, and float up to the fifth floor where I pull out a grimoire and lower back down to the floor.

Papa wrote that when he was dealing with time's bizarre and unusual behaviors, he and Aunt Citrine discovered that grandpa had made fifteen separate timelines. Pacing the floor, I review the pages as I think aloud.

"The fourteenth timeline is the actual true timeline, then the others were designed to throw Merlin off. I have the fifteen Curpendulums, but if things are to be different and we are to truly stop Merlin, thus allowing us to restore the timeline, once and for all, then I need to do the one thing that no one, not even Grandpa Yule, would have suspected."

Putting the grimoire on the table, I spin my hands in front of me as thousands of pieces of broken clocks circle in front of me. Surges of magic fly around the space encircling me, the room, and the Timekeeper. Throwing my right hand forward, the thousands of pieces merge, circling the Timekeeper. Rapidly gaining speed, the spinning pieces create a helix around the Timekeeper.

Magic may be bound by the rules outlined in the Curpendulums, but rules can be broken when needed. The Sanctuary disappears as I walk across the night sky, the stars flying around as I reach the Timekeeper. Touching the watch, it spins, flashes, then I land in a darkened room. Closing my eyes and opening them again, I light the torch basins circling the space, just by looking at them.

If this room grows any darker, there is going to be trouble. I have to keep the lights burning.

While standing in the middle of the circle, the pocket watch levitates above my hand as it slowly turns.

Magic, you have never failed me, do not start now. Timekeeper I imbue you with all the other clocks. Their magic and energy should keep you going.

The floor begins to shake under me as dark magic strikes a field of magic that the timekeeper is projecting.

Extraordinary. Now, time, you will listen to me. You are mine to control. Shall I fix this story?

&

A bone-chilling laugh echoes through the space.

"Ha, ha, ha, ha! Well, what do we have here? If it is not the annoying brat, Luciana" Merlin states, approaching me as I hold the pocket watch as still as possible, keeping time from advancing or rewinding.

"Your nightmare is what we have here," I reply, referencing the watch and smiling at Merlin.

"Child, my nightmare? Ha! My nightmare will end when you and the rest are dead, and I, the great Merlin, reign supreme, with every Arcane and Mundane alike, in shackles, bowing to me. Besides, you are growing weak. The muscles in your arm are starting to tighten. Soon, you will drop the watch. When that happens, it will be mine," Merlin remarks, raising his wand and pointing it at me.

"The watch will never be yours, Merlin."

"The pocket watch, if you please, child, and I will spare your pathetic life. You see, girl, he, whom you seek, is dead. You hold on to stupid notions of something that can never happen. This is pointless. Accept that you are the last Noble Elder, and you, like the two before you, will never stop me," Merlin says, smiling as flames begin to fly around me.

Turning my head quickly, I examined the flames, knowing all too well what it could mean when I notice a cloaked figure walking through the flames, taking various sizes, one minute they are tall, the next small, with every step they make between the flames. Spinning rapidly, the stone circle where I stand holding the pocket watch drops me in the middle of an American baseball field. The cloaked figure walks toward me. Their hand extends as the flames re-appear, circling me rapidly and picking up speed. With a flash, I am gone, flying through the flames, the Timekeeper spinning in my hands. Then, I reappear in the middle of a wedding ceremony. People get up screaming. Merlin appears, trying to grab the pocket watch but the cloaked figure's arms emerge from the flames and grab Merlin by the back of his hood, pulling him into the flames as the circle oscillates. I raise my other hand around the Timekeeper, trying to keep it safe as I land back in my original spot.

The flames reappear, circling me again, spinning quickly, creating a spiral column and flying into the sky. Watching the column, I again observe the cloaked figure walking in and out of the flames. Then, Merlin reappears, hand raised, striking the column of flames with dark magic. But it backfires and burns his arm.

"I have never seen magic like this," Merlin yells, holding his burned hand as he wraps it in a bandage.

What in the world...? I wonder, holding up my now free hand to examine the flames. Then, I notice something rather unusual about them. Suddenly, Merlin flies into the air, choking, and then, falling to the ground. Merlin scrambles to his feet. Blood runs from his nose as he observes the space. Then, wiping his nose and seeing blood, Merlin becomes furious as he spins his hands and multiple dark creatures and guards arrive.

"Tear this place apart and get me that watch! Kill anything that tries to stop you, except the girl. Bring her to me in chains," Merlin screams, wiping the blood again from his nose and stamping his foot. One of the dark creatures strikes the wall of fire as the flames protecting me explode into the air, creating a firewall. The flames spin and wrap around the creature, engulfing it as it transforms into a Mundane. The Mundane screams and runs, trying to escape.

Listening, I hear a voice talking through the wind. Then, I feel something that appears to be holding up my hand.

"It is time to let go of the watch," the wind tells me.

"If I let it go, time will shatter. The story will crash. It will never be put right, and Merlin will succeed," I yell.

"You have had faith and have done your job, protecting time. However, now it is time to channel that faith and trust," the voice on the wind directs.

"If I let go of time, I lose them all. I am doing more than stopping Merlin," I state, tears rolling down my face.

"You are afraid. You always have been. Time has played a twisted game with you. But, know this, you won't lose them because I am right here," the voice in the wind materializes as a figure, grabs my hand, steadying it, and, with their other hand, holds their palm to the pocket watch as it begins to pick up speed, spinning magic streams around it as the watch grows bright.

"How is it possible that the watch responds to you?" I inquire when the individual raises their cloaked head enough that I can see their face.

"Shh, do not say anything. I am right here. You are not alone, and you do not need to do this alone anymore. I think it's time for us to fix this story and save everyone," the figure says as I nod in agreement.

Standing and watching the cloaked figure, I look around as multiple grimoires appear, spinning around me.

"Those are not just any grimoires. They are the fifteen Curpendulums. So, Papa was right. You truly are the Master of the Curpendulums. But how do you control the Curpendulums that have yet to be discovered in the time you are from," I ask.

"Because, in the time realm, magic has no rules. We are both the Masters of the Curpendulums. There is not much that I cannot do. Besides, where do you think you get your magic from?" the figure asks, observing the darkness outside the flame column as the magical field of protection shakes.

"Is he that desperate to get his hands on the pocket watch?" the figure asks.

Merlin projects strike after strike of dark magic against the outside of the flame wall, trying to weaken it.

"General, this bores me. Bring it down," Merlin says, yawning and dismissing the wall with his hand, as an annoyance.

The dark creatures form a circle around the flame wall and start striking the flame barrier with their weapons in unison. Each strike shakes the inner circle where the cloaked figure and I stand.

"They will get through," I remark, raising my free hand as it starts to glow with an energy orb.

"They can try, but they will not succeed," the figure declares, kneeling and placing their fingertips on the ground as everything slows. The flames slow even further, to a snail's pace until they freeze. The dark creatures, outside of the field move slowly, then, like the flames, they also freeze.

"You can control time? How?" Luciana inquires.

"As I said, there is not much I cannot do with magic. It is the reason that I was not too fond of it. I have always been able to control time in bizarre and extraordinary ways. However, I never use the power of time magic," the figure explains.

"You gave up your powers because of that?" I ask, looking around in amazement as magic begins flying around me.

"I did and for other reasons. But now, I have them back," the figure remarks as the flames wrap around the frozen dark creatures and spiral up Merlin's wand.

"Now, if you will excuse me, I need to handle Merlin. Oh, and whatever you do, stay out of the line of fire of the Curpendulums," the figure warns as they raise their hands, causing the flame wall to disappear as, simultaneously, the dark creatures fly backward, exploding, and Merlin's wand dissolved.

"You?" Merlin yells, pointing at the cloaked figure, launching dark magic against them. The cloaked figure spins, their cloak catching the streams of magic flying toward them as it disappears into the fabric.

"My turn," the figure declares, lifting Merlin off the ground and lowering his hand so that Merlin hits the ground face first. Furious, Merlin gets to his feet and spins his hands as more dark creatures emerge, and he hurtles magic at the figure. Then, catching the magic in both hands, the figure spins it in front of them, sliding backward from its sheer strength as the figure absorbs the magic.

"I see that nothing has changed about you, Merlin," the figure laughs as Merlin throws blast after blast repeatedly at the figure and they catch each one, absorbing the magic.

"This is not possible. How can this be? How do you have the ability to stop me? I am the great and powerful Merlin. The greatest wizard who ever lived," he yells as the figure spins his hands, causing an energy ball to appear as he launches it at the figure.

But the orb of energy backfires, explodes, spinning magic around Merlin, seizing his arms, and binding them to his side.

"I have grown tired of you," the figure remarks, raising their hand as water flies up. Then, the figure throws their hands forward and Merlin is blasted off his feet. Merlin stands up quickly, brushing himself off. Then, he whistles, and several dark creatures emerge, one grabbing me from behind.

"General, bring the girl to me, *now!*" Merlin roars as the dark general drops to the ground, screaming as multiple grimoires strike him repeatedly.

"The Curpendulums," Merlin says as the figure lowers their hood, throws off their cloak, and raises their hands, spinning them as their eyes turn black and the Curpendulums circle them.

"Noel!" Merlin hisses through his teeth as the dark creatures all scramble backward.

Noel, the amazing Noble Elder, raises his hand and releases the fifteen grimoires. Each Curpendulum takes off, striking one of the dark creatures as Noel catches the blade of Merlin's sword in between his two palms.

Quickly, I pull my wand, running toward my dad as I blast the dark creatures, causing them to transform into Mundane.

Merlin raises his hand as the three of us teleport and reappear in the middle of a bridge, cars swerving to miss us. Merlin raises his hand, launching one of the cars into the air, and projects it at Noel. Suddenly, the vehicle shrinks. Holding up my wand, I catch the small car in my free hand, turn, and place it on the ground where it resumes full size and drives away.

"You see, Merlin, whatever you do, we have the counter for it," Noel explains as his eyes turn white and the fifteen Curpendulums fly around Merlin, creating a cyclone.

Merlin strikes the cyclone with the back of his closed fists, but the field continues to strengthen.

"You see, Merlin, each strike makes the field stronger. So, please, continue to strike it. You are just strengthening your prison," Noel explains, floating on air, sitting, smiling, while he rests his hands behind his back.

"You! I will have your head for this," Merlin screams.

"Luciana, my dearest daughter, look at me. You have done a great job, but now, it is time to go home. We have to fix the timeline once and for all. Please do not forget to gather up your cousins, and do not forget Alviss and his family. Note my dear child, our paths will cross again, and, the next time, it will be very different," Noel advises, raising his hand as the Curpendulums continue to spin. Merlin throws dark magic at the inside of the cyclone, but his magic does not seem to affect it. Noel stands, holding the cyclone in place as I run up and hug my dad.

"Good luck."

"Thank you. I have it from here," Noel remarks, raising his left hand and opening a field.

"Be careful," I say, stepping back, turning, and walking toward the portal.

"I will. Luciana, remember to get our friends and take them with you. Their place is with you. It is not here. Now go," Noel explains, turning and raising the cyclone in the air.

The winds rapidly pick up speed. As I prepare to leave, members of the Dark Council appear. Four of them throw dark magic at Noel, all at the same time, but it stops in mid-air. Confused, the four look around. Then, one of them slams into the ground as another member jumps in the air to avoid the arms that are reaching for them from the ground. Raising their wands, they attempt to cast magic but again, their magic freezes in mid-air.

Appearing was my Papa, who spins his hands, causing the dark magic to fall to the ground and dissolve. Next, the four council members spin their wands, casting dark magic. As the four Dark Council members attempt to combine their magic, they suddenly stop as everything freezes.

Looking around, I stop and raise the Timekeeper as I stroll through the space, examining the Dark Council members.

"You, sir, do not need that," I remark, taking the Dark Council member's wand. I walk toward each of the other three, doing the same thing. Holding the wands, I raise the Timekeeper next to them and they dissolve.

"Now, just a mere figment of time," I say smiling and raising my hand as I bind the four council members with magic, and then, walk over to the cyclone holding Merlin.

Observing the space, I raise my hand as the fifteen Curpendulums rise into the air, spinning.

"Things will be different this time," I say as the fifteen grimoires begin glowing.

Creo.

Create.

As the fifteen books spin, a new book materializes. I grab the new book and walk over to the four Dark Council members. Opening the book with both hands, the Dark Council members disappear as I seize them in the pages.

Closing the book, I walk toward the cyclone, raising the book, opening it again as time unfreezes.

"Luciana?" Papa yells, raising his arm over his eyes, trying to see as magic, fog, water, and sand emerge, spinning around the space.

"Dalton, do you see her?" I can hear Dad inquiring, his voice echoing through the space as lightning strikes the pages of the grimoire, burning the corners of the pages as I reach up with an orb, catching the cyclone.

"This time, Merlin, you will only be a fairytale," I remark as a giant clock appears, the hands spinning rapidly. As they slow, they slow the spinning streams of magic and sand to a crawl.

"Luciana," Dad yells as he runs up and grabs one side of the book, which the wind is snapping back and forth.

"We can stop this. We can stop Merlin. All we have to do is seize him in the pages, making him a thing of the past," I explain as lightning continues to strike the book's pages.

Dad holds tight to the other side of the grimoire and nods.

"Luciana, on my mark," Dad says and the two of us slam the book shut, sealing the cyclone holding Merlin in the pages.

Waving his hand over the book, a giant clasp appears, sealing the book. Then, holding the book in his hand, my dad raises his hand as the other fifteen Curpendulums fly into the air and disappear.

"That book should not be left out," Papa notes, approaching us, first hugging me and then Dad.

"It is good to see you, Hun" Noel replies, winking at Lord Yule.

Then the three of us teleport to the Sanctuary of Legend and Lore.

Carrying the book, my dad climbs the steps on the far side of the room, raises his hand as the wall slides open, and a small pedestal appears. He reaches in, places the book on it, and raises his hand, causing five small orbs to fall around it as the wall slides shut.

"A lore that will remain locked away for eternity," Dad declares.

"I take it that the timeline will restore itself?" I inquire, looking at both of my fathers.

"To a point. Once you return through time, the timeline will be fully restored," Papa explains.

"Well, I guess this is where we say goodbye," I remark, hugging both of them.

"Do you remember what I said?" Dad asks.

"I do. I will get my cousins, swing by to pick up Alviss and his family, and be on the way back to my own time," I reply, smiling as Dad and Papa raise their hands to open a portal.

"Oh, Luciana, you may need this," Papa says, throwing me a time orb.

"A time orb?"

"Once you have everyone, just drop it and say where and when you want to go," Papa explains as I disappeared through the portal. It shuts behind me.

"Merlin is gone," Noel remarks, smiling and kissing Lord Yule.

Suddenly, a portal flies open and Bardagul runs through.

"Lord Noel," Bardagul cries.

"What had happened?"

"It was horrible. The darkness attacked us, they shattered the timeline, and we all got separated," Bardagul replies, crying.

Noel turns, runs up the stairs and raising his hand, slides the bookcase open.

"Gone," he says.

"Then, our battle is just beginning," Lord Yule remarks.

"We missed something. Somehow, there was a hiccup. Merlin and the council got away," Noel says as he watches the Sanctuary start to freeze around him.

"Noel, it is a counter-time spell, you must…," Lord Yule begins to say, and then, he freezes.

"*Merlin!*" Noel yells, spinning his hands as the timeline starts rewinding.

"Merlin, if you want to play with time, then let's play. This time though, I am taking the story to a point, a moment you do not realize exists," Noel declares as he flies into the air, the sanctuary dematerializing around him as he walks among the stars, orbs flying around him and the Curpendulums appear, forming steps. Ascending to the top, Noel spins his hands as the stars begin to spin, and the story starts over again. Stars fly around his raised arm as he examines them. Reaching out, he plucks one out of the group

"The perfect star to begin the story," Noel says, holding the star in his hand as it grows bright.

"Fascinating, is it not? Shall we see where our story begins again? I ask because time alters and drops us in the middle of a coffee shop.

Chapter 2
The Coffee Shop

Sitting quietly and listening to the music playing overhead, I read an old grimoire. Now, don't worry, you know me, the great Queen Rose. I will disguise any Arcane book, so mere Mundane do not know what I am reading. Stopping to look over my book, I watch the rain come down as, outside the coffee shop where I sit, people bustle up and down the sidewalk, many entering the coffee shop and placing their orders. Behind a large group entering the shop, I see my guest has arrived when she pushes her way through the crowd to my table.

"Is this seat taken, My Lady?"

"Yes, Anwara, it is now. How are you?"

"Rose, my old friend, it is good to see you. I see life is treating you well."

"Indeed, Anwara it is."

Undoing her cloak's clasp, Anwara takes off her cloak and drapes it over the chair next to her. Then, she speaks.

"How are dear sweet Vivian and Bridget settling into married life? Their wedding was beautiful, fitting for a princess of the elves."

"They're doing well, Anwara. Thank you for asking."

The two smile as a server approaches.

"Morning, what can I get you two?" The server asks.

"For me, I will have a cup of black tea, with cream and sugar on the side, and for my friend, she will have coffee black, no cream or sugar," I reply.

"Of course, ma'am, I will have that right out," the server responds.

Then, as the server leaves, Anwara speaks, "I see you know my order well."

"I still do not understand, Anwara, how you can drink coffee without anything in it."

"I ask, 'How can Arcane and Mundane alike put anything in such a fascinating beverage as coffee.' But that curiosity can remain for now. I want to know why we are meeting in a Mundane coffee shop."

"Anwara, it is the furthest from the academy, and I wanted to meet in private, away from everyone."

"If that is the case, you should have just said something. Then, I would have arranged the location."

"Thank you, and while it is tempting, I cannot be in another realm and leave the academy unattended for too long."

As we speak, the server delivers our drinks.

"Thank you!"

"No problem, please let me know if you need anything else," the server responds

Then, quietly sitting back, I pour milk into my cup, followed by the sugar.

"You are quiet, and I know that look on your face. You're thinking. What is going on, Rose?"

"Anwara, do you believe that anything is possible?"

"I am a Celestial. So, yes. But is this Queen Rose asking? Is this the Headmistress Rose asking, or is this Grandmother, or Mother, Rose asking?"

"What if it was all three, Anwara?"

"What is it, Rose? I am listening," Anwara says, spinning her finger about as her coffee spins in her cup.

"His dreams are getting worse every night. I can hear them. As his grandmother, I respect the boundaries of not entering into his mind, but as the Queen, I have my duty to protect all people. So much so that I have asked Ethan to brew potions for sleeping. I've taken more these days than I care to count just to be able to sleep. I have been through every grimoire, trying spells to disconnect from hearing things, but my motherly and grandmotherly instincts are emerging. I want to run and jump into his visions to help him," I explain while Anwara sits and listens in all of her wisdom.

"Rose, this is the first time I have ever seen you like this. You don't know what to do?"

"In this case, Anwara, no, I don't."

"If it makes you feel better, Noble Elder is concerned also."

"Wait, why is Noble Elder concerned?"

"Rose, I can tell by your perplexed look that you're curious," Anwara notes, her right eyebrow raised.

"Yes, Anwara, I am. Does Noble Elder see the visions too?"

"He does but, then again, he does not. But this is Noble Elder we're talking about. Anything is possible with that man. For example, just the other day, he was rambling on about how Noel will return. But then, he speaks of a variance, an alteration if you would prefer to call it that. He rambled on about it being tied in time."

"Noble Elder rambling? That is not surprising. But him rambling about a variance in time? That does not make sense."

"Exactly, Rose. He came to us for guidance, and for the first time in eternity, none of us knew the answer, but I guess that's what makes Noel's situation so perplexing. The rules of magic have never applied."

"Indeed! But if Noble Elder also has had these visions, should we be worried?"

"You know Rose. I truthfully cannot answer that. No one can, the one person who can answer that gave up their power over six years ago."

"At this point, Noel alone is the only one who can answer that question."

"Indeed, Rose, and it has me concerned."

"You know Anwara, your daughter Meredith is also concerned."

"I know she is. Rose. I am appreciative that she has you and your son here. But, with me being away, it is difficult for my dear daughter to be Celestial and live on earth away from everything and everyone she knows."

"I thought it was bad carrying the weight of Ambrose's responsibility. No one truly understands that weight better than Meredith. Her responsibilities are far greater than any Arcane."

"About that, you are correct, Rose. Ambrose's situation is a difficult one. We thought Merlin was tough. But, unfortunately, this makes the Merlin matter look like it is nothing. Meredith will be worried sick about everything when it comes to Ambrose, and rightfully so."

"Anwara, I would not say that Merlin is not a problem. Remember, Merlin has twisted and corrupted everything. His actions have forever drastically altered the timelines and history. But I also understand from Nimuway that Ambrose can fix the echoes, the hiding of the Curpendulums, and the collective timelines altogether."

"Rose, Nimuway is correct on that, but also wrong. I do remember the concerns of both Merlin and Ambrose alike, but I also remember a time when Merlin wasn't always evil. Nimuway's love for him, has clouded her judgment. No matter what, she has always seen good in him. She struggled when he went dark. At one time, Merlin was the most trusted advisor to King Arthur and the Knights of the Round Table, but then something happened that none of us could have foreseen. The darkness corrupted him, and in doing so, we lost a genuinely remarkable wizard. But through all of this, we had gained another wizard, one of extraordinary power."

"Ambrose?"

"Yes, indeed, our dear grandson will be the one to save everyone. It breaks my heart that he wants nothing to do with his responsibility. But, Rose, I remember when days were simpler when Celestials did not have to worry about their safety. Neither did the Arcane or the Mundane."

"Simpler days? Anwara, my mother told me of them. But, then we have learned those were a thing of the past, and now, we all have to be vigilant, particularly when it comes to Merlin."

"I remember the day that Meredith told me she wanted to live on Earth. I nearly went out of my mind. The oceans rose, multiple countries flooded, I leveled several temples, and over fifty stars exploded. The thought of her living without the safety of the Celestial realm had me concerned."

"What changed your mind about letting her come here, then?"

"Believe it or not, Rose, it was you, Rusty, and, of course, Noel. I had seen a truly remarkable series of visions of you, your brothers, of dear Rusty, and Noel, coming to power. I knew if Noel were to succeed, I would have to let my daughter come to earth and become the Celestial she was meant to be."

"Anwara, answer this question. Noel is a Celestial, is he not?"

"Rose," Anwara pauses, taking a deep breath, then acknowledging, "Yes, he is. But as the head of the Celestials, I learned long ago that I could not force that responsibility on anyone. Noel's mother and my dearest daughter, Meredith, taught me that. Besides, I have learned that, with Noel, things are never what they seem.

"You reference him giving up his powers, but as a Celestial."

"Of course, I do. But that's different than any of us have ever seen. You, of all people, should know magic has and will always be bound by rules. Now, we know that your five children have broken these rules, time jumping. Also, you and your two charming brothers, the great Magical Three. But what if I told you that when the rules were written, Noel was excluded?" Anwara asks, sipping her coffee and gazing out the window, smiling. Sitting quietly, I watch Anwara as a tear rolls down her cheek.

"Anwara, if what you say is the case, then it was as if the Celestials knew of his coming."

"Yes and no. We knew of one who would be powerful. We just didn't know who they would be. However, Meredith did. Meredith has always known about Noel but has adhered to her duty as a Celestial and kept the earth safe. Somehow, it was as if she knew she would come to earth to prepare Mundane and Arcane alike for Noel's arrival. Lady Rose, I will share a story with you that no one has ever heard. It has only ever been spoken of by one person, and that was me. Meredith heard bits and pieces of it over the years, but it is time you know the truth of Noel."

"Anwara, I am listening," I reply as Anwara places her hands on the table, her eyes glowing white and everything begins to freeze. Looking around, I am amazed. Ice forms under our table as it begins to spread, reaching every corner of the coffee shop. Watching Anwara, sand spins around us as image after image plays out in the sand. The sand stops, hits the ground with a whoosh, and spreads everywhere.

Eventually, the entire coffee shop stands frozen. Anwara stands, brushing herself off and looking around. White magical streams fly around the space as her attire transforms, and she motions for me to follow her.

"I have never seen a vision like this," I say, looking around as the front wall of the coffee shop dissolves, revealing a distorted space. There, we stand in the coffee shop, and then, as we walk, we emerge into a field of snow.

"You are known as the great lady of visions, but a few of us can also control visions like you do. Who do you think taught the Arcane how to use this gift?" Anwara asks, winking as she walks in front of me, the scenery changing with every step she takes. Anwara's voice rings through the air as she begins telling a story as image after image appear in the fields around us, playing out quickly.

> *A great princess once lived. She loved and adored her people. She was considered a calm and caring ruler. As an only child, she knew her duties and responsibilities as someday, her father's throne would be hers. Then, one night, she fell ill. A week later, screams were heard ringing throughout the castle. As her ladies-in-waiting entered her room, one of the ladies threw a dagger into a dark creature as several guards and the king stormed the room and attacked the creature. At that moment, time changed, and several weeks later, it was discovered that the princess was pregnant with a child. Eight months later, Merlin was born.*
>
> *When Merlin was born, everyone rejoiced as he was a genuinely extraordinary child. The nobles, the appointees of the Celestial Council, visited the child and dismissed his power upon meeting him. They noted that he was of no concern. However, a compelling member of the Noble*

Council, a man by the name of Elder Illuminary, visited the princess several times. Over time, Elder Illuminary watched Merlin play and grow up. Finally, in his teen years, Merlin caught the attention of Balimore, which sparked Elder Illuminary's concern. So much so that Elder Illuminary kept a close eye on things.

One evening, when Elder Illuminary had left the palace, he was strolling in the gardens when a dragon appeared, soaring overhead. Now, this was no ordinary dragon, for she was the legendary moon, the majestic Dione herself. Dione was the most beautiful but also the most dangerous dragon. For you see, she was the first, the mother of the great Queen Belinda.

The dragon, in all of her magnificent power, landed and talked with Elder Illuminary. Unfortunately, Elder Illuminary was found dead in the gardens one hour after the dragon left, much to everyone's shock. Questions arose around his death, but no one could explain what had happened.

Twenty-five years passed, and the nobles went on living their lives. After the death of Elder Illuminary, the nobles were led by a new leader. Noble Elder continued to dismiss Merlin. Merlin tried to become a noble but was dismissed many times over by Noble Elder. Annoyed, the Nobles would laugh, mock, and ridicule Merlin for his feeble attempts.

While Merlin was a young adult, he continued trying to secure a place among the Nobles. It was during this time that his mother ascended to her father's throne.

Time passed, and the great princess, Phoenix, now Queen, was out in her garden strolling and looking around, when she found the necklace of Elder Illuminary. The queen knelt down and picked it up, holding the necklace of her closest friend in her hands, a tear dripping from her face and hitting one of the stones. Everyone close to her noted that, in that moment, she changed. She ran, retrieved her horse, and rode all night until she found the council chambers of the Nobles. Jumping off the horse, she ran through the archway.

"Elder Illuminary! Elder Illuminary!" she called repeatedly. As she ran through the space, she looked through

every part of the council chambers, continuing to call for him, crying hysterically. No one knew what to do. Finally, Noble Elder appeared. He had been watching her from afar.

"My lady, why do you cry?"

"Noble Elder, I am looking for an old friend, an old advisor. I found this laying in my garden next to the rose bush he so loved," the queen explained, holding up the necklace.

Curious, Noble Elder approached, and he looked at the necklace and, rather unimpressed, turned up his nose.

"It is just a necklace, my lady."

"My good sir, this is no necklace. It is the truth."

"The truth?" asked Noble Elder with an eyebrow raised.

"Noble Elder, yes! Elder Illuminary told me a long time ago that there would come a day, a single day, when magic would gain its champion. He knew of my son's dark tendencies and knew that a cure existed to stop him. And then, that night, he died suddenly. He was once a member of this council, and I hope he may have left clues with some of you. Merlin's heart darkens day by day, and I fear what is yet to come. Seeing this necklace has given me hope. It is a sign from the other realm, that my closest friend is sending word that he is alive."

"My lady, you are gravely mistaken. No such information exists, nor does Elder Illuminary."

At that moment, the queen fainted, losing her will to live. Defying the motion to stop by Noble Elder, several of the nobles approached and comforted the queen. Quietly, they helped her up and walked with her to her horse. They helped her mount the back of the horse as she clicked its side and rode off. Riding, the queen held the necklace in her hand, holding it to her chest, crying as she observed the night sky. At that moment, a star shot by her. Her horse spooked and threw her. Sitting up on the ground, the queen looked around, then she suddenly had a vision.

Within seconds, time froze around the queen and a cloaked figure approached, extending their hand, and helping her up. She took the figure's hand and rose to her feet as her attire transformed.

"You are not Elder Illuminary," the queen noted when the figure shook their head and lowered their hood. The young elf's distinguishing features, his pointed ears, his salt and pepper hair, and his goatee, were prominent. His attire transformed, and he dawned his traditional black pants, knee-high boots, white tunic, gray long-coat, and gauntlet gloves.

"No, my lady, but I am a friend," Noel stated, bowing, and kissing the queen's hand. Then, darkness appeared around them, running across the field, swords drawn, charging.

Spinning his hands, Noel summoned the stars around him and the queen. Then, the planets appeared, flying around the hill. The moon's light grew brighter as the planets circled Noel and Queen Phoenix. Finally, the darkness was lifted off its feet as it flew backward away from Noel and the queen. Furious, the darkness flew into the air creating a spinning column as it dove on the two. Raising his hand, Noel cast a light dome. As the darkness hit the dome, it exploded, dissolving instantly upon impact with the field.

Then, something that had never been seen, something that no one could explain, happened.. The dome, at that moment, grew so bright that the Celestials observed it from their realm. Noel stood on the top of the hill in a blink of an eye, the queen behind him as the great watch levitated in his hand. A flash of light occurred, and he and the queen were gone. The darkness lay dead on the ground as they transformed back into Mundane.

"Rose, you are the first Arcane ever to see that vision," Anwara notes, sitting back in the chair as the coffee shop rematerializes around them.

"So, Noel was there," Rose states.

"Yes, he was there. The Celestials also believe that the moment Merlin's mother, your great, great grandmother, disappeared was what prompted Merlin's journey to look for the Curpendulums, to be able to find her and get her back. You see, Merlin had given up trying to find the

Curpendulums. His youth had not been the most pleasant, but then, in that moment, his mother's disappearance changed everything."

"Oh my! Did Noel influence Merlin to become evil?" Rose asked.

"Yes and no. The only part I did not show you was Merlin's arrival on the hill. When Merlin got there, he ran into Lord Time Yule and the 'true' Noel. Furious, Merlin screamed and attacked them. Then, they were gone, but that is when we, the Celestials, saw the truth. You see, Balimore stood in the distance, casting the images of Noel and Lord Time Yule."

"Balimore is the puppet master behind all of this," I note.

"Yes. We discovered that Balimore had been the one causing problems for years. The Celestials believe that he may be the reason that everything has happened the way it has.

As we sit and talk, a commotion is heard outside the coffee shop. When Anwara motions with her head, I turn to look. The darkness is moving down the street toward the coffee shop until multiple Arcane materialize in front of them, casting magic against the advancing darkness.

"Anwara, we have to get you out of here quickly?"

With that, I raise my wand and a portal flies open. A few of the staff members of the coffee shop reveal that they are Arcane by raising their wands, quickly casting fields of protection as other staff members quickly hide the Mundane under the counter.

"You two, block the windows, and you, sir, if you can, cover the door," I order as Anwara stands behind me.

"I have never seen the darkness like this. They are different, Rose. It is as if they are possessed by incubuses."

"Well, you are not staying to find out."

Suddenly, an explosion in the middle of the street occurs as Zander, Oliver, and Ethan arrive and the darkness flies backward, many trying to escape quickly.

"Anwara, let's get you out of here."

"Rose, I'll give you this much. Noel will return. He will be opposed to it, but he will return. And, this time, things will be different, very different. You must protect him, continue to guide him. Tell my daughter that I will see her soon."

With that, Anwara raises her cloak hood and steps through the portal as it flies shut. No sooner do I capture the portal in my hands, sealing it thoroughly, than the darkness explodes into the coffee shop window and glass flies inward. Spinning my wand, the glass dissolves. Darkness enters the space as my wand lights, and streams of magic explode around the space. The darkness lunges for me but falls to the floor and dissolves. Oliver stands with an arm extended, wand in hand.

"Sis!"

"Dear Oliver, so good to see you."

"Get your stuff, and let's go. The magical law enforcement teams are arriving."

Turning, I reach down to grab my bag. I pick it up but find it heavier than usual. Flipping the flap of my shoulder bag back, I noticed a new grimoire. I flip the flap shut as Oliver extends his hands as Ethan and Zander approach. Grabbing Oliver's hand, we disappear and arrive back at the Ignatius' manor.

Cedric is standing in the grand entryway, arms crossed as he taps his foot.

"I was concerned that you four had been captured, and I would have to send in the cavalry."

"Cedric, we are fine, but thank you," I acknowledge, hugging him.

"Now that you are safe, I am heading to Parliament Hall to monitor the darkness," Oliver notes.

"Keep us posted, please," I ask as Oliver nods and disappears.

"I am heading back to the school. I left the science club with Lady Marybelle. I just hope she has not brought the science books to life. On that note, before I go, do you need anything?" Ethan inquires.

"No, we are good, and thank you," I reply, hugging him as he disappears.

"You okay?"

"I am fine, Zander, just annoyed with the darkness."

"When Esther sent word, we came immediately."

"I appreciate it. I wish I had had more time."

"Rose, how did your meeting with Anwara go?"

"Fine, until we were interrupted. Our conversation was getting… well, interesting."

"Did you learn anything?"

"Zander, love, please. This is Anwara we are talking about. She always provides useful insight on things. As always, vague or mysterious, but that is Anwara"

We walk down the hall to the back sunporch when, suddenly, a pop rings through the space, and our daughter, Hope, arrives.

"Mother, Father, good to see you both. The Aelfdene Council is convening."

"You two go. I have some work I need to do," I reply.

"Are you sure?" Zander asks.

"Yes, you and Hope go. Send my apologies and let them know that I am traveling," I say as Hope and Zander disappear on the spot.

Turning, I walk toward the study, push open the giant doors, and set down my bag on my desk. Opening the bag, I retrieve the grimoire and turn it over in my hand. Then, suddenly, I am startled.

"Sorry, my lady. I brought your afternoon tea," Cedric acknowledges, placing the tray on the credenza and walking toward my desk to look at the grimoire. Reaching into his vest pocket, he retrieves his monocle and places it over his right eye.

"I thought I read the title properly," he remarks.

"Thoughts?"

"I take it that Anwara gave you this grimoire?"

"Yes, Cedric, she did."

"Wasn't this stolen from the library nearly a decade ago?"

"Yes, but now we have it back. The *Chronica Senioris* (*The Chronicle of the Elders*)," I note, holding the grimoire.

"My lady, if Lady Anwara had it, I am sure there is something in the writing that we have simply missed. Otherwise, why would she take such a grimoire?"

"I am sure there is something we missed. If she had it, then I need to review it again. Cedric, I will be reading for the afternoon. Please let me know when dinner is ready."

"Of course, if any updates come in, I will keep you informed."

As I walk toward the credenza, the teapot flies into the air and pours tea into my cup as I catch the saucer and cup levitating across the room. I sit down in the old, overstuffed armchair and begin to read. The sun in the afternoon sky lowers as the moon rises into the sky and a knock sounds at the door.

"Hey, good evening."

"Good evening, love," I reply, yawning and closing the grimoire.

"Cedric says that dinner is ready. He told me what you were reading, and I figured that I would give you a little more time," Zander acknowledges.

"Thank you. I have poured through this grimoire and read every story, and I do not understand why Anwara would have taken it. I must be missing something," I explain as Zander stops and nods towards my desk.

"Why is the orb for your office at the school glowing?" Zander asks as we both approach it. Picking up the orb, I spin my hand over it, then notice that defensive lightfields have been activated around my office.

"Zander, we have a security breach," I note, raising my hands as the two of us try to teleport.

"That normally works," Zander remarks.

"Give me your hands, and hold on," I say as our eyes turn gray, and we teleport to the school, landing just outside of my study.

"Our grandchildren are grounded over this! Then, I will unground them and ground them again, their descendants, and their descendants' children."

"Rose, why would they lock down the study?"

"Zander, love, I am sure your guess is as good as mine at this point."

An hour earlier in the evening, Willow sits quietly. Raising her quill, she begins writing. Then she stops, raises her hand, and six balls of light fly into the air.

"Summon them. I need to speak with all five of them. Go! Miss Pixie, wait. Go check on Ambrose, but do not bother him," Willow demands as Ms. Pixie flies out of the window. Placing her quill back on the paper, she begins writing again.

Chapter 3
Willow's Journal I

Dear Journal,

The time has come to speak and write of many things again. Where does one begin to share such events of one's life or day? As always, I struggle to find the words to put on your pages.

As you know, I adore my job here at the academy, life continues to be good to me, and I continue to grow in my magic with each passing day. Father and Mother note that learning magic is a lifelong process.

As always, five of my six siblings are close by or up to no good. Isabella is busy with her two charming boys, my dear nephews, and Sophia and Kells are at the Council of Aelfdene, carrying out their duties. So naturally, the elves look to them for guidance. But then, there are dear Michael and Pete. It seems that trouble always seems to find them. That is the part that continues to remain unclear. The two are so much like Great Uncles Ethan and Oliver, who have a knack for getting themselves into trouble. That is Peter and Michael to a tee.

Then, of course, there is dear Ambrose. Where to even begin? I love my dear brother, but I wish the others could see what I see in him. He is truly extraordinary. I wish he was around the other day when I found an interesting text.

In my studies, I have recently come across an interesting piece of magic. Actually, calling it "interesting" is not correct. Let me think! It is a rather peculiar piece of magic. You see, time is constantly changing and in ways unexpected. However, Grandma and Grandpa are concerned that time has never changed like this before and at an alarming speed. It is altering, at various moments, in one day. We re-live that exact moment multiple times without any explanation. It is as if time is skipping, But why? If Ambrose was here, he would claim that he does not know, but then, would somehow find the answer.

Right now, it is as if time has changed around us without warning, continuing to alter its path. My siblings and I feel the change, but it leaves many questions, some that we can answer, but others that we cannot. Time has changed so much that it has altered everything it has touched, including our families and the Ignatius rose bush. But why? What does the simple family rose bush have to do with anything? Now, I know that time is bizarre. But I have to ask, why pick a rose bush to alter? It makes no sense. Indeed, this is perplexing. But it is also fascinating in some curious way. For magic, to pick a single item, such as a rose bush, can mean one of several things. I wonder if it is a sign of things to come.

Further, in examining one of the orbs from the rose bush, I discovered a cloaked figure walking across the air, grimoires forming under them as the stars spun around them in the night sky. Magic responded to them in a perplexing way. You see, the magic flying around them was that of elemental magic—earth, fire, water, wind, ether, and spirit. The figure seemed to control the elements and all magic with each step they took.

It appears to be a particularly fascinating figure of interest, about whom Grandmother and I have studied and learned everything we could. It has been our hope for years that this figure will return to power. However, while the figure walks in the image observed in the orb, darkness surrounds them.

Then, suddenly, a flash of light, then nothing. They were gone. The orb goes out. This is interesting. If what I have witnessed is true, then my summoning of the siblings is necessary. If time is sharing a story about a figure among the stars, it can only mean one thing.

Yes, indeed, I wonder if it can be. Has the time come to restore magic to its previous glory? Could it be that Noel is coming to power? Hmm. Indeed, it is time to summon the others and explore time!

~Willow

Chapter 4
A Twisted Beginning

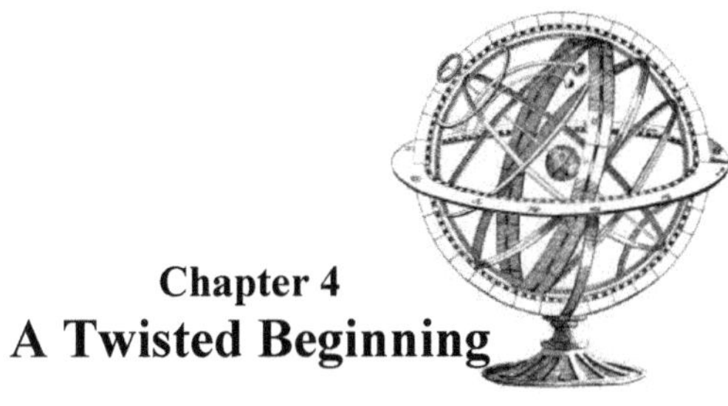

"Ugh, are you kidding me?" complains Michael, holding up his wet cloak sleeves as he stands in the middle of the giant study.

"Again, how do you always get wet?" Pete asks, laughing as he sits down on the couch and puts his boots up on the armrest.

"Every time I teleport, I swear I go through a waterfall, a rainstorm, or the ocean. It is the only explanation as to why I am always soaking wet," Michael complains when a loud pop echoes through the grand room.

"Please tell us that you two summoned us because of something important?"

Sophia approaches them as Kells nods his head in agreement, standing behind her, carrying his hammer over his shoulder.

"It was not us," Michael and Pete reply.

"Then, please tell us it was, Isabella. Whatever this summons is about, it is fine with me. Besides, I was getting bored listening to particular members of the Aelfdene council rattle on for two hours after the council meeting," Kells remarks.

"No, I did not summon. I was tucking your dear nephews in for the night. They recently discovered how to transfigure items in the house to make it look like they are sleeping when they are casting an invisibility spell to be able to stay up all night playing, just like their uncles did when they were younger. Thank goodness, Mom is there to help," Isabella's voice rings out over the space as she materializes, sipping her coffee.

"Us play all night? That is impossible," Pete laughs as Isabella rolls her eyes.

"If it is not the two knuckleheads and not you, then it could only be one other," Sophia laughs as Willow bursts through the door of the study, mumbling, carrying an orb in one hand, and her helmet on her head with the lens down in front of her eyes. Several grimoires fly in behind her.

Spinning her wand over her head, the shutters outside slam shut, and the room lights.

"You are all here. Good. Outstanding indeed," Willow remarks as the lenses raise, then fall over her eyes again. The lenses adjust as Isabella rolls her eyes at the ridiculousness of the helmet.

"Good evening, dear little sister. What is this about? Let me guess. You found the cure for being annoying?" smirks Isabella laughing and handing Willow a cup of coffee that has just materialized.

"Ha, ha! Very funny and good evening, my dear siblings. To answer your question, sister, no, I did not. I found something even better. Actually, it is remarkably fascinating."

"Willow, what new amazing thing do you have now?" Pete laughs, throwing popcorn in the air as Willow makes a potted plant appear.

"Oh wow, Willow. That is something you do not see every day. It is a plant."

"Michael, shut up," Isabella snaps, getting up from the armchair and circling her sister and the plant.

"That is the Ignatius rose from the manor courtyard. But it is…" Isabella begins when Kells interrupts.

"Why is it gray and wilted? It looks sick."

"It is frozen, a rather odd effect, wouldn't you agree? I particularly like the icicles dripping from the leaves. Don't you? I tested them for any chemical mixture we might use in potions and elixirs," Willow smiles, glancing at the group.

"Nerd," Kells says, shaking his head and smiling.

"Kells, I would have done the same," Sophia remarks, crossing her arms.

"The bush is frozen, but why?" Isabella inquires.

"Time has sent us a message. This orb is the message," Willow explains, pointing to the orb.

"What's the message?" the other five ask in unison.

"It is about a man who walks among the stars," Willow explains, smiling when the other five's faces drop.

"What? Your joking, right?" Kells asks.

"Willow, a man who walks among the stars is not a good thing," Isabella notes, the others nodding in agreement.

"None of you want to admit that it could mean the return of a particular Arcane," Willow explains as Sophia examines the leaves of the rose bush.

"Sis, may I see your helmet?" Sophia asks.

Willow nods as she takes off her helmet and hands it to Sophia. Sophia places the helmet on her head and lowers the lenses. Then, she holds her hand to her chest, gasping and backing up.

"What in the world? How is that magic possible?" she inquires as Willow nods in agreement.

"Seriously, what are you two babbling about?" Isabella asks, snatching the helmet off her sister's head and putting it on. She pauses and tilts her head in confusion. Then, raising the lens, she circles the plant, examining it carefully.

"Your response is identical to mine," Willow notes, watching her sister.

"Fascinating," she remarks.

Willow raises her hand, causing the plant to levitate across the space to the far side of the room and into an open area. Pulling her wand, Isabella lowers one of the lenses, points her wand, and speaks.

Manifesto.
Reveal.

Magic begins spinning around the space as the pot with the plant flies into the air, then falls to the ground. Crash! The plant explodes as it grows to five times in size. The six stop, jump, and back up as the branches from the plant reach across the room. The flower pods open when the branches finally stop expanding, revealing orb after orb.

"Wow," Peter and Michael remarks in unison, each reaching for an orb until Isabella swats at their hands.

"Touch absolutely nothing. We do not know what they contain. All we know is that they could be prison, or even poison, orbs," Isabella explains as she circles the plant, stepping carefully over the roots.

"They appear to be vision orbs," Sophia states, tapping one of them with her wand.

"Careful," Isabella says, hands up, motioning for Sophia to be cautious.

"Sis, seriously, they are just orbs with visions. We see weird things all the time. So, a guy is walking among the stars. Woo, big deal. Besides, what's the worst that can happen?" inquires Peter, snatching one of the orbs and tossing it up and down in his hands until it rolled out of his hand and falls to the floor. It stopped when Isabella spins her wand in mid-air, and the orb flies up into her hands.

"Sophia, seal the door. Willow, contain the plant. Michael, seal the fireplace. Kells, close the remaining windows. Peter, stand right there and well… do nothing!" Isabella ordered.

Magic flew throughout the room, sealing all aspects of it. Then, Isabella lowers her hand and points her wand at the orb, holding it suspended in the air.

"As the eldest of all of us, here are the rules. If what Willow saw is possible, then we need to investigate. Rule one, touch nothing. Rule two, stay together. Rule three, do not stop any images. Oh, and Peter, bring nothing to life, and I mean *nothing*. We are going in to look around. That is it," Isabella explains as the orb flies into the air and begins glowing.

Light flashes around the group as a giant clock appears beneath them. It rises to waist level as it begins to spin, and a lightfield rises around them. Smoke fills the area as the floor crumbles under their feet and they all begin to fall. The six are now flying in the air.

"Isabella, what is this?" Kells inquires, a hand resting on the handle of his hammer, ready to strike.

"It appears to be a vision but unlike anything we have ever seen," Willow explains as the six observe the space until the air falls dark around them, and they feel a surface materializing under them.

"Guys, are you there?" Kells asks as he holds up his wand, lighting the space.

"Yeah, this piece of furniture broke my fall," Peter remarks, brushing himself off as he looks around the space.

"This is weird. We normally cannot interact with anything in a vision," Sophia remarks as Michael and Isabella nod.

"Willow? Where is Willow?" inquires Isabella while the other five notice her standing on the far side of the room, peering through an archway.

Walking toward her carefully, they weave their way through the junked room and come up behind Willow, observing a great hall. Peter motions with his hand for his siblings to observe what he is seeing.

"Is that Mr. Cee?" asks Willow.

"It appears it is, and he looks ancient," Sophia notes as the cat slumps across the floor to the fireplace, laying down.

Quietly, the six slip into the room, looking around. Chattering could be heard in the space as they hide behind some old sheets covering furniture as two figures enter the room.

"I told you tampering with time would not work," the woman states.

"Do you always have to complain?" the man inquires as he raises his hands, and orbs appear, spinning throughout the room. The woman lowers her hood to examine the room.

"That is Lady Yule," Willow whispers as her siblings all shoot each other looks of curiosity.

"Dalton, will you just restore the timelines?" Lady Yule inquires.

"Sis, the timelines can't simply be 'restored.' You, of all people, should know that. Besides, my plans to maintain them is currently working," he explains, lowering his hood and smiling.

"Working?" Lady Yule inquires, spinning her hands as magic flies through the space, revealing multiple statues of various Arcane.

"Ugh, I hate when you do that. Did you have to reveal them?" Lord Yule inquires in an annoyed tone of voice.

"Brother, they are our friends," Lady Yule remarks.

"Yes, and here in the realm of time, you know what time does. It screws with everyone's mind," Lord Yule replies.

"You are still disappointed in them?" inquires Lady Yule.

"I would rather not discuss it," Lord Yule replies.

"All of them lost. If they had only had faith. But they did not believe in him," Lady Yule says, walking around the various statues.

"They made their choice," declares Lord Yule.

"Look, we have lost all of them. You can fix this, and your magic is strong enough to save them," she barks.

"It is not that easy, sister," Lord Yule responds, shaking his head.

"Easy, just make the clock appear, turn back the hands, and poof, we are done," Lady Yule suggests, crossing her arms and tapping her foot.

"Citrine, it cannot be done. The spell was shattered the last time it was cast," Lord Yule explains.

"The spell is broken? How? What are you talking about? Time spells do not break," Lady Yule declares as Lord Yule pulls the snow globe out from under his cloak.

"Big deal. It is a snow globe," Lady Yule states.

Rolling his eyes, Lord Yule spins his hand over the globe as the room darkens and a cold Christmas eve night appears. The six watch in amazement at what they witness until the room returns to normal.

"When? How?" Lady Yule inquires.

"Over one hundred years ago, when he ran away, he went to the park, met the other fourteen Ambroses of the other timelines, and, at that moment, confined his powers to this snow globe. When he did that, time changed. He did something to it, something no one can explain," Lord Yule explains.

"Then, Brother, just simply take it back to him," Lady Yule remarks, annoyed.

"Again, as I have already explained, it is not that simple. It is complicated," he explains, nodding his head back and forth.

"Complicated? Wait, you nodded your head back and forth. What happened?" she snaps.

"As I said, Ambrose cast a feat of magic so powerful that it has never been seen or even imagined. You see, we cannot just take it back. Time is… well, not broken, but changed. And, because of it, we cannot just give him the globe. He, at this moment, has to want it back and has to be ready. He tied the very existence of magic to this globe. So, if it is damaged, then so is magic. If it is destroyed, magic will cease to exist. Therefore, the globe has to be protected," Lord Yule states as Lady Yule backs up, her hand resting on her chest.

"How?"

"That, dear sister, I do not know. That is why I asked you to join me here. I needed to examine the magic around it to see if there is any way to stop magic from being tied to it," Lord Yule explains as Mr. Cee approaches, growling and stepping in front of them as Lady Yule flies backward across the room, and a hand appears out of thin air, grabs the snow globe, and throws Lord Yule out of the way. Mr. Cee lunges at the materializing figure, but the cat also flies across the room. A cloaked figure holds the snow globe up, looking at it when an arrow whizzes by the figure, tacking his cloak to the staircase.

"Pesty children," a man's voice declares as Sophia stands, bow in hand, lowering her arm. Kells helps Lady Yule, while Michael helps Lord Yule up off their feet. Willow kneels down to check on Mr. Cee, ensuring that he is okay.

"If that snow globe belongs to Ambrose. Then, you, sir, merely holding that snow globe, it is against the Arcane laws, and as a member of the Royal House of Ignatius, I place you under arrest. Hand it over," Isabella declares, appearing out of the ground, holding out her hand.

"Um, no!" the figure yells, pulling the arrow out of his cloak and spinning it around him as magic encircles the space.

The six raise their arms containing the magic and Lord Yule strikes the gauntlet on the figure's arm with his sword. Then, the figure flies backward as a woman rises out of the floor, pulling two swords from off her back and engaging Lord Yule in a duel.

Blasting magic at the woman, Lady Yule holds her wand as the woman raises her hand, catching the streams of magic with one of her blades as the other blade clashes with Lord Yule's.

Willow and Isabella join Lady Yule from the other side of the room, throwing magic at the woman. As she catches their magic with the blade of her sword, she is pushed back, the stone pavers of the floor piling up behind her as she slides backward.

"Stand down. I do not want to hurt anyone," the woman declares, spinning her hands and throwing them all backward, tacking Isabella to the wall with magic.

As the others rise to their feet, the woman snatches the globe out of the man's hand and ascends the stairs where Michael and Peter appear behind her. Willow releases Isabella, who flies into the air as the woman casts magic at the two brothers as she backs up the stairs.

Peter and Michael catch the magic in lightfields and dissolve it.

"You are not very wise," Michael remarks as Peter strikes the woman with his sword. As the blades collide, he is blown backward.

"Interesting," Willow remarks.

As Willow passes, Sophia grabs an elvish blade from her sister's belt, disappearing and, seconds later, reappearing, striking the woman with the dagger.

"Clang!"

"How is this possible?" Sophia asks, pulling her wand against the woman as she flies off the steps, dropping the dagger.

Willow stops, summons the dagger, and throws the blade in the air. Catching it backhanded, she makes her sword appear from under her sleeve. Charging the woman, their blades clash. Willow ducks the woman's blade, coming inches from her face when Willow catches sight of the markings on the woman's blade.

"You're an elf," Willow declares as she spins, striking the blade of the woman's sword for a second time. The woman backs up and tilts her head, looking closely at Willow.

"Why would you care?" the woman snaps, striking the dagger Willow holds.

"In the name of the Royal House of Ignatius, and as a member of the Elvish Royal Family, stand down. Give me the snow globe!" Willow demands as she peers back at Isabella and nods.

The other five siblings know what this means, and each one casts magic against the woman as she spins, catches the magic beams with her blade, and raises her other hand, causing a clock to appear.

"Time Magic?" Lady Yule asks, spinning her wand, attempting to contain the magic, and regarding her brother.

"I will handle this," he says, flipping his cloak off his back as he glides across the floor, palms out, trying to control the clock.

"Who are you?" he demands as he struggles to control the clock as a light column explodes behind him, and Rose appears.

"Oh, this will get interesting now," Peter laughs as the six Ignatius siblings back up. Furious, Rose spins her wand, slamming the cloaked man into the wall as she points her wand right at the woman.

"Stand down," Rose demands, her eyes glowing blue as she raises her hand, taking control of the clock.

"You, Great Queen, of all people, should know you cannot stop me and will not succeed. The hands of time are set, the wheels are in motion, and time is on its path. Stop it if you can, but if you do, you will destroy time itself and him," the woman taunts as the cloaked male appears behind her, raises his staff, and the two are gone in a flash of light. When the two disappear, the space spins and everyone is dumped back in the grand study.

❧

"Sealing the study? Whose idea was that?" Rose yells as she points her wand at the fireplace and the field of magic explodes.

"Hi, grandma," the six say in unison, smiling.

"Hi! Hi! Do not 'hi' me. So, you open a time orb in the study in this academy, seal the room, and think I will not figure it out? Are you all mad?" Rose yells, pacing the floor as Lord and Lady Yule quietly slip through the space toward the door.

"Lord and Lady Yule, freeze. Just one minute," Rose says as Cedric appears.

"My lady," he says, handing her an orb as he disappears again. She rolls it across the floor as Rusty and Meredith also appear.

"Ugh, we are so busted," Peter remarks as Rusty looks at the six of them.

"What were you six thinking?" their mother yells

"Are you mad? No, wait, maybe a bit crazy? Seriously, a time orb?" Rusty inquires.

"It was the plant," Willow points, making it appear when Rose backs up.

"Rusty, the Ignatius rose?" Rose inquires as he walks around the plant, examining it.

"Enchanted," he notes, then he raises his nose. "A hint of ginger. I would say twenty, no twenty-one orbs and an unknown magical signature," he explains, still circling the plant.

"Seriously?" Michael inquires as Rose glances back at him.

"Willow is this one of your plants?" her mother inquires.

"Mama, no. It is the one from the courtyard," Willow replies.

Then, Isabella interrupts, "I think everyone is missing the bigger picture here," Isabella says, leaning against the bookcase.

"And my dear granddaughter, what would that be?" Rose asks in a curious tone.

"While you are all doing your job, examining some enchanted family bush, a very dangerous relic tied to the entire fate of all magic has been stolen," Isabella explains.

"The snow globe," Rusty and Meredith say in unison, looking at each other concerned, and then at Rose for answers.

"One of the figures noted that it was Ambrose's," Sophia interjects.

"Seven years ago, on Christmas Eve, several of you, not to name anyone in particular, and your dear brother, Ambrose, ended up in one of your usual spats. Words were said, punches were thrown, and your little brother, Ambrose, ran out. We found him later that evening, in Central Park asleep, a homeless man protecting him, and that is when I discovered that your brother gave up his magic to live a normal life, a mundane life," their grandmother explains while pacing the floor.

"The prophecy of the Mundane?" Sophia and Willow inquire.

"Yes! Your parents, your grandfather, and I protected the snow globe until the time when Ambrose will need it," Rose exclaims.

"Well, someone has it now," Kells explains as his other siblings nod.

"We know. Lord Yule, would you care to explain?" Rose inquires.

"I borrowed the globe, Great Queen. I needed to examine it. As you know, Ambrose tied the fate of all magic to that thing. If it is damaged, so is all of our magic. If the globe is destroyed, our magic is gone. I do not know how, but, somehow, someway, he learned to control a powerful form of magic that has never been seen. Not even the Celestials understand it. That is why the Celestials granted me the ability to come back, trail him, and find out what can be and, if needed, protect him and the snow globe," Lord Yule explained.

Just as he finished, Esther appeared.

"Everyone," she acknowledges.

"Esther, what did you find out?" Rusty inquires.

"Dad found this," Esther notes, holding up an elf blade as Rusty hovers over the floor.

"That belongs to the cloaked lady we were fighting," Willow explains.

"Indeed, Cousin, and it is unique," Esther remarks.

"May I?" Willow inquires as Esther hands her the blade.

"Lightweight, cuts through the air with ease. The handle is made of Elfish Oak. Sophia," Willow says, tossing the sword to her sister.

"It is ancient, one of the original blades. The magic that flows through the blade is remarkable," Sophia states, her eyes glowing blue. The sword levitates in front of her as her hands circled the blade floating in the air.

Walking up, Kells points his wand at it,

Manifesto.

Reveal.

The blade flies into the air, spins, and images appear. Isabella strolls through the images that are dancing around the space as she puts on her glasses.

"Whoever she was, she is powerful. This blade has seen its share of battles and time," she notes.

"Indeed, it has, granddaughter," Zander declares, walking up, acknowledging the group, and floating into the air to examine the sword more closely.

"Hello, everyone. Rose, dear, I wish to take this to the Aelfdene for further examination," he remarks as Rose nods, and he grabs the sword and disappears.

"Lord Yule, thoughts?" Rusty inquires.

"I have my hunches but nothing definitive yet," Lord Yule responds.

"Grandchildren, the matter has grown rather urgent. I have known about the snow globe for some time and swore to protect it. Whoever has it knows of the power of the globe. Our job is to locate it, protect the Arcane, and protect Ambrose. There are still things about that snow globe that we do not understand. While you're at school, Peter, please keep a close eye on things. Dalton, you too. Esther, send word to Lady Fae. Let her know what is going on and let her know that I will be stopping in to visit. Now, go. All of you. Willow, a word?" Rose says, her hands resting behind her back.

Chapter 5
Perspective

"Really? Are we in a bad dream? This place looks as bad as Michael's and Peter's room. It also smells just as bad," Willow says as she regards her grandmother.

"Touch nothing," Rose says as the tip of her wand lights.

"Why would I want to touch anything? This place is rather gross, and I thought growing up with four brothers was bad. This place is so dirty that I would hate having to clean it. If Cedric saw this place, he would freak out," Willow remarks, moving cobwebs with her wand as she looks disgusted and shapeshifts into Cedric.

"My Lady Rose, this place is rather disturbing. Might you have a broom and dustpan in that bag of tricks, or would you like me to burn the room down?" Willow asks, pretending to be Cedric.

"Willow, he really isn't that bad," her grandmother says.

"Seriously, grandma?" Willow inquires, screwing up her face.

"Quickly, Willow, do keep up," Rose demands as Willow turns back into herself and the two weave their way through the dark space.

"Grandma, what is this place?" Willow inquires.

"An ancient tomb. It is said to hold the remains of a particular Arcane of interest," Rose explains as the two emerge at a crossway leading to four archways.

"An Arcane of interest?" inquires Willow, her right eyebrow raised.

"Oh dear, which way do we go?" Rose murmurs, trying to avoid Willow's question.

"Should we take creepy archway one, two, three, or four?"

Willow chuckles as Rose stands examining the space. Then, she closes her eyes. When she opens them, they glow white.

"Archway three," Rose says, pointing as the two descend the long corridor with Willow holding up her wand, several orbs flying into the air, floating above her head, lighting the way.

"So, grandma, you never answered my question. Who is this Arcane of interest? Also, of all of your grandchildren, why bring me?" Willow inquires as the two continue along the long dark corridor.

Rose stops and checks every aspect of the tunnel.

"How can you just poke your head in and out of things?" Willow asks, watching her grandmother examining the tunnel.

"You will learn, dear child, to examine everything," Rose stands, raising her wand.

Illuminare.

Illuminate.

Light flies around the two as the torches light in the corridor. "Better. And to answer your questions, I brought you because whether you want to accept it or not, you are next to your brother, Ambrose, in power, which means that, currently, you are the most powerful of your siblings. The other reason is that your helmet will prove invaluable in this journey," Rose explains as the two enter a giant room with six stone sarcophagi circling the room.

"Oh, what a charming place, who is their decorator? An undertaker or, perhaps, Gothic Depot?" Willow inquires turning up her nose at the sight of the place.

"Willow, touch nothing. We do not know what type of magic protects this place," her grandmother remarks as Willow nods.

"I have no plans to touch these graves," Willow explains as the two stroll through the space. Suddenly, Willow let out a gasp, backing away from one of the sarcophagi.

"Grandma?" Willow points as Rose approaches and spins her wand, revealing the markings.

The Lady Isabella Roslynn Ignatius

"Interesting. Willow, check that one over there," Rose says as she moves toward the next one. Willow approaches, spins her wand, and reveals the name on the lid.

The Lord Kells Ingálvur Ignatius

"This one is Kells. So, Grandma, please tell me this is not the burial site of my siblings," Willow says.

"It is believed to be. It is a break in time, but that is not why we are here," Rose answers.

"A break in time? What? I do not understand. What are we doing here?" asks Willow.

"I am looking for Ambrose's sarcophagus," her grandmother replies, strolling around the circle and examining all aspects of the space.

"Wait! What do you mean, Ambrose? He cannot die," Willow exclaims.

"So, we thought," Rose notes, carefully observing the walls.

Looking cautiously around the space, Willow comes upon some runes. Kneeling in the center of the circle, she places her hands on the rune markings as the circle shakes and the floor opens and multiple sarcophagi and statues appear.

"Would this be what you are looking for?" Willow asks as the floor opens and four more sarcophagi appear.

"Indeed, and this is why I brought you. Your siblings would have gone mad by now at the site of their burial spots," Rose remarks, climbing the steps to the four sarcophagi as she begins to examine the lids.

"Grandma, it is Ambrose," Willow notes, resting a hand on the lid. Rose walks over and points her wand at the lid as it explodes.

Oblitero.

Obliterate.

"Grandma," Willow gasps as Rose turns, motioning for Willow to look inside.

"It is empty," Willow says, looking confused.

"As predicted. Willow, your helmet, scrutinize the inside of the box carefully. Don't miss anything," Rose directs as Willow places her helmet on her head and switches the lenses back and forth, examining the inside of the sarcophagus.

"There are ancient markings here, writing I have never seen," Willow says as Rose continues to look around the space. Then, she retrieves a scroll from her bag and places it on one of the other sarcophagi.

"Hmm, ancient markings, empty sarcophagi, six on the lower level, four on the next. The one we are looking for is missing," Rose states as she looks around and walks toward a statue of Lord Yule. Rose examines the pointing statue. Turning and looking around, she is curious to see where the statue is pointing.

"Interesting," Rose says when she realizes that the statue is pointing directly at Ambrose's empty sarcophagus.

"Willow, where is the statue of your brother pointing?"

"It appears to be pointing here."

"Stay there. Let me check something. It appears that the four statues each point to a different aspect of the room," Rose notes.

"Grandma, the hexagon shaped stone in the floor is where the final statue is pointing," Willow states as Rose cautiously approaches the stone.

Looking around, Rose holds out her hand as her staff appears. When she taps the stone, the floor shakes and opens. Willow jumps backward as another sarcophagus emerges.

"Grandma? Who is that one for?" inquires Willow.

"That, my dear granddaughter, we are about to find out," Rose explains as the two ascend the last steps.

Magna rebellis protector lucis.

A great rebel protector of light.

"The great rebel protector of the light? Who is that, Grandma?"

"Luciana Luna Ignatius, your niece," Rose replies, peering down at the lid as Willow looks at her, confused.

"My niece? What? Isabella has two boys. Who has a daughter?" inquires Willow, even more confused.

"Ambrose and Dalton," notes Rose as she walks along the length of the box, studying the runes on the lid.

"Grandma, what do you mean they have a daughter?" asks Willow.

"The other night, when you and your siblings traveled into that vision, you met an elf that you all had the pleasure of fighting. She was trained in the old ways of the elves. Her magic was strong, equal to that of your brother, Ambrose, and your future brother-in-law, Dalton. Her fighting skills are unlike anything ever seen," Rose explains.

"Yes, Grandma. What about her?" Willow inquires as her grandmother looks at her steadily.

"Oh, no. NO! That girl who helped that cloaked figure who stole the snow globe?" Willow eventually yells.

"Yes. Your grandfather and I believe that she is the same. After your grandfather examined the blade, he took it to your great grandmother, Mora. Now, you know your great grandmother. She rattled on for about a half-hour as she circled the blade, examining it. Then, with one simple touch, your grandfather had to pick her up off the floor. At that moment, she saw…

well, knew, everything over five thousand years of history," Rose explains as she motions for Willow to help her remove the lid of the sarcophagus.

"If Lord Yule's hunch is correct," her grandmother remarks as they push the lid off, and it hits the floor.

Thud!

"Like the others, the sarcophagus is empty. The timeline has definitely been re-written, and all that remains is an orb," Willow remarks, reaching for it but it flies into the air.

"Willow, be careful. We do not know what type of orb it is just yet," Rose remarks as images begin dancing through the space.

"It appears to be a vision orb," Willow replies.

Sand spins around them as ghostly images begin appearing.

"I assume that would be Ambrose, only older?" Willow suggests, pointing to a much older elf in the images playing out.

"Yes. You can tell by how he pulls his hair back" Rose says as she and Willow look at each other and the image disappears

"Grandma?" Willow asks, her hand raised, trying to stop the vision.

"This is normal, particularly with vision or time orbs," Rose explains, holding her hands behind her back as various items materialize around them.

"Where are we?" Willow asks, examining a room with bookshelves seemingly reaching endlessly for the ceiling.

"The Sanctuary of Legend and Lore. The Sanctuary belongs to Noble Elder, passed from one Noble Elder to the next. It holds many more ancient Arcane texts than we can even begin to imagine," Rose remarks as Willow wanders about the space, examining many of the books.

"Grandma, these are the fourteen of the fifteen Curpendulums," Willow declares, shocked.

"Your brother Ambrose hid the fifteenth Curpendulum in the Sanctuary to protect it," Rose explains, running her hand over the cover of one of the books. As the two observe the place, a young woman appears, the Lady Yule accompanying her.

"Your father and papa had hoped that someday they would give this place to you," Lady Yule remarks, looking at Luciana.

"What is this place? Wait, Aunt Yule, these are the Curpendulums, the most ancient of all magic texts," Luciana says, her hand resting on the cover.

"And now, they are yours!" Lady Yule exclaims, looking at her.

"Thank you, but I wish they were here," Luciana says sadly as she strolls through the Sanctuary.

"They are always with you. Oh, by the way…" Lady Yule says, handing an orb to Luciana. "I will let you be. This is meant for you," Lady Yule explains as she disappears.

The orb rises and flies out of Luciana's hands and across the room as Ambrose appears.

My Dearest Luciana,

Your journey, my dear daughter, has just begun. I am so sorry that I am not there to help you. My heart breaks recording this, but I failed to muster the magic I needed to save the Arcane or magic. You see, the love of your papa was not enough. Let me share with you something from which I had protected you. I have kept this from you but, growing up, my siblings never cared for me. They were dreadfully afraid of my magic, and I realized that there was no way to stop Merlin without their help.

Not to speak ill of your aunts and uncles, I hope you have gotten to know them better than I ever did. We hardly grew up together, so the trust we had for each other was never there. It was hit and miss, and, many times, we all struggled to get along.

In the darkest of hours, when I needed them the most, when I needed their strength, they were not there. But, contained in the walls of this Sanctuary is magic far more significant than any could imagine, a magic that will forever be yours. Not only are you my daughter, but you are the one true successor of the Noble power.

Your papa and I love you, my daughter, but know that things for my siblings and myself…

"Grandma, the vision," Willow says as the room spins around the two and they find themselves on the floor in the Sanctuary, a blade at each of their throats.

"Oh my! You are the great queen, my humblest apologies," Luciana says, stowing her blades quickly and bowing.

"Thank you, child."

"You are Queen Rose, which means…" Luciana declares, hugging Willow and never finishing her sentence.

"Well, enough of this. I am sure there is a reason why you two look so young and are here."

"We are looking for information," Rose explains as the chair at the table pushes back magically, and she sits down.

"The truth about the whereabouts of the snow globe," Luciana remarks.

"Yes, to a point. There is more though," notes Rose as she sips from a cup of tea that had just appeared.

"Me?" Luciana asks, observing both of them.

Rose sips her tea again, keeping a straight face as she speaks, "Yes."

"Grandma, you did not…" Willow begins to say when Luciana interrupts her.

"Papa sent you?" she asks.

"He did. You see, in the time I am from, your destiny is not yet written. Your fathers have not even married yet, at least not in our timeline," Rose explains as Luciana walks toward where the Curpendulums stand.

"The timeline can be altered still?" Luciana asks, running her hand over the cover of one of the Curpendulums.

"It was your dad who saw to that, somehow, your father, in this time, was able to seek out the other thirteen Ambroses, and the fourteen traveled through time, using their magic, and creating the snow globe," Rose replies, standing.

"He gave up his powers because none of the others understood," Luciana remarks.

"I understand," Willow speaks up.

"Not you, Auntie Willow. The others. Aunts Sophia, Isabella and Uncles Michael, Peter, and Kells were afraid. Dad's magic is unlike anything ever seen, known, or even written about. My dad defied all known laws of magic, and he struggled with another concern," Luciana remarks, a tear running down her face as she holds a portrait, hugging it. Rose reaches into her bag, pulls out the elfish blade, and places it on the table in front of Luciana.

"I believe that this is yours. Given to you by your dad," says Rose as Luciana's hand runs lovingly over the blade.

"It was a relic of a time gone past, a time when magic was beautiful and when it was powerful," Luciana remarks.

"That magic can be powerful again," Willow explains.

"Indeed, Willow, it will be. But, Luciana, you mention a concern," Rose asks, an eyebrow raised.

"Oh dear, you know he is afraid, terrified of the bloodline," Luciana explains.

"The House of Phoenix and Ignatius?" Willow asks, confused.

"It is not that. It is something else."

"What is it?" Willow asks.

"The blood of the incubus," Rose says, looking at Willow.

"Merlin?"

"Yes. Father believed that the incubus blood fueled his magic," Luciana explains, pacing around the space and examining the writing on the walls.

"Where is the snow globe?" Rose inquires.

"Safe, Great-grandma, safe with a friend," replies Luciana as she looks back over her shoulder.

"A friend, Luciana? That globe contains magic beyond anything," Willow replies with concern as Rose raises her hand, stopping her.

"Why would this friend want it?" Rose asks when Luciana walks out from behind the desk, smiling.

"In time, the prophecy will occur. Ambrose will become Noel, the most powerful Arcane ever to live, and, when that occurs, it is said that it will be the very last time. You see, time will be restored, and the timelines will fall into alignment," Luciana remarks as Rose turns to address Willow.

"Willow, get ready to leave," Rose nods at Luciana.

"You know, don't you?" Luciana asks.

"I do, child. Yes," Rose replies, taking a deep breath.

"He can win. But he cannot do it alone," Luciana remarks.

"I know. He will need all the help he can get," replies Rose.

"Can you help him?" inquires Luciana.

"Indeed, that is my goal. It is why I am here. Your papa says that your magic can help with that," Rose continues as she regards Willow.

"You came by way of the tomb?" Luciana inquires.

"We did," Rose responds as Luciana spins the dial of the watch in her hand, the hands of the watch spinning out of control.

"Time is a fascinating feat of magic, wouldn't you say?" asks Luciana as the watch flies into the air, and the Curpendulums fly around her and her eyes glow blue. The winds in the room pick up and papers begin to fly everywhere. Willow quickly moves across the floor and grabs onto her grandmother's hand.

"Care to explain what is going on?" Willow asks as books begin flying off the shelves spinning in the space as they dissolve.

"No. Just hold on," Rose says, looking at Luciana, whose eyes are now glowing white.

Per magicam terrae, per magicam domuum Drake, Fae, Pendragon, Yule, Elder, Ignatius, and Phoenix recipio iter tutum nam haec due sino tempus esse fixa per eos. Sino alios meminisse. Tempus est.

By the magic of earth, through the magical houses of Drake, Fae, Pendragon, Yule, Elder, Ignatius, and Phoenix ensure a safe journey for these two, allowing time to be fixed through them. Allow the others to remember. It is time.

Luciana's voice echoes through the space and all that can be seen is a being of glowing white light as the Curpendulums spin around the space.

"Grandma, what is she doing?" Willow inquires, holding her arm over her face.

"She is using her magic to fix time and send us back," Rose says as she and Willow fly into the air, the Curpendulums spinning around them as a vortex opens and starts to consume the space. Turning her head and looking up, Luciana catches the vortex with her hand and pushes it back, fully controlling the strength and size of the vortex.

"The Curpendulums will protect you. Get out of here. I have this," Luciana's voice echoes through the space. Black vines explode through the vortex, grabbing and beginning to wrap around Rose.

"Willow, get out of here. Now! Get to safety," Rose yells as Luciana spins her hands and the multiple Curpendulums strike the vines descending from the vortex.

"Grandma," Willow yells, her hand extended as she raises her wand and points it at her grandmother.

Funis.

Ropes.

Multiple ropes fly from Willow's wand and wrap around her grandmother, preventing her from disappearing through the portal.

"Hold on. I am not letting go," Willow calls as she pulls toward her grandmother. Luciana takes to the air, spinning magic around her as the darkness climbing through the vortex dissolves instantly.

"Willow, let go. I will get back to you. Get to your siblings. It is up to you to protect Ambrose and guide the other five," says Rose who pulls her wand, the tip lights, and the vortex begins to spin.

Illuminare.

Illuminate.

The light hits the vortex as the vines holding Rose begin to snap.

"I cannot let go. I need help. I need the Ignatius siblings," Willow yells as lightning strikes around her and a hand reaches out, grabs her hand, and steadies it as she is pulled to the ground.

"I got you, sis," Kells calls as Isabella and Peter appear.

Funis.

Ropes.

The four pull down on their wands, fighting against the winds of the vortex, holding tight to the ropes.

"We've got you, Grandmama. We are not letting go. We are all in this together," Michael says, helping the others to pull down on the ropes.

"Willow, get us out of here," Isabella demands as Merlin and the Council of Darkness begin to climb through the vortex.

"Not in my sanctuary," Luciana screams, her hair standing on end as static sparks fly between the tips. Her eyes turn black, and she flies across the space, riding one of the Curpendulums as the other fourteen Curpendulums strike Merlin, the members of the Council of Darkness, and the vortex repeatedly.

"Everyone, hold on. Good luck, and remember, time is on your side. It will be there to guide you," Luciana directs, holding the pocket watch in her left hand as it rapidly spins. She captures a star flying and, around the ceiling, a light flashes, and the six land in the grand entry of the school with their grandmother.

They scramble to their feet as Zander approaches, helping Rose up.

"Did you find them?" he inquires as Rose nods in reply.

"Are you six okay?" Rose asks, brushing herself off.

"Yes. That was freaking crazy, seeing the fifteen Curpendulums flying like that," Kells remarks.

"Is that what Ambrose can do?" Sophia asks.

"Who was the girl?" Michael inquires at the same time.

"Stop! All of you are talking at once. Seriously?" Rose replies, motioning for them to settle down.

"Willow and I will answer your questions momentarily but not here in the entryway of the academy," their grandmother declares as they all disappear and reappear in the study.

"Zander, my love, summon the children. Willow, summon your great grandparents, please. Isabella, summon Cedric," Rose directs as she walks behind the desk, spinning her wand as the shutters slam shut over the windows. The fire in the fireplace explodes into flames, the candles light, and the room expands with chairs appearing everywhere.

Within seconds, a commotion ensues as members of the Houses of Phoenix, Drake, Knight, and Ignatius appear. Weaving her way through the group of people, Rose reaches for an orb. When she rests her hand on it, it suddenly flashes. Turning it in her hand, she examines it, then raises the orb as it flies into the air and projects an image on the ceiling, and the story of what she and Willow had just witnessed plays out in front of everyone.

Later that night, Willow retreats to her study where she begins to write.

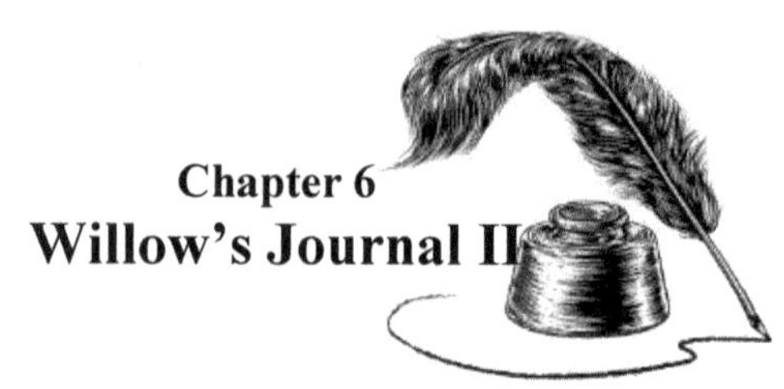

Chapter 6
Willow's Journal II

Dear Journal,

How when I was younger, I used to fill your pages about my family's many adventures, the various things I have learned, and my feelings. But recently, I have not had the opportunity to write because of my duties with the Academy. Being a teacher at the Arcane School of Magical Teaching has its moments. Unfortunately, Grandpa, Grandma, and the faculty did not prepare me for the joy teaching brings, nor the sheer headache.

Tonight, I dare venture into this endeavor of writing again. If I only knew where to begin. Time is rapidly changing around us, and none of us know what to think, what to do, or how to respond. One minute time is fine as it works beautifully then, the next time, like today, it wants to play its many bizarre games. Time travel is a fascinating feat of magic and one that I do not fancy as it should be reserved for only a few. I understand what my family means about not meddling in the past or the future. Time, in its ever-unique glory, is a magic that is enough to cause an Arcane, gifted with the ability, to want to go out of their mind.

A rather complex situation with time but, nevertheless, eye-opening. So many questions arise around the events of today, but where does one begin to process them? Let's start with my siblings. Now, that is a good spot. While I love them, I am frustrated that they do not see Ambrose the way I do. Did he have to die in that timeline without our help? I know that the other timelines are inaccurate, but now, that realization will haunt me for the years to come.

Ambrose is charming, witty, athletic, always getting into trouble, wise beyond his years, and has one of the gentlest of hearts. I am proud of my little brother but very hurt by the actions of my other siblings. Yes, I know, Ambrose's magic was not balanced when he was younger, which caused many challenges, but the others never gave him a chance.

While Sophia and Isabella have been like me, more nurturing, trying to help him learn, Pete, Michael, and Kells, our dearest older brothers, were nowhere near supportive, In fact, they were the opposite. So, I understand Ambrose's disdain for them, more and more.

On another note, I am curious about the family rose bush. Those orbs were placed there for a purpose, which was not a coincidence. Neither was Ambrose's snow globe going missing. These challenges tend to be exceptionally interesting as they all lead to different outcomes, none of which our great seers have predicted accurately, and none of which are noted in the great texts. I know for sure that what I have to do to help Ambrose, I will do it, even if the others are afraid. It will take a lot of convincing, but now, more than ever, he needs us.

Willow

Chapter 7
College

Across the countryside of England, rising out of the ground, a majestic grand clock tower rises over the land. Small balls of light buzz around the tower as wizards and witches on brooms can be seen flying around it. The great tower sits at the heart of a bustling university campus and is flanked on either side by rows of two- and three-story brick buildings. The grand clock tower watches over the central courtyard below, providing minute-by-minute details of the time for the campus.

Fountains stand as resting places to sit and talk throughout the courtyards, while oak and pine trees line the walkways. Students, faculty, and visitors bustle about on the ground below, darting in and out of the various buildings. Groups of students sit in the square, engaging in conversations or various activities. The Arcane and Mundane students go about their day as they all interact.

The grand clock tower chimes every hour and can be heard inside the student apartments. An alarm sounds, indicating that it is 7 AM. RJ rolls over, hitting the snooze button.

"Are you kidding? Did I oversleep? Not good, not good at all. I will be late for class and on the first week," RJ exclaims, jumping out of bed and dashing across his room, throwing on his clothes.

"Meow."

"Good morning, Mr. Cee. You are supposed to wake me."

Grabbing his bag, hopping on one foot, putting his boots on, RJ dashes out the door.

Seconds later, RJ emerges through the double doors on the main level and runs across the courtyard to one of the academic buildings on the opposite side from his apartment building.

❧

"With one minute to spare before class, I run down the hall to find the professor pulling the door shut and waving as he smiles."

"You're late. Goodbye!"

Ugh! Seriously? It will be a long semester if he is going to lock us out a minute before class starts.

Anyway, I guess I am heading to work. Hello, I am RJ, and this is my story.

You have been led to believe that this is a story about magic. Can I interject and note that that is boring? A word of advice, magic is not all that they say it is.

"Where to begin? So, yeah, you saw I was locked out of class, so I walk out of Griffin Hall and down the walkway to work at the Dwarfbrew."

"Fascinating place" is all I hear during my shift. Dwarfbrew is the hippest coffee shop in the Arcane world. The owner has mastered the form of coffeemaking, and their coffee is all the rage among students at this school. All I am asked all day is, "Can I get a mocha Frappuccino?" and "Do not forget those cute dwarf sprinkles." Arcane and their fancy drinks. Blah!

If their fancy drinks are not enough, try working for the grumpiest dwarf around, Mr. Brewer himself! Talk about a dwarf who loves money, and he won't spend a dime to fix anything. He has hooked the counter together with duct tape. He has the coffee machines strung together with string. To get water in the sink, you have to use the water pump outside, and his poor wife complains to him about everything breaking. If you know of Mr. Bruin from the Arcane Academy of Magical Teaching's library, then you know Mr. Brewer, who is Mr. Bruin's cousin and the absolute opposite of him.

BOOM!

"Not again! That makes it the seventh time in two days," Lyle declares as he holds the espresso machine together as I come around the corner, set my bag down, and try to help him put the machine back together.

"Thanks, RJ," Lyle says.

"That there is Lyle. He is one of the other workers here and like me. We both think Mr. Brewer is cheap. But, yes, the dwarf has figured out how to use magic to, somehow, hold together the espresso machine. But you could say that the spell does *not* work.

If Mr. Brewer is not enough to drive me crazy, it is this coffee house's Arcane, magical atmosphere. Welcome to Dwarfbrew, the hottest, hippest place on campus. Yes, I work here, to my bad luck. You try being one of two Mundane working in an Arcane coffee shop. The newspaper buzzing with the latest Arcane gossip from the village is delivered every morning, the walls are covered with old tapestries, and certain parts of the sitting area smell like something has died, and whatever you do, please do not use the jukebox. The old ghost who haunts this place will get mad, fly into the air, screaming, then dive into the machine as the music changes. To top off the wonderful décor, standing dead center is every Mundane and Arcane student's dream, a life-sized statue of the Magical Three. You can even take pictures with them.

But it was either this job or the job at the pool being a lifeguard. I figured this would be safer. At 6'4", I did not want to swim in the pool, and, at least here, I can roll my eyes at the Arcane and not have to save them from drowning.

Oh wait, I am so sorry. Were you expecting a cute story about the Magical Three? Well, that is not going to happen. If you want their story, visit the library at the Arcane Academy of Magical Teaching and look for the Volume on *The Rise of the Magical Three*. Besides, they will come along later. But for right now, you have me.

Oh, where are my manners? I almost forgot! But, yes, you have figured it out. I am Mundane of Arcane experience. You can imagine my parent's reaction. However, I was not always Mundane. I was born Arcane of magical heritage but decided to give up magic over a series of events that occurred in my life.

If you have not figured it out yet, my parents are none other than Lord Rusty and Lady Meredith Ignatius, and my dear dad is the crown prince of the elves, the last royal Arcane of magical and mystical families still reigning as the other significant and prominent Arcane families have dissolved or have been wiped out. My mom comes from an ancient Arcane bloodline, one that, to date, remains very mysterious and makes the Houses of Phoenix and Ignatius look normal.

Because of who my family is, I was admitted to The Institute of Arcane Studies here at the University. The University of Arcane and Mundane Studies is the only one where Mundane and Arcane can integrate and study together. It also does not help that my grandmother's first cousin, Lady Bethany Phoenix Fae, is the Chancellor of the University.

You probably wonder why a Mundane would come to such a university. No, it is not because of who my family is, actually. The university is the only one with my major. I graduated from high school at fifteen, finished my undergraduate studies in three years, and now, at eighteen, I am doing my graduate degree in Arcane cultural anthropology and archeology. Yup, I am the only Mundane doing such a degree, and I plan to be the Mundane to find every Arcane artifact and—how do I put this gently?—well, dispose of them.

Anyway, life has not been easy for me. How do I put it? The Arcane make things look easy. Those of us who are Mundane have to work for everything we have. We do not have luxuries, such as wands, that we can wave around and, presto! Or brooms or even magical creatures to zoom around on.

For us Mundane, we do not have any of that.

Arcane and their magic? Blah! For me, I am distant from my family. I hardly see them, like ever. My parents have always been busy working, my siblings all had their own lives, and I've been left to the books. So, you can say that the books are my only friends, unless you count my cat, my family's butler, bodyguard, and guardian, Cedric, and my one best friend, Amelia.

"Who are my siblings?" you ask. Well, they are none other than the Ignatius Six, who are loved by the elves and the Arcane. But, if you ask me, they are rather annoying.

Growing up, the most dangerous arguments I got into with my siblings involved words. My understanding of the world was far different than theirs because I read and study anything and everything I can get my hands on. Although my family has money, status, and great wealth, I could care less about it. On the other hand, several of my siblings have been consumed by our family's status, whereas I just want to be left alone. So, when I was offered the chance to move here to the university, I jumped at the opportunity immediately. Although there have been days I wish I had not.

You see, the campus is enchanted. The halls of the buildings continuously move. One minute, your class will be in one building, and the next time, it has relocated to another building altogether, making it next to impossible to know where your class is from one moment to the next. Construction around campus is crazy. Chancellor Fae points her wand, and presto! a magical building appears. The books in the library are enchanted to rotate hourly. The campus is magically booby-trapped. You walk from class to home one minute, then poof! you are now walking in the forest. The charms in this place are enough to drive anyone mad. Every time I turn around, I seem to be getting hurt or lost. I have tripped multiple times because of the moving pavers on the sidewalk. I've fallen into holes in the ground, and do not get me going about the screaming plants. I am surprised that the Arcane are not deaf.

While I am not a fan of the campus, I am, however, a fan of where I live. It is the one true perk of the campus. It is an old stone and brick five-story resident building with various things to do. Living across the hall from me in the apartment building is my best friend, Amelia. She and I have known each other our entire lives. We grew up together. She is more like a sister to me than my own siblings. She and I… well, we both attended the Arcane School of Magical Teaching. But wait, you are asking yourself. I thought you were a Mundane, RJ? Well… that is where the story gets interesting.

I am, as I said, Mundane of Arcane experience. But, then again, I am not. I was born Arcane and with that came great responsibility, one that I did not want, so I simply made a choice and stopped being Arcane. You see, I was born Arcane, but when I was younger, because of a horrible argument with my siblings, I made a simple choice. I gave up my powers. Problem solved.

Anyway, where was I? Oh yes, Amelia comes from a unique family. She is none other than a Pendragon. Her grandmother, Brooke, is the sister of Lady Olivia Phoenix. Yes, that is right, as in the Lady Olivia married to Lord Oliver Phoenix of the Magical Three, and Brooke is my grandmother, the Lady Rose's, best friend,. That makes Amelia and I related, but it does not matter to us. We are the best of friends.

Amelia finds it rather annoying that her great uncle is the head of the Arcane, as their president. I have laughed and told her "Welcome to the club." Although our great-uncle is the head of the Arcane, Amelia is not a magical Arcane. But do not get me wrong, Amelia can fight, and she comes from mystical Arcane heritage. She spent her summers growing up in Camelot and training with King Arthur. Her family does not know what to do with her, though.

She is in school studying nanotechnology and can build anything she wants. So, while the Arcane are using their magic to bring hexed items to life, Amelia makes robots. The funniest moment with her robots was the weekend she and I went to catch the band SmashVamps, and we left one of her robots to care for my cat. Let's just say that, by the time we came home, he was hiding in the back of the closet, and the robot had poured a pile of food on the floor where the cat's bowl was. Mr. Cee was not very happy about that.

I joke with Amelia that she is at least far enough removed from Oliver Phoenix that she can slip by without people knowing. On the other hand, everyone knows you when you have my grandfather and grandmother for your grandparents. It is next to impossible to get away when your family is in the reigning elfish monarchy. You are pretty much like a celebrity. Everyone wants your picture. Everyone wants to discuss world peace with you. And everyone expects you to do magic."

So, you are probably wondering, if my grandparents and family are Arcane, then why do I dislike the Arcane so much?"

"That is easy. Try growing up with my siblings. Of course, you would hate everything about magic if you knew what I know. But it is much more complicated than that.

"It is bad enough that I grew up hating magic, but then, I was introduced to my roommate, the Residential Assistant, who is as Arcane as they come. A rather awkward wizard who is scary to be around, his magic is… well, how do I put it nicely? Weird! Downright weird. A nice guy who, and please do not tell anyone, but I do fancy. So, it is rather awkward with him being Arcane of noble heritage and me being Mundane of Arcane experience. What's worse is he is some living elder of magic, and we are destined.

But do not get me wrong. I have a fantastic two-bedroom, one-bathroom apartment on the fifth floor of the building, overlooking the campus and the fields, but imagine my daily dismay having an Arcane roommate. Amelia and I often ask if his magic backfires on simple spells on purpose or if he just failed Wizarding 101. What's worse is I, somehow, ended up with him in every one of my classes. It is cute because he is rather distracting, charming to look at, and easy on the eyes, but also annoying.

For the most part, the apartment building is quiet, except for one particular Arcane. Then, on cue, there's that music again, all hours of the day and night, from the miserable lad living next door. A fifth-year senior who happens to be Arcane and an elf, who doesn't get along well with anyone. You can imagine my joy to find out that one of my egocentric older brothers lives next door. It was bad enough growing up with him at home as the two of us never got along. But, to my dismay, I still have to deal with him here. College was supposed to be my escape. At least, I am relieved to know that I am not the only person who does not like him.

Pete is an interesting chap. He does not like any sort of Mundane. He despises them. He goes out of his way to make their lives miserable. So, I avoid him at all costs, and so does Amelia. As a child, he never played nice. He always caused trouble, and always was mischievous, a trait that has followed him into young adulthood. Amelia and my older cousin, Martha, claim that Pete is the strange one in the Ignatius family, and I could *not* agree with Cousin Martha more.

As I noted, it was bad enough to grow up with him. But, to my overall joy, he comes into the coffee shop and is always difficult. Every one of my co-workers hates him, and Mr. Brewer has told everyone quietly to overcharge him for being a pain. The only time Mr. Brewer is not grumpy is when he is tormenting Pete at the coffee shop.

The only saving grace about him coming to the coffee shop is that Martha works there with me and has been known to hex Pete. Then, there is Mr. Brewer, who has, on occasion, gotten into arguments with Pete. Now, dwarfs are the one Arcane creature with whom you do not want to get into an argument. First off, they are resistant to magical spells, and secondly, they have exceptionally mean tempers and great strength. The entire coffee shop went nuts and broke into cheers the day, a week ago, when Pete got out of line, and Mr. Brewer hoisted him over his head, carried him outside, and threw Pete, face first, in the mud. To my delight, I got some great pictures, and it made my heart flutter with joy to see such an event befall such a nice person. Please do not repeat that to anyone in my family, with maybe the exceptions of Martha and Amelia. For the past week, the entire fifth floor has buzzed in amusement. It took everyone's attention away from the fact that Pete is a ladies' man and has ladies coming and going daily. I have had these same ladies all come into the coffee shop, telling me how lucky I am to have him as my older brother. Then, they ask me for his number.

So, you have heard about my second eldest brother and the third eldest of the seven. Let me tell you about my other siblings. The eldest of all my siblings is Mrs. Perfect, my dear sister Isabella. She married her husband, Bradley, three years ago, and they have two sons, my charming little nephews, Bradley Jr. and Edwin. My sister is a master of magic and must get every spell correct. She spent hours practicing every spell and mastering every potion. Her husband, an Arcane of magical heritage, even laughs at how perfect her spells and potions must be. As the eldest, she feels she has to be motherly to all of us, and it gets rather annoying. Isabella has even been known to drive my other siblings, parents, and grandparents nuts as she has to correct them on everything.

Michael comes next, then there is Pete. My two eldest brothers, I do not see eye-to-eye with about anything. Michael, although the eldest, while growing up, he was that brother who always did what Pete dared him to do.

Michael, like Pete, has never settled down. Michael is an exceptional weapons master and can fight with any weapon you give him, whether trained or not. When Pete is not around, Michael and I can tolerate each other. Of all of us, Michael is the one who is less academically inclined and hates school. After graduating from the Arcane school, he took a career with the parliament, traveling the world and working with the Arcane to form partnerships with the Mundane. Of the seven of us, he is the only one who lives full-time at the Aelfdene Village, when he's not traveling, and helps oversee the village.

Next, are the twins Sophia and Kells. They take after Aunt Vivian and serve on the Council of the Elfish Priory. The Elfish Priory is where the elite guard of the elves train and is known for its monk warriors. The priory is the oldest building in the village and has been in the Ignatius family for centuries. Both Kells and Sophia are trained in all twenty-five styles of elfish combat and are the masters of weapon and non-weapon combat.

When Sophia and Kells are away from Pete and Michael, they are delightful. Dad used to pair Kells and I off during training as we are the closest in age and size. Sophia inherited magical skills that make Lady Marybelle and Ms. Adwin look weak. Sophia can animate anything with her magic, both paintings and books.

After the twins comes, my sister, Willow, to whom, of all my siblings, I am the closest. Willow is the only sibling in my family who understands me. She teaches at the Arcane School of Magical Teaching and helps to oversee elemental magic training. She has a green thumb, and she can control nature through her magic. Of all my siblings, Willow is unique. Like my other siblings, she can fight with or without weapons, but she is the only one who can manipulate magic in fascinating ways and create gadgets. She is also the one living Arcane and elf, who is a master archer and can shoot an arrow around the globe, controlling it with her mind. When none of us could master archery, Dad and Grandpa always had Willow step in to teach us.

Throughout my life, I have always found magic interesting, but I have found many Arcane to be boring. They're always zipping and zapping here and there, and, heaven forbid, they have tempers.

So, as you can see, my life is okay for the most part. The less I hear from my family, the happier I am. So, a little secret about why I'm interested in Arcane studies. I mentioned that I wanted to learn everything I could about the Arcane, the history of magic, and Merlin. The faster I can find the artifacts and destroy them, the sooner I can go about living a quiet, peaceful life, away from magic and the Arcane. I am thinking somewhere in the mountains. I am sure my grandmother would not be thrilled to hear me say that as she feels every book should be preserved and every artifact should be put on display. However, I see it as a waste of time, and, besides, I am sure Cedric hates cleaning all of it.

While this semester has just started, it cannot end fast enough for me. My family does not know this, but the Manhattan Center University has started an Arcane Studies program to draw Arcane to New York City. I hope to apply to that and if accepted, go there, leave this university, and live a normal life among the Mundane. I have not spoken of this yet with Amelia as I know she will try to talk me out of it. However, between school and work, I take every opportunity to save every penny, even picking up extra shifts so that I don't have to rely on my parents or family to help me move.

Well, that is my life, pretty uneventful and boring, just the way I like it, except for the annoying dreams I get. Amelia bugs me that I should see one of the great Seers, such as the Lady Divinity. Still, I would rather deal with the annoying dreams than have my family find out anything about the content of them, particularly about who I was destined to become before I gave up my powers."

After finishing his shift at Dwarfbrew, RJ walks across campus, grabs dinner at the campus eatery, and heads home to do his homework. Upon finishing dinner, he sits down at his desk and begins working when he dozes off, falling asleep on his textbook.

Chapter 8
Nightmares

RJ looks around as his dream spins, dumping him in a forest. Standing, he brushes himself off, then starts to walk, but his dream spins again, dumping him in the middle of a field of sheep.

Seriously? This is going to be a long, annoying night, RJ thinks when the dream spins again.

"*Enough!!*" RJ yells as everything finally stops spinning around him.

Looking around, RJ finds that he is standing in an old village.

Not again. Why do my dreams insist on dumping me in some Arcane fantasy. Put me back in the field of sheep! Even worse, I am dressed like my siblings. Yuck! How can they wear these robes? RJ wonders as he walks down the path, exploring the village.

Well, let's get this dream over with. I wonder what it is going to throw at me today. Hmm. Let me guess. Creepy dolls will chase me. But, no, that is too easy. Maybe a dragon needs help. Ha, like that will happen! This is going to be interesting.

Oh, look I'm in an old Mundane English village. What? Is a creepy psycho clown going to jump out at me?

RJ shook his head and then started to stroll the path looking around. Then, he shrugged his shoulders.

This place is boring. Nothing is happening. It is dead, a village that is not bustling. But wait, how fascinating," notes RJ as he stops and watches a young elf child skipping in the distance. *Well, that sure was not me when I was younger. I would not have been caught dead wearing anything like that! It looks like the young elf robbed a Mundane closet from the 1600s."*

RJ laughs to himself as he watches the child.

By the looks of it, that is not any of my siblings either.

Quietly, RJ walks along behind the young elf who skips down the path to an old cemetery. The child stops and looks around. An arrow whistles by RJ's head as he jumps out of the way.

"What the heck? Now, that is *not* boring," RJ states aloud as he turns and sees an older elf standing with a bow raised.

RJ, it is only a dream. It is only a dream. You will wake up in your bed and presto, he thinks as the elf walks up, pulls a blade, and attacks RJ, who catches the blade in both hands.

Not a dream. This definitely is not a dream. I hate it when this happens," RJ notes, spinning and kicking the elf.

"A dream? Far from it, kid," the elf says as they throw a dagger at RJ, tacking him to the tree.

"Seriously? By order of your prince, stand down," RJ demands as he pulls out the dagger, spins it in his hand, and catches the elf's blade again.

"You smell like an elf. You fight like an elf. But you are no elf. You lack magic, and your ears are rather disgusting. Mundane ears! You are a disgrace to the elves, and I take no orders from the fake family," the figure remarks as they pull their staff and prepare to strike RJ.

Catching the end of the staff, RJ spins, snaps the staff out of the elf's hands and backs up, spinning the staff.

"A disgrace? Let's talk about a disgrace. You attack me, a member of the Elvish Royal family. Who is the disgrace?" RJ inquires as he blocks the elf's sword.

"Heed my warning, Mundane, a war is coming, and when it does, Merlin will have you in chains," the elf declares as they jump in the air, flip backward, and lob three arrows at RJ.

Then, suddenly, the elf disappears.

"Charming," RJ remarks, looking displeased and holding his arm as he notices an arrow sticking out of it, blood dripping down his arm.

"Damn! Are you serious? This will be fun to get out," RJ says as the area begins to spin around him.

&

"Ugh, are you freaking kidding me?" asks RJ as he lands on the floor with a thud in his family room, causing Dalton to jump off the couch.

"RJ, are you okay?" Dalton inquires as he helps RJ up off the floor. Then, his eyes narrow.

"I am fine," RJ says, pulling his arm away.

"Fine, you have an arrow sticking out of your arm and it is bleeding! You think that is fine?" yells Dalton when his staff appears.

"No, you are not taking it out. I am going across the hall to see Amelia. She will be able to take care of it," RJ says as he moves toward the door, but his knees buckle, and he collapses.

"You are in no shape to walk," Dalton remarks, helping RJ to the couch.

"Then, get Amelia for me, and only Amelia," RJ insists, grabbing Dalton by his shirt collar. In a flash, Dalton disappears as Mr. Cee runs into the room and jumps in RJ's lap, holding a vial.

"Thanks, buddy," RJ says, petting the cat as the door flies open and Amelia runs into RJ's apartment, Martha trailing behind her.

"Oh dear! What the hell happened?" Martha asks, pointing her wand at the arrow as it dissolves.

"I would rather not talk about it," RJ replies and grits his teeth as Amelia sprays the wound with antiseptic spray. Martha searches the apartment, then stops and glances down at the same thing Dalton is observing.

Kneeling, Dalton examines a dagger, waving his hand over the blade as it begins to glow.

"Do not touch it. We do not know if it is hexed. It appears to be extremely old," Martha cautions, waving her wand and levitating it.

"If it is glowing like that, it must be hexed," Dalton remarks as he and Martha turn to observe Amelia and tearing tape can be heard. As Amelia pulls surgical tape with her teeth, wrapping the bandage on RJ's arm as he swallows the potion in the vial.

"A healing elixir?" she inquires.

"Yes, I have a batch in my room," RJ responds.

"I will have to tell my mother," Martha says as RJ stands up.

"Martha, my dear cousin, I would rather you did not. If you do, we will have the entire Arcane Parliament arriving, and making a fuss," RJ exclaims.

"RJ, you had an arrow in your arm. There is an elfish blade laying on the floor. What next," Martha asks.

"Not to mention that you appeared magically and fell from a portal in the ceiling," Dalton adds.

"What? Oh no! Hearing that, I am calling for help," Martha declares as she glides across the floor as the French doors to the balcony blow open. Raising her wand, sparks fly into the air.

Concalo.

Summon.

RJ scrambles back to his feet and runs toward the balcony as an explosion echoes around them, and a ray of light hits the balcony.

"Shit," RJ shouts as multiple individuals appear. Members of the Arcane Law Enforcement and protection guild step out of the field, raising their wands as magic flies around the balcony. In the middle of them all is Lady Gwen.

"Mom," Martha says, hugging her mother as Gwen looks around cautiously.

"Cousin Gwen," Amelia acknowledges.

"Children," Gwen replies as she notices RJ standing and holding his bandaged arm.

"Guards continue to secure the balcony and keep an eye on things. Call Queen Rose immediately if anyone moves against this place," Martha and Gwen order as several fairies buzz the balcony.

"If we did not wake the entire school, the rest of my family will surely know what is going on. But, unfortunately, the fairies are here, which means my family will know within a matter of minutes. I am surprised the Chancellor is not knocking down my door," RJ grumbles.

"Inside, all of you, Now!" Gwen commands, shooing them inside.

"Mom, I am so glad you are here," Martha begins to say when Gwen raises her hand, silencing her.

"Yes, Martha, dear. I am here. RJ, you are hurt, and what is that?" Gwen asks, pointing her wand at the dagger.

"He fell from the ceiling with an arrow lodged in his arm. His roommate, Dalton, found the dagger," Martha explains. Suddenly, the room freezes around them before anyone can say or do anything. RJ stands looking around as sand appears, spinning around him. A light flashes and RJ is standing back in the apartment. Time unfreezes as Martha approaches him.

"RJ, let me see your arm," Gwen demands, reaching for him as RJ pulls away.

"Cousin Gwen, it is fine. Besides, it is 3:46 in the morning. Shouldn't you be in bed?" RJ inquires, smiling sweetly.

"Good point, everyone, to bed now. I have this," Gwen directs.

"Cousin Gwen, I am staying," Amelia protests.

"Amelia Genevieve Pendragon! Do not make me call your mother," Gwen threatens.

"Well then, on that note, good night," Amelia replies.

"Martha, take your cousin home. I have this. I will call for assistance if I need anything," Gwen snaps as Martha and Amelia nod, knowing that tone all too well.

"I will be fine, thank you," RJ says, hugging Amelia as he falls back onto the couch.

Dalton quietly slips into the kitchen and sits on one of the barstools as the door closes.

"You, sir. Your name is Dalton, correct?" Gwen inquires, pointing at him.

"Yes, ma'am," he replies.

"Would you mind leaving RJ and I to speak, please?" Gwen suggests as Dalton gets up, walks across the room, and disappears down the hallway. Gwen checks the area, walks across the floor, and sits down in the armchair.

"Russell Ambrose Alezander Elderchild Ignatius Jr., start talking. Do you care to explain what has happened?" she demands.

"It was nothing," RJ responds.

"Nothing? Nothing?! RJ, your arm is bandaged. There is mention of an arrow, an ancient elfish dagger lying on the coffee table that looks to be from the 10th Century. But it is nothing," Gwen yells as she raises her wand and levitates the dagger into the air, examining it.

"It is 10th or 11th Century by design. But, clearly, the markings are elfish," Gwen remarks.

"They are high elfish," RJ exclaims.

"Well then, that settles it. But, of course, King Ignatius will want to see this immediately," responds Gwen.

"Cousin Gwen, it was a dream. It was nothing," RJ says, trying to change the conversation.

"Cousin, this is no dream. The dagger would not be lying here on the coffee table if it were a dream," remarks Gwen, obviously annoyed.

"I do not want to talk about it. I said it was nothing," RJ snaps.

"RJ, I will have to take the dagger to my aunt, your grandmother. Do you know what is going to happen? She will be down here in the blink of an eye. So will my parents, Uncles Ethan and Sebastian, and your grandfather," Gwen replies.

"Exactly my point. No freedom No independence. I am 19 years old, and you all treat me like a child. If I say it is a dream, grandma will be sending armies into my dreams."

"You are 18, dear little cousin, although you *will* be 19 in a few weeks. Until then, your grandparents need to know. Besides, I will be in trouble if I keep this from them. I am not as worried about keeping it from your grandparents as I am of keeping it from my dad."

"If you have to run and tell your aunt, my grandmother, do so, if you must. But it does not mean I am saying anything about it. It was nothing," RJ reiterates, standing, but his legs go out from under him.

"If you are going to be difficult, let me help you to your feet and to your room," Gwen remarks as she supports RJ and walks with him to his room.

"Good night," he says as he reaches the door. Gwen turns and walks towards the family room and balcony.

"Mr. Cee, keep an eye on him. If he is not better come sunrise, send for help immediately," Gwen commands as she glances down at the coffee table.

"Odd. The dagger is gone," she remarks as she walks through the French doors, raises her hands, and the doors fly shut. Turning, she examines the area. Then, she acknowledges a cloaked individual on the next balcony with a nod and disappears with the guards. The cloaked individual examines the space, then raises their wand, causing a lightfield to rise over RJ's balcony door. Walking to the balcony railing, the figure raises their wand, and two orbs appear in the potted plants by the door. They glow, then return to normal. Nodding, the figure knows that they have done their job.

"Security orbs are set. Let anyone try to breach that apartment," the cloaked individual notes.

Turning, the figure pulls the dagger from under their cloak. Examining it, they wave their hand over the dagger as the markings begin to glow. The figure raises its wand, spins it, and disappears on the spot with the dagger.

It was a quiet, wet Saturday at 7:00 AM. Amelia and RJ walk across the campus, the wind howling behind them. The two have not spoken about what happened the night before. Instead, they descend the hill toward the large field. RJ carries a duffle bag over his right shoulder. His left arm is still bandaged. They reach the bottom of the stairs and walk toward the bleachers. RJ sets the bag down and bends over to tie his shoes.

"RJ?" inquires Amelia.

"I am fine, Amelia," answers RJ.

"Are you okay, RJ?" she inquires, pulling her hair back and tying it into a ponytail.

"You too? Did Cousins Martha or Gwen put you up to this and ask you to check on me?" he inquires.

"RJ, I am asking as your best friend," Amelia snaps.

"I am fine, just annoyed," he responds, pulling a bow out of his bag.

"I am going to practice," he says as he walks toward the middle of the field where he throws the bag down and taps the bow against his side. Watching from a distance, Amelia begins to stretch. RJ closes his eyes and takes in a deep breath, listening. In the distance, he can hear the voices of spirits chattering, the hooves of centaurs galloping, the buzzing of fairy wings, and the songs of the mermaids echoing around him.

੭

Stepping forward with his eyes closed, RJ feels his weight shift to his right foot as he snaps the bow up and begins spinning it over his head and in front of himself. The wind is howling around him as it speaks.

"You are the great master of time," it echoes around him as he opens his eyes, throws the bow in the air and does a back handspring toward his bag, grabbing his sword and spinning it around, cutting through the air with the majestic blade.

Spinning, he throws the blade in the air. It lands, standing straight up in the dirt. RJ runs across the ground, scoops up two arm blades, spins them, and they run along the length of the back of his arms.

"Elvish arm blades, the most powerful weapon imbued with the magic of the elements," Amelia remarks, walking up.

"You forget that they are activated by the power and magic of the spiritual elders of my people," RJ replies, smiling.

"For someone who hates magic, you sure have a bag of goodies," Amelia says.

"Just because I hate magic does not mean I do not like the weapons or culture of my people," RJ responds.

"Do you need someone to practice with?" Amelia asks, smiling and winking at him.

"Thank you, and while you know that usually I do not mind, today, I want to practice on my own. I am trying to process the dream, my arm, and everything that is going on," RJ replies, setting the arm blades down and sitting on the ground. Approaching, Amelia sits down in front of RJ.

"Dreams? Are these the same ones you have told me about before?" she asks.

"Yes, but they are becoming more vivid and real. Each time I am in them, it is as if something has changed. I cannot explain it, but they become more real," he explains.

"Is that what happened last night?" inquires Amelia.

"Indeed, it is," he says, sitting quietly as Amelia places a hand on his leg.

"I have an idea," Amelia suggests, standing up.

"What are you doing?" RJ asks as holding her phone in her hand, Amelia taps on the screen. Suddenly, flying across the field are small black objects that transform into a suit of armor.

"Wow, impressive," RJ says, standing and walking around the suit of armor, tapping it with his finger.

"It is my latest project. I programmed them in the lab the other day. The nanobots interlock and can create anything we need," she explains.

"They are amazing."

"After last night, I spent the rest of the night getting these guys ready," she remarks, pulling a watch from her pocket.

"Ready for what?" RJ inquires.

"This," Amelia says, picking up RJ's wrist and placing the watch around it as the nanobots break formation and fly around the two of them.

"I designed them to respond to you. The watch is designed to track you and your emotions. If your dreams are becoming real, if you get hurt or get stuck, the nanobots will be able to track you, telling me where you are, and I can send for help. Also, if you are without your bag of tricks, they can become your weapons. Moreover, I designed them to protect you against magic," she explains, smiling.

"How do they work?" RJ asks as the bow flies from the ground into his hand.

"They respond to your emotions and thoughts," she replies, laughing.

"Wow, I was right, science is more efficient than magic. Ha!" RJ remarks.

The two smile at one another as the nanobots continue flying around them, picking up speed.

"Amelia, what is going on?" RJ asks when Amelia picks up RJ's wrist pointing to the watch's face, which is flashing green. Suddenly, a blast of magic strikes the field of nanobots. The two look at each other, kneel, and RJ picks up his arm blades. As they stand up again, a cackle rings out over the field.

"Look, Liam, two filthy Mundane," Raven remarks, walking up and turning up her nose in disgust.

"Filthy Mundane? Really? Amelia, do you see filthy Mundane here? I only see two filthy Arcane!" RJ declares, mocking Raven.

"No, but I see a cranky old witch," Amelia responds as Raven raises her wand.

"Witch, that would not be a wise idea. To attack students of this university is asking for war. Besides, the Chancellor does not take nicely to Dark Arcane," Amelia notes as Raven releases dark magic against the two. The magic strikes the field of nanobots and disappears. Turning, Raven snaps her fingers and dark creatures appear. Snarling, they rise from the ground.

"Kill them, my pretties, then find the bunker," Raven commands as a dark throne made of skulls appears, and she sits down on it while the dark creatures continue to emerge. As two dark creatures approach, they drop to the ground, screaming and holding their severed arms.

"A Mundane with blades that can defeat the darkness? That is impossible," Raven screams as her eyes narrow on the blades.

"Ma'am, those are elfish," Liam notes, backing up cautiously.

"I can see that, you idiot," she remarks, pointing her wand at RJ. Then, she flies backward in the throne and tumbles across the ground as balls of light fly around the field and begin transforming as fairies dressed in armor appear. When Liam draws his wand, he finds a blade held to his throat as one of the fairy guards holds a sword to it. Two other fairies stand by with spears pointed at Raven.

"A dark witch attacking students. This is unacceptable," the Chancellor declares, appearing with her eyes narrowed at the sight of RJ. Before anyone can say or do anything, a loud pop sounds over the field as the Chancellor's husband approaches.

"Lord Phineas, what do you want us to do with her?" the two fairies inquire, still pointing their spears at Raven as Chancellor Fae walks up and picks up Raven's wand.

"She will be dealt with when King Ignatius arrives," Chancellor Fae declares as she snaps the wand in half.

"Dealt with? My brother does not dictate rules to me. He is no King," Raven cackles as Chancellor Fae raises her wand right in the face of Raven.

"Give me one reason, just one, to drop you here, witch!" The Chancellor says.

"And him, ma'am?" the fairy holding the sword to Liam's neck inquires.

"You're a filthy traitor," Liam spits at the Chancellor.

"Traitor? Liam, you sided with Morgana. I sided with my family," Chancellor Fae responds as Liam throws the fairy back and charges her but finds a blade in his gut.

"Now, I believe the Chancellor made it clear that you were not welcome here," RJ remarks, pulling the blade from Liam's gut as RJ's ears start to transform.

"An elf! He is an elf!" Liam yells as he collapses.

Raven reaches up and tapping the spears' tip, throws the two fairy guards back.

"An elf! You will either bow to your queen or die," Raven yells as she begins to charge RJ.

Suddenly, a column of light explodes in front of her throwing her across the field.

"No!" Raven screams, hitting the ground with the backsides of her closed fists.

Vines explode out of the ground as arrows scream through the air. Stepping out of the light column are Cedric, Willow, Rusty, Rose, and Zander.

Willow runs to RJ and steps in front of him to protect him when his bandaged arm catches her attention. Rose regards Chancellor Fae and the others, nodding her head and acknowledging them as Zander marches past her.

"Raven," he yells as she scrambles to her feet and begins running away, but vines wrap around her legs and slam her face-first into the ground. Zander looks back at Willow as her eyes stop glowing green, and she lowers her hands.

"Seriously? Do you mind?"

"Sorry, grandpa," Willow replies as she winks at RJ who smiles back at her.

Zander points his wand, and the vines explode, and Raven disappears on the spot. All that remains is a single orb. Zander reaches down and picks up the orb, turning it over in his hands a few times. Raven's face is pressed up against the inside of the orb and, when he throws it into the air, it disappears.

Turning, he looks at Liam. Zander's eyes narrow. Walking towards Liam, Zander is feet away from him when a voice stops him.

"Zander, brother-in-law, stop, please. Liam is my responsibility," Sebastian says, materializing.

"Brother," Liam snarls, spitting blood on Sebastian's boot.

"You have been stabbed and, by the looks of it, with an elvish blade, which means you messed with RJ," Ethan states, laughing and materializing next to Sebastian, his wand lifting up Liam's chin.

"Ethan, what should we do with him?" Sebastian inquires.

"Maybe hang him from the rafters of Camelot. Or Cedric is standing over there. I am sure he is hungry," Ethan jokes.

"Oh, I like that one," Sebastian concurs, raising his wand and levitating Liam into the air until he is stopped by a voice from behind them.

"Let him go."

"Let him go? Are you mad?" Sebastian asks, confused. Turning, he looks at his nephew RJ.

"I said let him go," RJ repeats, blades in front of him, ready to fight.

"RJ? Are you feeling OK?" Sebastian asks.

"Yes, Uncle. Let him go," RJ repeats with annoyance as Sebastian drops Liam.

RJ lowers his blades and walks across the field, kneels in front of Liam, and raises his chin with the tip of one of the blades.

"You have one chance, wizard. Either denounce your allegiance to Merlin, or I cannot stop those two," RJ says.

Liam starts laughing as dark magic flies from his mouth and spins around him and RJ.

"I have had enough of this," Rose declares, pointing her wand as RJ jumps back and a vortex portal opens under Liam, and he disappears.

"What's your issue?" Sebastian asks, looking at RJ.

"My issue? My issue? Is it so hard to show mercy? Why do all of you have to resort to magic?" yells RJ as he stumbles backward, fainting. The nanos activate and fly around him, catching him as he falls and, instead, he is lowered gently.

Chapter 9
Questions

Several hours later, RJ awakes to Mr. Cee purring next to him as he sits up in bed.

"Careful, you took a bad spill," his grandmother states, handing him a cup of tea and sitting down in the armchair next to his bed.

"Thank you. How long was I out?" RJ inquires as he takes the cup, his hand trembling.

"You were out for five and a half hours. You collapsed because it appears the arrow that punctured your arm last night was a poisoned arrow. Thank goodness your sister is a master herbalist," his grandmother remarks.

"Ugh, that probably explains the headache, but thank you," RJ says, sipping his tea.

"No need to thank me, you need to thank your sister. I am glad we got here when we did. Why didn't you call last night?" his grandmother asks, looking at him with her right eyebrow raised.

"It was early morning, and I did not want to hear any fussing over my dreams," RJ explains when a knock echoes through his room.

"Come in," says Rose as the door opens and Pete appears.

"Seriously, what are you doing in my apartment?" RJ mumbles.

"Grandma needed a way to get in, and since your bedroom balcony is next to mine, I levitated over and let her into your place since magical teleportation into your apartment is blocked," Pete explains.

"Wait! What? You let yourself in? I need to change the locks," RJ continues to grumble, somewhat annoyed.

"Pete, what is it?" their grandmother inquires, redirecting the conversation.

"Grandpa, Cousin Fae, and Willow have secured the University. New defenses have been installed, and the students are safe," Pete remarks.

"For the love of things good, please tell me you did not help," RJ asks.

"Yes, why?" Pete inquires.

"That means we are all doomed. Someone is sure to be hexed," RJ replies, annoyedly sipping his tea.

"Russell Ambrose Alezander Elderchild Ignatius, Junior, apologize to your brother for that comment," their grandmother demands.

"No!" RJ declares, slamming his cup down on the saucer.

"It's fine, Grandma. I guess he is getting back at me for all those times I mentioned that his magic is possibly going to kill us," states Pete, half smiling as he leaves, shaking his head.

"Russell Ambrose, what has gotten into you?" Rose demands.

"First off, I do not go by Ambrose. I do not use that name as a Mundane. Second, I go by RJ. How often do I have to explain this to everyone, and third, when has Pete's magic amounted to anything? I seem to remember that, as a child, the only thing his magic was ever good for was hexing me. Lastly, this was my time to get away from home and from magic. But no," RJ notes, crossing his arms.

"RJ, I am sorry. I know you want your freedom. At least, your brother is trying. You have to give him that much," Rose replies, smiling.

"Trying? Trying? Oh please! When you are not here, he is causing chaos, like when we were children. The only difference is that we are older, and he is not breaking my toys or hexing them or me," RJ barks as he gets out of bed, grabbing his shirt from his dresser and putting it on as the room begins to spin around him.

"No, no, no, no! I hate it when you do that. Take me back to school," RJ yells. The room materializes as Rose walks toward her desk.

"Not until you answer some questions," she replies, pouring a new cup of tea.

"Ugh," RJ moans as he throws his head back until the fireplace mantle catches his attention.

"What the…? Wait? When? Grandma?" RJ inquires.

"Yes, RJ?" Rose responds, calmly stirring her tea.

"Where is the snow globe?" RJ asks, pointing at the empty spot.

"Sit. We need to talk," Rose says as RJ walks toward the fireplace mantle, examining it. He pushes the griffin statue's leg down and steps back. The bricks in the fireplace begin moving to create an archway. RJ descends the stairs as Rose appears at the bottom of the stairs behind him.

"It is not down here. RJ, stop. It was taken," Rose explains as RJ stops, spins, and looks at her.

"Taken? How? When? By whom?" he asks.

"Please come back upstairs, and let's chat," Rose suggests, setting down an orb as RJ nods.

When the two emerge in the study, Cedric is standing there.

"Hello, Master RJ," Cedric says.

"Hey, good chap," RJ replies, smiling.

"See, Grandma, he calls me RJ," RJ remarks, sitting down.

"Yes, Cedric, what is it?" Rose inquires as she raises her hand, causing the teapot to float in the air over the two cups.

"Excuse me for the interruption. The Lady Esther needs to speak with you. I will let her know you're busy," Cedric says, regarding RJ carefully, then disappearing.

"Now, where were we?" Rose inquires.

"The snow globe?" RJ prompts.

"Yes, I will answer your questions, but, first, what happened last night? Gwen says you were badly banged up, and, by the way, your wound looked… well, it looked horrible. We were concerned it was from a poison arrow. It had started to spider out, and your veins were turning green. Please explain," Rose remarks, picking up her cup and saucer.

"It was a dream. Some elf attacked me," RJ says.

"An elf?" she asks, looking confused, her eyebrow raised as she stirs her tea.

"You look as confused as I am," RJ replies, taking a sip of tea.

"Did they know who you were?" she asks.

"I do not know. They were a crack shot, fought in the old ways, and carried this crazy old dagger on them," RJ explains.

"I heard from Gwen about the dagger being 10th or 11th Century, with writing in high elfish. The dagger's whereabouts are currently unknown," his grandmother notes.

"Unknown?" RJ inquires.

"According to Gwen, it went missing off the coffee table," his grandmother replies.

"Great! So, an ancient elfish dagger and my snow globe are both missing," RJ says annoyed.

"RJ, how often do your dreams become real?" his grandmother inquires as RJ sits quietly drinking his tea.

"A few times," he mumbles.

"What? I did not hear what you said. You seemed to have mumbled. But, dear me, I thought your grandfather and I taught you to articulate more clearly."

"A few times," RJ sighed again.

"A few times? RJ, this is serious!" Rose declares.

"I do not think so," RJ responds.

"Am I good to return to school?" he asks.

"Not yet," Rose replies, walking over to her desk as her grimoire appears.

"For the love of all things, Mundane, I have homework," RJ grumbles.

"And I have questions. Besides, the Mundane have computers, or you can take some automatic writing quills or a typewriter with you. You can get your homework done that way," Rose responds.

"We know the dagger is missing, and we know the snow globe is missing. So, big deal. What else do you need to know?" RJ asks.

"RJ, when you decided to contain your magic in that snow globe, the very fate of magic was tied to it. If the globe is destroyed, so is all magic," Rose explains, concerned.

"Good. That means, no more magic. We all can live normal lives," RJ quips.

"You do not mean that!" Rose declares.

"But I do. Have you met my siblings?" RJ inquires, sitting back and crossing his arms.

"So, that is what this is about? Your siblings?"

"Yes and no. But they are part of it."

"What is the other part?" Rose inquires, sitting across from RJ and placing a hand on his knee.

RJ gets up and walks toward the window, watching students zip by on brooms.

"I do not want the responsibility. The prophecies for the future are unclear. We do not have a clear answer about Merlin. With magic gone, the Curpendulums will have no power. None. Which means everyone is protected," RJ explains, his hands resting behind his back.

"RJ, Lord Yule reset time. He used the last of what time magic he could to make sure that you would return and save the Arcane," Rose says, leaning on the arm of her chair.

"That is what I am doing. Saving everyone, my way," RJ says.

Frustrated, Rose closes her eyes and sighs as the room spins. Leaning back in the chair, she touches her fingers of both hands together and rests her chin on them as the room dematerializes, and she disappears.

"Seriously? Dropping me in a vision is not going to help. My answer is still 'no!'" RJ calls, walking across the courtyard and looking around.

Examining the space, he runs his hand along the wall as his fingers dance over the runes written there.

"The story of time," RJ reads aloud.

"Oh joy, another boring story of magic," RJ laughs as an older version of himself walks through him towards Dalton.

❧

"You're late," Dalton notes, his back turned to Ambrose.

"I hate when you do that. For once, can't you note when I am on time?" Ambrose notes, approaching Dalton and looking out over the valley as he leans on the rock wall in front of him.

"You will never be on time, love, accept it."

"Besides, I thought you said time stands still here?"

"It does but, remember, time acts differently for both of us even when you are Mundane."

"What? Wait. What did he say?" RJ asks, walking toward Lord Yule.

"Indeed, it does. You know that I hate this, right?"

"I know, but you've hated magic all of your life."

"You are right about that."

"Ambrose?"

"Yes, Dalton."

"You know we can stop this battle with Merlin."

"I know, but I am afraid."

"Ambrose, I do not blame you for being afraid. Merlin is unpredictable."

"It is not that. Merlin is the easy part. It is my power, my magic… It is unpredictable. One minute stable, the next in chaos," Ambrose explains, holding up his hands and looking at them. RJ stands there mimicking the same motions as Ambrose.

"Your magic and power are fueled by them," Dalton remarks, placing his hands on top of Ambrose's as RJ stops, drops his arms, and looks at Dalton in shock as the image freezes. Dalton walks across the space and circles RJ.

"You believe that they do not understand?" Dalton asks aloud, circling RJ.

"Yes. Not another dream that turns real. Ha, ha! Funny, Grandma," RJ remarks, looking on in disbelief.

"No, I am actually here. You are interacting with me. This is not a dream," Dalton explains.

"How?" RJ asks.

"Do you have to ask? You should know. It is by the power of time," Dalton says.

"I cannot do this," RJ replies, sitting on the stone ledge of the rock wall overlooking the valley.

"That is not the RJ I know," Dalton says, circling the older version of Ambrose.

"He lacked confidence, hated magic, and wanted magic to go away. And yet, he took back his power. He held faith. He believed. And do you know why he believed?" Dalton asks as RJ gets up and walks away across the courtyard, passing a fire pit that is dimly lit.

"How do I get out of here?" RJ demands as Dalton stands on the other side, shaking his head.

"He is not ready," Dalton remarks aloud as several figures of light appear, materializing into complete forms.

RJ stops, turns, and observes the beings.

"I am not ready. Far from it. But neither are they," Dalton says as the flames in the pit jump as the beings regard one another.

The last of the beings materializes, revealing a woman who is familiar to RJ. She walks across the ground to the fire pit.

"Hi, Grandma Anwara," RJ says, approaching her and hugging her.

"My dear boy," she acknowledges, regarding him kindly as she spins her hands over the flames and conjures up a number of different images.

"Throughout the timelines, magic has shattered, been broken, torn apart, and used as a weapon. But through all that, magic remained strong. It persevered. It did this because one man, who had faith in themselves, and, when they gained that faith, so did everyone around them," Anwara remarks, looking up at RJ.

"It cannot happen. You do not know what it is like. They should have embraced me. Instead, they feared me. I am glad the snow globe is gone. I am glad it may be destroyed, and magic will cease to exist," RJ says.

"It is time to tell him," Anwara declares as the others regard one another and then look at Dalton.

"I screwed up," Dalton says, looking over his shoulder.

"Screwed up? You're the Great Lord Yule," RJ replies, half laughing, half confused.

"Yes, but when I merged the timelines, I created the one in which you reside. You are the true Noel. The others were never destined. They are there, but then, they are not. So truthfully, the true story is about you," Dalton explains.

"And...?" RJ asks.

"You grew up. You became Noel. You changed time. However, we learned that things are never what they seem. An alternate part of the story existed, one that, if played out, would destroy the very essence of time and, hence, would forever change it," Dalton explains as an image of an elf girl appears.

RJ's eyes narrow.

"She is stuck in time. She got stuck trying to save you," Anwara noted as RJ held out his hand.

"Me? Why me?"

"Because when you stopped believing, she did not. She believed in you," Dalton continued.

"She believed in both of us, and she knew that your heart would change if she could reunite us. She saw the good in you. She jumped through time to help you regain your magic, and she knows that you can stop Merlin," Dalton explains as he takes RJ's hands in his, leaves spinning around them.

"Your siblings may fear you, but I do not. Amelia, your best friend does not. Luciana, our daughter does not. She needs you. I need you. Amelia needs you. And, believe it or not, your siblings need you," Dalton declares as lightning strikes the leaves, causing them to burst into flames as fire flies around RJ.

"Dalton?" RJ yells, holding his arm up, shielding his eyes as the flames grew brighter around him. Suddenly, the nanos activate, spinning around him and creating a field protecting him.

"Go to New York City, go to find what you are looking for. Magic is always with you, even when you cast it out," a voice echoes as RJ feels the floor materialize under him. Then, the light flashes. Then, darkness.

"What the…?" RJ declares, sitting up on his bed, moving his hands over his shirt. "I am here. That was the strangest dream," he remarks, looking at Mr. Cee. Getting up, he walks over to the bedroom door, opens it, and looks out, observing his apartment. Then, he closes the door, walks over to his desk, and retrieves his journal.

Chapter 10
RJ's Journal

Journal,

    Where to begin is always the question. My dreams, if you would even call them that, are getting worse with each passing day. I just awoke from a dream that made no sense. But, then again, do any of my dreams ever make sense? I have filled your pages over the years with the complexities of each of them and how weird their mysteries are. So, to answer my own question, dreams often do not make sense. They are troublesome, and they always lead to many more questions than answers. But, of course, if I said anything about them to Grandma, she would want to jump into my dreams and meddle. She would want to explore and understand every aspect of what is going on. Then, of course, she would investigate everything and drive me nuts in the process, something I would rather her not do. Now, do not get me wrong, she can meddle in the ones involving magic, but I would rather her stay out of the ones that mainly involve Dalton.

    As always, time, in its infinite wisdom, is acting bizarre, yet I am still left to figure things out. Even as a Mundane, this is rather annoying. If my dreams are any consolation of what is yet to come, I wish time would just break once and for all, and all magic would cease to exist.

Just the other day, Amelia and I were attacked by Great Aunt Raven. She is now Merlin's second-in-command. When Grandmama, and Great Uncles Oliver and Ethan defeated Morgana, and sealed her away, it caused Raven to step into her spot. In my studies of history, I think dealing with Morgana would be more pleasant, then Raven. To date, I am still perplexed as to why the Aelfdene Council has not ordered her to be captured and locked up, but, hey, what do I know? However, Raven did say something of interest during her attack on Amelia and myself. She noted something about a bunker.

Now, Great Aunt Raven is the younger sister of Grandpa Zander. Her attack, the other day, caught my attention. You see, it was the first time that I have seen him so angry in a long time. His ears turned red. The last time, he was this angry, I was twelve and broke the Aelfdene Urn.

Now, if Raven is looking for some "bunker," it has to be here somewhere on this campus, and, if that is the case, why? Or, better yet, where? Thus far, I have hunted high and low, examining the various parts of the campus and nothing appears to be out of the ordinary, no tunnels, nothing that would show that a bunker exists or ever existed on campus. Although, the challenge still exists that things move and rotate on this campus. If a bunker exists, I have probably walked by it many times without realizing it because of how this campus behaves. So, I will have to head to the library instead to do some research.

Like the Sprite and Academy Libraries, the library on this campus holds various texts about every secret of this campus, the Arcane, and the campus's rare forms of magic. So, there should be at least something noted about this bunker in one of the texts in that library. If I have to pour through every book, I will.

And, yet again, there goes another explosion from the kitchen. One of these days, Dalton will finally figure out how to use simple magic without setting off the smoke alarms. He got so annoyed with the microwave the other day, that he lit it on fire with magic. Simple magic for him is rather confusing, but what I have seen is that complex spells are what he is the master of. It is actually rather odd, but that is what makes Dalton who he is.

While I find him rather cute, his magic, on the other hand, is rather annoying. For a High Arcane, his magic is weird and does not follow the traditional magical rules. But, then again, neither does mine.

I have been afraid to ask him out, even though I know we are "destined." I am really into him, but I am still scared. Dalton is sweet, very attractive, and always has the right words for the right moment in time. For me, I find myself attracted to him and on more than one level. He is smart, has a beautiful, caring heart, and is physically attractive. I laugh that when he is shirtless, he can give any of the elf warriors and monks, during practice, a complex as they look horrible next to him. I have been amazed at how well Dalton can keep up with me at the gym. He matches me move for move. I am fearful of asking him out because I feel it would give my family the impression that I am willing to take back my magic. I often wonder whether I can be with Dalton and not have to deal with everyone questioning me about magic.

I wish, Dalton and I could slip off to my beautiful cabin in the mountains of Montana, away from everyone. The siblings still do not know that I bought the place, and I plan to keep it that way. The cabin has just enough magic protecting it that I can disappear there and never be detected. It is sufficiently far away from Aelfdene, the Arcane villages, and the Academy so that no one would be able to find me and, thank you to a neat little magical artifact that Uncle Sloan, my mother's brother created, the magic protecting the place is untraceable.

Well, for now, I am off to the library to see if I can find anything about this rumored bunker or any reference to Merlin hiding things around the campus. I can only imagine the great horrors and obstacles that await in that bunker. Although I will say this, because this is Merlin we are talking about, nothing would surprise me. With that said, it becomes critical to find the bunker in order to maintain peace. Then, I might consider going to visit New York. Actually, no!

~RJ~

Chapter 11
Life on Campus

Leaving the apartment building, RJ walks quickly across campus, then climbs the stairs to the library's double doors. Zipping behind him is a small ball of light. RJ stops to listen.

"Weird, I thought I heard something," RJ remarks as he enters the library.

Entering the grand hall of the library, students bustle about up and down the stairs as RJ steps onto the circle platform in the middle of the hall as it levitates up to the fifth floor to the history of the university section. Strolling along the tall bookshelves of the library, RJ quietly runs his fingers over the spines of the books. Then, examining the spines, he pulls out a book, thumbs through it, then places it back on the shelf.

Hmm. Raven mentioned a bunker the other day. So, there has to be something in this old library that references some sort of bunker. This is annoying. I wonder if they have other books that are not out.

Quietly, RJ looks around. He descends two flights of stairs and approaches the central reference desk.

"Excuse me, ma'am? Can you tell me if everything is currently out on the floor, or is there a restricted section?" RJ inquires.

"Yes, young man, there is a restricted section. However, it is only accessible to the faculty and staff. I am sorry, but it is impossible to grant your request for access without their permission," the librarian explains, looking at RJ.

"Thank you."

The faculty or staff have to grant permission. Hmm. I wonder…

RJ sets off out of the library and down the path, wandering the campus, until he reaches the agriculture building.

Office 4A. Where is 4A? Ahh, here it is.

RJ knocks several times until the door opens, and several fairies buzz at the door.

"Hi, I am so sorry to bother you but is Professor Fae in?"

"RJ, come in."

"Hi, Professor," RJ acknowledges as several fairies take complete form. One of the fairies stops, examining RJ as another smiles, trying to flirt with him.

"Fayette, seriously? He fancies men. Go help my mother at Glenoaks or do your homework," Professor Fae remarks, laughing, "besides, he has no interest in females, let alone a fairy."

"So, what brings you out to my part of campus?"

"Would it be possible for me to trouble you for a favor?" RJ asks.

"Depends. What is the favor?" Professor Fae responds.

"I am writing a paper for my Arcane archeology class. Unfortunately, I seem to be having trouble finding any good information, and I need permission from a faculty member to enter the restricted section of the library," RJ explains.

"Ahh. No!"

"What? Why professor?" inquires RJ.

"One, my wife would kill me if I granted any student such access. Second, did your grandmother approve it? Third, NO! I thought you were coming to ask me for something more useful, like to hex your brother."

"Seriously? Wait! Hex, my brother? Can you do that? But, wait. Never mind. We can discuss that option later. But even with my grandmother over at the Arcane Academy, she is still dictating the rules, even here," RJ complains, rolling his eyes.

"Oh, look at the time. I am sorry, RJ. I would love to help but, no. Why not ask the Chancellor? Besides, if there were any books about a particular—oh I do not know—bunker, they would not be here. Maybe one should inquire with Cedric," Professor Fae remarks, winking as his wings appear and he shrinks and disappears.

"Thanks, Professor."

"The professor could not be more helpful," Fayette remarks, dropping a marble as she shuts the door.

▲

I am so going to regret this. Ask Cedric? Really? RJ hesitates, scooping up the marble and throwing it down the hall as a portal opens.

RJ walks toward the portal, passes through, and arrives in the manor's kitchen.

Smells good. What is cooking? Picking up the lid, RJ examines the pot. *Nice. Cedric is making duck. No RJ. Focus! Leave the duck alone. You need to find Cedric.*

Leaving the kitchen, RJ enters the hallway, looking around when he hears voices and slips behind one of the suits of armor, listening.

"Oliver, I want as many investigators looking for that bunker as possible. Even if you have to pull other departments, need I remind you that if the texts and prophecies are true, the bunker will be a gem among gems. The artifacts reported to be in that place are priceless, Arcane artifacts. Remember, our great grandfather, Merlin, stole, killed for, and hid the relics in his lust for absolute power. If my crazed sister-in-law, Raven, wants them, we have to find them before she or Merlin does," Rose says as Oliver and Bethany stand nearby listening to her.

"You know, sis, Bethany is the Chancellor of the University, and, as the Arcane President, I must follow Arcane law. I cannot just order the investigators on campus, not without her permission, just like at the academy," Oliver notes as Rose raises an eyebrow toward Bethany.

"I will allow it only if they are unseen. I do not want the newspapers all over this. That is all we need, the papers reporting that the campus may have a secret bunker with multiple Arcane artifacts. Do you realize the mess we would have on our hands? There are not enough fairies to guard the campus or the students. Besides that, the Arcane Tribune would send their top reporter Ms. Claria, and you know the issues with her," Bethany remarks as Cedric approaches.

"Cousin, I understand none of us like Ms. Claria, but I am not asking for the laws to be broken, just for things to be investigated," Rose explains.

"Hello, Cedric," the three acknowledge.

"Lord Oliver, Ladies Rose, and Bethany, my apology for interrupting," Cedric says, handing a letter to Rose, which she opens and starts to read.

"Not again! This makes the fifteenth time in two weeks that fifth graders are upsetting Mr. Giggle. This is going to be a long year with them. I will leave you two to speak," Rose explains.

As she disappears, Cedric catches a glimpse of RJ hiding on the other side of the hallway.

"Lord Oliver and Lady Bethany, while I always enjoy your visits, I have much work to do," Cedric remarks, grabbing the two by the arms and marching them toward the door.

"Cedric, you are in a hurry," Bethany remarks.

"My lady, I do not want to be rude, but the light, yes, the light in the hallway is perfect at this time of day for me to dust the suits of armor," replies Cedric as the three stop in the entryway.

"Cousin, you have my permission. As I have said, you can send in investigators, but I do not want them seen. Understood? If I find that nosey know-it-all, Ms. Claria, on my campus, I will be hexing you," Bethany remarks, wrapping her scarf around her neck as she disappears.

"Good day, Cedric," Oliver says, rolling his eyes as he disappears.

Cedric raises his hands as the shutters slam shut, and he turns.

"Master RJ, to what do I owe this visit?" Cedric inquires, arms crossed, tapping his right foot.

"Cedric, hello. I happened to be in the area," RJ smiles.

"Master RJ. Have I not taught you anything? You may be able to lie to your parents, your siblings, your family, and hell, even yourself, but I see through your lies. Just call it a sixth sense for vampires," Cedric replies sternly.

"You talk about me lying. You told my grandmother, her cousin, and my great uncle a lie. The lighting in this hallway is horrible," RJ replies, shaking his head, running a finger down the coat of arms and picking up his finger to examine it.

"See, no dust."

"Master RJ, if any of them had seen you, there would be thousands of questions."

"Well, thank you for getting rid of them and sparing me the headache. I am heading to the library," RJ says as he walks past Cedric, patting him on the shoulder.

"No, you're not! Your grandmother locked it."

"Okay, that is a new one. Anyway, Cedric, don't you have the key? I am writing a paper for my Arcane archeology class and need some materials."

"Master RJ, yes, I have the key," Cedric notes, pulling it from his vest pocket and holding it up.

"You're the best, Cedric," RJ says, walking back and grabbing the key from him.

"Oh, and Master RJ, if you are looking for texts on the bunker, they are not here," Cedric remarks as RJ pauses in the central section of the staircase.

"Of course, they would not be here. How silly of me. Why would I think they are here?" RJ replies as Cedric appears next to him.

"I shall join you in the library. Maybe I can help you find what you are looking for," Cedric explains, walking with RJ.

The two stroll down the long hallway quietly until they reach the library.

"Master RJ, I gave you the key, correct?" asks Cedric.

"Yes, you handed it to me as I walked by," RJ replies.

"Ah yes, That appears to be the key for the secret study. Silly me! This is the key for the library that you will need," Cedric replies, pulling a second key from his pocket and unlocking the door.

"A secret study?" RJ asks, eyebrow raised.

"Did I say a private study? Why, whatever do you mean?" Cedric asks as the two enter, looking around as RJ begins strolling along the bookshelves of his family's private collections.

"Hey, Cedric, do we have anything on ancient ruins?"

"I believe your grandmother files them over there in the bookcase next to the fireplace," Cedric remarks, pointing.

"This one?" asks RJ as he approaches the bookcase and starts scanning the spines.

"Cedric, are you sure this is the correct shelf?" RJ asks as his eyes wander over the books. "Never mind," RJ continues, running his hand down the spine of a book titled *Secrets*.

Examining the spine, RJ pulls the book and notices a keyhole hidden behind the book. Retrieving the key from his pocket, he places the key in the hole and turns the lock.

When the lock clicks, the bookcase slides open, and RJ looks back at Cedric, who is gone.

"Cedric?"

Well, I guess I proceed through the secret door.

As RJ descends the spiral staircase, the torches pop on, lighting one after another as the walls are made of various bookcases holding ancient texts and various artifacts. Reaching the ground floor, RJ observes that the room goes on for miles.

This place must be the private holdings of my grandparents. Interesting vials—the scale of dragon, blood of centaur, feathers of phoenixes—these shelves are filled with the ingredients needed to make many of the high-level potions the Arcane use.

Then, RJ sees it, the pedestal with a giant book.

That has to be it.

Wow, grandma, what an exciting book to leave in the house. Is that natural skin? Eww, and the mouth being sewn shut is a classic touch. Definitely must be either Merlin's book or something about him. Unfortunately, it appears the book is asleep.

Stepping back, RJ examines the spine, *The Inventory of Merlin.*

Yes, it is Merlin's book. That explains the weird cover. Hmm, I wonder. Let me see. The feather, that's it.

RJ strolls across the space, retrieves the jar of feathers off the shelf, takes one out, and goes back to the book. When he moves the feather over the cover, the book flies open.

It worked. How interesting.

Over the next few hours, RJ goes through the book, page by page, examining the inventory, writing down some of the essential items noted in Merlin's inventory.

"Are all of these items in Merlin's collection?" RJ asks aloud, not paying attention or realizing that he is not alone.

"That is why the book is here," Cedric remarks.

"Are all of these items in the bunker?" inquires RJ.

"Yes, we believe they are. That is why the book was brought here. Your grandmother and grandfather have been studying every page," explains Cedric.

"This is why I hate magic," RJ mutters quietly under his breath.

"You hate magic because of magical artifacts, Master RJ?" inquires Cedric.

"No. I am reading the description of this item. Why would this even exist? I have counted at least twenty different items that should not be in the general public. Look at this, an elf sneer. Great grandpa Ignatius banned those things. A singing harp. Wow, that needs to be burned. Get this, 'If allowed to sing, it will render any attacker unconscious.' Why do these things exist?" asks RJ.

"They are the items of the times of old. The harp would be nice to have against the legions of the dark," Cedric replies, running his hand down the page.

"Are you kidding me? These should all be destroyed," RJ declares, turning the page, which he stops and examines.

"You have the same look in your eye that your grandfather did when he was younger and read about that item in the Sprite Library," Cedric remarks, watching RJ.

"The Elven Star. The beacon of hope. That is the lifeline of the elves. So, Cedric, why does Merlin have this?" asks RJ.

"That Master RJ, we are still trying to figure out," Cedric replies.

"The Elven Star has unbelievable power for healing, time manipulation, and control of all forms of elemental and celestial magic. The Elven Star is believed to be over two thousand years old and was given to the Arcane Mystical Race of Elves to guide them on their journey," RJ reads aloud, looking up from the book at Cedric.

"Cedric, could it be possible that this item is no longer in Merlin's control?" RJ inquires.

"We do not know. But, if he has the star, that will be his prized possession next to the pocket watch, if he ever gets his hands on it," Cedric remarks as RJ begins examining his ring.

"Master RJ, is everything okay?" Cedric inquires, watching as RJ continues to examine the ring with a puzzled look on his face.

"Yes, Cedric, it is. Question for you?"

"Proceed, Master RJ."

"Cedric, what if Merlin did not have the Elven Star? What if, by fate, it was hidden from him? What if he needs the bunker because, without the star, he is vulnerable?"

"It is a possibility, but the star, if returned, would certainly be detected. Your grandfather has multiple spells and charms in place to locate it."

"Cedric, I understand that, but what if it is not meant to be found?"

"Master RJ, is there something you are not telling me?" Cedric asks as RJ glances down at his ring yet again. Cedric approaches, picks up RJ's hand, and examines the ring.

"Master RJ, if the star exists and is in the control of a particular Mundane, then it would be safe."

"Sorry, Cedric, you know how I get with the books. It was just a crazy idea. Forget I ever mentioned it," RJ remarks, pulling his hand back and closing the book.

"Well, not to rush things, but I came down to get you home. Your grandparents will be back in the hour, and they will be here, in this library, studying. If you are found down here, you will be in more trouble than any of us could imagine."

"Understood, and, Cedric, thank you," RJ says hugging him.

"Master RJ, I have sworn to keep these things a secret, but I also took an oath to protect your family. Young Master, I have known about Lord Time Yule, securing his necklace's stone with you and I suspected that your ring is extremely old, keep them with you. Although, you hate magic, you must protect both. No one is to know what that ring truly is until the time is right."

"Understood," RJ responds, smiling as Cedric holds up an orb, as it grows bright, flashes, and RJ disappears.

Within seconds, he is back in his apartment. Looking around, RJ walks toward his chest and taps it. As it opens, he pulls a key from his pocket and opens the hidden chamber where he takes off his ring, places it in the chamber, locks the door, and then, closes the chest.

"Cedric is right, that ring needs to remain hidden, for now at least."
Sitting on his bed, RJ yawns, then falls asleep.

Chapter 12
The Festival

BUZZZZZ!

"Ugh, what time is it?" RJ asks, hitting the alarm clock when he picks it up.

"7:00 AM on a Saturday! Are you kidding me? Why is my alarm set for a Saturday?" RJ asks, rolling over.

"Wait, my apartment. I am in bed. That was the weirdest dream yet. I dreamt that I was in a secret room in the library at the manor, reading about the bunker. What do you think, Mr. Cee? Was it a weird dream?"

RJ puts on his shirt and walks out into the family room to find Dalton making breakfast.

"Good morning," RJ yawns, opening the cupboard and pulling out a mug.

"Good morning," Dalton acknowledges.

"I see you are making breakfast," RJ remarks, pouring coffee.

"Yep, I figured I would eat a good breakfast before we went out on our date," Dalton replies.

"Date? That's right! Our date. Sorry. I am not fully awake yet," RJ remarks as Dalton looks at him, perplexed.

"Are you okay?"

"Yeah, just trying to wake up," RJ laughs.

Bolting to his room, RJ shuts the door.

Okay, breathe, Russell Ambrose, breathe, you have a date. What should I wear? Where are we going? Ahh. Stop. Calm down.

Twenty minutes later, RJ re-emerges from his room, his hair spiked, and wearing a nice pair of jeans, boots, a nice shirt, and his long coat, sunglasses hanging from his shirt front.

"You look nice," Dalton remarks.

"Thanks," RJ responds.

"Give me a minute, and I will be ready," Dalton says, standing and transforming his clothes with magic as RJ rolls his eyes.

"Magic, seriously? Anyway, where are we headed?" RJ askes

"Man, you must be tired. Remember we talked about the festival?" Dalton explains.

"I remember. I was trying to see if you remember and are as excited as me," RJ says, smiling and holding the door for Dalton.

RJ leans against the wall as Martha and Amelia greet him and Dalton as they turn to lock the door.

"Morning," the two women say in unison.

"Morning," Dalton and RJ reply when, suddenly, yelling is heard.

Martha and Amelia regard one another, then look at RJ, who rolls his eyes.

"This goes on at all hours of the day and night," RJ remarks as his brother's apartment door flies open.

"Creep," the woman yells, throwing a drink in Pete's face as she leaves.

In just his boxers, Pete sees everyone in the hallway, staring. Then, he slams the door.

"I am sure your grandmother would love hearing about this, Martha remarks as RJ shrugs, and the group walks downstairs, out the door, and across campus to the path leading to the festival.

Martha and Amelia are watching every move Dalton and RJ make. Several times, Dalton attempts to sneak in holding RJ's hand but is unsuccessful as RJ realizes what is occurring and does something to avoid holding Dalton's hand.

The four are chatting and laughing until they reach the gates, when RJ suddenly stops and the other three become aware of what has caught RJ's attention.

"Guys, I do not want to deal with anyone. Let's get our tickets and go," RJ says just as the other three notice Michael, Sophia, and Isabella standing with a group of students from the Arcane School of Magical Teaching, while Ms. Destiny, Lady Marybelle, and Ms. Tulip are fussing at a group of fourth-graders who have just transfigured a bird into a goblet.

"Then, we will not engage them, dear cousin," Martha says, taking RJ by the arm and walking toward the ticket window while Amelia and Dalton follow closely behind them.

"Can I have four tickets, please?" RJ asks at the ticket window.

"That will be forty dollars, sir," the clerk replies.

Just when RJ hands her the money, the four hear a loud pop, followed by his sister's extremely loud voice behind him and his group.

"Drunk? Seriously? There are rules," Isabella remarks loudly as Pete stumbles backward.

"Here are our tickets. Let's get out of here before the magic starts flying," RJ remarks as they each hand their tickets to the young man who is checking them at the gate, leaving the crowd that is starting to form behind them.

"I see nothing has changed with Pete, still as difficult as ever. He will never learn," Martha laughs, trying to make light of the situation, but Amelia and Dalton give her a stern look.

The four wander through the festival, stopping at various vendors and strolling through the booths. Dalton examines a moon dial in one of the booths. When he puts it down and walks away, his attention drawn to the carnival games, RJ quickly walks over, picks it up, takes it to the register, and pays for it.

Walking out of the booth, RJ smiles and hands the bag to Dalton.

"I wish you had not," Dalton says, kissing RJ.

"From what I saw, you were interested in it," RJ replies, smiling as Dalton takes his hand and drags him off toward the carnival games.

RJ and Dalton laugh together as they play a few carnival games. Martha and Amelia are making bets on how long it will be before Dalton starts messing with time in order to win the games. However, the two realize that RJ is a natural at many of them and does not need magic to win.

After a while, the four stop playing and stroll down the row of food vendors where they grab some lunch and eat at one of the picnic tables.

"Are you two going to be okay here for a few minutes?" Martha inquires.

"Yes. Why?" RJ asks.

"Amelia and I are going across the way to look at that booth," Martha replies as the two get up and head for the booth.

"RJ, sit right there. I will be right back," Dalton says as RJ sits quietly, observing the area. Several Arcane students are playing with dragon gliders. When one lands by RJ's foot, he reaches down, picks it up, and hands it to the approaching student.

"Is this yours?" RJ inquires, handing it to the first-grader.

"Thank you. I am so sorry that it flew into your foot, Lord Ambrose," the child replies.

"It is okay. Besides, I used to play with dragon gliders when I was your age. So, you might want to get back with the rest of your class," RJ responds, smiling and handing the glider back to the kid.

"Thank you again, Lord Ambrose," the kid says, skipping back to his friends.

"Lord Ambrose," Dalton says, smiling and holding an ice cream sundae.

"Are you planning to eat that whole thing?" RJ inquires, smiling back at Dalton.

"No. It is for us to share. I did not realize you still went by Ambrose," Dalton remarks.

"Ugh, I do not. But many of the younger kids have, at some point or another, heard me referred to as 'Lord Ambrose,' and that is what they call me. I prefer that they do not, but I will not sit here and argue with them," RJ replies, grabbing one of the spoons. The two smile at each other and start eating the sundae and laughing.

Across the way, Martha and Amelia stroll through the booth until Martha speaks up, "What do you think of the two of them?"

"Martha, they are cute together, but please stay out of their business," Amelia responds, looking at one of the necklaces on the table.

Suddenly, Martha elbows Amelia.

"That is adorable. They are sharing an ice cream sundae," Martha says as Amelia and Martha regard one another.

"It looks like they do not need magic to like each other," Amelia remarks, smiling.

"Oh no, dear cousin, there is no spell or potion we can use to make two people fall in love. It defies all the rules of magic," Martha explains in a serious voice.

Then, after exchanging glances, she and Amelia, set down the items they are looking at and run out of the booth.

"Well, what do we have here?" Pete asks, patting RJ on the back.

"Hi Pete," Dalton responds as RJ ignores him.

"Not saying anything? What, does Mr. Cee have your tongue?" Pete asks as RJ says, "Let's go!" to Dalton.

"Go, baby brother? Why not come hang with your siblings?" Pete suggests as RJ stands.

"No!"

"Are you serious, RJ?"

"RJ, we have our duties. We have to greet all of the people," Pete remarks but is interrupted.

"Hello, Pete. How are you, cousin?" Martha inquires, approaching with Amelia in tow.

"Martha," Pete acknowledges, obviously displeased.

"Good, you two are back. Let's go," RJ says.

"Dude, I asked if you wanted to join us?" Pete repeats.

"Pete, he said 'no,'" Martha replies as Pete raises his wand. Amelia quickly steps in front of RJ as Dalton stands with his hands raised.

"Stand down, Pete. Hexing RJ is not the answer," Martha declares as Pete spins his wand.

As he opens his mouth to speak, time freezes. RJ, Amelia, and Martha regard each other as Dalton steps over the bench, his hands glowing as he steps between RJ and Pete.

"Dalton? I wish you had not done that," Amelia remarks, observing the reaction on RJ's face.

"Magic! Magic! Is that all any of you can resort to? Magic! I can handle myself," RJ yells as he looks first at Dalton and then approaches Pete. He grabs Pete's wand, snaps it in half, and throws the two pieces in opposite directions.

"RJ, I have always told you that I would respect your request for no magic, but he was casting magic against you. I am not going to let that happen," Dalton responds.

"For once, I wish everyone could just be normal. I am done with magic. It is easier to slug him in the face than deal with magic," RJ remarks as he walks away.

Amelia regards Dalton, and Martha shrugs her shoulders. The two motion for Amelia to follow RJ. Lowering his hands, Dalton unfreezes time and Pete.

"My wand! Where is it?" Pete demands and Martha shakes her head.

"Peter Kelvin Bair Ignatius, over here. Now!" Ms. Destiny barks, tapping her foot.

"Aunt Destiny, I was trying to get rid of a bug that was flying around," Pete explains as Sophia, Michael, and Isabella approach.

"Oh, this is not good," Sophia remarks as Destiny shoots her an annoyed look.

"You, of all people! You know the rules. The repercussions of your actions could have been catastrophic if you had hit your brother with magic, so help us all," Destiny declares as the sky lights up and a column of light descends.

"I was coming over to speak with my brother. But, jeez, I was not going to hex him," Pete grumbles.

"That is not what it looked like to us…" Dalton began until a very disgusted voice was heard.

"Peter Kelvin Bair Ignatius, please explain to me why am I being pulled out of the library? I am told that you are being disrespectful to your brother," his grandmother's voice booms around him.

"Hi, Grandma. I was trying to handle a bug," Pete mumbles, looking down at the ground.

"A bug, a hex, a magical water balloon fight. I do not care what you want to call it. The alerts sounded that you had raised your wand against Ambrose," Rose remarks, stepping out of the column, materializing along with Zander, Rusty, and Meredith.

"Hi, Grandma," Isabella, Kells, and Sophia acknowledge.

"Isabella, Kells, Sophia, Aunt Destiny, please join the rest of the faculty and students and continue your day. Martha, I advise you to find your cousin. Make sure he is calm. Lord Time Yule, thank you. Please join Martha, and go after him," Rose commands, tapping her foot, arms crossed, and looking angrily at Pete.

When only Rose, Zander, Rusty, Meredith, and Pete remain, Rose spins her hands and all five disappear.

❧

"I would suggest you sit down," Zander remarks to Pete as Rusty leans against his mother's desk and Meredith quietly pours cups of tea for everyone, shaking her head.

"I was trying to take care of a bug?" Pete protests.

"A bug? Seriously, Peter? We have been through this time and time again…" his grandmother begins when Rusty raises his hand, interrupting her.

"Mom, may I?"

"By all means. Go ahead, Russell," Rose replies, stepping back from Pete, walking over to an armchair and sitting down.

"What were you thinking? No, wait! You were not thinking, were you? You were just angry," Rusty yells as Pete slumps into an oversized armchair.

"Dad, I was joking with him. You know, good ol' brotherly joking. The way you and Uncles Ari and Theo do," Pete replies, trying to make light of the situation.

"Joking? Joking?! I do not believe my pointed ears. Pointing a wand at your brother is not joking! My brothers never did such a thing. Lord Yule having to freeze time is joking? Seriously, Peter?" Rusty screams as items in the room start to levitate and fly around him. Meredith and Rose gently raise their hands, trying to lower items back down into their proper places but only getting about a quarter of them under control.

"Dad, I know you're getting upset. Your ears are getting red. Why don't we talk about this calmly?" Peter inquires, trying to remain calm himself. Suddenly, a pop echoes through the room as his Uncle Ari and Aunt Vivian arrive.

"Oh dear, items floating. Not good," Vivian remarks at the sight of her brother, Rusty.

"His ears are red. That is not good at all," Ari notes.

"Yes, my ears are red because this clown wants to continue to hex his brother. NO!! I do not want to hear you explain to me, Peter. Some stupid excuse. It's always some stupid excuse. For seventeen years, I have maintained my temper, Peter. I have listened to and sought the counsel of many around me. I have meditated and been patient. But enough is enough. This ends today. If I hear about you stepping out of line again, whether it is about the ladies in and out of your apartment, the drinking, skipping classes, or hexing your brother, I will bind your magic like I should have done seventeen years ago. You have tormented Ambrose for seventeen years. Enough is enough! You are the second eldest boy, Peter, and RJ has looked up to you. Your other siblings have looked up to you and Michael to set the example. Instead, you insist on being a pain. RJ was on a date, and he told you 'No.' But instead of listening and being respectful, you ignored your sibling's request and continued to push. Do you know why he ignored you? Do not answer that! I will tell you," yells Rusty as items in the room begin flying for a second time.

"Mom?" Vivian inquires as Rose raises her free hand to lower the items, while she chokes on her tea, trying to maintain her composure.

"Rusty, dear, you're upset. Shouldn't maybe your parents speak to Peter, dear?" Meredith inquires gently.

"No, dear. I have this, but thank you," Rusty responds.

Pete attempts to speak, but Rusty continues yelling.

"Silence! You will not interrupt me. Ambrose feels that he does not have a relationship with five of his siblings. Put your hand down. Do *not* interrupt me!" Rusty commands, raising his own hand as his eyes begin to glow. Peter quietly lowers his hand and slumps down lower in his chair.

"Ambrose looked up to you. Of all his siblings, you. He idolized his older brother. He used to wait by the door for all of you to get home and then cried when you, Michael, and Kells went off to do things that never included him. All he wanted was to be with his brothers. But no, instead, you and your brothers have ignored him and called him names like 'Freaky Merlin twin.' Peter, we are all 'freaky Merlin twins.' Incubus blood runs from Merlin through our entire family line, or did you forget that?" Rusty rants on as the others stand by, quietly listening.

"Dad…?" Pete begins to say.

"I know I did not give you leave to interrupt me," Rusty yells as he turns to the others in the room. "Did any of you hear me give him permission to interrupt?"

"Rusty, Brother, breathe. He does not understand. He is not like the five of us," Ari suggests, trying to calm his brother.

"No, Peter would have no clue what the five of us were like. You four could have hexed me all day long, particularly since I am blind. But, instead, you all taught me how to use my magic, unlike Peter, who simply wants to torment his brother," Rusty exclaims as the giant oak doors of the study fly open to reveal Isabella, standing in the doorway, lightning flying between the tips of her hair as Michael, Kells, Sophia, and Willow appear behind her.

"Please tell me someone has already hexed him. If not, I would be more than happy to do so now," Isabella remarks, pulling her wand and pointing it directly at Peter.

Willow grabs Isabella's arm, trying to control the situation.

"Isabella, wand down. NOW! No one is hexing anyone! So help me, I will bind all of your magic," Rusty barks as the remaining four siblings back up.

Isabella lowers her wand and stows it when she notices that her grandmother's wand is out.

"Oh, sorry, Dad. It appears that you have this situation under control," Isabella says, backing up toward her siblings.

"Peter, this is the last time that I am saying this. Not a toe out of line, not one toe. Is that understood? If I hear a spirit, a fairy, an elf, anyone, say anything negative about you, I will bind your magic and show you what it means to take on the next future king of the elves," barks Rusty.

"Yes, Dad. I understand," Pete responds, his voice shaking.

"Now, the last thing I strongly advise is that, until Ambrose cools off, you stay away from him. Is that clear? If not, and you choose to mess with him, then all I can say is that I hope for your sake that he does not choose to destroy *all* magic. Is that clear?" Rusty inquires sternly.

"Yes, sir, it is," Peter replies, chastened.

Then Rusty turns, acknowledges his parents, wife, siblings, and other children with a nod and disappears.

"Mom and Dad, Vivian, if you will excuse me, I will check on Rusty and make sure that he is okay," Ari remarks, tugging on Vivian's sleeve and both of them disappear.

"Peter, my dear boy, fix this. Do you understand me? You fix this. I suggest you start by listening to your father. Then, when the time is right, and I mean the time is right, you apologize to your brother," his mother directs, patting him on the shoulder as she also disappears.

Rose rises from her chair and walks toward her desk, steadily regarding Zander.

"Grandpa, you two are not going to say anything?" Peter inquires.

"Peter, I have learned that there are two people who I do not challenge, your grandmother and your father. You just saw a side of your dad that I do not think you knew about. I would strongly advise that you listen to him. Otherwise, who knows what he will do to your magic," Zander remarks calmly.

"Dismissed. All of you. Peter, you stay," Rose commands, her hands resting behind her back as she gazes out the window.

"Come on, let's go, you four. We will see you later, Grandma and Grandpa," Isabella declares as they all disappear.

Swallowing hard, Peter stands, quietly waiting.

"Peter, I would advise that you lay low and not get into any more trouble. Now, have a good evening," his grandmother says calmly as she raises her hand, and Peter disappears.

"Do you think things will change?" Zander inquires of Rose after Peter is gone.

"For the sake of time, our family, and everything yet to come, I hope so. Ambrose already has his struggles. Peter mucking things up does not help. I hope that for the sake of magic, Ambrose and Peter can learn to trust each other and work together," Rose replies as Zander nods in agreement.

Chapter 13
Siblings

After leaving the study of the Arcane Academy, Peter ends up back at the University of Arcane and Mundane Studies. He looks around, then spins his wand as a portal opens, he steps into it and disappears. Arriving in the greenhouse, he looks around cautiously.

"Willow?" he calls as he taps the leaves of one of the plants with his fingers.

"Pete, what are you doing here?" Willow asks as she emerges from behind one of the shelves of plants.

"Can we talk?"

Sitting down on one of the stools, Willow motions for him to sit on one of the others.

"What's on your mind?"

"Everything. I do not know where to begin," Pete replies, confused.

"You're upset about Dad being tough on you?" inquires Willow.

"Yes. I have never seen him that angry before. Have I really been that difficult?" he asks.

"At times, yes. But that is what makes you who you are as one of my older brothers. Pete, you have to remember that Father has always been very reserved, but Dad has also always expected all of us to get along the way he and his siblings did. Our parents have carried a great responsibility on their shoulders for years," Willow remarks, smiling and placing her hand on top of his.

"Do you believe that Dad and our aunts and uncles all get along and never fought?" Pete inquires.

"My understanding from Grandma is that our dear uncles and aunts went out of their way to make sure Dad was taken care of and included. Dad is who he is because of the care of his siblings. Grandma said that as Dad got older, he found independence, and, at times, it scared Uncle Ari to death.

Grandma explained that there were many occasions when she had to take Uncle Ari or Uncle Theo's wands as they would hex someone just for messing with Dad."

Willow waves her hand, and a sandwich tray appears.

"You always know how to calm a situation," Pete remarks, picking up a sandwich.

"I watched Mom and Grandma over the years," Willow laughs.

"So, let me ask, sis, did I screw up?" Pete inquires, taking a bite of the sandwich.

"To a point. It was not easy for any of us with Ambrose. We all care for him dearly, but the magic our brother holds is far beyond anything we have ever seen, or that we were ever taught about at the Academy or by our family. When his meltdowns occurred, they made his magic even worse. Remember, our entire family has remarked on not having seen anything like Ambrose's magic before. But, Pete, it was also difficult. Ambrose looked up to you. He idolized you more than even Michael or Kells. He spent hours copying you in combat form. Why do you think he fights the way he does?" Willow inquires.

"Idolizing me? But why?"

"Because you were the one who, even though you two fought more than any of us, were there to protect him. He will be angry at me for telling you this, but he still remembers the day you messed up Braggish for messing with him," Willow replies, smiling.

"Braggish? How can I, or anyone else, forget him? Nasty chap, and ugly to boot," Pete laughs.

"Ambrose hid the day you told him to run, the day Braggish came after him. Ambrose watched as you alone, single-handedly dealt with Braggish. It was in that moment, that our dear brother realized that he wanted to be able to fight like you," Willow explains taking a bite of her sandwich and watching Pete as he sits quietly looking up out of the roof of the greenhouse.

"Willow, I never knew," Pete says sadly.

"Ambrose never spoke of it until much later," Willow explains patting the top of Pete's hand.

"I want to touch on something else you said. If Ambrose's magic is the way it is, there must be a reference to it somewhere in the texts," Pete says.

"Pete, no. Grandmama, great-grandmas Nadia and Mora and great-aunt Destiny have spent years pouring through the books, the texts, everything they could to find, for anything about Ambrose's magic. They have spent countless hours in the Sprite Library, and even in the Temple Library of

Athena. There is nothing," Willow declares as she waves her hand, causing an orb to appear.

The greenhouse darkens and the blinds close over the windows.

"What is that?" Pete inquires, pointing at a projected document on the table.

"A secret. The only text that exists that speaks of Ambrose's true power," Willow explains.

"Wait! The only text? You said nothing exists. Where and how did you get this?" Pete asks curiously.

"That, dear Brother, is my secret. Do not worry about it," Willow replies.

"Does Grandma know?" Pete inquires.

"Yes, she was with me when it was discovered."

"Why didn't you tell any of us?" Pete asks, annoyance in his voice.

"The time had to be right. Besides, the group that gave us this orb, did so at a great cost," Willow replies sorrowfully as she flips the projected image up into the air and Pete reads it aloud. As he begins to read, the words fly around the space, playing out around the two of them.

The Tale of the One

A truly remarkable story and a unique one that began many moons ago. The great Celestials gave the earth magic, and the seers were entrusted with visions to see, predict, and share the prophecies of many events to come, but the great seers were unable to see one event, the birth of an extraordinary man, the next Noble Elder, his successor, Noel.

Now, it was known that Noble Elder had planned to be a council member, but the Celestials had something different planned for him. So, agreeing to take the mantel of Noble Elder, he agreed that he would be the head and oversee the council but would, eventually, step down, and that a new individual would take his place.

Many believe that, somehow, he knew who his successor would be from the beginning, but none of the seers were sure. So, the great seers, the mystics, even the oracles, and the divines themselves, all gazed into their crystal balls, read countless runes, looked to the stars, and deciphered the numbers in numerology. Still, nothing pointed to the successor until one night when the great Anwara, herself, had the only vision of who the successor of Noble Elder would be.

A sorcerer born of immense power, so powerful, in fact, that even the incubuses and all immortals feared this sorcerer. For, you see, there will come a moment when one individual will change the fabric of time as all The Arcane know and understand this. This individual will be the King, the ruler of all forms of magic. This Arcane is said to be the one who will bow out of respect to magic, not showing they are above it, but rather, equal to it. They will forge a never-ending friendship that based on their respect for each other, a friendship that will stand the test of time's bizarre behavior, still a friendship that, at times, will have its moments.

The seasons change throughout time, people will come and go, and the earth will age, just like Mundane and Arcane. The Elders, the guardians of magic and earth, lived among the Mundane, teaching them of the earth. Their magic would be that of legends and will inspire all around them. But that magic sometimes changes for the better and, sometimes, for the worse, for no individual Noble knew when (or how) it would change.

In the darkest of times, when a person might know evil, one thing will light the way, a force of power so unique that it ages differently. It transforms earth and time in ways not explained.

Time can change and alter at the drop of a dime, but this individual does not affect time in the same way. This individual, a child who will grow into a man, is said to be destined to be so powerful in the magical arts that no rules will exist for them. They will surpass all of the known rules that govern magic.

Protected by an ancient secret, the power of the Magical Three and this child are destined to forever change the way the earth knows magic. Time has always acted bizarrely, but this child will balance time. Together, they will be the ones who change time, fix it, and make it work properly again.

It is said that this individual is destined to bring balance to the ever-changing nature of time, the one who, in their lifetime, will learn to balance and control time's chaotic dysfunction.

Declared from their birth to be the only one of their kind, a Grand Arch Sorcerer, their magic will defy the very essence of every magical rule. Their magic will be unlike any other, a magic so raw in form that it has no beginning or end but flows continuously. Magic driven by light, love, family, and friendship will change, sometimes growing, *sometimes weakening, depending on ongoing interactions with light, love, family, and friendship.*

With every passing moment, the person's magic will change, morph, adapt, and change again, stagnating one second and extremely active the next. Yet, through them, magic is simple!

It is said that a great army that has lain dormant will awaken at their command, the elements will merge and bow to their command, and they will control magical forces and energy far more significant than anyone can explain. This magical power is the very same power after which Merlin lusts. He craves it. He desires it. He wants it.

This one individual is bound to time itself through love, passion, and heart, and this individual will experience times of good and evil. This individual is said to be neither good nor evil, light nor dark. Instead, they will be the center, the very balance of both. The ArchSorcerer will be so unique that they will stand at the heart of the yin and yang.

"Interesting," Pete notes when he finishes reading.

"Grandma thought so," Willow remarks as Pete stands up and begins pacing the floor.

"So, Grandma has seen this?" asks Pete.

"Yes, and I will say no more about it," Willow acknowledges.

"Willow, sister, can I ask why is it that you and Ambrose get along so well?" Peter inquires as he stops pacing to listen to her response.

"How do I explain it? I have always taken time to be gentle with him. I have always listened, and I have had to learn to let go," Willow replies.

"Let go?" Peter asks.

"Whenever Ambrose amplified my power, I stopped and trusted him to resolve the issue. It is why I do not fear it when my magic grows in strength.

Think about the times when any of you would grow in power. What was the first thing Ambrose would do?" Willow explains as Pete stops and thinks carefully about her question.

"He would stop what he was doing and check on us," Pete finally replies.

"And in those moments, he cared less about his own magic and what he was going through, and cared about us," Willow remarked.

Then, they heard a voice behind them.

"Pete, it has taken me years to realize that Willow is right. Finally, our baby sister has been the one to help us all realize what we have or, in this case, have not, done," Sophia says as Kells, Michael and Isabella appear behind her.

"Wow, you guys too?" asks Pete.

"Yes. But we have each had to understand our relationship, or lack thereof, with Ambrose in our own way. The weekend he moved out, we lost a part of ourselves," Sophia explains.

"You three were always getting into trouble, always blowing something up, always making mischief. Then, Ambrose came along, and you guys did not know what to do. He was different. He could fight, he could play sports, he loved his toys, but he was also glued to the books. He wanted to cook with Cedric. I will never forget when he came to play dress up with Willow. Our brother was not bound by any rules. He just loved his life," Isabella remarks, picking up a sandwich and taking a bite.

"You see, the six of us can get together and do things like this, sit here, talk, laugh, and be siblings. But Ambrose never could. He always struggled with socialization in large groups, but he was terrified of his magic. He looked at the world differently. I have always believed that he was aware of the responsibility that he was born to, but all he wanted was to be like the three of you," Willow explains, pointing at her brothers.

"Michael, what is it? You're sitting there quietly eating?" Isabella inquires, seeking answers from him.

"I am trying to figure out if there is a way to fix our mistakes," Michael responds.

"We could start by apologizing to Ambrose," Pete says.

"While I agree, I do not think you going anywhere near Ambrose right now would be a good idea," Sophia suggests.

Willow gets up from the stool and walks over to the window.

"Willow, what is it?" Isabella inquires, watching her sister.

"The way to fix this will be difficult and practically impossible on many levels," Willow remarks, turning and regarding her siblings.

"Impossible in what ways?" Kells asks.

"First off, Ambrose is stubborn. Second, it will be easier for Sophia, Isabella, and I to speak with him than you three, and, finally, one wrong move on any of our parts, and he could choose to let the snow globe be destroyed," Willow explains.

The others regard one another and, when they finish eating, bid each other good night. Isabella is the last one remaining.

"Willow, a word?" Isabella inquires.

"Yes, Isabella?" Willow replies.

"Would Ambrose respond if I go to speak with him?" she asks.

"Depends. What are you thinking?"

"Taking him lunch and talking with him."

"Possibly. But I will warn you, Isabella, he may not respond well."

"I have to try, Willow."

"I know, and while he will listen, be gentle. Our dear brother, Ambrose, as you know, does not like to be handled. Remember, he grew up away from us. So, he responds to things differently. We may go to speak with him with good intentions, but he may perceive it differently," Willow explains as the two nod at each other and Isabella takes her leave.

The following day, descending the front steps of her home and pulling her traveling cloak around her, a portal flies open and Isabella steps through, arriving at the university. Strolling across campus, she stops in at Dwarfbrew.

"Isabella, cousin," Martha says, wiping her hands and coming out from behind the counter to hug her.

"Hello, Martha," Isabella replies.

"What brings you here?" Martha asks.

"I am an alumnus of the university. But I am on a mission today. I have some business here on the campus," Isabella replies.

"Oh, what business?" Martha inquires as Isabella regards her with a raised eyebrow. "Oh, I know that look. RJ."

Isabella nods.

"Martha, can you get me two of whatever he drinks and one of whatever Dalton drinks, please," Isabella asks, taking off her traveling gloves and looking around at the coffee shop.

Martha goes back behind the counter and starts making the coffees.

"You know, RJ is not a big fan of coffee," Martha remarks.

"What does he drink, then?" Isabella inquires, circling the statue in the middle of the coffee shop.

"How tacky!" Isabella remarks out loud, wrinkling her nose in disgust.

"Your brother thinks so as well," Martha replies, approaching Isabella with three large cups in her hands.

"Thank you, dear cousin, and these are?" Isabella asks.

"Two vanilla and cinnamon iced coffees with goat's milk and pumpkin whipped cream. It is the only one RJ will touch. This other one has a triple shot of espresso and a double pumpkin spiced coffee with chocolate foam. Dalton loves the pumpkin coffee, and it does not affect him. I, on the other hand, drink it and blah," Martha explains, handing the cups to Isabella.

"Martha, thank you, dear cousin. By the way, my brother is correct. Burn that damn statue down when I leave. It is rather tacky. Whoever sculpted it made my nose too big, my grandmother looks horrible, and I will not say a thing about the way your grandfather looks. Anyway, where might I find my dear brother?" Isabella laughs as she takes the drinks.

"It is 8 AM on a Thursday, he will be home or at the library," Martha suggests.

"Does he live in the old student hall?"

"He does. Fifth floor, end unit. The fancy penthouse apartment," Martha remarks, smiling.

"Thanks, love, and I will see you Saturday at Grandma and Grandpa's for the family dinner," Isabella calls over her shoulder as she walks toward the door. "Oh, and Martha…" says Isabella.

"Yes, cousin?"

"Has Cedric seen the sculpture?"

"He has not," Martha remarks, smiling.

"Take it to him. I am sure Cedric would love it for target practice," Isabella smiles, walking out the door.

Observing the campus, Isabella turns her nose up in the air.

This place is rather gross. Do they idolize the Ignatiuses this much? That statue in Dwarfbrew is nothing like that statue of Grandpa and Grandma over there. It is even worse. They should level them all. Clearly, the artist has no talent.

Isabella chuckles to herself as she teleports, arriving at the food court. She walks through, looking at the food vendors. She buys lunch, turns, puts her sunglasses on, and throws her hair back as she teleports again. Arriving outside the student hall, she walks to the far side of the building. Then, snapping her fingers, she arrives on the end balcony on the fifth floor, coffees in hand and a bag with lunch in the other. She takes a deep breath.

"I hope this works," she says to herself as she knocks on the double doors.

"Hello?" Dalton inquires, opening the French doors as Isabella strolls in, pushing past him, and handing him the large cup of coffee.

"Pumpkin spiced coffee with chocolate foam just the way you like it. Is my baby brother home?" Isabella inquires, looking around, smiling.

"Yes, I think so," Dalton replies as a loud hiss is heard.

"Charming, Mr. Cee, always having your say," Isabella laughs as RJ emerges from his bedroom.

"Hi," he says, drying his hair, a towel over his shoulders.

"I brought coffee and food," she says, holding up the bag and the coffees.

"I can see that. Thank you. Let me get my shirt on," RJ remarks as Dalton watches him walk away.

"I saw that," Isabella says, smiling.

"Hush, it is not every day that a shirtless, 6'4" elf walks by you," Dalton replies.

"Half-elf. Remember that we also have human in us," Isabella remarks, sitting down on the couch and laying out the food on the coffee table.

Walking behind the couch, Dalton makes a face at her just as RJ returns down the hall, stopping to observe Dalton. Then, he smiles.

"Your coffee," Isabella says, handing him the cup.

"Thanks," RJ says as Mr. Cee walks over and sits down between the two, his eyes glowing green as he watches every move.

"Mr. Cee," RJ commands in a stern voice as the cat meows and, lying down, begins licking his paw.

"Do not worry. He is fine. Besides, I brought some Mr. Kitty catnip," Isabella remarks, putting it down in front of Mr. Cee.

"You shouldn't have," RJ interjects.

"I don't mind," Isabella replies.

"So, what brings my sister here today?" RJ asks, sitting back in the armchair.

"I wanted to bring you some lunch and have a visit," Isabella explains, smiling, but looking annoyed at his question.

"Really? How interesting," RJ replies.

"Am I not allowed to come to visit?" she inquires.

"No. Of course, you are allowed to visit. It is just… well, never mind," RJ says.

"It is just what?"

"Why start paying attention to me now? You, Pete, Michael, Kells, Sophia, it is like I never existed to any of you. So now, suddenly, you want to bring me and my roommate lunch?" RJ replies.

"I cannot speak for our dear brothers, but I can speak for at least Sophia and myself. We are sorry we never spent more time with you. I am trying to make things right," Isabella explains, handing him his food and reaching across the couch to hand Dalton his.

"Thank you, Lady Isabella," Dalton says as RJ nods at Dalton.

"You're welcome," she replies when yelling suddenly breaks out in the hallway.

Dalton and RJ shoot knowing looks at each other, and then, RJ rolls his eyes.

"What is all that noise about?' Isabella inquires, getting up and walking toward the front door and opening it. Michael has a dwarf and a goblin pinned to the wall in the hallway.

"Michael, what is the meaning of this?" Isabella snaps.

"What in the world?" Dalton asks, coming out of the door.

"Filthy, Arcane," the goblin shouts when RJ appears in the doorway.

"What is going on here?" a stern voice asks as Chancellor Fae approaches wand drawn, several fairy elite guards with her.

"I came by for a visit and caught these two trying to break into Pete's apartment," Michael explains as RJ turns to walk back into his apartment.

"And we would have succeeded," the goblin notes. "But the little, filthy princess elf will do instead," the dwarf mocks, pointing at RJ.

Before anyone can say a word, Isabella pulls her wand and places it at the throat of the dwarf.

"Make one wrong move," Isabella remarks but finds a hand on her arm.

"He is not worth it, Izzy," RJ remarks as she smiles at him.

"Look, the ugly, royal princess thinks she can take me. Oh, how Raven would love to tear you apart," the dwarf sneers as he finds himself slammed against the wall.

"Dwarf, I may not have magic, but that does not mean I cannot kill you," RJ states, holding the dwarf by his collar against the wall.

"Guards, get them out of here," Chancellor Fae commands, motioning for the fairy guards to take the two away as RJ drops the dwarf to the floor.

"Guards, wait," RJ says, approaching the goblin.

He kneels and examines the goblin's bag, pulling out the dagger from his dreams.

"Merlin will come for you," the goblin threatens as he is dragged away.

RJ walks toward Chancellor Fae and hands her the dagger.

"See to it that this is handled properly. Make sure my grandmama knows that it has been found."

"Of course, RJ," she replies

Then, RJ turns to his sister and says, "Shall we finish lunch?"

"Everyone back to your apartments," Chancellor Fae remarks, disappearing with the guards.

"Come along," Isabella says, pulling Michael along with them.

"I need to check on Pete," Michael protests.

"He has magic, right?"

"Yes, he does."

"Then, he will be fine," Isabella remarks, pulling on Michael's arm and giving him a stern look.

Isabella re-enters RJ's apartment with Michael in tow.

"You do not mind if I join you two, do you?" Michael asks, guardedly, watching for RJ's reaction.

"You can have half of my sub," RJ replies as Michael sits down.

"Dalton, come sit with us?" RJ calls, throwing a pillow on the floor and sitting down on it as Dalton joins them. The four sit eating and talking when a knock is heard at the door.

"I'll get it," RJ says.

"Hi, RJ. Sorry to bother you," Pete says, tripping over his words.

"Yes, Pete?"

"By chance, do you know what happened to my apartment? Did you hear anything?" Pete asks as Isabella appears behind RJ.

"Can he come in?" Isabella inquires, resting her hand on his shoulder.

RJ steps aside, allowing Pete into the apartment.

"Michael?" Pete remarks.

"I came to visit you and let myself in and found a dwarf and goblin tearing up your place," Michael explains.

"My place looks horrible. They tore everything up," Pete complains.

"Nothing could be as bad as the treehouse," RJ laughs, then takes a bite of his sandwich.

"You know, it could probably hold a close second right now," Pete replies.

"Treehouse?" Dalton asks, his eyebrow raised.

"Ask me later?" RJ says.

"Our father built a treehouse for the seven of us. RJ, when he was younger was afraid of the place. So, Pete, Michael, and Kells trashed it to keep us all out. RJ refused to go in it after a while," Isabella explains.

"I will take the treehouse at this point," Pete remarks.

"Does it appear they got anything?" Michael asks.

"A few things," Pete replies nervously.

"They were after the dagger," RJ replies, chewing.

"Wait! The dagger?" Pete asks.

"Don't worry. It is an ancient elvish artifact. I gave it to Chancellor Fae. Which means, 5-4-3-2-1," RJ says, counting down until a portal in his apartment flies open, and out steps their grandmother.

"Called it," RJ declares.

"Grandmama," Isabella acknowledges.

"Am I interrupting something?" their grandmother asks.

"I came to have lunch with RJ and Dalton, and then, we heard a commotion. We have handled the issue. Michael joined us, then Pete came, inquiring about his apartment. I think that sums it up," Isabella remarks.

"It does. Thank you. RJ, where did you find the dagger?" his grandmother inquires.

"It was in the goblin's bag," RJ explains.

"Interesting."

"Grandmama, it was an older goblin, spoke of Merlin. Mean little bugger. He carried a dark amulet, and I assumed that was how he and the dwarf teleported," Michael explains.

"The dwarf with him was rather rude and made Mr. Giggles look nice," Isabella remarks.

"I see," their grandmother says, pacing the floor.

"Is something wrong, Grandmama?" Isabella inquires.

"I am trying to sort through all of this, particularly I am trying to gain an understanding of that dagger," their grandmother replies.

"Michael and Peter come with me. Let your brother, Dalton, and sister finish lunch," their grandmother says.

"Grandmama, it is okay. They can stay and finish before I head out to class. Then, they can come to help you once they're done with lunch," RJ responds as Isabella sits down and rejoins Dalton and RJ.

Rose looks at Michael and Peter and motions for them to go.

"Peter," their grandmother says, looking at him with a stern look.

"I know, Grandmama," he replies as she disappears, and he walks over to join the others. Holding up her hand, Isabella waves it over the food and it multiplies.

Chapter 14
Unexpected Help

Several days pass as RJ attends his classes and work. No one says anything to him about walking out of the festival or his siblings having lunch with him. Finally, confused and frustrated, he rises at the end of class and walks out the door. He is quietly strolling along the path by the lake when Amelia approaches him.

"Hi! How have you been? Are you okay?" she inquires, handing him a wrapped sub-sandwich.

"I am fine," he responds, keeping it short and accepting the sandwich as he sits on a rock overlooking the water.

"You have been quiet these past few days. Something seems to be bothering you," Amelia remarks.

"It is nothing," RJ replies, turning his head and wiping a tear.

"I saw that. It isn't nothing. RJ, you are crying. I know you too well. It is never just nothing," remarks Amelia.

"I have something in my eye," RJ replies, redirecting the conversation.

"Mmm hmm," Amelia sighs as she takes a bite of her own sandwich.

"Amelia, all right. There is something. First, there have been the weird dreams that I have been experiencing. Then, everything that happened with the festival and the issues with magic. Then, the other day, my sister brought me lunch and several of my siblings joined us," RJ remarks.

"RJ, wasn't it nice that Willow brought you lunch?" Amelia replied.

"Willow? Oh no. It was Isabella and then Michael and Peter," RJ explains.

"Wait! You let Peter in your apartment? Wow!" Amelia remarks.

"It was nice having lunch with them. But I was on edge the whole time, from the minute Michael and Pete got there," RJ says.

"Do you think Isabella would have allowed anything to happen?"

"No, but, Amelia, come on, we are talking about Pete. My siblings always have an angle."

The two sit quietly eating. Amelia is the first to notice the water of the lake moving.

"RJ, what is that?" Amelia inquires, pointing at a blurry haze floating over the water. Raising to his feet, RJ walks toward the edge of the rock as the image continues to float over the water.

"It appears to be a figure," RJ remarks as he and Amelia discover that the floating haze is pulling them toward it.

"Take my hand," he says.

As the two hold hands, the wind begins spinning water around them and they hear screaming.

"Help! Help! Help!"

"RJ, someone is in trouble," Amelia yells, clicking a button on her watch as nanobots fly around them, creating suits of armor. They examine the area carefully, then notice, a figure that appears to be fading in and out of the floating haze in the distance.

"It is a woman," Amelia says.

"Amelia, that is my… my daughter from the future. Oh dear! Time has to be on the fritz," RJ declares, pushing off into the air towards her.

"Father," Luciana calls, holding out her hand.

When their hands touch she fully materializes. Holding up her hands, she examines them.

"You are, as they say, truly powerful," Luciana states.

"How is that possible? I am without my magic," RJ explains as Luciana backs up.

Amelia pulls at RJ's shirt.

"I do not mean to interrupt, but what is that?" Amelia asks as her nanobot armor begins to activate, scanning the area.

"Get behind me, both of you," Luciana demands, catching dark magic in both hands as it pushes her back.

An eerie laugh rings out as Luciana absorbs the dark magic.

"You two must get out of here! The darkness is coming," Luciana commands, spinning her hands as streams of magic fly around the three of them.

"We cannot just leave. As I have said, I do not have magic. Neither of us does," RJ says as Luciana looks back at him as she holds the darkness at bay.

"Then, it looks like I will have to get both of you to safety," Luciana remarks as magic spins around her materializing her armor as she lifts her right hand and opens a portal.

"RJ look," Amelia says.

"Go! I will buy you some time. I can hold the darkness, but you must get to New York City. Find your snow globe and save time. The fate of the Arcane and Mundane rests with you. GO!"

As Amelia grabs RJ's hand to pull him towards the portal, Luciana is struck with dark magic, flying backwards. Then, the darkness turns its attention to RJ and Amelia. Raising her hand, Luciana causes the sky to turn black. Then, it returns to normal.

As the darkness is about to strike RJ, the dark magic suddenly stops flying and explodes in midair. Streams of magic circle around the three of them until Amelia looks over to see RJ flying into the air, magic spinning around him. At first, his eyes are flickering, then they begin to glow white.

"Get out of here!" RJ yells as a wand appears in his hand. Spinning it, he catches the dark magic in a field of light and redirects the dark magic that is flying at him, and it dissolves.

"How?" Amelia inquires as she reaches Luciana's side.

"I have pulled us into the zone of time. Here, his magic is limitless, even though he gave up his magic, here he is unstoppable. The rules do not apply here," Luciana explains.

"Amelia, we cannot leave him," Luciana declares as Amelia helps her up. Magic fills the area spinning as RJ's hand starts to glow.

"Ahhhh!" he yells, holding his hand with the other one.

"Amelia, was he poisoned?" Luciana inquires.

"Yes, with an elfish arrow," Amelia says.

"It is still in him, and rapidly spreading. Look at his face," she says, pointing at the green veins that are spiderwebbing over his face. Magic continues to circle the area as RJ floats in the air.

"Amelia, I am going to get him down. Look at me. Take this orb. Get through the portal and throw the orb. It will take you both to safety, to the one person who can help him," she says, handing the orb to Amelia as she flies into the air.

"Father, take my hand," Luciana says, holding out her hand as RJ reaches for it. The instant their hands touch, RJ passes out and Luciana lowers him down. Amelia gets under RJ's arm and supports him.

"Good luck," Amelia says.

"You too, and be safe," Luciana responds, picking up the wand that RJ has dropped.

The darkness dives on the three of them as Luciana raises her hands and forms a magic dome over them. Holding up RJ, Amelia runs toward the portal when a figure appears.

Amelia stops and observes the cloaked figure approaching.

"I have him," the woman says, pulling her wand as all three go through the portal, landing in a field.

"Do you still have the orb?" the figure inquires.

"I do," Amelia answers, holding it up as the figure places a bag over RJ's head and onto his shoulders. The figure pulls out a vial of a purplish liquid from their pocket, pulls the cork, grabs RJ's mouth, and pours the liquid into it.

"This will stabilize him," the figure explains as the field goes dark.

"Amelia, get him out of here. Take the bag and get him to safety. NOW!" the woman shouts, spinning her wand as the darkness strikes a magical field.

"He is waking," Amelia remarks.

"Where am I? Why is everything fuzzy?" RJ inquires, swaying and holding his head.

"I am right here, RJ. We are getting you out of here," Amelia says as she bowls the orb across the ground. A portal flies open as the light strikes down around them. The orb stops and the figure lowers its hood.

"Lady Nadia," Amelia bows.

Magic Terrae, Tuere Ilos.

By the magic of the earth, protect them.

Magic flies around Nadia, spinning through her hands as she raises them, forming a protective field around Amelia and RJ.

"Amelia," RJ says weakly.

"Yes?"

"Leave me. Help her, please. The darkness is different this time," RJ says weakly.

"My orders are to get you to safety," Amelia replies as the darkness attacks them. Then, as a sword of darkness lowers upon them, the blade is stopped in mid-air, mere inches from them. When they look back, Nadia is holding the blade with her magic.

"Russell Ambrose Alezander Elderchild Ignatius, Jr., I am not saying this again. Get out of here, now! You must protect your ring, the family, magic, and all Mundane and Arcane at all costs. Your ring, the one you are wearing, is the key. Do you hear me? It is the key," Nadia declares as she flings a dark general backward with her magic, away from Amelia and RJ. The dark general hits the tree as Nadia raises her hand, capturing the dark general with its roots. As they wrap around him, preventing him from moving. Then, turning, she looks at the two of them.

"Great-grandma, we cannot leave you," RJ declares.

"My boy, my dear, sweet Ambrose, I have my duties as you have yours, including the power to protect everyone. The time has come. If no one else will tell you, then I will. I have faith in you, RJ. Even when you are scared, remember that you are invincible. I have faith that you will make the right decisions. Become the man you are meant to be. Become Noble Elder and save the earth. Now, get to New York City. Help is there. The poison is spreading through you. Find…"

But before Nadia can finish, she catches the dark magic flying toward them and throws it back at the dozen dark creatures that are descending upon them. Suddenly, she flies into the air fighting the darkness off. However, multiple dark guards appear, throwing magic at her, and when she is caught off guard, they overwhelm her, striking her with dark magic.

"No…Great-grandmama," RJ calls, falling to the ground.

"RJ, we cannot help her," Amelia cries, trying to help him up.

The darkness dives on Nadia as nanobots appear, circling her and creating a shield. RJ looks around and sees Amelia standing with her phone in her hand, controlling the bots.

"Get her out of here now," RJ yells weakly, rising to his feet. "It is me they are after," he declares, whistling and limping toward the portal. Reaching it, he falls through as the darkness chases after him and the portal seals. Running across the field, Amelia reaches the Lady Nadia.

"My Lady! Oh, not one iota of being good. The queen and my uncles will fly off the handle," Amelia says, kneeling and holding Nadia's hand.

"Child…" a weak Nadia says.

"My Lady, hold on! Please hold on. Cousin Gwendolyn!" Amelia screams as the clouds spin in the sky.

Gwen materializes just as darkness dives on Amelia and Nadia. Screams ring out as Gwen stands, eyes glowing red, wand in hand, flames flying around her, her cousin, and her grandmother. The darkness rears back and charges as Gwen raises her wand, and the darkness explodes. Running across the field, Gwen reaches the other two.

"Oh damn! Grandma," Gwen declares, kneeling as she touches Nadia's other hand. The area spins around the three of them and they arrive in the grand parlor of Ignatius Manor. Several of the manor staff jump back in alarm at their arrival.

"Cedric," Gwen yells as a pop rings through the space, nearly deafening everyone.

"My Lady," Cedric says as he races across the floor to Nadia's side. Gwen raises her hands, spinning her wand as fireworks fly toward the ceiling and disappear.

"Brace yourselves. This is going to get interesting," Gwen remarks as several staff race past her carrying rags and potions.

"Cedric…"

"Rest, My Lady, rest."

"My old friend, he is on his way…" Nadia says, holding up a hand and placing it on Cedric's face. When Cedric looks across at Amelia, he sees that she is dressed in her armor.

"I see, My Lady," Cedric replies, placing his hand on top of hers.

"Protect him. You must promise me, old friend, that you will protect him. Cedric, he has the ability, even without his magic, to be great," she says weakly as multiple pops echo through the room.

"Mother," Ethan yells, lowering his bag and running to Nadia's side.

"Ethan," she replies, smiling at him.

"No, no, no! Where is Rose?" he yells as Oliver appears, bolting across the room. At that very moment, a light column strikes the floor as the six Ignatius children, their parents, and their grandmother arrive. Before anyone can say anything, Rose is across the room at her mother's side.

"Mom," Rose says, taking Nadia's hand as Amelia and Rose make eye contact. Instantly, Rose knows everything that has happened without either of them saying a word.

"Rose, help her," Ethan says.

"My children, it is okay. Time…" Nadia stops to catch her breath.

"Mom, save your strength," Oliver says when the room shakes and Kelvin bolts across the room with Zander immediately behind him.

"My love, my dear, sweet Kelvin," Nadia says, smiling at him.

"Nadia, what has happened?" he inquires as he hugs her.

"My love, he is on his way. Promise me, promise me that you will guide him. Kelvin, the time of the Phoenix has come," Nadia replies quietly.

"Sis?" Oliver begins to ask as Rose stands holding out her hands.

"Follow my lead," she says as her brothers take her hands.

Avalon, audi nos. Et nos Magus Tres praecipimus tibi

protego sua, protego nos mater.

Avalon, hear us, we the Magical Three command you to protect her, protect our mother.

Magic flies around the room, as the three cast the spell together, speaking collectively as one voice, their eyes glowing as light flashes around them, and Nadia is gone. Then, closing their eyes, Oliver and Ethan opened their eyes at the same time, looking around as Rose stands quietly, her eyes closed.

"Mom?" Hope inquires but Zander raises his hand, stopping her.

Breathing in, Rose opens her eyes.

"Mom?" Vivian asks, hugging her mother for comfort. Rose hugs her back as Amelia sits in an armchair and begins to cry.

"Child," Cedric says, moving across the floor to comfort Amelia, placing his hand upon hers as his eyes narrow. He turns, then, looking back at Rose with a concerned look.

"Old friend, do not give me that look," Rose says, taking a deep breath as she regards the others in the room.

"Gwen?"

"Yes, Aunt Rose?"

"Take Amelia home. Go to RJ's apartment. Find Mr. Cee and keep him with you. Do not leave Amelia or Mr. Cee until further notice. If the journey through time has begun, Mr. Cee will surely sense it and go looking for RJ," Rose orders as Gwen and Cedric help Amelia up and the two disappear.

"Mom, what are your plans?" Hope asks, her armor materializing.

"War is upon the Arcane and Mundane. If the darkness attacked my mother, they are coming for everyone," Rose explains.

"Ari and Theo, suit up. Get to the village, and ready them," Zander orders as the two disappear instantly.

"You all have this here. Your mother gave me orders, and I plan to see them through," Kelvin says, rising to his feet and wiping his face.

"Orders? Dad, you are in no condition to go anywhere," Oliver protests.

"Oliver, no!" Rose says, raising her arm to stop him.

"Oliver, even as we speak, RJ is out there. He is on the brink of regaining his powers. Besides, your mother would not sacrifice herself if he were not. She has known for some time that this day would come," Kelvin explains.

"But you do not know where to begin looking," Ethan declares.

"Master Ethan, this is RJ we are talking about. Besides, when I touched Miss Pendragon's hand, I saw everything, which confirms that he went through time. Moreover, he drew the darkness away from Amelia and Nadia in order to protect them," Cedric remarks as Kelvin and Zander regard one another.

"I will notify the Elder Council, Kelvin. How many of them will you need to help you?" Zander inquires.

"It will be Cedric and myself," Kelvin replies as he and Cedric disappear.

"Grandma, what of us?" Willow asks.

"Willow, get to the Magic Nexus and work with your cousin Esther to try to find your brother and keep your great-grandfather notified of anything weird. You and Esther are his magic eyes and ears now. Isabella, Pete, and Michael, get to the university and begin preparing the campus for any movement the darkness may attempt. Sophia and Kells, get to Cousin Fae and tell her what has happened. She and Phineas will send word to the fairies and alert Queen Amaryllis," Rose commands.

"Ethan, I will be back. I must notify the Arcane Parliament and put them on alert," Oliver says as he disappears.

"Mother, Vivian, Rusty, and I will go to notify the covens and the Lords Leo and Leaf, and Lady Leonia," Hope says as the three disappears.

Rose and Ethan watch as Sebastian and Matthew arrive.

"Everyone will need to see this," Sebastian remarks when Zander, Oliver, and Olivia appear. Olivia hugs Rose as Matthew approaches them.

"This was found in the field," Matthew says, handing Nadia's wand to his aunt.

"Mom's wand," Ethan remarks as Rose holds it in her open palms. Oliver walks up and waves his hands over the wand causing the room to darken and a ghostly image of Nadia appears.

My Children,

Although I am not there, my wisdom and teachings will always be with you. You three, your spouses, children, and grandchildren, have brought me the greatest joy. I have watched all of you grow for years, but I have known that the time will come when a series of events will need to be set in motion. This time would mean the moment of truth, the return of the darkness to full power. Oliver, Ethan, and Rose have always borne the most significant responsibility, but you do not have to do it alone.

Noble Elder is sick, which is unheard of for any Elder. He is dying. He is holding on as long as possible to transfer his magic to an unwilling successor. Everything, as I have taught you, happens for a reason. Merlin will return, and his fury will have no bounds. He will kill, destroy, and devastate everything.

My beautiful great-grandchildren, the Ignatius Six, are soon to be the Ignatius Seven. Hear me. Your brother needs you. He needs you to believe, and he needs you to not be afraid. Each of your greatest fears is not his power but what your powers do around him. For many years, none of us understood, but then a dear caring friend showed me everything. Ambrose amplifies each of your powers in ways that none of you understand, and that frightens you.

The six regard one another as Isabella and Sophia break into tears. Willow waves her hand, freezing the image.

"It is okay. Ambrose enhances all of our magic. Your grandfather, your parents, none of us could explain it. We experience the same thing much like you six," Rose explains, walking up and hugging them.

"It can be frightening. We know that, but you six have a bond that we know will help your brother. He needs you to be there to help him and guide him. Time is going to be trying for all of us. How we manage it and support each other will be critical," Zander notes as magic flies around the space and the image unfreezes.

You six must help him. Alone, he will eventually fall. But, together, with all of you, he will succeed. Your brother amplifies your powers, and your magic helps fuel him in return. So, as one might say, it is a reciprocal relationship. There are and will be many uncertainties ahead. But from what I have foreseen, you six will be his balance, and he will be yours. So, find him, help him, and stop Merlin. Each of you has a gift.

Remember, your magic is always with you. It is in everything and runs through all things. In the darkest of moments, it can be the beacon that lights the way and guides you. Good luck.

Love,
Your Mother,
The Lady Nadia

When the image of Nadia finished playing out, it disappears. Rose closes her hands around her mother's wand. It glows, then appears in the glass case next to Rose's desk.

"You six, have your orders. Now go," Rose says as she turns to look out of the window.

"Zander, Brothers, summon all remaining Arcane. We need to buy Ambrose as much time as possible," Rose remarks as the others nod and begin disappearing. Rose turns and walks out onto the balcony as the French doors fly open. Whooshing wind is heard as Rose flies up over the railing, landing on the back of Autumn, the dragon, who roars and takes to the air. The two disappear into the night sky.

Within seconds of falling through the portal, RJ appears, landing on the ground in the park. Slowly, he pushes himself up and brushes himself off as he limps toward the pond.

"Great! The park," RJ says, sitting down and catching his breath. Suddenly, multiple dark creatures encircle him. A laugh rings out.

"Weak, dear Noel?" Merlin laughs, appearing with a grin on his face.

"No, just catching my breath," RJ explains, raising his hands in a boxer's stance, ready to fight.

"Pfff, you are going to fight me? My poison, running through your veins, will kill you when you throw one punch, unless you give me what I want," Merlin sneers, holding up a vial.

"And what would that be Merlin?"

"Your magic and the Curpendulums. I will give you the antidote in trade."

"Merlin, I would rather die than ever help you."

"So be it. Take him," Merlin motions as the darkness advances on RJ.

Inches from RJ, the darkness flies back, sliding across the ground as two figures appear. RJ drops to one knee, trying to hold himself up, his head spinning.

"What is going on?" RJ asks.

"Get him out of here now. The poison has kicked in," one figure addresses the other.

Merlin screams in rage as he flies backward as one of the cloaked figures casts magic around RJ to protect him.

"Sir?" the other figure asks.

"Get him out of here. I have Merlin," a man's voice declares as the first figure raises his hand, and the darkness explodes. Then, spinning his wand over his head, a circle of flames appears, creating a protective barrier around RJ and the other figure.

The second figure reaches RJ, places its hand on his back, and the two disappear. The other figure stands looking around them as more dark creatures materialize. Then, raising his hands, the cooing of pigeons can be heard and, suddenly, the birds appear, flying around the darkness, and a hundred cats run through the park, also attacking the darkness. The tree roots spring from the ground, the branches hitting the darkness and throwing them back.

The figure turns, forming an army from the fountain's water. They point their wand, and the ducks fly from the fountain hitting the darkness repeatedly. Finally, spinning their wand, the figure causes the wind to pick up.

Merlin laughs, waves his hand, and throws the figure into the stone ledge of the fountain.

"Getting old, aren't we, Noble Elder?" Merlin mocks when he raises his wand and throws black magic at Noble Elder. The magic explodes as everything freezes around Merlin. The air grows cold, and Merlin's eyes narrow as his breath can be seen. Noble Elder backs up, observing the space and casting a shield in front of himself.

"Lord Yule, come out, come out wherever you are," Merlin hollers as vines explode from the ground encircling him and binding his arms to his sides.

"You killed her," a voice echoes around him. The darkness holds their ears as the voice echoes even louder, "You killed her."

"Killed who? I kill anyone who stands in my way."

"You killed her."

The voice was so loud that it shook the ground and, as the vines explode, Merlin doubles over, holding his ears.

"You killed her, the Lady Nadia," Luciana screams, walking up, wand drawn, as Merlin flies into the air, choking. Her eyes turn black, and the ground shakes for a second time, throwing the darkness off their feet.

Two dark Arcane Council members appear, aiding Merlin as they cast dark magic at Luciana. As she catches their magic with her free hand, she continues to hold Merlin in the air with her wand.

"Who is she?" one of the dark Arcane Council Members asks when a giant clock appears, the hands spinning out of control. As the clock grows brighter, the dark creatures begin marching backward, Merlin turns young, and the two dark Arcane freeze.

"Noble Elder, please go to help RJ. It is time. I will hold time in limbo until the moment is right. Save him, and, Noble Elder, give him this," Luciana declares. She turns her back to Noble Elder as a box appears, levitating in front of Noble Elder, who reaches up and grabs the box. Two dark generals appear throwing magic at Luciana, but she snaps her fingers, and they disappear. The clock holds everything still as Merlin turns old again and casts magic at Noble Elder, who catches and redirects the magic into the ground.

"I see, Merlin, that your moves are still as predictable as always," Noble Elder exclaims as a flash of light occurs, and Merlin finds his magic intertwined with Kelvin.

Cedric approaches Noble Elder.

"Quickly, get out of here. We have this," Cedric says, grabbing a dark creature and slamming it into the ground at exceptional speed. Cedric grabs a second dark creature that was advancing on him and Noble Elder and snaps it into the ground. Reaching down, Cedric rips the creature's throat out and throws its lifeless body aside.

"Grandfather, your creatures killed her," Kelvin declares, spinning his wand as if fencing, exploding Merlin's wand and flinging him across the park into the side of a stone bridge.

"Noble Elder, whatever you do, guard that box with your life," Cedric acknowledges handing the box that he had dropped back to him.

"Thank you, vampire," Noble Elder nods as Merlin hits the ground. A scream sounds and the area grows dark as Raven and Liam appear. Raven hisses as she helps Merlin up. Liam stands by, his wand pointed at Kelvin.

"Kill him," Raven snaps

Liam tightens his grip on his wand, and, in one quick motion, he spins on the spot and blasts her, raising her off her feet and slamming her headfirst into the stone bridge. But she disappears. Several dark guards surround Merlin lowering their spears, protecting him, as Liam backs up toward Cedric and Kelvin.

"Thanks for the help," Kelvin remarks as the darkness flies into the air, spinning and merging.

"Any time, Lord Kelvin," Liam says, spinning his wand and causing light to fly around the park.

"Kill them all, including that traitor," Merlin snaps as the darkness charges and Liam, Kelvin, and Cedric combine forces to hold the advancing darkness back.

"Noble Elder, we are not saying this again. Get out of here! This is not your fight," Kelvin advises as Noble Elder holds up his hand, lightning strikes the ground around him, and he disappears on the spot.

"Cedric, Liam, we have to buy Noble Elder as much time as possible," Kelvin declares as time freezes.

Chapter 15
The Sanctuary of Legend & Lore

Noble Elder appears at the Sanctuary of Legend and Lore within seconds of leaving the park. First, he places the snow globe on a pedestal. Then, gliding across the floor, he reaches the bedside of RJ.

"How is he, Minnie?"

"Stable, but the poison is strong. It is moving rapidly through him."

Raising his wand, a flask flies from the shelf across the way from him. Noble Elder pulls the cork with his teeth. He pulls back RJ's shirt. As he pours the potion over the wound, it bubbles.

"Sit him up and pinch his nose," Noble Elder orders as he dumps some of the potion into RJ's mouth.

"Will that save him?" Minnie inquires.

"Yes. Merlin's poison is strong, but I learned the antidote to counter it decades ago. Now, we wait. The antidote responds differently in each person."

"Noble Elder have you seen his ring?" inquires Minnie.

Reaching down, Noble Elder takes RJ's hand and examines the ring.

"Fascinating," notes Noble Elder as he attempts to remove the ring but finds that it cannot be removed.

"I already tried to take the ring off to examine it further," Minnie remarks.

"For now, we leave it. That ring will prove to be interesting," exclaims Noble Elder.

Minnie nods as she summons a chair next to RJ's bed and sits down, causing a book to appear and she begins to read. Noble Elder pats RJ's hand and walks across the room, climbing the stairs to the second-floor walkway, where he begins to pace. The next few hours pass slowly until the Sanctuary begins to shake. Noble Elder quickly teleports back to RJ's side in order to examine him.

"Sir, what is going on?"

Noble Elder places his hand on RJ's forehead, "He is dreaming."

"Dreaming?"

"Yes, Minnie. He is dreaming, but it is hard to enter his mind even without him having magic. I will stay close by to keep an eye on him," Noble Elder remarks, checking the spot on RJ's shoulder.

"It looks worse than before," Minnie exclaims.

"I have never seen anything like this. Normally, the antidote clears it up quickly. We will have to continue administering it to help treat it fully," Noble Elder explains.

Minnie and Noble Elder jump back as RJ suddenly begins to levitate into the air.

"Sir?"

"Fascinating," Noble Elder says, putting on his glasses and examining RJ carefully, running his hands between RJ's floating body and the bed.

"Since he is floating off the bed, he, somehow, appears to have magical powers. We know that he gave up his powers. But did he? Hmmm."

Noble Elder teleports up to the seventh-floor balcony, running his hands along the spines of the books. He pulls one from the shelf and levitates back down to the main floor.

"Here it is. *Somnia Ambulans*, the ability of an elder to walk through dreams. If asleep, the individual will levitate in the air and fly around the space as a form of protection. For the dreamers, the dreams become reality. They have to wake from it on their own."

"If he is dream walking, then how do we help him?"

"We cannot. He is on his own. To wake him would be catastrophic. So, all we can do is wait."

∿

Waking lying in a field of long grass, RJ sits up and looks around.

What a weird dream. Where am I?

Then, climbing to his feet, he observes the area.

There is Grandma and Grandpa's place in the distance.

Walking across the field, RJ makes haste toward the estate. Then, he stops, kneels, and examines the ground.

"This is weird. The grass has always grown on this hill. It has never been barren like this. The whole area looks like it is dying."

Rising, RJ walks more cautiously as he approaches the estate. He notices broken glass and vines growing through the windows.

"Hello. Is anyone home?"

What in the world has happened here? Why is this place so dark?

"Cedric? Grandma? Grandpa?"

RJ strolls around the main floor, looking around until he reaches the study.

Dang! Cedric, how long has it been since you dusted? This place is trashed. Wait, the windows are broken, the home is dark, and the library is a mess. Did someone tear this place up? Hmm. What is going on here? The globe...

Approaching the globe, RJ places his hand on it as it flies off of its stand.

At least the magic of this place still works.

"Now, where are they?" he says aloud, spinning the globe as it is floating in the air.

This is weird. There are no signs of any of them. Hmm.

RJ steps back and rubs his chin as he thinks. Then, circling the globe, he spins it several more times, examining it further.

No signs of magic. No signs of the Arcane. No signs of anyone. Hang on, the globe is only showing the Mundane. No. magic! This is amazing. Finally! I could get used to this."

Sitting on the sofa, RJ looks around, then, dozes off.

Several hours later, he is woken by the sun shining through the library windows. Getting up, he yawns and walks towards the kitchen.

Hmm, is there any food in this place? Wow, this room looks worse than the library and the rest of the house. This is weird. The cabinets are empty. The whole place looks as if it has been ransacked.

RJ's eyes narrow as he looks through the kitchen door into the main entry. A young dwarf stands there, frozen, looking at him. Several items fall out of the dwarf's satchel, and he scrambles to pick them up.

"Hello," RJ says as the dwarf's face twitches.

As RJ walks through the door, the dwarf suddenly runs off, up the stairs. RJ follows. He runs his hand along the wall, following burn marks, until he reaches the main hall on the second floor.

Where did the dwarf go? Wow! RJ wonders.

Then, he backs up and gasps.

That is not good, not good at all.

Looking up, he regards the space and notices markings of the darkness burned into the ceiling.

Either I am dreaming, or time is playing a fickle game with me. The room is destroyed, the tapestries are in ruin, and the artifacts are all missing! Merlin, you foul monster, you better not have...

RJ runs down the hall and turns down a second hallway, bolting for the study.

Where is it?

RJ's hands dance over the spines of the book and when he pulls down on a giant leather book, the bookcase flies open. Descending the stairs, he comes upon a long hallway.

Fourth archway. Here it is. The armor of an elf general. If I remember correctly, tap the sword handle.

RJ steps back as the wall slides open, and he enters the next room.

Hmm, the magical nexus is still working, but Lady Esther is not here. Where is everyone?

The central orb lights and flies into the air as lines appear, spinning in the orb.

I see that it still works. But this is weird. Where are they? There is nothing. How is it that I am not finding anyone? What is going on?

RJ walks out of the room taps the sword handle again, sealing the room, and turns into the adjacent archway across the hall. Then, picking up a cane, he taps the wall three times, and it slides open, revealing an armory.

Something is going on here, and I will find out what. Let's see, orbs, bow and arrow, and I will take the sword, and, ah yes, that staff will work. Wait, that is Willow's helmet. Hmm. That goes with me too. She is never without it. Something is not right if that is here.

Turning, RJ leaves the room, walks down the long hall, and climbs up a ladder, arriving in the old carriage house.

Mustang? No. Lamborghini? No! Skateboard, are you kidding me? A carriage would be fun, but if only I had a horse. Hmm. I know. Let's see if this still works.

Walking up to the wall, RJ steps down on a giant stone at the bottom and the wall comes ajar. Pushing it open, he reaches in and retrieves a broom.

I cannot believe I am going to do this. If the siblings were here, I would never hear the end of it.

He throws the broom in front of him, pulls a pair of goggles off the shelf, puts them on, and tightens the straps on his bag.

"Okay. Goggles, check. Bag tightened down, check. Boot laces are tucked in, check. If I remember correctly, it is 'Mount the broom and kick off.'"

Mounting the broom, RJ looks around, ensuring that he hasn't forgotten anything. As he kicks a lever with his boot, the ceiling of the carriage house opens, and he kicks off, rising into the air. Soaring into the sky, he quickly looks around.

The landscape appears to be the same, but it seems that the Arcane School of Magical Teaching is in ruins, RJ remarks to himself.

The broom carrying him takes off as he races across the sky toward the academy. He circles the school several times, observing the grounds below until, suddenly, a spear flies past him.

Wow! Athena," RJ notes as he dives down and lands.

Athena backs up, watching RJ cautiously.

"Athena?" inquires RJ, raising his hands.

"Yes," she replies.

"The Arcane School of Magical Teaching, what has happened?"

"The Arcane School of Magical Teaching has been gone for years," a confused Athena responds.

"Wait! Years? That is impossible! Oh no! Time?" RJ says as Athena tilts her head to one side, gazing at him quizzically.

"Time is gone. Everyone is gone. When you are a goddess, like me, you live forever and, in many cases, you outlive everyone," she says sadly, walking toward RJ, circling, and examining him closely.

"You are an elf?"

"I am," RJ replies, touching his ears.

"You carry elfish weapons?" she points out, examining the staff strapped across RJ's back.

"That staff, where did you get it?" she inquires, suddenly holding a blade to his throat.

"Please, Athena. I mean no harm. I got it from my family's estate," he replies, his hands raised.

"Your family's estate?" Athena asks, lowering her sword. "That is impossible."

"What is impossible?"

"If you are who I believe you to be, then either my uncle is playing a weird game from the underworld, or you are really standing here," she says.

"May I ask who you think I am?" RJ inquires as Athena continues to look at him, her eyes narrowing.

"Are you not Lord Ambrose?" she demands.

"Well, I am RJ. The non-magical side of Ambrose," he replies.

"The non-magical one! Great Hera! This has to be a joke!"

"I do not understand, Athena. Why a joke? I gave up my powers seven years ago," he explains.

"I see. Seven years. Which means you are nineteen. Interesting, I suggest that you follow me," Athena says, raising her eyebrow as she stows her sword and walks toward her temple. Picking up his broom, RJ follows Athena quietly. Looking around, he stops and kneels down to touch the land where statues of his family used to stand.

"Athena, where are the statues?" RJ inquires

Looking around, he notices that she is no longer there.

"Ugh! Are you kidding me?"

Ascending the steps, he enters the temple, then gasps.

"What happened here?" he asks, observing that the temple is also torn up.

"Devastation," Athena replies as she disappears behind a pile of books.

"These are the books from the Academy's library," RJ says, picking up one of the books and turning it over to examine it.

"Preserved. I saved as many texts as I could," Athena replies, re-emerging and carrying a chest. RJ drops the book and his eyes narrow as he approaches the chest.

"That is the chest called 'Hope,' the one that the Magical Three used many years ago to enter the Arcane realm," he states.

"Yes. I hunted high and low for it."

"Athena, where is my family?" RJ inquires.

Athena stops and looks toward the ceiling as the temple darkens and the ceiling lights with the stars.

"They are all among the stars. You are the last living Ignatius," she replies.

"Impossible."

"No. It is possible. You were poisoned over a hundred years ago and went missing. Your family fought to save time, but when Noble Elder passed away, the snow globe was lost. Merlin found it. But, at that moment, he died, and his lifeless body fell to the ground, dropping the globe. When the globe hit the ground, it exploded, sending the Arcane world into chaos. Magic was lost forever," Athena explains as she leans against the table.

"But magic still exists. The estate still has its magic," RJ exclaims, confused.

"Yes. That is something that I cannot explain. It is as if the home knew that… well, you were alive and would return," Athena remarks.

"Return? Wait! I am confused. A hundred years ago?" RJ exclaims, pacing the floor.

"The last I remember was my great-grandma yelling at me to get to safety," RJ says.

"RJ, tell me. Do you remember exactly what she said?" Athena inquires as RJ sits down abruptly on a chair.

"Think, think, think!" RJ says aloud as he closes his eyes, trying to remember. Then, he speaks.

"'Russell Ambrose Ignatius, Jr., get out of here now. You must protect your ring at all costs. It is the key. Do you hear me? It is the key.' She also said, 'My boy, my dear, sweet Ambrose, you have the power to protect everyone. The time has come. If no one else will tell you, then I will. I have faith in you, RJ, to make the right decision. Now, get to New York City. Help is there. The poison is spreading through you, find....'"

"The poison," Athena repeats as RJ jumps to his feet.

"Athena, I was hit several days before with a poisoned arrow from an elf. Grandma and Willow treated the wound, or so I thought. Athena, what happened to my great-grandmother that night?" RJ demands.

"She passed away several hours later. She became a Sister of Avalon," Athena explains.

"A Sister of Avalon? Hmm. Has Lord Yule been seen?" RJ asks.

"No," replies Athena as the room re-lights, and she watches RJ pick up his broom.

"Athena, I need 'Hope.' I am going to Avalon," declares RJ as he walks towards the chest.

"RJ, I understand that you want to find Avalon, but Avalon would cease to exist without magic," Athena explains.

"Pallas Athena, while I understand what you have said, there is one thing you are forgetting. If time is altered again, which it appears it has been, then, with or without magic, I am the one who can make it work," RJ declares.

"You make a valid point. The Hope chest will take you where you need to go, but I do not know if it has enough magic to teleport you to Avalon," Athena says, reaching for a box on the table.

"If it drops me anywhere close to Avalon, I can find it. Besides, I have Willow's helmet," RJ remarks, clicking the clasps on his bag and flipping the flap back, revealing the helmet.

"Then, you will need this," Athena says, handing him the box.

Opening it, RJ looks down at the items inside.

"One remaining magical spell, preserved in each of them. The wands belonged to your parents and grandparents. I could never find your siblings' wands, and as you are without power, they may come in handy," Athena remarks as RJ runs his hands along the length of the wands.

"Four wands, one spell each is all I need," RJ states as Athena hugs him. Then, pulling back, she places a scarf around his neck, pulls his jacket collar up, and smiles.

"That is the Ambrose I know. Sorry, I mean RJ," Athena remarks.

"Athena, it is okay at this point. But, unfortunately, it looks like Ambrose is going to have to return. And, unfortunately, to fix this, I will have to do things that I do not want to do," he replies.

"Ambrose, there comes a time in one's life when they may not want to do things. But I have known you your entire life. I know you will make the right decisions, and, if not, you will just mess with time until you get it right," explains Athena, winking at him.

"Thank you, Athena. I hope I can do this," Ambrose replies.

Kicking the side of the chest of Hope with his boot, the lid flies open and lightning strikes down around him.

"Good luck, Ambrose. May the powers of time be with you and protect you."

Athena waves goodbye as Ambrose yells.

Accipe me, Avalon.
Take me to Avalon.

Sand spins around him as the winds pick up. Then, a giant storm forms and orbs fly out of the trunk, spinning around through the sand and lighting the area.

Chapter 16
The Juncture

Sand continues to spin as Ambrose looks around, raising his hand and running his fingers through the sand until the lid of the chest of Hope slams shut. He finds himself standing in a dark hallway, the only light coming from the moon through the windows. Picking up the chest, Hope, he looks around, reaching into his bag with his other hand, and retrieving a lighter. Strolling down the walkway, he finds a stick and, reaching into his bag again, pulls out a torn cloth and makes a torch. Lighting the end of the torch, Ambrose looks around. Finding a candle stand, he lights four candles, then walks toward the other side of the room.

This place is creepy, he says to himself, chuckling. *And dirty. Wow, have they never heard of dusting?* he wonders, running his fingers along the tabletop and examining the dust.

"Well, it is empty. I might as well move on," he says aloud.

Then, he sees the spirit of a woman floating on the far side of the room, watching him.

"Hi," he says as the spirit tilts its head and flies toward him.

Quickly, he dives under the table and the ghost disappears.

What was that about?

Getting up and brushing himself off, he turns to find a cloaked figure standing in front of him. Backing up, he watches the figure as they lower their hood.

"Russell Ambrose Alezander Elderchild Ignatius, Jr., can it be?" inquires Nadia.

"Great-grandmama. You're here," Ambrose exclaims, hugging her, a tear rolling down his cheek.

"Are you crying?"

"No. Okay. Yes, I am. What is going on?"

"Time altered."

"I can see that. One minute, I am in the field with you and Amelia. Then, I wake up in a field down from the estate, and the home is trashed."

"Time is altered."

"Where is everyone?"

"As the Arcane died, they joined the stars. Earth is very different now. It is barely holding on. With magic gone, the symbiotic balance is altered. Floods, tornadoes, famine, disaster after disaster, plague the world and the Mundane," Nadia remarks as she begins walking and Ambrose follows.

"I do not know what to say," Ambrose says.

"I know you would never take magic back, but the world needs you. The world needs Noel," Nadia explains, stopping to look out over what remains of Avalon.

"It is ruined. I remember you and great-grandpa would bring me here. This place was one of the most beautiful ever seen," Ambrose says.

"Yes, when magic left the earth, the Sisters of Avalon channeled what magic we could to save Avalon. But, unfortunately, with each day, more of it fades. It will only be a matter of time before Avalon will cease to exist, the last remaining remnant and hope of magic for the earth," Nadia sighs.

"I made a mess of things," Ambrose remarks.

"Not exactly. Your siblings did not help," Nadia explains as they sit side-by-side on a bench.

"They were always difficult," Ambrose says, looking out over the vista. "It is beautiful here. Well, what is left of it," he says, smiling.

"It is indeed," Nadia sighs.

They sit quietly together for a while until Ambrose suddenly stands.

"No! Avalon has always been the true realm of the exceptional magic of earth. The Sisters of Avalon have always guarded magic. If the estate has retained its magic, and this place has magic, we can still save the world," Ambrose remarks as Nadia watches him closely.

"The manor still has magic?" she asks in confusion.

"Yes! I went there. The nexus still worked. So, I grabbed a broom and flew to the ruined Arcane School of Magical Teaching. Athena is there, her temple is a mess, but she gave me Hope, which I used to come here?" explains Ambrose.

"Follow me," Nadia says as she rises to her feet and glides over the ground quickly with Ambrose trailing behind her. Finally, Nadia reaches an old priory.

"The Priory of Avalon," Ambrose declares in amazement, looking up at the old priory.

"Yes, the heart of Avalon," Nadia replies, throwing the doors open as they enter.

Several women rise to their feet when Nadia enters.

"Nadia, what is this about? Is everything okay?" Lady Flora asks as Nadia steps aside, revealing Ambrose.

"Wait! The Lady Flora?" Ambrose says, stopping and acknowledging everyone in the room.

"It is Ambrose. He is alive," Dawn remarks, disappearing from her spot and reappearing next to Ambrose, examining him closely.

"Indeed, he is, Mother. Indeed, he is," Nadia says, rummaging through a chest and throwing items around her on the floor.

"Nadia, what are you looking for?" Flora inquires as Ambrose walks slowly through the space, looking around.

"I recognize this place. It is the priory from my dreams. This is where it happens," Ambrose exclaims, examining the space further.

"What is he talking about?" Dawn inquires.

"He refers to himself returning to power," Nadia answers, holding up an orb.

"An orb?" Ambrose asks.

"Yes. It is what we need to fix time and get you home," Nadia explains.

"Wait! Get me home? Great-grandmama, what are you talking about?" Ambrose asks as Nadia throws the orb into the air and it triples in size.

"Nadia, would you care to explain what is going on?"

"Lady Flora, as Ambrose has noted, the manor still has magic. If the manor has magic, he feels it," Nadia remarks, moving her hands around the orb as an image appears.

"Wow, that is me," Ambrose exclaims.

"You do not look so good," Lady Flora says.

"Because, at the time we are viewing him, he is sick. The poison has him trapped here in a bad dream," Nadia explains, looking around the orb.

"Trapped? I do not understand," Ambrose responds.

"The arrow that hit you held a powerful poison. Your grandmother could not contain it. But Noble Elder has the cure, the antidote. He gave it to you, and, as a result, you are here," Nadia explains as she taps the orb.

"So, I am having an out-of-body experience?" Ambrose asks.

"No, your mind is trying to fight the power of the poison," Nadia explains as the priory begins to shake.

"What is going on?" Ambrose yells.

"The magic is weakening. Ladies, we must hurry," Lady Flora declares, spinning her hands.

"What are you doing?" Ambrose asks.

"Getting you out of here," Lady Flora explains.

"But your magic…" Ambrose interjects.

"Will be restored when we get you back. Dawn, Nadia, help me," Flora calls as magic flies around Ambrose.

"Ambrose, you can do this. Your siblings… They fear your magic, but not because they are afraid of you. They are afraid of what your magic does to theirs," Nadia explains.

"What my magic does to theirs? I do not understand," Ambrose cries, raising his arm over his eyes.

"You amplify their magic. They are afraid of what their magic transforms into. You have to teach them, Ambrose. You have to teach them," Nadia replies as the three women raise their hands and lightning strikes down around Ambrose.

ॐ

Back in the Sanctuary, the wind picks up speed as it blows through the shelves, as the books, grimoires, and scrolls begin to fly everywhere.

"Noble Elder, what is happening?" Minnie inquires, standing.

"Brace yourself, Minnie," Noble Elder advises as the winds blow even faster.

"What in the world…?" Minnie asks as she grabs ahold of the railing.

Books and scrolls are flying out of control. Ambrose levitates higher into the air and a flash of light occurs. Noble Elder loses his grip and starts to fly up into the air.

"Got you," Ambrose says as he holds Minnie tightly by the hand.

"Stay here, both of you!" Ambrose commands as he runs across the floor, jumps on a chair, and flies into the air, his arm extended, reaching for the globe that is spinning in the wind high above the floor.

"Got it," Ambrose announces as the wind stops suddenly, and everything falls to the floor. Getting up, Minnie and Noble Elder brush themselves off and regard one another.

"Well, that was interesting," Noble Elder remarks, watching as Ambrose examines the globe.

"You seem taken aback by it," Minnie observes.

"It is not that. It is hard to explain," Ambrose replies.

"Part of you wants to drop it on the floor and destroy all magic, but now, you know what will happen. The other part of you is curious to see what is yet to come," Noble Elder states.

"Unfortunately, Noble Elder, even if I destroy it, somehow, magic will still exist, and inevitably, I will still have to take magic back. There is no clear path where magic ceases to exist," Ambrose says, setting the globe on its stand on the table and sitting down on the steps.

"I am curious about why you hate magic," Noble Elder remarks.

"Who said that I hate it?"

"Giving up your magic is not hating it?" Noble Elder inquires.

"No," Ambrose replies, rising and walking away with his hands behind him.

When Minnie begins to ask a question, Noble Elder raises his hand, stopping her.

Leaning over, he whispers, "Let him be."

"Noble Elder?" Ambrose inquires.

"Yes, Ambrose?"

"You have been the reigning Noble Elder. Why me? Why now?" Ambrose inquires as he stops and leans on the handrail.

"Hmm," sighs Noble Elder. "There comes a time in every Noble's life when they ascend to the stars to guard the universe. My time is upon me. Although, truthfully, I was never meant to be the Noble Elder, the Nobles appointed me until the true Noble Elder came along, the one who would be called Noel," he explains as Ambrose rolls his eyes.

"You doubt him?" Minnie confronts Ambrose.

"No, it is not that. I roll my eyes because all I have ever heard, throughout my life, is about my duty and who I am to become. I thought giving up the power would solve that, but even as a Mundane, I see it doesn't," Ambrose exclaims, descending the steps, walking toward the table, and picking up the globe. Minnie and Noble Elder stand quietly observing Ambrose as he holds up the globe.

"Is something supposed to happen?" Minnie asks.

"I do not understand," Ambrose mutters, examining the orb closely.

"Noble Elder?" Minnie inquires, glancing at him.

"Interesting. Very interesting indeed," Noble Elder says, putting on his glasses and walking toward Ambrose, who is still examining the globe.

"Sir?" Minnie asks, raising her hand.

Noble Elder stops, pulls his wand, and points it into the open space in the middle of the room as a portal flies open. Within seconds, Nadia and Nimuway arrive.

"Noble Elder," they say in unison as Nimuway glides across the room, levitating above the ground and circling Ambrose.

"Interesting. The globe is here, but it does not work," she remarks, placing her hand on its surface.

"It will not work," Nadia says, pouring herself some tea.

Stopping, Nimuway looks back at Nadia as Ambrose approaches.

"How do I get it to work?" he asks.

"That is going to be the trick," she replies.

"Trick? What sort of trick?" he inquires.

"It is not enough to simply want your magic back. You gave it up willingly. So, the globe is protected by six magical layers," Nadia explains.

"Six layers? The magic of siblings," Ambrose says as Nimuway raises an eyebrow.

"Your magic is powerful, but their fear is what protects it," Nadia explains.

"So, I have to convince them not to fear it?" Ambrose asks.

"We are doomed," Minnie mumbles as everyone turns to look at her.

"Do you have an opinion on this?" Nimuway inquires, looking annoyed.

"I would rather not say," Minnie interjects.

"No, wait, Minnie. I want to hear your thoughts," Ambrose says smiling at her while the others look at him, confused.

"Of course. Ambrose, you are the most powerful Arcane ever to live. The years of torment caused you to give up your magic. They fear your magic because of what it does to theirs. Your siblings do not always have the best track record," Minnie remarks.

"Minnie!" Noble Elder declares sternly.

"No, Noble Elder. She is correct. While Willow has loved me unconditionally, no matter what, the other five have been afraid. Terrified, even in the other timelines," Ambrose explains.

"Other timelines?" Nimuway asks.

"This would be easier to explain if I had magic to show you. But the night I ran away to New York City, I met the other Ambroses, fourteen of them to be exact. We all talked, and I learned something. In every timeline, my siblings feared my magic. In every timeline, when they died, they had no relationship with the Ambrose of that time. So, I did something the others did not expect, I chose a path with which the other fourteen Ambroses of the other timelines did not agree. I gave up my magic to show them that I cared," Ambrose explains, a tear rolling down his cheek as he turns away from them and, leaning his hands on the mantle, gazes steadily into the fire's flames.

The four regard each other sadly, looking for the right words to say. Suddenly, the room darkens, and an orb emerges out of the floor.

"What is going on?" demands Nimuway. Ambrose turns to watch the orb as Noble Elder approaches, his hands spinning as an image appears.

"It is Luciana," Minnie remarks.

"Is she okay?" Nadia inquires.

"The darkness is moving in on her," Nimuway declares as Ambrose approaches the orb.

"She is holding time still. But why?" he asks.

"She is doing it for you," Minnie exclaims as Ambrose glances over his shoulder at her.

"She won't be able to hold it still forever," he says, scooping up his bag and grabbing the broom.

"What are you doing?" Nadia asks, rising to her feet.

"I need to help her," Ambrose replies.

"Without magic?" Minnie asks, confused.

"What would you have me do? Nothing?" he snaps.

"Ambrose, she is holding time still for you. She is buying you the time you need to restore your magic," Noble Elder explains.

"Help him!" Minnie demands of Noble Elder.

"It is not that simple, Minnie," Ambrose notes, placing his hand on the orb. He cannot simply transfer his magic. Even now, magic will follow the rules. When it is least expected, the magic of Noble Elder will transfer to me, and when it does, all hell will break loose.".

"He is right, Minnie," Nadia concurs.

"Everyone, create a portal for me, please. I need to speak with Willow. She will be at the greenhouse of the Arcane School of Magical Teaching. If Luciana is in the time realm holding time still, then I will need the others to help me," he explains.

Hugging Ambrose, Minnie speaks up again, "I will keep an eye on things and help Noble Elder."

"Thank you," Ambrose says as Nimuway and Nadia touch hands, and a portal spins open. Ambrose throws the broom in front of him and leaps on it as it takes off. Soaring through the room, he swoops down, grabs the globe off the table, and disappears through the portal as it seals shut behind him.

☙

Ambrose looks around as he soars through the sky, high above the clouds, on his broom.

You know, this is the one thing I do love, flying.

Flying into the field behind the Arcane School of Magical Teaching, Ambrose pulls up on the handle of his broom as he soars up the hill. Then, he quickly dives off the broom as it hurls itself into one of the trees at the edge of the forest.

Ha! On the other hand, I hate flying for that very reason. Landings always suck, he laughs to himself as he gets up off the ground.

Then, looking around, he notices that the field is empty.

Woohoo! At least, I wasn't seen.

Ambrose runs across the field toward the steps climbing up the hillside to the main level of the Arcane School of Magical Teaching. Stopping, he gazes back across the field and trees as he feels as if he is being watched. And, indeed, someone *is* watching him from the trees.

Weird, he thinks, running up the stairs. Reaching the top, he notices students bustling about. Weaving his way through the groups of students, he notices Athena entering her temple. Quickly, he chases behind her and enters the temple.

"Pallas Athena?" he hollers as he looks around for her. Then, turning, about to leave, a flicker catches his eye.

"Well, I guess no one is here," he declares aloud as he walks towards the entrance. Once outside, he ducks behind one of the pillars, watching the doorway. Emerging, Athena looks around cautiously as she picks up a scroll, her back turned to the entrance.

"Why did you hide?" Ambrose asks.

Startled, Athena drops the scroll.

"Hello, RJ. How are you? Hiding? No. I was in the back of the temple. I am sorry I did not hear you," Athena replies, laughing but looking somewhat nervous. Leaning down, Ambrose picks up the scroll and examines the seal.

"This is the seal of the Nobles," Ambrose exclaims, looking at Athena.

"Ah, look at that. So it is," she replies, her hand shaking.

"Are you okay?" he asks.

When she looks at him, she motions with her eyes to the right and up. Carefully so as not to draw attention, Ambrose follows her glance and notices an owl, sitting in the rafters.

"Hello, Ms. Hoot," Ambrose acknowledges, walking toward the rafter where the owl sits. Just as he reaches the spot, the owl hoots and takes off and flies out of the door.

"Great Hera!" Athena declares, breathing a sigh of relief.

"Care to explain?" Ambrose asks.

Athena points her finger. They reenter the temple, and the temple doors swing shut behind them.

"I would, but then it would be unwise to assume things," Athena responds.

"Assume what?" he asks regarding her curiously.

"It is nothing," she replies and turns to walk away.

"That I am not RJ?" Ambrose asks as Athena freezes in mid-stride. Turning, she scans the area cautiously, as Ambrose flips the flap of his bag back, revealing the globe.

"Ambrose? Praise Zeus!" Athena declares.

"Yes, but without power for now," he remarks, flipping the flap of his bag shut again, re-engaging the clasp, and picking up a book.

"I see. How much do you remember?" she asks, watching him.

"If you are asking about that dream, everything. Athena, you are the greatest mind in the universe. How do I get the globe to work?" Ambrose inquires.

"You don't remember?" she asks.

"Remember? What?" Ambrose replies with a confused look.

"Not here. There are too many watching," Athena cautions as she walks past him and hands him a scroll, which he stows in his bag. She opens the door to the temple as soon as the scroll is out of sight.

"Good day, RJ," Athena acknowledges.

"Have a good day, Pallas Athena," Ambrose replies, walking out the door.

Strolling across the Arcane School of Magical Teaching grounds, Ambrose walks out the back gates toward the field and descends the hill to the greenhouse. Quietly, he slides through the backdoor as Willow is busy teaching a class of fifth year students.

"Class, would anyone mind explaining the difference between gray and green roots?" she asks as several students raise their hands.

Then, the bell chimes over campus.

"We will start with that question next class. Hurry. Move along, all of you. You should not be late for your next class," she directs as the students bustle out the door.

Ambrose smiles as Willow comes over to hug him.

"How are you?" he asks.

"Dear Brother, I am fine. So, I see you are up and doing better?" she says, smiling.

"Doing better?" he inquires, puzzled.

"Oh, you must have hit your head harder than you remember," she replies, pulling out a chair and inviting him to sit.

"Yes, there are moments I do not remember anything," he says, playing into her concern.

"I am just glad to see that you're okay. So, what brings you here?" Willow inquires.

"I just came to say 'hi.' I had the day off from work and class," Ambrose explains when Lady Marybelle barges into the greenhouse.

"Lady Ignatius, some assistance, please. Lady Marybelle notes that five third-graders are trying to burn down the owl hut again," Lady Marybelle declares.

"I will see you later," Willow says to Ambrose as she hugs him and heads out.

Ambrose looks around the room, then quietly walks out the door. Observing the grounds, he heads off down the back path that leads to the village. Once he reaches the village, he turns down one alley that comes to a dead end. When he taps the stones, the sand falls away out from under him and he walked down a set of stairs.

Once his head is below the level of the ground, the opening seals, and the alley stands empty. Then, several minutes later, Ambrose emerges from the forest. Walking along the path, he stops at the cliff's edge and looks out. He hears rustling from the bushes behind him. Reaching under his cloak, he places his hand on his blade.

"No need to draw your weapon. It is just me," Athena says as Ambrose removes his hand from the blade's handle.

"Now, how is it that you remember what happened, but no one else is aware of anything?" inquires Ambrose sitting on a log.

"Your daughter. She is very adamant that you will return. She rambled on about how I was the greatest of the ancient goddesses, that she could only entrust the secrets with me," Athena explains, walking to the edge of the cliff, her hands resting behind her.

"Well, what did she have to say?" Ambrose asks but Athena simply turns and walks into the woods. Getting up, he picks up his items and follows her. The two walk quietly for a while. Then, they come upon an ancient cave.

Backing up, Ambrose freezes.

"What is it?" Athena inquires, watching Ambrose closely as his eyes narrow.

"I know this place," he says.

"How do you know this place?" Athena inquires.

Ambrose closes his eyes and then opens them. The area spins around him and Athena. Turning and observing the area, Athena stops and gazes at Ambrose. They have arrived in a dark cave.

"Never try to enter the cave through the opening. It is a trap designed to detour anyone seeking answers," Ambrose explains as he sets his bag down and walks toward the stone table. Then, brushing his hand against the stone, he bends over and blows on the stone. As dust flies around the room, an image of Luciana appears.

"How did you know to do that?" Athena asks.

"It is just like in my dream," he remarks as he looks at Luciana.

"Hello, Dad," Luciana greets him.

"Hello," Ambrose says as seven orbs fly around Luciana.

"Throughout history, time has changed rapidly. It has bent, broken, rebuilt itself, and, for fun, broken again. But, in all that, one thing has remained the same, your magic. With each passing year, your magic grew. Then, one day, nothing. Finally, magic went dark, and it stopped working. You had fallen at the hands of Merlin," Luciana's voice echoes through the cave as image after image play out around them.

Ambrose walks through the space exploring the images as Luciana continues, "Although you and Papa fell to Merlin, something that was not expected happened. You altered the timeline and altered it in a unique way that would forever shape the story."

The seven globes fly into the air, and light explodes from them, revealing Ambrose and his six siblings.

"My brothers and sisters," Ambrose says as Athena acknowledges them.

"When you chose to give up your magic, something happened. The magic that bound your siblings to your magical fluctuations left them. So, you see, somehow, when you separated your magic from you, the parts of your magic that resided in them also left. Thus, for your magic to return, each of them must give you back the power," Luciana explains as the image of the six play out, each one returning the power to Ambrose.

"You do realize that, logically, we are doomed," Athena exclaims as Ambrose nods in agreement. Upon leaving the cave, Athena teleports Ambrose back to the campus, just outside the student union.

Chapter 17
Cool-Down

After returning, Ambrose strolls down the path of the dark campus, the only light illuminating from the glow of the streetlamps. Reaching his apartment building, he ducks behind the shrubs and watches as Michael and Pete walk into the building.

He sneaks around the corner, peering into the lobby. When he sees no one is there, and that the coast is clear, he slips in and runs up the back stairs of the emergency exit. When he reaches the fifth floor, he stops, places his ear to the door, and listens. Opening the stairwell door, he observes the hallway, then walks out into it. He goes to his apartment door, opens it, and slips in quietly, shutting the door behind him. Turning on the light, he looks around.

Dalton is not even home., Bah! How am I to have a conversation with him? This is frustrating. At the very moment I need him, he is not around.

Walking down the hall, Ambrose reaches his bedroom. Throwing his bag on a chair, he rummages around, throwing things into his sports bag. Stopping, he starts to cry as his heart tells him one thing while his mind is telling him something different.

"Hi, Mr. Cee. It has been a long week, buddy. Let's get out of here," Ambrose says, scratching Mr. Cee on the back of the head.

"Meow," Mr. Cee acknowledges as the cat sits on his bed watching Ambrose as he starts digging through his closet, throwing things out of the way.

"Where is it?" Ambrose asks as he pulls out a vast steamer trunk from the back of his closet.

"I hate this damn thing," he says, scooping up his bag from the floor, walking toward the trunk. Kicking the latch with his boot, the chest flies open, and he and Mr. Cee disappear.

❦

They land in a field and Ambrose walks toward a giant gate, pushing it open. The glow of candlelight shines from the windows of the homes lining the street, lighting the way as Ambrose walks along with Mr. Cee at his side. Several individuals look out of their windows and doors as tiny fireflies fly from the windows and take to the air.

"Look, Mr. Cee, the night sky is perfect here, and it is so quiet," Ambrose remarks as the two reach the end of the street.

Ambrose reaches into his jacket pocket and pulls out a giant skeleton key, which he slides into the lock of a door and turns three times. Click, click, click. On the third click, the light in the overhang of the building turns on and Ambrose pushes the door open and walks into the entryway. Closing the door behind him, Ambrose advances down the hallway, past ancient elfish columns rising out of the ground and reaching for the never-ending ceiling of the structure. Ambrose enters a courtyard as the fountain springs to life, and the candles light.

"Come on, Mr. Cee, keep up," Ambrose says as he enters a room on the far side of the courtyard. There, he throws his bag on the ground and takes off his jacket, followed by his shirt. Then, reaching into his bag, he retrieves his staff and walks into the center of the floor. Mr. Cee meows, then jumps up onto the ledge, watching over the space. Ambrose bows to himself in the mirror as he snaps up the staff and spins it.

Ambrose practices various forms of elf combat for the next hour, after which several of the practice mannequins lay on the floor in pieces. Then, snapping his staff down, he spins it, striking one of the combat mannequins, the head of which flies off and stops floating in midair.

"Remind me never to upset you," Sophia remarks, watching her brother. He rolls his eyes and walks back towards his bag, throwing his staff down and picking up his shirt.

With his back turned to Sophia, he speaks, "Good evening."

"Ahh. So, you do speak?" Sophia replies, handing him the combat mannequin's head. He takes it, walks over, and puts it back on the mannequin's body. Then, he leans down to pick up the broken pieces.

"What brings you here this evening?" Sophia inquires, leaning down to help him scoop up the pieces.

"I have it," he snaps as she stands back, looking at him.

"I was only trying to help," she explains as he walks across the room, throwing the pieces into the wooden bin.

"If you must know why I am here, it is because I need to clear my head," he states with a straight face.

"I know that look all too well," she responds, sitting on the second step and motioning for him to sit beside her.

Ambrose strolls over and sits down, leaning forward and resting his arms on his knees.

"You make that face when something is bothering you," she remarks, looking at him.

"I would rather not discuss it," he replies.

"Ok. Do you remember how dad used to bring us all here to practice?" Sophia asks, raising her hand as various images play out in front of them.

"Yeah, it was rather annoying," Ambrose remarks, leaning back as Mr. Cee walks across Sophia's lap and climbs over onto Ambrose.

"I see that he is still protective of you," Sophia says.

"Yes. The only one in the family, except for Willow," Ambrose replies, standing and picking up his bag.

"'Night," he says, throwing the bag over his shoulder and walking out the door with Mr. Cee in his arms.

"RJ, wait," Sophia calls, chasing after him as he picks up speed. Raising her hands, she throws up a field, blocking the door.

"Not this again! Are you serious?"

"I asked you to wait."

"Why, Sophia? So, you can lecture me about coming here. Oh wait! I know, I need to clear coming here with the Elfish guard, or is it that I need all of my sibling's permission to come here?" Ambrose yells, pulling the key from his pocket and tossing it in the fountain.

"Russell Ambrose Alezander Elderchild Ignatius, Jr.," Sophia yells back.

"Lower the field, Sophia, now!" Ambrose shouts, throwing his bag on the ground and pulling his arm blades.

"RJ, stop!. I just want to talk to you," Sophia pleads.

"Nope! Lower the field," he demands, striking the field multiple times with his arm blades, causing the building to shake.

"RJ, you will bring the place down. This is one of the oldest buildings in Aelfdene. Please, stop," Sophia cries as she runs up behind him and hugs him.

"Let go," he yells.

"Not until you stop and listen. Please," Sophia replies as she lowers the field.

When she lets him go, Ambrose throws his arm blades into his bag.

"What gives?" he asks.

"I have something to say. Please, hear me out," Sophia replies as Ambrose looks at his watch.

"You have a minute," he says, holding up his watch and observing the hands.

"RJ, I am sorry! I am very sorry! I never stood up to the others. I am sorry that you hate us, and I am sorry that you had to move out," Sophia says, holding her hands up as a tear rolls down her face.

Lowering his arms, Ambrose stops, closes his eyes, and takes a deep breath.

"I do not hate you guys. I always looked up to all of you. We had our differences and I needed you guys. I needed my siblings to help me understand my magic instead of arguing with me. My magic was different, and I lived my entire life in fear because of it," he replies as Sophia comes up and hugs him again.

"We were all scared. You would have a moment, and our magic, whoever was closest to you at that point in time, would feel it. Our powers would feel it," she says.

"I know. I left for that very reason," he explains as they stop hugging, and he turns to pick up his bag again.

"Wait! You knew?" Sophia inquires as Ambrose reaches for the doorknob.

Stopping, he looks back, "Yes. Good night."

Walking down the path, Mr. Cee strolls next to him.

"Meow."

"Don't you start, Mr. Cee! I do not want to hear it."

Reaching the gate, Ambrose pushes it open and begins to walk down the path. Stopping, he looks back toward the village when he hears a creepy laugh.

"Ahh! How cute the Mundane Ignatius and his cat. Kill them," the voice commands as Ambrose drops his bag, spins his spear, and strikes two dark creatures.

"Oh look, Mr. Cee, it is the ugly witch," Ambrose mocks.

"Ugly? Ugly?! How dare you! I am the most beautiful in the land, unlike that filthy grandmother of yours. It doesn't matter. She, like the rest, will be dead soon enough, and when they are, I will be the queen of the elves," Raven laughs as she flies backward, avoiding the magic flying at her.

"Is she annoying you, dear Brother?" Sophia asks, appearing as her clothes transform into elfish armor.

"Two of them. This will be double the fun. General, kill them," Raven screams, licking her lips as a spear appears in her hand.

"Raven's mine. Give me cover against the others," Ambrose says, taking his jacket off and spinning his spear as Raven charges him. Simultaneously, the dark creatures glide across the ground at Sophia as she spins her wand, creating a lightfield and pushing them back.

The blades of their spears clang. "You know I am the best spear mistress that ever existed," Raven brags, holding down Ambrose's spear as flames explode around the area, and elfish guards appear. Dodging multiple flying arrows, Raven jumps backward, blocking the arrows with her magic.

"Captain, get my brother out of here," Sophia orders.

"No, I am not a child, and I can handle myself," Ambrose declares, catching a magical blast with his spear.

"Fine! I am not going to argue with you. Just do not get hit with magic. I will never hear the end of it from our parents and grandparents. Captain, stay close to RJ," Sophia commands as she spins her wand, creating an arm shield of magic.

When magic strikes the shield, Sophia holds her position firm, sliding backward across the dirt. Then, spinning his spear and striking multiple dark creatures, Ambrose drops to the ground, doubled over.

"Ahhhh!" he yells, holding his hand as it starts glowing.

"RJ?" Sophia yells as her eyes turn blood red and the dark creatures all drop to the ground screaming.

Ambrose remains doubled over, holding his hand when Raven is suddenly launched into the air as the dirt under her explodes and Minnie runs up to Ambrose.

"Noble Elder, can you help him?" she inquires as Noble Elder redirects multiple dark magic blasts from every direction.

"I am kind of busy here," he says, spinning his hand as he throws the dark blast into the ground.

"Brother, are you okay? What can I do?" Sophia asks, placing her hand on his back as her eyes start to glow white and she pulls her hand away.

"Little Brother, I understand. Hang on," Sophia declares as she regards Minnie.

Sophia smiles, stands, and raises her hands above her head, lightning striking the ground and throwing the darkness back. Energy flies back and forth between her hands until a quick flash happens, and an orb appears. She lowers it in front of her.

"I think you may need this, Brother. Ambrose, I give you the ability to protect all," Sophia declares as the orb flies up into the air, flashes, and is gone. Ambrose remains doubled over. Minnie remains close to him as

Sophia and the Captain cast lightfields to protect themselves, RJ, and Lady Minnie.

"Lord Noel, come on. We need you," Minnie calls as Noble Elder flies into the field and hits the ground. Peering up, Ambrose raises his hand, concentrating as flames explode around the group.

"This is about to get interesting," Minnie notes, smiling

Then, RJ pushes himself up, rising to his feet.

"Lady Sophia…?" The captain began to inquire, backing up at the sight of RJ.

"Captain, whatever you do, stay focused on holding that shield," Sophia directs as she gazes at Ambrose.

"My turn," he says, flying into the air and raising his hand. Ambrose's eyes turn purple as magic flies around him. The dark creatures start exploding and dissolving into dust as light beams spin around the area, signaling the arrival of help.

An arrow screams, flying across the ground and bursting into flames, striking three of the dark creatures and going completely through two of them, and dropping the third. The dark creature drops its sword, falling over backward, dead. Sophia and Minnie give each other side looks upon the arrival of help. Zander, Rose, Cedric, Conrad, Conway, and Willow stand back-to-back, as the light beam lifts.

Willow lowers her bow as the darkness dives on the group but strikes the field and is launched into the air. Zander and Rose observe Ambrose standing tall, his right arm raised as magic flies from his hand, creating a field pushing the darkness high into the sky.

Turning to acknowledge the arrival of help, Ambrose looks at his grandmother, Rose, who notices that his eyes have turned solid black.

"Alezander, look at Ambrose's eyes," she remarks.

"I see them," he replies, his blade catching the blade of the dark general inches in front of Ambrose's face. Tilting his head, Ambrose looks at the dark general who flies backward, the general's sword glowing orange.

Screaming, the dark creature throws his blade down, holding his hand. As Ambrose raises his fist, the dark general dissolves just as Raven strikes Ambrose with dark magic. Unfortunately, the stream of magic backfires as Ambrose turns and walks toward several of the dark creatures causing them to explode. Backing up, Raven falls back to Merlin, who has been watching what has been happening. When Merlin turns away, he finds himself face-to-face with Ambrose.

"Going somewhere?" Ambrose asks, moving his hand by his side as the flames encircle him and Merlin.

"What is he doing?" Sophia asks as Ambrose raises his hand and starts bellowing fire. Merlin trips backward, falling through the flames until he points his wand at Ambrose and yells,

Finiendum Vitam.

To take the life of.

Deflecting the blast, Ambrose walks through the flames. Raven charges him, but Ambrose flicks his finger, and she is blasted off the ground into the air and is gone. Again, Merlin scrambles backward, trying to get away from Ambrose. He points his wand, but, this time, vines wrap around Mr. Cee as two dark generals strike Ambrose' gantlets, trying to draw his attention.

"Willow?" Sophia notices that her sister is holding an orb in her hand.

"By the magic of the Arcane, I give you back the magic you need to stop them," Willow commands as she launches the orb across the ground. It takes to the air and flies rapidly around Ambrose. Suddenly, the vines holding Mr. Cee dissolve as the orb strikes the darkness multiple times. Ambrose reaches up, touches the orb, and turns to solid light.

The two dark generals look at each other as they explode and are transformed into two Mundane. Jumping back, they look around as the light where Ambrose had been standing disappears. Several of the Dark Council members are engaged with Rose and Zander in a duel when one of the Dark Council members falls to the ground screaming. Ambrose appears and touches the shoulder of the individual. The spiritual force of the individual flies out of their mouth. The dark creatures begin to disappear. Merlin spins his cloak, disappearing on the spot.

Turning, Ambrose snaps his fingers, and all of the darkness disappears. Looking around, he nods to Mr. Cee, raises an orb, throws it into the air, and a portal opens. Walking toward it, he disappears along with Mr. Cee, and the portal spins shut. The area is left standing still as the others look around.

"Rose?" Zander says as they regard each other, acknowledging what has just occurred.

Chapter 18
Dream Destruction

Papers lying on the floor begin to fly around the hallway as a portal spins open, and Ambrose emerges with Mr. Cee in tow.

"Mr. Cee, no wandering off. Stay close," Ambrose directs, descending into the hall.

"This place is still a mess, I see," he says, walking down the stairs into the basement. Walking through the fourth archway, Ambrose bends the leg of the griffin statue, and the wall slides open. Ambrose drops his bag and raises his hands as the weapons in the room fly into the air, spinning. Ambrose points his finger, and the items disappear and immediately reappear in his bag.

"Do not look at me like that, Mr. Cee."

Leaving the room, Ambrose restores the leg of the statue, then walks further down the hallway, and taps a picture that slides back. Raising his hands, the orbs in the room fly into the air, and then, into the bag with the weapons.

At the end of the hallway, Ambrose sets the bag down, climbs a ladder, and disappears through a hatch. A second later, he reappears carrying multiple brooms. As he drops them down through the hatch, they disappear in midair and reappear in his bag.

"Thank goodness I remember the expansion spell," he laughs, looking at Mr. Cee.

Continuing to stroll down the long hallway, he ascends the stairs, follow by Mr. Cee where he places the bag on a desk, then, presses a button on his watch as a nanobot appears, landing in his palm. Picking it up with his other hand, Ambrose examines it.

"This should be interesting."

Walking over to a suit of armor, he places the nanobot on the back of the armor, and it comes to life.

"Soldier, defensive mode," Ambrose commands as the suit of armor takes a defensive stance at the door.

"It works. Wow! Amelia's tech is not half bad. Soldier, stand guard," Ambrose directs as the suit of armor salutes, then goes back into a defensive stance, holding its spear at the ready.

Ambrose lies down on a loveseat, yawning as he dozes off. Waking, he opens his eyes to find the room lit by the moon. A fire pops in the fireplace and Ambrose looks around.

The guard is still here, but where did this fire come from?

Getting up, he walks over and examines the fireplace.

Weird.

"Hiss."

"Mr. Cee, what are you hissing about?"

Turning, Ambrose sees a young dwarf boy standing at the other end of the room, holding a pile of wood in his arms.

"Oh, hey. It's you again. Hello," Ambrose acknowledges as the young dwarf pushes past him and throws the pile of wood into the fireplace. Reaching down, Ambrose picks up one of the sticks that the young dwarf has dropped and hands it to him.

Cautiously, the young boy takes it, his hand shaking.

"It is okay. I won't hurt you," Ambrose says soothingly as the young man crouches, obviously afraid and hiding behind the arm of the couch.

"You are an elf?" the boy askes observing Ambrose's ears. Before answering, Ambrose stops, listening.

"Bardagul, where are you?" a voice echoes through the space as the young boy runs toward the door.

"Wait," Ambrose calls, raising his hand as an older dwarf appears holding a mace.

"Who are you?" the dwarf demands, snarling and swinging the mace.

"Please, sir. I mean you no harm," Ambrose explains, his hands glowing as light spins around him.

The older dwarf stops and looks at him awkwardly.

"Sir?" the dwarf asks, confused.

"Yes, sir," Ambrose responds, tilting his head toward the dwarf, also confused.

"I have not been referred to by the term 'sir' for years," the dwarf explains, lowering his mace.

"Years?" Ambrose inquires with his eyebrows raised.

"Aye, it has been years since I have met anyone nice," the dwarf explains.

"This is an interesting place. How is it that there is no one nice here? Oh wait. I almost forgot. Magic is gone from here," Ambrose remarks.

"Aye. I see Bardagul has set the fire. I hope the lad did not bother you. Where are my manners? I am Alvíss," the dwarf says, stowing his mace on his back.

"Nice to meet you, Alvíss. I am Ambrose."

"Aye. I see. Very interesting. Nice to meet you, Ambrose," Alvíss replies, circling Ambrose and examining him.

"Papa?" Gorodra, a young dwarf girl, inquires as she enters the room.

"Oy! I am right here, daughter."

"Papa, this is a Mundane. Get back! I will protect you," Gorodra declares, pulling a dagger.

"Put it down, you fool. He won't hurt anyone. Run along and help your mother with dinner, children," Alvíss says, smiling.

"Indeed. May I ask you a question?" Ambrose inquires.

"Aye, go ahead."

"What brings you and your family here?" Ambrose asks.

"That, fine sir, is a fascinating question," Alvíss replies.

"I am listening."

"I do not know if you have ever heard the story of the Magical Three. They were considered the greatest wizards and witch. They were kind, gentle, and very focused. The youngest of the three, the queen, sought out the help of the dwarves. The elves and dwarfs have always had a special relationship, sometimes friends, sometimes enemies. As the queen of the elves, she called in some favors, and one was a rather weird favor at that. My father, a high-ranking member of the Dwarf Council, was fascinated by the Queen's request. You see, he owned a coffee shop. Maybe you have heard of it? Dwarfbrew?"

"That, good sir, I have," Ambrose acknowledges.

"Well, that owner was me father. He worked for the queen. Time passed, and, for many years, he kept an eye on things for her. I was just a wee lad when my father died," Alviss explains, sitting back and smoking his pipe.

"Anyway, after me father died, me mother, siblings, and I went to live in the Aelfdene village. When the battle of darkness arose, the queen moved me, my wife, and children here. So, you could say that we are the keepers of this place."

Quietly, Ambrose rose to his feet, walking over to the fireplace and gazing into the flames.

"Magic died, didn't it?" he inquires.

"Aye, it did. But it has recently returned. We do not know how, but this place has been coming to life. First, the cupboards started slamming open and shut. Then, the suits of armor sprang to life, and then, all the books began to chatter," Alviss explains.

"Interesting," Ambrose remarks, stroking his chin as a crash sounds through the room.

Ambrose raises his index finger to his lips to signal silence as he and the dwarf hide behind the furniture. A gang of four men enter the room.

"Look, boss, a fire. Someone is here," one of the men says.

"Search the room! Grab anything of value!" the man who is clearly in charge says.

"Boss, look. A dwarf."

Before Bardagul can move, one of the men grabs him.

"Ugly little thing he is. Do you think he will fetch us a good price?" the man inquires as Mr. Cee jumps on the desk, hissing.

"A black cat," another one declares as he pulls out a switchblade.

"Should I gut him?"

Before anyone can respond, the room goes dark. All that can be seen are two glowing white eyes. A scream is heard as the lights come back on. The man with the switchblade finds himself suspended in the air, his two buddies lay dead, and the leader is hunched on the floor spitting blood.

"Let's get the hell out of here," one says to the other, pulling him down. The two look at each other and run.

"This place is haunted," they declare in unison.

When they have gone, Ambrose appears holding Mr. Cee. He points his wand at the two dead bodies, and they dissolve.

"Father, was that magic?" Bardagul inquires.

"Aye, son. It is a rare form of magic," Alviss acknowledges.

Ambrose gazes at Alviss, considering his comment as he places Mr. Cee on the back of the loveseat, wipes the blood off his blade, and stows it away.

"Ambrose, I cannot thank you enough for helping my son. Please, come to meet the Mrs. and have dinner with us," Alviss suggests as Bardagul runs up and takes Ambrose's hand.

"Come on, Mr. Ambrose. Mama will like you."

The three walk to the other side of the estate where Alviss taps a panel behind the grand staircase three times, and the wall opens. The three descend a staircase when a brightly lit room comes into view.

"Chalia, we have a guest," Alviss exclaims when his wife stops what she is doing and drops the pan in her hand.

"Gorodra told me," Chalia explains as Ambrose wanders around the space, observing all the old pictures of his family.

Suddenly, he stops and his eyes narrow when he sees a particular picture of Alviss and Noel.

Pointing at it, Alviss explains, "A dear old friend."

"He and me papa were best friends. They did everything together. That was before either of us was born. Papa has taught me how to fight like him," Gorodra remarks, swinging her sword like an elf.

Ambrose smiles and sits down at the table. Being 6'4", it is not easy for him to fit in the space. Bardagul and Gorodra fight among themselves to sit next to Ambrose as their parents join them and their guest at the table.

After dinner, Chalia and Alviss put the children to bed and wish Ambrose a good night. Laying down, he looks up at the ceiling, his mind racing. Suddenly, he sits up.

"I have made a mess of things, Mr. Cee," Ambrose declares, getting up and walking up the stairs.

Mr. Cee follows behind him when Ambrose clicks the button on his watch and multiple nanobots appear. He places one on each of the eight suits of armor lining the hallway. Raising his hands, he spins them, and the home begins to restore back to normal, but, suddenly, Ambrose collapses to one knee, holding his shoulder. Pulling back his shirt, he examines the shoulder.

There is nothing there, but it hurts like the poison is still there, he thinks as he sits on the floor, looking around.

Then, quietly, he works through the night until Alviss appears at 7 AM in the morning, carrying a mug.

"I thought you might want some coffee," Alviss remarks, handing the mug to Ambrose.

"Thank you," Ambrose says, raising the lens on his helmet as he takes a sip.

"By your facial reaction, I can tell you are him," Alviss states.

"That I am who?" Ambrose inquires, an eyebrow raised.

"Noel," Alviss states, taking a sip from his own mug as Ambrose chokes on his.

"Yes. How long have you known?" Ambrose inquires.

"I knew last night when the room darkened. I have often seen you do that trick in the past," Alviss explains as his wife and two children come into the room.

"The home is fixed," Chalia states, looking around.

"It is the least I could do," Ambrose explains as Bardagul backs away from the window, pointing.

"Papa, we have trouble," the young boy says as Ambrose gets to his feet, takes off his helmet, and observes the group outside. He waves his hand and the helmet, and all his materials disappear. Lowering his arms to his side, two elfish arm blades appear.

"Alviss, take your family and hide," Ambrose orders.

Alviss walks up next to him, mace in hand as he lowers his helmet.

"Aye, I would, Ambrose. But I will fight alongside you. The wife knows what to do," Alviss remarks as Chalia grabs the two children and bolts for their hiding place.

"It looks like they have two elves tied up," Ambrose remarks as he looks down at Alviss.

"Alviss?"

"Aye, Ambrose."

"I will hold that gang off. Get the two elves to safety. Mr. Cee, protect Alviss' family while I am out there," Ambrose directs as he raises his hands, and the suits of armor come to life. Clicking the button on his watch, the nanobots circle him as he hands Alviss a medal.

"Put this on. They will respond to you," Ambrose explains as a brick flies toward the window and, then, stops. The double doors fly open as Ambrose levitates above the ground, appearing in the doorway as he walks across the air and down invisible steps to the ground. Alviss places the medal on his shirt as the nanobots circle him, forming protective armor on him.

"Seriously? You're throwing bricks?" Ambrose says, looking around.

"Boss, there are people here," one of the guys yells as four of them charge Ambrose.

Alviss runs towards the two elves, sliding under the legs of a Mundane and striking him with a mace. Turning, he pulls a dagger and cuts the ropes that bind the elves. The two elves regard one another, and then Alviss.

"Thank you," the female elf says, kissing Alviss.

Suddenly, one of the Mundane falls inches from them. The girl looks down and gasps at the sight of an elfish dagger sticking out of the man's chest.

"Dwarf?"

"The name is Alviss. Master Elf," Alviss replies, striking another attacker with his mace.

"Mr. Alviss is the elf your friend?" the young elf man inquires.

"Aye, and one of the most interesting ones you will ever meet. Quickly, inside," Alviss shouts as two more Mundane begin to attack. Soon, they find spears in their chest as two suits of armor throw spears at them. A scream rings over as two more attackers fall dead, with arrows sticking out of their backs. Ambrose lowers his bow, steps over the dead men, and walks toward Alviss and the two elves.

"I thought I said to get them inside?" inquires Ambrose as the elf girl points behind him.

"I think that would be a great idea. Look," she declares.

When Ambrose turns, he sees over fifty Mundane running across the field, carrying clubs and pipes, advancing toward the manor

"Inside. Quickly!" Ambrose commands as the group runs through the double doors.

Turning, Ambrose shuts the doors, then raises his hand sealing the door with magic.

The elf girl stops, watching Ambrose. The two stand in amazement regarding one another.

"What do we do?" Alviss inquires.

"I am getting you all out of here," Ambrose declares as his eyes start to glow white.

"Brother, the magic of the ancient ways," the girl gasps, backing up as Ambrose kneels and places his hands on the floor. The two siblings look through the archway and out of the window as sand spins around the house.

"He is moving the house," the young man shouts as Alviss' children and wife appear. Standing, Ambrose looks around as a flaming bottle flies through the glass at the front door. Before hitting the ground, it flies right back out of the window, and the glass is instantly repaired as if the event that just occurred was rewinding. Ambrose raises his arms, causing the manor, the grounds, and the carriage house to disappear from the hillside.

"What sort of magic is this?"

"Magic of the ancients," explains Alviss, smiling.

As everyone looks around themselves, a clock appears on the floor, the hands spinning.

"Look, Brother" the young girl points as her brother kneels, placing his hand on the ground, magic spinning around him.

"I am Elvey Peter Ignatius, and this is my sister Nordika Destiny Ignatius. I demand to know how you are doing this?" Elvey declares as Ambrose gazes over his shoulder at him.

"Master Elvey, may I suggest that we do not interrupt him while he is doing magic," Alviss remarks, redirecting the elf just as a crash echoes through the space.

The group looks around when, suddenly, Bardagul flies into the air.

"Papa," the young dwarf yells, his hands out, reaching for his father when a laughing, dark creature appears.

Nordika grabs the young dwarf's hands, and her eyes start to glow. The creature explodes.

"What in the world?" Nordika inquires as she lowers the dwarf back down to the ground.

Raising her hands to examine them, the magic begins to fly around her and the group. Ambrose raises his hands, and the house drops out of the air, spinning.

"If I were you, I would hold onto something. This might get bumpy," Ambrose's voice is heard.

The others look around, but he isn't there. Within seconds, the manor stops spinning, and the group finds themselves standing up and brushing themselves off.

Observing the area, Alviss is the first through the archway, looking out the window as Ambrose pushes the doors open. The manor sits in a field, a river running by as multiple elves appear pointing and chattering among themselves.

Emerging, Elvey and Nordika push past Ambrose, and the elves around the manor bow at the sight of the two young elves. The ground begins to shake as darkness flies around the area, laughing.

"Take cover!" one of the elves yells as Ambrose and Alviss appear, standing back-to-back as the darkness dives on them. The area darkens, but then, the dark creatures fly straight into the air, screaming, as light spins around. Spinning his hands, Ambrose is protecting everyone. Repeatedly striking the light field, the darkness charges until one of them slips through and goes after Alviss. Flying backward, it flies into the barrier of light. It screams, begins to shake, and explodes. As Ambrose lowers his hands, the light barrier grows brighter, dropping the darkness where it is.

Suddenly, Ambrose collapses, leaning on his staff.

"Lord Ambrose?" Alviss inquires.

"Ahhh! My shoulder," Ambrose says.

"You do not look too hot," Nordika declares as Ambrose falls to the ground.

"Ambrose, no! We have to help him," Alviss yells but the two elves look at each other and shrug.

"We would, but we have no magic," Elvey explains as Ambrose reaches into his pocket and hands a key to Alviss.

"My old friend, the building at the end, please get me there," Ambrose begs, hunching up and holding his shoulder.

"Aye. Bardagul, you carry the bag. Gorodra, dear, carry Mr. Cee. Chalia, help me lift him," Alviss orders as Elvey and Chalia help Alviss carry Ambrose. Nordika runs toward the building and unlocks the door as magic spins around. Stepping back, she watches as two beings of solid light appear.

"We are the Guardians. Please state your emergency," one of them says.

"My great-uncle, he needs help," Nordika explains as the Guardians disappear, scooping up Ambrose and reappearing in the doorway.

The others follow the two beings of light into the structure.

"Wow! This place is amazing," Elvey remarks, examining the markings on the pillars.

"Brother, this is ancient elfish, the story of our people," Nordika says as Mr. Cee bolts out of Gorodra's arms and runs toward the fountain where the two beings of light are lowering Ambrose into the water.

"What is going on? Elvey inquires when a ghost appears standing next to him.

"Fascinating, isn't it?" the ghost says as everyone else jumps back.

"Grandpa?" Elvey asks as the ghost smiles and flies across the room toward the fountains.

"The Guardians activated? Ambrose, no! How is this possible?" the ghost asks.

"He moved the manor to the village…" Alviss explains when the ghost interrupts.

"Help him!"

"We are unable to. Our job is to guard Ambrose. We are not able to heal him. Our magic is not designed to heal," the Guardians remark in unison.

The ghost flies across the courtyard.

"You, kid, is that Ambrose's bag?" the ghost yells.

"Yes, sir, it is."

"May I?" the ghost asks as he begins digging through the bag, throwing things everywhere.

"Aye. But what are you looking for, Peter?" Alviss asks.

"His globe. Where is it? Where is it?"

"Meow."

"Mr. Cee, the globe, where is it?" Peter barks as Mr. Cee jumps into the bag and reappears, a minute later, dragging a box. Picking up the box, Peter flies over to where Ambrose is lying, and opens the lid. The globe glows and launches into the air. Light flashes, and Ambrose stands, restored, in the courtyard. Looking around, Ambrose notices Peter as he walks past, and, placing a hand on Alviss' shoulder, bids the group, "Good night."

Chapter 19
The Elf Priory

The following day, the courtyard of the elf priory stands quietly in the crisp morning air. Chalia is busy cooking breakfast as Bardagul and Gorodra still sleep. Alviss sits in the courtyard smoking his pipe, watching as Ambrose levitates in the air during his meditation.

"Good morning," Elvey greets Alviss, who motions for him to be quiet.

Nordika emerges carrying a basket and walking across the courtyard. A crash rings out over the space, and Peter appears.

"'Morning," he says softly as Ambrose lowers to the ground and opens his eyes.

"Do I smell coffee?" Ambrose inquires, trying not to show that he is displeased with the interruptions.

Chalia emerges carrying a tray. "Good morning, Lord Ambrose. Did you sleep well?" she asks.

"Good morning, Chalia. Yes, I did. Thank you," Ambrose replies as he sits on the bench quietly. An awkward silence falls over the courtyard when Mr. Cee emerges. Crossing the courtyard, he begins to grow in size, but then, shrinks again.

"What is going on?" Nordika inquires, observing that magic is flying around her and the courtyard.

"The magic is returning," Peter explains as Ambrose sips his coffee and rolls his eyes.

"Sis, I think we need to check on the village," Elvey says, pulling his sister along as they leave their grandfather and great-uncle to speak.

"Alviss, would you mind giving Ambrose and me a chance to speak in private?" asks Peter.

"No, he stays," Ambrose replies, annoyed.

"Are you serious? You are still as stubborn as ever," Peter declares as Ambrose gets up and walks toward the fountain. He places his hand in the water, and it wraps around his arm. As he raises his arm, the water spirals up it.

"Elvey has your ears, and Nordika has your nose, Grandpa," Ambrose laughs, peering back at Pete.

"Their father had a sense of adventure like his uncle Ambrose," Pete remarks, walking towards Ambrose as he disappears and then reappears, holding his cup and sipping his coffee on the opposite side from where he had been standing.

"You know that I am happy to see you," Pete says.

Ambrose stops sipping his coffee, puts down the cup, and the water starts spinning around Ambrose's arm again.

"Happy. Happy? Let me say, that is a first. You are happy to see me? Wow!" Ambrose remarks, rolling his eyes.

"You always roll your eyes," barks Pete.

"Because you play off hundreds of years like it is nothing. Like nothing happened," Ambrose yells back as he suddenly has Peter pinned to the wall with a blade at his throat.

"Brother, that blade can hurt a ghost. Please lower it," Pete begs.

"Lord Ambrose," Alviss speaks up as Ambrose lowers the blade and drops Pete back to the ground.

"Wait! I am confused," Pete says, puzzled.

"Confused about what?"

"You can touch me without falling through me," Pete says.

"It's called necro magic. Maybe you have heard of it?" Ambrose responds sarcastically.

"Yes, but how?"

"That, Brother, even I am still trying to figure out. You see, I am only at partial power. With each passing day, I feel more of my magic returning. But until I am fully restored, my magic is chaotic," Ambrose explains as Pete backs away.

"Isabella's prophecy."

"Pete, what are you rambling about?"

"Brother follow me, please?" Peter asks as he disappears through the wall.

"Alviss, I will be back," Ambrose says, displeased, as he walks across the courtyard and enters the hallway.

"Pete?"

"I am here, Brother."

"So, what is this prophecy you are rambling on about?" Ambrose demands.

"Several years before she died, Isabella had a prophecy. It was one of the last feats of magic she was able to do before her magic went completely out," Peter explains, handing the orb to Ambrose.

Ambrose raises his hand as the orb levitates in the air. Within seconds, the room spins, and Ambrose disappears.

Walking through the sand, Ambrose waves his hand back and forth as an old building comes into view.

"The old priory of Avalon."

"This is Isabella's dream," Ambrose notes as the rain falls.

"Wait! The vision is real?" Ambrose asks, ducking under the archway and holding out his hand as the raindrops fall onto it. Listening, Ambrose hears the rain hitting the ceramic roof tiles and bouncing off, as the sound of dripping water can be heard—drip, drip, drip. Looking around, Ambrose observes a door and pulls it open, entering the priory.

As he looks around, a hooded figure appears. The pipe organ begins to play enchanted mystical music. Ambrose sees that the ruined parts of the priory are reassembling as stones fly around the space. The cloaked figure watches, running their hand over the surface of the stones as each takes its designated place.

Walking down the long aisle of the priory, the stone columns rise toward the mystical ceiling. Looking as if they are descending from the sky, the columns are lit by the glow of candlelight. Stopping and looking around, the figure lowers its hood. Ambrose's eyes narrow as he watches a version of himself flip one of the pews into the others in front of it, causing them to domino through the room.

Screaming, the Ambrose in the vision falls to their knees, crying as magic spins around him. His cries echo through the priory as spirits materialize around him, comforting him. Finally, the figure nods.

Standing, he wipes his tears from his face, spins his hands in a clockwise motion, catches the magic flying around him, controlling it, and levitating into the air. Then, spinning the magic in his hands, the figure watches as it dances through his fingers. The Ambrose of the vision continues to watch as the magic gains speed, flying around his hand. Then, he redirects it, projecting the magic away from himself.

The magic spinning throughout the old priory, every remaining candle explodes into flame and everything in the area comes to life, and music begins to echo over the space, emerging from the glowing pipes of the organ. Then, closing his eyes and raising his arms, the Ambrose of the vision allows the magic to fly around him.

Bringing his right hand in front of him and raising it, the water of the baptism font flies down the center aisle as fire from the candles circles Ambrose. The organ pipes blare even louder as the maple and birch doors of the priory fly open, and leaves sail down the aisle, spinning in the wind. Wind, water, and fire now encircle Ambrose as he tilts his head, looking down the central aisle as the stone floor turns to grass and flowers blossom.

Raising his hand, everything instantly stops moving, and the priory falls silent, nothing moving, nothing sounding. Even the vision of Ambrose freezes as the Ambrose who is watching the vision walks through it, studying the various aspects of it.

Hmm. He looks to be about my age. His magic is powerful. The spirits respond to him, which means his necro magic is strong. This is the ancient priory, but why here? It appears as if I am restoring magic. Hmm, I wonder…? Ambrose thinks.

With that, waving his hand, Ambrose unfreezes the vision.

The Ambrose of the vision spins, observing the space as he raises his hands, his attire changing into long robes. He raises his hands over his head and a star appears and begins flying above the figure. Then, another star appears flying in the opposite direction of its counterpart. Then, a giant clock appears, the stars serving as the tips of the hands. The Ambrose of the vision spins his hands over his head as the clock flies down around him and lifts him back into the air. Watching from the ground, the spirits all start to bow. As they bow, the magic spinning around them causes them to rematerialize, bringing them back to life.

Seconds later, Ambrose spins his cloak and disappears from the vision. He reappears in the hallway, hands resting on his knees as he catches his breath.

"Interesting. So, my magic can raise the dead," Ambrose remarks.

"Have you seen the prophecy?" Ambrose inquires of Pete.

"No, I was only told about it," Pete replies.

"I cannot believe I am going to say this to you, but thank you," Ambrose says, stumbling over the words as Pete stops, looking confused.

"Wait! You just thanked me," Pete stammers.

"Yes, and I won't be repeating it. Now, I have to figure out how to get back to my time," Ambrose responds.

"Brother, what about Avalon?" Pete inquires.

"Weak, they barely had enough magic to get me back last time," Ambrose replies.

"Wait! Last time? You have been here before?" a puzzled Pete inquires.

"Yes, several nights ago, in a dream."

"Okay, wait. What do you mean in a dream? How? What did you learn from it?"

"At first, I thought it was a dream, but it appears it is not," Ambrose exclaims.

"Ambrose, you mentioned coming back here several nights ago. What were the magic levels then?" Pete inquires.

"Virtually non-existent. The magic was extremely low," Ambrose replies.

"Brother, since you have been back, magic has been returning. Maybe, just maybe, enough magic will have returned for them to use the priory stone to get you back," Pete suggests as Ambrose stops and thinks carefully.

"It is possible," Ambrose remarks, beginning to pace back and forth.

"You're pacing, which means you're thinking. Are you trying to figure out how to supercharge the stone and get the hell out of here," Pete asks, laughing.

"You're crazy. You know that?" Ambrose says, stopping and looking around at the space. "But wait."

Ambrose walks down the hallway and pushes open two doors.

"Ambrose? What are you doing?" Pete asks, a hand raised.

"It was me who created this mess, and it will have to be me who fixes it," Ambrose replies.

"What are you doing?"

"Pete, tell the others goodbye for me. Heck, I will see them soon," Ambrose remarks as Bardagul runs through the door crying.

"No, you cannot leave us. What do we do if those mean guys come back?" he asks through his tears. Ambrose kneels and places a hand on Bardagul's shoulder. "Then, Master Bardagul, you will fight them."

"Take us with you?" Bardagul asks, pulling on Ambrose's arm as Alviss comes through the door.

"Oy! Me son! He is not from this time. Besides, if he did what you ask, it would alter the timeline and could have catastrophic implications," Alviss explains as Ambrose looks at him.

"Alviss! Altering the timeline! You are a genius," Ambrose declares, rising to his feet and smiling.

"Pete? Last night you saved me. Why?" Ambrose inquires.

"Well, Brother, I made a mistake many years ago when I never stood with you. I was so afraid of your magic that I did not know what to do. I watched as all of our family died around me, and I could do nothing to stop it. Without magic, it was horrible. But, seeing you here has given this old ghost hope," Pete replies, sitting down on a bench.

Looking at Alviss and his family, Ambrose notices Nordika and Elvey lingering in the background near the door. Ambrose motions them to come closer.

"Okay, here is what is going to happen. I am going to return to the time I come from. I have to save Luciana this time. So, I am taking you all with me for safety. But the minute I can hand the six of you off to her, I will do so, sending you all back. Is that understood?" Ambrose explains.

The six regard one another and nod as Ambrose cringes, holding his shoulder.

"Your shoulder?" Pete asks, moving quickly toward Ambrose, circling him.

"Yes. I do not think Noble Elder's potion worked," Ambrose remarks.

"It will only work when you have fully restored your power. By the way, about that…" Pete says, looking up at the ceiling.

"Pete, what did you do?" Ambrose asks.

"I gave you back your power. I slipped my orb into yours, last night, when I gave you the orb to restore you. I knew my younger self was too stubborn to help, so I made the decision," Pete explains as Ambrose hugs him.

"I appreciate this. Nordika and Elvey, say your goodbyes for now," Ambrose directs, pulling his pocket watch and clicking open the lid.

Gorodra smiles as she picks up Mr. Cee, who is purring and rubbing against her leg.

"Gorodra, I need you to do me a big favor," Ambrose says, making a bag appear, placing it over her head, and resting the strap on her shoulder.

"Yes, Lord Noel," she says, smiling.

He pauses for a minute, taking in a profound breath upon hearing himself called that.

"Mr. Cee is your responsibility. Please keep him safe. He will ride in the bag. If he senses danger, let him out. He'll know what to do," Ambrose explains, helping her place Mr. Cee in the bag.

Ambrose winks at the cat, and Gorodra smiles as she pets Mr. Cee's head.

"Mr. Cee, old friend, you know what to do if trouble emerges," Ambrose remarks, reaching down into his bag and pulling out an elfish bow and arrow and handing them to Elvey.

"I assume you know how to use this?" Ambrose inquires as Elvey swallows heavily, nodding solemnly.

"I do, sir, yes," Elvey replies.

"Remember, what your father taught you, Elvey," Pete says as Elvey nods.

"Nordika, I believe these will suit you," Ambrose says, handing her a pair of elfish arm blades.

"Thank you, Lord No… I mean, Lord Ambrose," she replies, taking the blades and unwrapping the leather from around them.

"I will say this to all of you. Please, just call me 'Noel.' 'Lord' is not needed. Do not be afraid to speak that name, as Merlin will surely not back down when he hears it," Ambrose says, regarding all of them.

"Nordika, be careful with those blades. They are sharper than you are used to," Pete explains, cautiously raising both hands.

"Pay no attention to him. He could never use them and was always afraid of them," Ambrose laughs as Nordika spins them in her hands.

"Alviss, for you and Chalia," Ambrose says.

"Aye, me friend, the wife, and I know how to use these," Alviss replies as he and Chalia hold giant hammers, throwing them over their shoulders.

"What about me, sir?" Bardagul inquires, tugging on Ambrose's cloak.

Ambrose reaches into his bag and rummages around until he pulls out an orb.

"Bardagul, I need you to keep this safe for me. I want you to promise me that, in a time of danger, you will throw this right at the danger and yell at the top of your lungs, 'Help is needed.' Or, it can be used to share information with my family. Deal?"

Bending over, Ambrose holds out the orb with one hand and extends his other hand to shake Bardagul's hand. Then, standing upright, Ambrose pats Bardagul on the back as he slips one of the nanos under Bardagul's collar.

"Are we ready?" Ambrose inquires as the ghost of Pete flies across the space to stand beside Alviss. Leaning over, he whispers, "Alviss, he is sick, as you know. The poison is spreading. Make haste and find help upon your arrival."

"Aye. Good luck, Lord Pete," Alviss waves as Ambrose stands, arms crossed and tapping his foot, waiting.

"Ready?"

"Aye."

"Ready, everyone?" Ambrose inquires as he raises his hands and sand begins to spin around the group. Their outfits transform into traveling attire with armor appearing over it. Looking around, the others are shocked as a phoenix emerges, flying out of the sand, its tail dancing in the wind as it turns vivid colors, reds, blues, and purples while it circles. As the phoenix flies the length of the sand funnel, its tail grows in length, protecting the group with a column of feathers. Ambrose looks up as he slams his hands together above his head. Then, looking down at the six, lightning appears in his eyes and the group disappears.

The six find themselves standing on a stone floor, water, sand, fire, and feathers circling around them. Ambrose's ring starts to glow as he suddenly raises his hand, and a star shoots from the stone.

"It is beautiful," Gorodra declares.

"Is that a star?" Nordika inquires.

"That is not just any star. It is the Elven Star. It is the beacon of safety that will get us all home. I would recommend grabbing each other's hands and holding on tight," Ambrose advises as he starts to glow bright white.

Under the full moon's light, the elfish priory stands rising out of the landscape as multiple elfish monks stroll the halls of the ancient place of prayer and serenity. Eight elves float in meditation in the courtyard as six others practice with weapons. In the distance, Isabella and Sophia can be seen walking down the corridor carrying a tablet and speaking, when suddenly the sky over the priory darkens.

"Sister?" Sophia remarks, reaching for a spear as lightning strikes the courtyard, causing the elves to jump. Scrambling to their feet, the elves run for cover as lightning continues to strike the courtyard, strike after strike, and the clouds circle in the sky.

"I have never seen a storm this bad," Isabella says. Horns sound in the distance and yelling can be heard. A bright star explodes in the night sky, lighting the area.

The two sisters regard each other knowing all too well that the star is the Elven Star. They run quickly down the corridor, their outfits transforming on the spot as brooms appear. Upon reaching the doorway, the two sisters take to the air on their brooms, soaring high above the village.

Motioning with her head, Sophia points out a part of the sky, behind the star and over the village where a vortex appears to be forming. The two bolt toward the vortex where they are caught up in the wind and whipped about. Emerging from the elf palace, Maria and Alvina raise their wands and stabilize Isabella and Sophia. The two sisters regard one another and dive for the ground, landing near the palace.

"What was that about?" Alvina inquires as Maria points toward the sky where the vortex blows open.

"Isabella?" Sophia calls.

"Alert the family immediately, sister. I will help cousins Alvina and Maria protect the village.

Sophia quickly runs across the stone bridge, throwing her broom in front of her. Leaping on it, she takes off, soaring across the ground as Isabella turns to nod at her cousins.

The three nod at one another as they amplify their voices magically, sending a message out over the winds.

"Quickly! Everyone, take cover! Get inside immediately!"

Lightning strikes the ground inches from where Maria is standing as Isabella raises her hands and speaks.

Clipem.

Shield.

A giant shield of magic begins forming as Isabella throws up her arms, and the shield flies up into the air. Maria and Alvina join her, expanding the shield. The lightfield soars into the air high above the village, forming a dome, then lowering to the ground, shielding the village from the elements. The three continue to hold the field steady as lightning strikes the lightfield repeatedly, causing Isabella, Alvina, and Maria to be pushed down onto one knee.

"I have never seen lightning this intense," Maria exclaims, annoyed when the field begins to crack under the continued lightning strikes.

"I do not know how much longer the lightfield will hold. Between the lightning strikes and the wind throwing things at the field, it is weakening," Alvina shouts as multiple pops can be heard behind them. Looking over her shoulder, Isabella smiles.

"Well, it took you all long enough."

Magic flies around inside of the field as it begins to repair.

"Stabilize the field. Protect the villagers," Rusty directs as Rose races by him on a broom, launching up into the air.

"What is that?" she asks as Zander flies up next to her.

"You know, Hun, I hate brooms. You could have observed the vortex from the ground," Zander remarks, laughing.

"Zander, that is not just any vortex, particularly not with that star above it. Look!" Rose declares, pointing as two giant beings of light emerge from the vortex, landing on the ground as the winds pick up further, spinning around them. Trees are uprooted. Then, the darkness appears, screaming and, diving on the two giants made of light. Looking up and raising their hands, the darkness explodes.

"Rose, those are Guardians," Zander exclaims.

"Indeed, they are, Hun," she notes, leaning forward on her broom and zipping toward the lightfield.

"I hate it when she does that," Zander remarks, chasing behind her as the darkness appears in the sky, charging the vortex.

Each blow on the vortex from the darkness causes lightning to strike the lightfield.

"When did the darkness grow brains?" Michael inquires throwing roof tiles out of the way.

"I know. It is as if they know the lightning can destroy the field," Pete explains when Rose suddenly explodes through the field. Her wand, which is pointed to the sky, lights as the darkness drops to the ground below, dead. Walking through the crowd of elves, who are now looking on, Ethan and Oliver emerge and raise their wands as a being of light appears. The being drops from the vortex, falling rapidly until they materialize. It is Nordika. Holding her arms in front of her, she descends in free fall until Zander catches her by her leg.

"Wow! I've got you," Zander says.

"Thank you, sir. But where am I?" she asks as the sky flashes.

"Where are you?" Zander asks puzzled.

The sky flashes again, and a young elf boy appears falling rapidly until, suddenly, the area above him grows and he flies back up into the air as Autumn snatches him out of the sky.

"Get them to the ground. We have this," Belinda roars as she flies into the vortex and disappears. Seconds pass and she re-emerges, flapping her wings mightily as the four dwarves ride on her back.

"Mother, I am scared," Bardagul yells.

"Child, I will not let anything happen to you," Belinda reassures him, roaring as she glides towards the ground.

"Father, where is Lord Ambrose?" Gorodra inquires.

Belinda glances back. "My dear, sweet dwarf, did you say Lord Ambrose?" Belinda inquires.

"Aye, Great Queen," Alviss replies, bowing his head as Belinda rears up roaring.

"That is the key word. We do not have time to get you to the ground, Master Dwarf. Hold on, the four of you. We are taking a detour," Belinda warns as a meow is heard.

"Mr. Cee is awake," Gorodra squeals as Mr. Cee meows again, and Belinda races toward the vortex.

"Master Dwarf, where is he?"

"I do not know, Me Lady. We got separated."

Belinda picks up speed, racing toward the vortex as it begins to spin closed. Belinda soars to the spot where the vortex had been, but it is as if nothing had been there. Roaring, Belinda circles in the sky as multiple dragons appear.

"Check the sky! Ambrose is missing!" Belinda directs as the dragons bow and soar off in different directions. Belinda glides toward the ground where Michael and Kells approach, offering hands to the dwarfs, helping them to dismount. Willow pushes past them, noticing that Bardagul is holding an orb. Kneeling, she pulls a handkerchief out of her pocket and wipes the young dwarf's face while Autumn approaches with Elvey, holding tightly to her back. Then, Zander lands with Nordika.

"Hello. I am the Lady Willow Ignatius," Willow says, greeting the young dwarf who is still sniffling. Elvey and Nordika regard one another when they hear Willows introduction. They stand quietly, side by side, observing the area and the others.

"Oh, this should be interesting," Nordika remarks as Alvina circles her, examining her attire.

"Rather odd-looking, wouldn't you say, sister?" Maria says.

"Alvina and Maria, leave her be," Willow directs as she looks at the dwarf again, wiping his face once more.

"Thank you. I am Bardagul, ma'am. You're an elf and pretty," he says, holding tight to the orb.

"That orb, where did you get it?"

"A very nice man gave it to me," he explains, holding it more tightly and moving away from her as Mr. Cee stalks up, purring and rubbing against Bardagul's right leg.

"Well, hello, Mr. Cee. What mischief have you been up to?" Willow inquires as Kells approaches from behind her, placing a hand on her shoulder. She reaches up, pats his hand, and stands upright. Bardagul, upon seeing Kells, becomes more frightened, turns, and runs right into Queen Rose.

"It is okay. I know he can be scary. But he towers over everyone," she remarks, smiling.

"Yes, ma'am, he is tall but not as…" Bardagul starts to say but stops.

"As who?" Rose inquired, kneeling down.

"Aye, Me Lady. I am Alviss. This is me wife, Chalia, me daughter, Gorodra, and me son, Bardagul. Those two elves are me friends," Alviss interrupts, bowing.

"Great dwarf, you do not need to bow. However, I am curious about who it is that your son was referring to?" Rose replies as Ethan approaches.

"Well, I am sure they have a fascinating story, and I know we all want to hear it. May I suggest, having witnessed that vortex, that we take this discussion indoors?" Ethan suggests, picking up Bardagul and carrying him inside.

"Well, I guess Ethan has spoken," Oliver chuckles as the others follow.

<h1 style="text-align:center">Chapter 20
Time Awakening</h1>

The group enters the great hall of the elves. Nordika and Elvey stop and observe the space in amazement.

"Brother, the tapestries of the ancients," Nordika declares, running her hand over the fabric as she darts across the room.

"The purge of darkness, the story of Elders, the creation of dragons. These are all the old stories of the past. They are all here and preserved. If father saw these…" Nordika remarks as Elvey stands shaking his head and the others look on.

"I take it you kids have never seen this cool elfish stuff," Pete laughs when he, suddenly, finds himself tacked against the wall, a blade at his throat.

"Stand down, sister" Elvey commands as Rose, Oliver, and Ethan all regard one another with confusion on their faces.

"Do not move, anyone," Rose states firmly, walking up to Nordika and examining the blade she holds to Pete's throat, and then, examining the stance Nordika has taken.

"Is there a concern, sis?" Oliver asks.

"No. I'm just fascinated," Rose replies, "You can drop him now."

Looking perplexed, Nordika lowers her blade and releases Pete.

"Wow, someone has a temper," Pete quips, rubbing his neck as Sophia walks over to Nordika, raises her arm, and examines one of the blades.

"Willow, what do you see?" Sophia asks as Nordika pulls away.

"It is okay," Willow soothes, approaching Nordika with her hands raised.

"May I?" she inquires, her hand held out to Nordika, who turns the blade up in her hand and hands it to Willow.

"Thank you," Willow says, taking the blade and examining it as Pete trips, crossing the floor, trying to observe what his sister is seeing.

"Ha, ha, ha," Bardagul laughs, hiding behind Ethan.

"Hey kid, what's funny?" Pete inquires as Bardagul peers out from his hiding place behind Ethan.

"You are, sir. He, he," Bardagul laughs.

"Charming child," Pete remarks, rolling his eyes as his siblings join in the laughter.

"Father, he is identical to the other," Gorodra notes, looking at Pete.

"Like the other?" Kells inquires, his ears perking up.

"I would advise not asking," Zander says.

"I agree with your grandfather. They are from the future," Rusty explains, regarding the visitors as he circles them, leaning on his staff.

"Father, that elf is blind. That would be King Russell," Gorodra says as Rusty stops, then smiles.

"Indeed, I am Russell but not king. At least, I am not at this time," he replies, continuing to smile and looking back toward his parents.

"Elvey, Brother, if he is a blind elf, then he is High King Rusty, Nordika explains as she bows.

"High King? Wait! From the future? How?" Michael asks.

"Lord Ambrose," Nordika replies as the room falls quiet.

"I think they all know who he is, sis," Elvey smiles.

"Where is he?" Rose asks, breaking the silence.

"Doing some magic that we have never seen. There was sand, fire, a giant phoenix, water, all flying around us, he said that he was taking us to Luciana. Then, somehow, we ended up here," Nordika explains as Zander, Rose, Rusty, Meredith all regard one another.

"He is coming back into his power," Rusty and Meredith say in unison as Rusty walks past everyone, reaches the table and picks up his cloak.

"Where are you going?" Isabella inquires.

"Isabella, go with your mother. Take your siblings and go home. Do not leave there," Rusty orders.

"Russell, freeze. You don't even know where to look," Rose says.

"Besides, your grandfather, Kelvin, and Cedric are looking for him, and, knowing them, they will have found him by now," Zander remarks.

"He should not be hard to find. He has activated the Elven Star. All one needs to do is look for it," Nordika suggests.

"That will be easy to spot," Rusty replies.

"My Lady, I am the Queen Roslynn," she says, regarding the two elves and not paying any attention to Rusty.

"Ma'am, I am Nordika, and this is my brother, Elvey," Nordika responds.

"Keep me out of this. I told you this was a bad idea," Elvey declares, crossing his arms.

"Oy! You two! Lord Ambrose is lost, and you two choose to be difficult. Besides, I do not remember hearing you protesting when me friend said we were coming here," Alviss remarks as the room grows bright.

Everyone stops what they are doing and look back at Bardagul as the orb he holds begins to glow more brightly.

"Aye, me son! What are you doing?"

"I do not know, Papa. It just started glowing."

"May I?" inquires Ethan.

Bardagul nods and hands the orb to Ethan, who turns the orb in his hand and throws it into the air as images appear.

"That is the manor," Willow says as darkness falls over it and the staff can be seen running away while others are consumed by the darkness. Screams can be heard as the dark consumes everything in sight. The group backs up, watching. Then, a small flickering light appears. Then another.

In seconds, the darkness flies in a cyclone in the sky, screaming. Then, it dives, exploding or dissolving as it hits the light. The staff return to normal as a being of light spins their wand, opening a portal. The staff can be seen getting up and running, disappearing through the portal, as the figure takes the darkness on alone, fighting and holding them back, destroying many of them in the process.

Suddenly, the orb flies around the room as it spins and turns in the air, readjusting the image. Then, at the center of light, stands an elf, spinning a wand as the darkness dissolves.

"It's Ambrose," Willow points out just as her father disappears.

"Zander?"

"Hun, I know. We dare not intervene for fear of upsetting the balance of magic. I guess we watch."

Landing on his feet, Rusty's ears perk up as he listens carefully. Turning his head, he hears the screams coming from the cyclone as he moves toward it.

Raising his hands, he stops and listens again. Then, he speaks in a deep voice.

Illustro Clipem.
Illuminate Shield.

Light flies around Rusty as the dark launches into the air, screaming.

"What are you doing here? I have this," Ambrose declares as he and his dad turn back-to-back. Then, raising their hands in unison, magic flies around them, turning into a ball of energy. When the two released it, the darkness dissolves.

"You looked like you could use some help, son," his father laughs.

"Hardly," Ambrose responds as he spins his wand over his head, flames circling above him and, when he snaps his wand down, the fire launches at the advancing darkness.

Rusty spins his staff in his hand and slams it against the ground.

Terrae Motus.

Earthquake.

Shockwave after shockwave roll through the land, causing multiple earthquakes. Finally, when Ambrose points his wand, light explodes around him and his father, causing the darkness to disappear.

Stowing his wand, Ambrose looks around, then collapses.

"Ambrose," Rusty cries, kneeling to support his son in his arms. Then, the two disappear.

&

A loud thud echoes through the Sanctuary of Legend and Lore as books fly off the table. Minnie pops her head up from over a pile of books. Not seeing anything, she stands up to look over them.

"Oh, dear! Ambrose! Noble Elder!" Minnie yells as she runs to help him.

"Hello," Minnie greets Ambrose.

"Dad, this is Minnie. Minnie, my dad, the future king of the elves," Ambrose says, half grimacing as Noble Elder appears.

"Ambrose, dear boy! What has happened?"

"The poison is back."

"Impossible. The counter antidote always works."

"Really?" Ambrose asks, pulling back his shirt from his right shoulder, revealing the poison's mark.

"Oh dear! I have never seen it this bad," Noble Elder declares as Rusty moves his hand over Ambrose's shoulder.

"Hmm? It appears to be potent, a poison made with a silver base. That would paralyze any other sorcerer. It seems to have a hint of oak. No, wait… maple. It appears Merlin is using old alchemist-based potions to poison," Rusty explains.

"A silver-base is the one thing that can weaken a Noble or Celestial," Noble Elder notes with concern.

"Wait! You saw all that by moving your hand over his shoulder?" Minnie inquires, puzzled.

"His magic amplifies his other senses," Ambrose explains, wincing as his father digs a dagger into his shoulder.

"Ouch!" Ambrose cries, looking at his dad.

"Hush, I almost have all the poison out," Rusty replies, humming and turning the blade as Ambrose grits his teeth.

Noble Elder stands, watching in amazement as Rusty's hand dances over the wound, removing a broken-off fragment of the arrow.

"I think that should do it. The antidote does work. However, it will only do so if no fragments remain in the wound," Rusty states, wiping the dagger blade as Noble Elder helps Ambrose up. Suddenly, a large globe flies into the air, lighting.

"Minnie, the globe," Noble Elder says.

"Sir, you will want to see this," Minnie replies, tripping over her words.

Observing the globe, Ambrose steps back in amazement, speechless. Magic is flying around the world, fixing everything, spinning around both Arcane and Mundane alike.

"Time has reawakened," Rusty says, his hands behind his back as he paces around the room, watching the globe.

"Noble Elder, how?" Minnie asks as Noble Elder points at Ambrose.

Watching the globe, Ambrose turns and walks away. Minnie raises her hand, but Noble Elder stops her, shaking his head "no."

"Noble Elder?"

"Yes, Ambrose?"

"I will be back. Keep magic safe for me? Dad, thank you! I will be back soon enough. First, I have to find the answers to unlocking the snow globe," Ambrose says, holding it in the air as the light around him flashes, and he is gone.

"Good kid. He will make us proud," Noble Elder says.

"I guess we wait," Rusty replies, pulling up a chair.

❧

It is early evening as Mundane walk down the sidewalks of New York City. Diners sit outside restaurants in the cool crisp evening air as cars and pedestrians bustle by in a hurry. A scream lets out as people back up at the sight of a giant griffin approaching. The creature rears up when it is, suddenly, lifted off the ground, flying backward and crashing into a concrete wall.

The Mundane stop what they are doing and look around as the creature gets up and starts flapping its wings. A giant clock appears. The griffin freezes, then shrinks to a miniature griffin, which falls to the ground as a cloaked figure appears, picks up the tiny griffin, and disappears. Reappearing, a second later, in a field, the figure flies backward when streams of magic come hurtling toward them. Raising their hand, the magic freezes and disappears as the cloaked figure notices a sorcerer standing opposite them in the field. The cloaked figure throws the griffin into the air as it resumes its full size and flies off.

"Fascinating feat of magic when one freezes time, wouldn't you say?"

"Can I help you with something, sir?" The cloaked figure inquires, and the sorcerer lowers their hood. The cloaked figure lowers their wand and then, reaches to lower their own hood.

"Ambrose," Dalton acknowledges.

"Hello, old friend," Ambrose smiles as the two approach each other and hug.

"You are coming into your power, I see," Dalton says.

"To a point. I am still trying to figure things out, and everything is a mess," Ambrose replies.

"Time is always a mess. Why do you think I gave up trying to fix it?" Dalton inquires as Ambrose takes Dalton's hand, and the two disappear.

Seconds later, they reappear in the old cave.

"It is the only private place I know of that takes my magical signature off the globe's view," Ambrose remarks as Dalton smiles.

"If you wanted privacy, you should have said something. I could have taken us to the variance of time," Dalton laughs, leaning against a stone table. An awkward silence falls over the space. Then, they both begin to speak simultaneously and start laughing.

"You first," Ambrose says.

"I wanted to say that I am sorry," Dalton replies.

"For what?"

"For using magic around you. I also have not been a decent boyfriend. I have not been there to support you with many things. But, as you know, I have my responsibilities," Dalton explains as Ambrose sighs.

"Here we go with the magic talk," Ambrose grumbles.

"Ambrose…" Dalton begins to say when he is stopped, knowing Ambrose's facial expression all too well.

"Do not 'Ambrose' me," Ambrose says, sitting down on the steps.

Quietly, Dalton comes to sit next to Ambrose. Several minutes of silence pass before Ambrose says anything.

"You are not going to lecture me?"

"Ha! No. I learned never to do that long ago," replies Dalton, smiling.

"I have made a mess of things," says Ambrose.

"No, you have not. In the other timelines, I would say 'yes, you have' and agree with you, but here, in this timeline, no," Dalton exclaims.

"Magic is a mess. Time is broken. The darkness killed my great-grandmother. There is an alternative timeline where magic does not exist. Not to mention our daughter," Ambrose declares, getting up and walking toward the center of the cave waving his hands.

Images fly around him as he starts to turn his hand, changing the images, and throwing them into various parts of the room.

"What are you looking for?"

"Answers, Dalton."

"I did not want to tell you, but I think this will help," Dalton says, raising his hand as the room darkens and begins spinning around them until they land back at the elf palace, right after Rusty left seeking Ambrose.

The group stands watching as Ambrose spins the flames in the air.

"Wow! His magic is not even at full power," Oliver remarks as Willow sits watching and smiling.

The six siblings stand in amazement, watching what is occurring until Rusty and Ambrose disappear.

"Wait! Where did they go?" Kells asks, concern in his voice.

"It could be one of several places," Zander replies.

"Mother, how do we help our brother?" Willow asks.

"You heard our dad, Willow, we are to go home with mom," Isabella replies as Nordika starts laughing.

The siblings stop arguing among themselves and look at her.

"What's so funny?" demands Isabella.

"You all. Nothing has changed," Nordika replies. Then, she stops speaking when she realizes what she has said.

"What does that mean?" Michael chimes in as Nordika covers her mouth with her hands.

"Children, I believe your grandparents made it clear not to inquire about the future," their mother declares.

The orb lowers to the floor where Ethan picks it up and hands it to Bardagul.

"Thank you, kind sir," Bardagul says, bowing as Pete laughs.

"What's funny?" Rose asks.

"The dwarf bows. That is something you do not see every day," Pete sneers.

"You also do not see a pointed eared elf like you alive," Bardagul laughs.

Pete stops and backs up.

"What?"

"Oy, me son. Not another word," Alviss interjects.

Gorodra asks, "Why?"

"Me daughter, no," Alviss replies.

"We are here because of those five anyway," Bardagul says as Willow makes a chair and a side table appear, with a tea pot on it.

"Tea, anyone?" Willow asks sitting down at the table.

"How can you drink tea?" yells Isabella.

"Enough, everyone" Rose declares.

Bardagul was holding the orb, looking at it. "That's it! I remember what he told me," he says, rolling the orb across the floor. "Help is needed."

The room begins spinning and lightning strikes the floor around the group.

Rose raises her wand, then it disappears.

"What magic is this?" she asks as Ambrose appears.

"Guys, look. It is our brother," Kells says.

"I see that you figured it out, Bardagul," Ambrose comments.

"Your wands and magic will not work against the orb, and you cannot freeze this vision. So, pay attention closely. The magic I placed in this orb is too strong for even the combined magic of all of you."

"Now, to business. Things are a mess, and I do not know where to begin. But I know one thing. If the seven of us do not work together, we will lose. I do regain my magic, but at a great cost. But that is something that we can still change. Look, I am as frightened as the rest of you. I have feared my magic for years, but do you know what made me not afraid?"

"This should be interesting," Michael chuckles as he flies off the ground and is hung upside down.

"Now, do you want to interrupt again? You can hang out there for a few moments and not another word out of you," Ambrose says as Rose, Zander, Oliver, and Ethan all laugh among themselves.

Willow stands up from her chair, walks over and circles Michael.

"Excuse me for a minute, Ambrose, Fascinating," Willow remarks, poking Michael with her finger.

"Hey, what gives?" Michael barks.

Ambrose's eyes narrow as he looks at Michael.

"Just making sure this is real," Willow says as she motions for Ambrose to continue.

"As I was saying, I was afraid of my magic. But the one thing that did not frighten me was being with each of you. Growing up, I idolized the six of you. Although we had our differences, I looked to each of you. Your failures and successes with magic taught me more than anyone will ever know. I saw the confidence each of you had, and I was so afraid that I would never be that confident," Ambrose explains.

"Wait! You idolized us?" Isabella interrupts.

"Yes! A shocker, I know. I gave up my magic to protect the six of you. I thought that if I gave it up, it would allow the six of you to enjoy your magic without worrying about your magic being affected by mine. But I was wrong," Ambrose continues.

"We screwed up," Pete exclaims as the area near him begins to grow bright. Kells is standing there, holding a glowing orb. The room grows silent as Isabella does the same. Holding out her hands, an orb appears, glowing like Kells'.

"I think it is time we fix this," she remarks as Michael, now right side up again, also makes an orb appear.

"Pete, what are you doing?" Isabella demands, tapping her foot as he continues to move his hands forward, but nothing happens. No orb appears.

"Pete, are you kidding me?" Kells asks.

"It is okay. Do not be hard on him. He gave me back my magic. He used his orb to restore me to health in one of the other timelines," Ambrose remarks as the others turned to look at Peter.

"I do not remember that," Pete exclaims as Alviss coughs and clears his throat.

"Just go with it."

"Willow, Sophia, and Pete can you help us out?" Isabella asks as she raises her orb above her head and it levitates into the air where Kells and Michael combine theirs with the others, and the orb on the floor flies up and merges them into one orb.

The orb grows brighter. Then, it flashes and disappears.

"Grandma…?" the six inquire.

"On its way. You will know when he has his full power," she says as the vision spins, and Ambrose and Dalton land back in the cave.

☙

Holding up his hand, Ambrose closes his eyes and the contents of his snow globe appear, spinning as it glows.

"Holy smokes!" Dalton says, backing up as magic spins around Ambrose and he levitates into the air.

A second orb appears and flies through the cave, combining with Ambrose's snow globe and the space begins to fill with the elements, spinning around them. Earth merges with water, which then merges with wind, and the three merge with fire. The elements dance around the two until a light appears. Ambrose is lifted off his feet, his hair turns brown, his ears fully transform back to their elfish state, a male diadem with green inlayed stones appears across his forehead, and his attire begins to transform as he lowers back down, arms raised, and magic continuing to spin around him.

Dalton's attire also transforms into beautiful purple, blue, and black robes with white inlay. Examining his attire, he looks down at the sword by his side.

"My father's sword," Dalton says reverently, touching the clock medallion on the sword's handle.

"It looks good on you," Ambrose says as he strides across the floor, his attire transforming.

"I like the robes," Dalton smiles, kissing Ambrose.

"Thank you, but I dislike them being this long," Ambrose remarks, holding up his sleeves. When he snaps his fingers, his cloak transforms into a long coat.

"How do you feel?" asks Dalton.

"Weird. The magic is strong. This will take some getting used to, again," replies Ambrose.

"What are your plans?" Dalton asks as Ambrose throws an orb into the air, moving his hands, and expanding the orb.

"The plan, my dear love, is to locate Luciana, send the six back with her, while saving the world, locating this hidden bunker, and then starting the journey for the Curpendulums," Ambrose explains.

At that moment, the orb starts to flash.

"Dalton, look," Ambrose points.

"Merlin. He is starting to gather an army. But for what?" Dalton asks.

"Dalton, take this. Alert my family, the council, and the parliament. I will find Luciana," Ambrose says, removing his ring as it transforms back into a necklace.

"You have this. Remember, time is yours to control and, Noel, be safe."

"I will. Let my family know that Noel has returned and is on his way to fix time," Ambrose replies, breathing in, pulling his hands together in front of him as lightning strikes the ground around him, and disappearing.

Magia, tempus adest, amoremque meum defende, et eos incolumes serva.

Magic, the time has come. Defend my love and keep them safe.

Dalton speaks the spell while spinning his hands in front of him. Magic streams circle the space. Then, Minnie arrives.

"Lord Time Yule, where is he?" she asks.

"He, as in Ambrose?" Dalton inquires.

"Yes, where is he? It is urgent, Minnie says, upset, her hands trembling.

"He just left. Minnie, is everything okay?" Dalton inquires with a concerned expression.

Chapter 21
The Council of Darkness

The flames dance in the various fire pits around the room as two griffins sleep quietly. Then, an explosion is heard in the distance and dark magic flies around the chamber. Members of the Dark Council sit in the chamber circle as the doors fly open, and Merlin storms into the room.

"Lord Merlin, to what do we owe this visit?" Balimore, the head of the Dark Council, asks.

"Great Balimore, I come seeking more individuals for the armies," Merlin remarks with a grin.

"But Merlin why should we grant you more individuals for the dark army?" the council query in unison, looking rather displeased.

"What if I told the council that I have a Curpendulum in my control?"

"You have our attention, Merlin. Proceed."

"I need more troops. I need the largest army you can conjure for me so that I may secure the magical bunker."

"A bunker? Why would we grant you an army simply to secure a bunker?" a female council member asks.

"Merlin, you would dare to waste our resources on a pathetic bunker?" one of the other council members inquires.

"Yes! I make such a request as this bunker, if you all must know, holds the lost artifacts of the Arcane and is where the Curpendulum is currently located," Merlin explains.

"So, you don't actually have the Curpendulum?!" a male member of the council shouts, smashing his hand down on the arm of his chair.

"No, But if the council grants my request, it will be magnificent," Merlin replies.

"If we chose to grant your request, Merlin, how do we know that we won't have more of our armies destroyed?" the council members roar in unison.

"Because once I hold the Curpendulum, along with the weapons in that bunker, no one will dare to stand against me, the master of all magic."

"You have said this many times in the past. However, each time, Merlin, you have failed. We grow exhausted with you," several council members mutter, mocking him.

"Time, as you know, Merlin is not something you want to mess with. You, of all people, should know that. However, we are willing to make a fair trade with you," Balimore says, grinning.

Merlin listens, stroking his beard. "Trade? What sort of trade?" Merlin inquires with an eyebrow raised.

"It is simple this time, Merlin. We will, as always, give you an army. In return, you deliver the Curpendulum to us. We see it as collateral. So, you go and get the Curpendulum. Bring it here, and you can have all of the armies you need. We will even create more individuals for the army," Balimore explains.

"Did you not hear me?" Merlin snaps.

"We would advise you to watch your tone! We hear you, Lord Merlin, but the Council does not trust you," Balimore replies.

"Trust me? Ha! You do not trust me? I would advise this council to choose their next actions wisely," Merlin snarls, raising his wand.

Immediately, the Dark Council members transform into black shadows, flying from their chairs and circling the room.

"Are you threatening us, incubus?" The council members scream, landing on the floor, materializing wands, their staffs pointed at Merlin.

"You may be an incubus child, born of darkness, but you forget the Incubus King appointed us to the council. We can take your magic easily, Merlin," the council members respond in a single collective voice, speaking through Balimore. Their eyes glow red, and flames explode around the room as a dark column strikes the floor, and a woman steps out.

"A crone! Here? To what do we owe this visit?" The members of the council inquire, bowing.

"Lords and Ladies, I bring word from the Incubus King himself," the woman says, hissing through her teeth.

"Crone, we do not take orders from the Incubus," Balimore explained, pulling his sword and holding it to her throat.

"Charming," she scoffs, raising her hand as the eight council members levitate off the floor, choking. Then, she lowers her hands, dropping them to the floor again.

"What sort of magic is this?" the members of the council demand.

"The magic of the true darkness, the magic of the incubus. This council does not need to worry about their precious army. The incubus, while they cannot walk on earth, will possess your army, and give them extra strength, thus giving those Arcane a true challenge," the crone remarks, smiling as bugs run through her teeth.

"Crone, we hear you, and while we agree, we need collateral. Merlin has made many promises that he has repeatedly failed to keep," Balimore declares as the Crone holds up her hand, making a watch appear.

One of the council members rises from their chair and walks toward the crone, circling her and examining the watch.

"Fascinating, truly extraordinary," the woman council member remarks.

When she reaches for the watch, the crone closes her hand, and it disappears. The woman council member looks back over her shoulder at Balimore.

"Crone, that watch is not the Timekeeper," Balimore points out.

"How do you know this?" the crone asks, smiling.

"Merlin will have his army. But either way, we will eventually have the Curpendulums with or without his help. And when we do, you will bow to us. But, in the meantime, we accept your offer, crone," Balimore declares as the crone opens her hand and the watch floats across the room to Balimore.

Consumed by greed, Balimore snatches the watch out of the air. Screams ring out through the chamber, and dark magical streams fly out from the watch, encircling council members as their eyes turn red and all of the members freeze. Laughter rings throughout the council chamber as the crone strolls across the room, picks up the watch that has fallen to the floor, and smiled wickedly.

"Not so tough now, Balimore?" the crone sneers.

"Merlin," the crone hisses.

"Yes, My Lady?"

"Your father has bought you time. Do not screw this up, or your father will have you in chains," the crone remarks as she runs her nail down the face of one of the council members, drawing blood.

"Mmmm. Blood. Come, my children, feeding is now," the crone calls as multiple incubuses appear.

"Leave them," Merlin yells as the crone snaps her head back and raises her hand, halting the incubuses.

"You would spare them?" she asks, circling Merlin, who is unphased by the crone.

"For now, at least until my father has full control of them. They will prove useful during the battle. Send them to lead the army of darkness. Let them be killed. That will buy me the time I need to reach the bunker with the Curpendulum," Merlin remarks.

"Ahh. Are you getting soft, Merlin?" the crone asks, gliding across the floor, examining the different council members. She steals a bracelet off the wrist of one of the council members and slips it into her pocket.

"Remember, you have always been a disappointment to your father," the Crone states, smiling as she examines the pocket of one of the council members' cloaks, removing coins from it.

"Enough, crone," an intense male voice echoes as Merlin bows.

"Crone, prepare the armies for my son. Now!! Also, put back everything that you stole," the Incubus King commands as the crone bows, smiles, and snaps her fingers, returning everything.

Then, she disappears along with the council members. A second later, a cloaked figure appears.

"Rise, my son, you do not need to bow to me," the king commands, motioning for Merlin to stand.

"Father," Merlin acknowledges.

"Your time among the Arcane and Mundane has not treated you well, my son," the king remarks, walking toward Balimore's armchair and sitting down. Magic spins around the room as the other chairs dissolve and the room begins to transform becoming young again.

"Better. I hate that chamber," the king remarks as Merlin looks around the room in which they now sit.

"The Palace of the Incubus," Merlin states.

"Indeed," the King confirms, petting the head of a griffin seated beside him.

"Tell me, Merlin, why is it that you always seem to fail? I keep the Council of Dark at bay. I tear holes in the fabric of time. Yet, you seem unable to complete a simple task," the king snaps, looking at Merlin.

"The Timekeeper and Noble Elder are the problems," Merlin explains.

"Indeed, I have heard both can cause problems. But you are an incubus. So, they should be easy to handle," the king declares.

"They are next to impossible to stop. You know that," Merlin whines.

"Excuses," the king yells and the griffin growls.

"It is okay, my pet. Merlin will *not* upset you again."

Standing in the center of the room, Merlin's eyes narrow, then he sighs. "I cannot kill Noble Elder, and the Timekeeper is protected by a magic the earth has never seen."

"Merlin, you are looking at it all wrong. Noble Elder controls the Timekeeper. Bring the young Elder to our side, and we have both," the king says.

"He would never come to our side. His magic is unstoppable," Merlin explains.

"Lies! Anyone can be killed. Anyone can be brought to our side. Figure it out. Besides, if you do not succeed, you will never see her again," the king declares, holding up an orb with a sleeping woman stuck inside.

"Mother?" Merlin inquires as the king laughs.

"Now, that I have your attention, the incubus will again reign supreme with you as their king. Get me what I want, and I will release her," the king explains. Then, he waves the back of his hand, dismissing Merlin, who lands back in the Dark Council chamber. Pulling an orb from under his cloak, Merlin raises it and disappears arriving in an old castle. He raises his hands and the double oak doors fly open.

Marching down the hall, he yells, "Raven!" as she scrambles out of her chair to her feet.

"Lord Merlin," she acknowledges as several dark guards stand behind her.

"Go to the rally point and meet with the crone and the Dark Council. Take control of the army and bring that university down. I want that bunker," Merlin commands, waving his hands over the bubbling liquid in a cauldron.

"And Raven, if you fail, your fate will be worse than death," Merlin declares, examining the cauldron's contents as he dips a leaf halfway in, and it melts.

"Perfection," Merlin notes.

"You all heard Lord Merlin. Get the armies assembled. Now!!" Raven screams.

She and the dark creatures disappear, leaving Merlin to do whatever he is doing. Quietly, Merlin stands gazing into the cauldron until he hears a voice.

"Hello, Merlin. You do not look well."

Turning, Merlin holds a fireball in his hand as he glares at Nimuway.

"Nimuway," Merlin snarls.

"Is that any way to speak to your wife?" Nimuway inquires, gliding across the floor and circling Merlin.

Then, she glides back to the table and sits, floating above it.

"I see you have not changed. You've just gotten older and grumpier," Nimuway laughs.

"What do you want? Are the graces of Avalon driving you crazy?" Merlin snarks back at her.

"They are the Sisters of Avalon. But that is beside the point. I came to check on you. I have heard chatter."

"Chatter?"

"Merlin, dear, it does not have to be this way. You know that if you stop this ridiculous hunt, Noel can fix anything and everything."

"There you go again, Nimuway, always believing in the great Noble Elder. Why don't you trust in me for once?"

"Merlin, I still believe that, although it may seem that everyone else has failed and has lost trust in you, our son still believes in you. So, why do you need the Curpendulums, Merlin? No one can control them."

"Lies, the prophecy foretold that Noel can, and he will do so."

"This is *not* about him. Your thirst for power, dear, is actually about her. Isn't it?"

"Nimuway, stay out of this."

"Merlin, stop being stubborn, and, for once in your life, ask for help."

"No! I will be king as I should be, and, when I am king, I will kill anyone who stood in my way."

"Merlin, do not be like your father, Balimore, the King of the Incubuses. His mind is twisted in darkness. He plays games with people. He has enslaved the Council of Darkness. He changes his name as he pleases to create a false sense in himself. But, Merlin, my love, you cannot stop him alone. Noel has the power to help you. Noel has the power…."

"*Enough!* I do not need Noel, Rose, or any of them. My magic will be unstoppable, and they will all bow to me," Merlin screams as lightning strikes the floor around him repeatedly.

Then, he disappears and arrives at the rally point.

The armies of darkness stand in rows as Raven walks through them, screaming as Merlin appears.

"Idiots," Raven screams.

"Raven, are they ready?"

"Yes, Lord Merlin, they are, and more are on the way," Raven replies, smiling.

"Then, bring down that university, find the bunker, and bring me those weapons, every last one of them."

"It will be my pleasure," Raven remarks, smiling and raising her wand, launching magic into the air as the griffins fly overhead, leading the way toward the University.

"General?" Merlin inquires.

"Yes, Lord Merlin," the general snarls.

"Take your elite group and go to the Academy. Bring them down! The Phoenixes and Ignatiuses will be so distracted by protecting the university that they will not expect an attack on their precious school. See to it, personally, General. You get into that library and bring me all of the Curpendulums in that school. Leave no one, and I mean no one, alive," Merlin commands.

As Merlin, the General, and Raven walk along the front of the army, one of the guards toward the back turns their head and as their cloak hits the ground, a small ball of light floats into the air, then takes off quickly.

Flying through the sky, the ball of light causes magic from the earth to fly everywhere. The ball lands and speaks to a squirrel that takes off running, as the ball of light is off again.

Arriving at Glen Oak, the ball of light transforms.

"Where is the queen?" the fairy asks as the guards point.

Hurrying down the hall, the fairy flies into the grand hall.

"My queen?" Marigold calls.

"My dear child, Marigold, what are you doing here? You were supposed to be tending to the flowers in the fields," Queen Amaryllis replies.

"My queen, I was. But it is horrible. Merlin has amassed a large army. They are planning to march on the university and academy," Marigold explains as three sparrows fly into the hall and land, chirping. Queen Amaryllis approaches the birds and listens as they chirp away.

"My dear friends, one at a time, please," she says kindly as the birds continue to chirp rapidly all at once.

"Ms. Marigold is right. It is horrible! We must quickly send word through the nexus. That is the fastest way to alert the Arcane," Queen Amaryllis declares, raising her tulip wand in the air as magic flies from it, and multiple elegantly dressed fairies arrive.

"You summoned, Our Queen?" the fairy council ask.

When they see Marigold, they all stop.

"Magical Nexus, do you copy? I repeat, do you copy? War is on the horizon. War is on the horizon!" Marigold yells into an orb.

"Marigold, dear, let me?" Queen Amaryllis says raising the orb into the air as a ghost-like image of Lady Esther Ignatius appears.

"Queen Amaryllis, is everything okay? That dear fairy child was yelling into the orb about war. I was not aware of any drills being run," Lady Esther remarks.

"Lady Esther, this is no drill, and it isn't a joke. Word is coming through all forms of communication. Merlin is marching a large army, which he is directing toward the Arcane Academy and the university. Alert all Arcane immediately! I am sending word to all corners of the globe, alerting all the fairy tribes," Queen Amaryllis explains as Lady Esther immediately disappears.

"Our Queen?" the fairies ask in unison.

"Yes, you heard me. This is not a joke. We are on alert. Get word immediately to all fairy tribes. Everyone is to meet immediately. It is time for all of them to suit up."

In the magical nexus, orbs fly around the space as bells chime, and dwarfs begin filing into the space, running toward various orbs. Lady Esther stands in the middle of the room, hands raised as her eyes glow white. Orbs circle as her hands glow.

"Touch the orbs and immediately be ready to send the messages," Mr. Bruin directs, standing next to the Lady Esther as the dwarfs around the room touch the orbs simultaneously.

"All Magical and Mystical Arcane, this is Lady Esther Ignatius, Mistress of the Nexus. War is on the horizon. Merlin's army is marching toward the academy and university. All groups converge on the field of the academy. Immediate assistance is needed. All groups report. Magic is in danger. The Arcane are in danger."

As Esther finishes speaking, multiple pops are heard as her father, Ari, her mother, Amber, her aunts, Vivian and Hope, and her uncle, Theo, arrive.

"What is going on?" Ari asks as he ducks several orbs that are flying close to his head. As image after image flash in the orbs, Esther's eyes turn blue, and the images of the armies of dark, led by the Dark Council, appear.

"Brother?" Hope says concerned, looking around as Amber runs after one of the orbs and begins waving her hands over it, examining the contents.

Amber glances back at her husband with a look of concern.

"Theo, get to Aelfdene village, alert everyone and rally the armies. Hope, call the covens. Vivian, notify our family, and Amber, love, help our daughter," Ari orders as Theo, Hope, and Vivian disappear.

"Father, take my bag. You may need extra help with the army guildsmen," Esther says, raising her hand and throwing a glowing orb into the air. She catches another one with her magic as it spins.

"Thank you. Esther, you are our eyes and ears," Ari replies, bowing and disappearing. Then, spinning on the circular platform in the middle of the room, as orbs fly, circling the room, Esther casts magic streams connecting the orbs.

Chapter 22
The Armies Gather

Birds chirp as moonlight shines over the night sky. Bats appear, flying toward the back fields as mermaids, appear at the water's surface, singing. Rose suddenly awakes to the sounds of bells chiming and multiple horns sounding. Jumping to her feet, Rose runs to the double doors and opens them, looking out over the backfield, observing a large group of various Arcane from all over as more arrive. She turns and runs back inside to wake Zander.

"Hun, we have company. Wake up. Get the others," she says, snapping her fingers as her outfit transforms, and she teleports to the field. Looking around, Rose finds armies of covens, vampires, and elves already assembled as others continue to arrive.

"Headmistress," Ms. Tulip greets Rose as she approaches.

"Good morning. What is all of this about?" Rose asks.

"Help has arrived. The covens and the armies have started arriving," Ms. Tulip remarks.

"I can see that, but why?" Rose inquires just as Lady Yule appears.

"There you are, Lady Rose," she acknowledges, looking at Rose. Oliver, Sebastian, Ethan, and Zander also arrive with a second wave of Madeline, Gwen, Matthew, Ari, Theo, Hope, and Vivian behind them.

"Lady Yule, why is an army of covens, fairies, elves, dwarves, and animals arriving on the back lawn of the Arcane School of Magical Teaching without permission from my office or the parliament this early in the morning?" Oliver inquires, yawning.

"Permission? Permission is *not* needed when my dear brother sends word that Merlin has amassed a large army and is preparing to march on the university," Lady Yule explains.

"Uncle, like Lady Yule, Esther has received word from the fairies of the same thing," Ari remarks.

"Lady Yule, do not forget that Marigold sent word from Glen Oak, and the magical nexus has been activated," Ms. Tulip explains as a pop rings over the area and Conrad approaches.

"Phoenixes and Ignatiuses, Cedric sends word," Conrad declares as Rose takes a letter from him and reads it.

"It appears that Merlin is marching, all right. Father and Cedric have counted over two-thousand dark creatures moving from the north and another five thousand from the east. All are moving toward the university," Rose says, handing the letter to Zander.

"Why march on the university? This place I understand, but the university still does not make sense," Theo declares.

"There is a legend of an ancient bunker there, holding some powerful magical artifacts that Merlin hid. If he wants them, you know he will do everything he can to get them," Zander explains, pulling back his hair into a ponytail.

"Ms. Tulip, alert Prince and Chancellor Fae, immediately. They need to know of the concerns," Rose orders.

"Already done, My Lady," Ms. Tulip replies.

"Very well. Then, make sure that they can hold out until we can all get there. Conrad, alert all remaining vampire covens, please," Rose instructs as Ms. Tulip takes off, followed immediately by Conrad.

"Sister, plans?" Ethan inquires.

"Merlin is after the hidden artifacts. This is not good at all," Lady Yule remarks.

"Ari, Theo, Hope, and Vivian, you know what you must do. Go!" Rose commands as the four raise their staves as the elf army follows, all of them disappearing.

"'Morning," Alviss greets the group as he walks up.

"'Morning, Sir Alviss," the group replies in unison.

"I am here, ladies and gentlemen, to help," he declares.

"Aunt Rose, Matthew, Gwen, and I, will take the covens and start forming protective fields of magic around the university so that no one gets hurt. We will keep the darkness at bay for as long as possible," Madeline replies.

"Madeline, Gwen, Matthew, buy your cousin as much time as possible, please," Rose directs.

"Madeline and Gwen, be careful. Not a mark. You hear? Not a single mark. Your mother will never let me hear the end of it if either of you get hurt," Oliver remarks.

Gwen kisses her father's cheek, "Thank you, Dad. But remember that Madeline and I are not children anymore. We are adults now," Gwen reassures him as the three spin their wands. Fire flies into the air as they and the covens disappear.

"I will inform the parliament and get them to secure the villages," Oliver declares.

"Wait for me. I am coming with you. I will activate the magical investigations and law teams," Sebastian remarks as the two disappear at the same time as the Lady Mora, Lady Meredith Amser Ignatius, Lady Marybelle, and Aunt Destiny arrive.

"Good. You four are here," Rose remarks when she hears…

"No, actually five. You missed me," Mr. Bruin declares.

"Aye," Mr. Bruin greets Alviss.

"Aye, are me wife and daughter in place?" Alviss inquires.

"Indeed, they are," Mr. Bruin confirms.

"Lady Mora, faculty members, please immediately secure the school, enchant the grounds, activate all defenses, and do not let the darkness breach this place," Rose orders.

"We will keep the school safe. Ladies, shall we?" Mora replies.

"Lady Marybelle?"

"Yes, Headmistress Ignatius?"

"I cannot believe I am about to say this, but this is the one time I will ever authorize this. Get whatever books you need from the library," Rose directs as Marybelle looks at her excitedly.

"Yes. Finally! It happens on the brink of a war that she grants me access to the books. I finally get a chance to enchant the books. It is about time," Marybelle giggles as Destiny shakes her head.

"Lady Marybelle, take this and give it to me niece-in-law and tell her I sent the authorization for you to have the books," Mr. Bruin notes as Rose gives him a stern look.

"Lady Marybelle, you do not have access to the battlement. So, those books remain completely off-limits," Rose instructs.

"Oh, and Lady Marybelle, if you mess up my library or damage a single book, I will either have Mr. Giggle and Ms. Hoot tear up your classroom, or I will turn the kindergartener's loose and tell them you hid puppies for them in your room," Mr. Bruin declares, smiling.

"How charming! Grumpy old dwarf!" Lady Marybelle mumbles as she disappears along with the others. No sooner are they gone than fields of magic start appearing around the grounds.

"I heard that," Mr. Bruin says, laughing.

"Ethan, dear, would you be a love and sound the horns, please?" Rose says as Ethan pulls the bellowing horn, sounding it just as Queen Amaryllis appears.

"I have sent word for help, and I am here now, my dears," she declares, hugging Rose.

"Vines?, Poppycock! That will not hold against the darkness. General, take the earth and wind fairies and fortify this place. Do not give the darkness an inch of opportunity to get into the school. Water and fire fairies, get to your prince now, and, darlings, light the darkness up," Queen Amaryllis orders, flying into the air and shrinking into a small ball of light as the fairy elite guard follow.

"What about us, ma'am?" Alviss asks.

"Mr. Bruin and Sir Alviss, I have a very special task for the dwarf army," Rose explains as roars ring over the land.

"It looks like the cavalry has arrived," Ethan points as a giant lion approaches, centaurs flanking him on both sides. The lion stalks across the ground as it begins transforming. Then, the animals bow.

"My friends, it is good to see you. Word has come through the forest that the darkness is advancing at an alarming speed and multiplying as they come," Leaf says, taking complete human form, hugging Rose, and bumping fists with Ethan and Zander.

"It is good that you are here," Rose says.

"Yes, the horn sounded. We animals will always come when the horns sound," Leaf explains.

"Lord Leaf, take the animals and go to the university. Provide as much support as possible. Oh, and, Lord Leaf, this is Sir Alviss," Rose explains.

"Good day, Sir Leaf," Alviss replies.

"Mr. Bruin, accompany them, please. I want you and Alviss to go with Leaf and work with the animals. The dwarf's expertise in animals and the earth will prove significant against Merlin. Whatever it takes, trenches, holes, mountains, whatever, create them. Do not let Merlin reach the school," Rose explains.

"Me lady, it will be our honor," Alviss declares, bowing to his uncle as they run with the animals into the forest, the other dwarfs following closely behind them.

"Rose, what would you like me to do?" inquires Ethan.

"Dear Brother, we may have to take on Merlin ourselves," Rose says.

"Any word from Rusty about Ambrose?" Ethan asks.

"Only that he has jumped through time and has disappeared," Rose remarks, looking concerned.

"Should we let dad know?" Ethan inquires.

"For now, no, he may still be able to find him," Rose says as Oliver appears.

"Parliament is on alert. They are securing the villages, and the council is also aware of the situation. Also, there is chatter," Oliver remarks.

"Chatter?" Lady Yule inquires, approaching the group.

"Ambrose has been seen," Oliver explains as Rose looks at him closely.

"Where?"

"Something about him time jumping," Oliver explains.

"Lady Yule, can you get me to your brother? We may need his help to track Ambrose," Rose declares.

"Oliver and Ethan, get to the university. See what support you can provide to Cousin Fae," Rose orders as Lady Yule spins her hands. A portal opens and Lord Yule steps out.

"Ladies," Lord Yule acknowledges, tipping his hat and placing his monocle over his right eye.

"Time jumping?" Rose asks.

"He is looking for Luciana. We have to buy him more time," Lord Yule explains.

"I understand that. But Merlin is on the march, with his forces multiplying with each step. They will be upon the university soon, and the one Arcane who can stop this instantly is time jumping," Rose remarks with frustration in her voice.

"When he returns from time jumping, the matter with Merlin will be resolved," explains Dalton.

Rose nods, indicating that she understands. Then, she raises her hand and all three disappear. Seconds later, they emerge at the university amongst the hustle and bustle of armies securing the campus against the darkness. Examining their surroundings, Rose begins to walk quickly through the crowded courtyard. Arcane students bustle everywhere, wands drawn and moving items to create barriers with land and various items around them. Other students enchant the barriers, securing the campus further as the faculty evacuate the Mundane students to safety in the buildings. Upon seeing her cousin Bethany, Rose approaches her.

"Cousin, how is everything?" inquires Rose.

"Things would be better if I didn't have our great-grandfather trying to attack my university and half of the arcane community here," replies Bethany somewhat crossly.

"Chancellor Fae, the fairies report that multiple defensive outer fields are in place," one fairy guard announces.

"Thank you. Please remind my dear husband that this is Merlin we are dealing with. If he wants to get through, he will. Tell him the current multiplied fields may not be enough. We will need more. Tell him to triple the current fields, and once those settle, triple them again. He should repeat this process no less than twenty-five times," Bethany directs as the fairy bows and flies off.

"How many fields are you planning to put up?" Rose inquires.

"Enough to stop that old and cranky wizard in his tracks and buy us time to defeat him. Besides, you know my husband. With each field comes a different obstacle for the darkness to work their way through," Bethany replies.

"Any updates on Merlin's whereabouts?" Rose inquires of Oliver as he approaches with Ethan in tow.

"His legions of the dark guards have stopped moving," Oliver reports.

"Do we know what he is waiting for?" asks Rose.

"No one knows," replies Ethan.

"At least the university is secured now," Oliver remarks, chuckling.

"To a point. We still do not know where this bunker is on the campus. I'm worried it could be in one of the unprotected areas, giving Merlin direct access to some dangerous Arcane artifacts," Bethany explains.

"Bethany, would you excuse Ethan, Oliver, and I for a few minutes so that we can speak?" Rose asks.

"Sure. I will go to see what Phineas is doing and make sure he has tripled every field again," replies Bethany.

As soon as Bethany disappears, Rose turns to speak quietly with her brothers.

"We need to find that bunker before Merlin does," she says.

"I had a feeling you were going to say that," Oliver replies.

"Dear sister, do you think we haven't been looking?" Ethan inquires.

"I know everyone has. But we have to find it! I'm thinking that some of the army of animals may be able to use their underground systems to find out where the bunker is. Also, the trees may be able to send their roots out," explains Rose.

"I wish it were that easy," Oliver replies.

"Nevertheless, Oliver and I have been thinking. There may still be one way to find it," Ethan remarks.

"Bardagul," the two say in unison.

"No, no! Absolutely not!" Rose protests.

"But he is a dwarf, and you know they can find anything," Oliver exclaims.

"Yes, but I do not want to hear what Ambrose will have to say if he gets hurt. I learned from Alviss that Ambrose is Bardagul's godfather," Rose explains.

"Then, we send Mr. Bruin or Alviss with him," Ethan suggests.

"I will go," a voice says from behind Rose.

"No! I forbid Amelia from going. If she gets hurt, her grandmother, my sister-in-law, Brooke, will never let me hear the end of it," Oliver declares.

"Uncle, this fight is not just an Arcane one but a Mundane one as well. Ambrose needs time, and if I can help get that for him, then, by all means, I must," Amelia remarks, clicking the buttons and turning the face on her watch as armor appears on her.

"You know, she has a point," Rose declares.

"If she gets hurt, Brooke will strangle me, followed by Olivia, who will also strangle me," Oliver exclaims.

"Brother, as the president of the Arcane, you of all people should know that we will have casualties if the fields are breached," Ethan remarks, looking concerned.

"Hence, I would rather Amelia not be here," Oliver declares.

"Uncle, I am going to help the dwarf. Besides, my nanobots have proven impervious against magic," Amelia remarks.

"I will be back soon," Rose declares, holding her hand out as Amelia grabs ahold and the two disappear.

⸮

"Willow, adjust the lever up there. Michael, kick that orb. Isabella, tighten down that smoke pipe," Esther orders as Rose and Amelia arrive.

"Wow! This place is amazing," Amelia remarks, looking around in awe of everything happening in the nexus as Esther's head pops up from behind a medium-sized orb.

"Grandma, absolutely not! I am at capacity here in the Nexus. So, no more people, please," Esther declares.

"Oh, I am not bringing another person. I am taking a few," Rose replies.

"Finally, we get to go," Pete says, standing up.

"Not you. I need Master Bardagul," Rose states as the dwarf pokes his head out from behind one of the giant armchairs.

"Me, My Lady?" he asks, pointing to his chest.

"Yes. I have a special task for you and Amelia," Rose explains as Bardagul runs up excitedly.

"If he goes, we go," Nordika declares.

"No. I need you and your brother here helping Esther. When Merlin launches his full attack against the university and school, she will need extra help and eyes on everything. It is also the safest way to keep the two of you protected since neither of you have magic. I do not want either of you hurt," Rose explains as she raises her hands, spinning them and Bardagul's attire is transformed.

"This is cool," he says, smiling, as his outfit turns into armor.

"Grandma, do not encourage him," Sophia says, kneeling to adjust Bardagul's chest plate.

"So, what's the plan?" Kells asks.

"The six of you will stay here. The minute your brother shows up, teleport to him. As for Amelia and Bardagul, you are with me," Rose directs, holding out her hand.

Amelia reaches down and takes Bardagul's hand, then grabs Rose's other hand as they teleport.

"Why do they get to have all the fun?" Pete grumbles.

"Seriously?" Willow says, hitting him upside his head.

"Fun? You think Merlin is fun?" Sophia asks, rolling her eyes as she sharpens her sword blade.

"No. I mean they get to go do stuff, and we are stuck here," Pete complains, sitting down in a chair.

જ

With a sudden pop, Rose, Amelia, and Bardagul arrive at the courtyard of the university.

"Oy! No, no, no! Why is me son in armor?" Alviss complains as he approaches them.

"Papa, look at this amazing armor," Bardagul says as screams are heard.

"The darkness is here," Rose remarks, looking up as several dark creatures strike the magical barrier that is protecting the university.

"Sis, we need to move and fast," Ethan declares, summoning his wand.

"Alviss, you, Bardagul, and Amelia are traveling underground, looking for the bunker or anything resembling a structure," Rose explains.

"They are not going without help," Matthew remarks as he approaches them.

"Be careful, all of you," Ethan cautions as Matthew spins his wand, and the four shrink, run toward an open tunnel, and jump into it.

No sooner did they leave than a second strike on the field occurs.

"Lords Oliver and Ethan and Lady Rose, you three might want to see this," one of the elves says as the three push their way through the crowd as over fifty individuals materialize, Sebastian standing with them in the front of the group.

"Take your places," Sebastian yells as Ethan comes up and hugs him.

"Any news?" Oliver inquires

"The villages and the Arcane School of Magical Teaching are secure. No way in or out! Lady Mora has gone freaky divine Elder Magic on the place. I have never seen anything like it," Sebastian explains.

"Thank you for bringing backup," Rose remarks.

"I brought the best of the best," Sebastian states as elfish horns sound and multiple elf guards are heard in the distance phasing through the magical fields.

"Darkness is attacking the far side of the field," Rose declares as the Arcane all begin drawing their wands and tightening their grips. Several dragons strike the field as the Arcane raise their wands.

"Hold your fire until absolutely necessary," Oliver commands as a sudden flash of light flies across the dome, and the dragons disappear.

"What was that?" Ethan inquires.

"No clue. But whatever it is, the dragons are gone," Oliver remarks.

"Quickly, keep up," Bardagul shouts, running along the tunnel.

"Aye, any ideas of what is occurring above ground?" Alviss asks and Amelia pulls out her phone.

"Master Dwarf, to answer your question, the fields are still in place with no concerns," Amelia says, watching what is going on above ground through her phone.

"So, you have those fancy robots everywhere?" inquires Matthew.

"Yes, they are small enough until needed. Then, they will be my eyes and ears," Amelia replies.

"Papa, look," Bardagul points as Matthew moves in to examine the wall closely.

"Brick," Matthew declares.

"Oy! It appears to go on for a distance," Alviss says.

"Shall we follow it?" Amelia asks as the nanobots begin flying around her.

"What does that mean?" Matthew inquires, watching the nano-bots.

"That, Lord Matthew, means that magic is nearby," she exclaims.

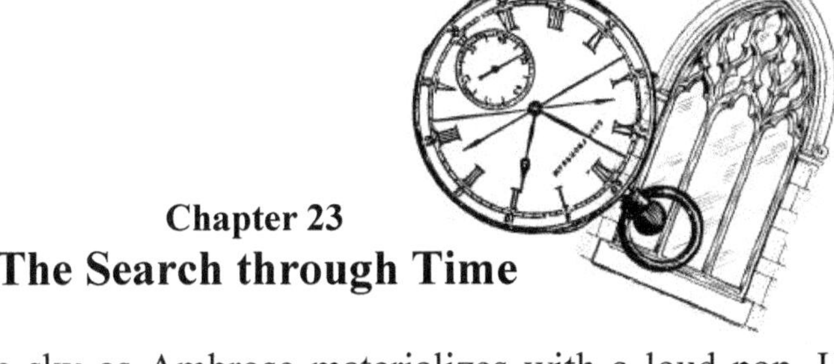

Chapter 23
The Search through Time

Birds fly into the sky as Ambrose materializes with a loud pop. He observes the quiet street.

It appears I am in New York.

Walking and regarding the environment around him cautiously, Ambrose stops in front of a familiar building.

Yup, it is New York. This is the old Library where I first met Minnie.

Walking through the door, Ambrose comes into the grand foyer of the library. Looking around, he notices that time is shifting around him rapidly, the people, their attire, and their age shifting right before his eyes.

Hmm. Time is changing, which means Luciana must be holding time still. But where is she?

Wizards and witches buzz by him as they come and go from the library. Then, Ambrose notices a young wizard who catches his attention.

❧

"Excuse me. Excuse me, ma'am?" a young Kelvin inquires of the woman behind the counter.

"Ahh, Your Highness, good day. What can I do for you?" the librarian inquires.

"I am looking for this book," Kelvin says, handing a note to the librarian.

"*The Search through Time*," the librarian reads.

"Yes, ma'am. I was told you had a copy of it," Kelvin replies.

"Your Highness, at one time we did. But that is a very dangerous book, and, under orders, I am not allowed to give anyone access to that type of book," she explains.

"Orders from whom? That book is for a school project, ma'am," Kelvin replies.

"I am sorry, Your Highness, but it is simply *not* allowed. Your Highness, you will need to come back with your parents, and they will need to get permission," the librarian explains but stops speaking as a man approaches.

"Master Kelvin, did you get everything you need?" Cedric inquires as the librarian backs up behind the counter.

"No. I am not allowed to see the book I need for my project," Kelvin remarks, lowering his head.

"Master Kelvin, will you please go and wait over there with your brother? I will be there in five," Cedric directs as Kelvin obediently walks away.

"A word, ma'am?" Cedric inquires.

"Yes, sir. What can I do for you?" the librarian asks as Cedric smiles, revealing his fangs.

"Am I to understand that you have denied the young prince access to the book he requested for a project?" Cedric asks as the librarian's hands begin to tremble.

"Sir, that book is perilous. I am not allowed to give it out," she replies, trying to keep calm as Cedric taps his fingers on the counter.

"Now, I am sure this is a misunderstanding. You see, if Master Kelvin returns without that book, his father and mother, the king and queen, will be down here," Cedric remarks, polishing one of his fangs with his tongue.

"Sir, the king, and queen can come down here, but I cannot release that book, by special orders," the librarian replies.

"Orders from whom?" Cedric asks.

"I am not allowed to share that information, sir," swallowing hard, the librarian explains.

"Very well then. I will be back," Cedric declares, turning and walking away.

Raising his hand, Ambrose freezes time.

Cedric, if Kelvin needs that book, then he should have it. Let me see. Time is frozen. If I spin my hands. Okay. Great! Now, I look like royalty. Ugh, how do they wear these things? Note to self, the first thing to do as Noble Elder is ban the wearing of robes with trains. Yuck!

Okay, let's see. If I remember correctly, Grandma always taught me that, to interact with a vision, one must simply raise their left hand and turn it counterclockwise four times, and there we go.

Time unfreezes as four buglers appears and start playing as Ambrose throws open the doors and marches into the library. Everyone stops what they are doing and bows.

"Hear ye! Hear ye! Announcing his majesty, King Titus Phoenix," one of the buglers states as Ambrose, posing as King Titus, strides into the library.

"Father," Wade yells, running to the king as Kelvin stands beside the table, watching. Cedric stands quietly behind Kelvin, observing carefully as his eyes narrow on Titus.

"Wade, my boy, are you listening to Cedric and your brother?" Titus asks as he hugs Wade, who nods in the affirmative, and the wizards and witches whisper amongst themselves. Then, carrying Wade, Titus approaches Kelvin and Cedric.

"Kelvin and Cedric," Titus greets them, nodding at them both.

"Father," Kelvin replies, making the same head gesture.

"Sir," Cedric says, wrinkling his nose and sniffing the air.

"How are things?" Titus asks.

"Good, Father. Look, we got books and lots of them," Wade says, pointing to a pile.

Noticing that Kelvin is looking down, Titus moves around the table, lowers himself down to Kelvin's level, trying to prevent himself from making eye contact with Cedric, and says, "Kelvin, my son, didn't you get any books?"

"No, Father, the librarian would not let me have the book I need," he replies softly.

"What book do you need, my son?" Titus inquires, standing up and snapping the clasps of his robes shut.

"The *Search through Time*, sir," Cedric explains, continuing to observe Titus's every move as he circles him cautiously.

"I see. I shall speak with the librarian," Titus declares as he turns toward the counter, running straight into Cedric, who snarls.

"Young Master Kelvin, will you take your brother and go to find the book of the Grimm Tales, please? I wish to speak with your father," Cedric says, tapping his fingers together.

"Cedric, what can I do for you?" Titus asks.

"Sir, follow me, please. I wish to have a word in private," Cedric says as Titus cautiously follows him into one of the side hallways out of sight of everyone.

Entering the hall, Cedric grabs Titus by the throat and picks him up.

"I will tell you this only once. You will not get near enough to touch the royal children again, or I will tear your throat out. I do not care if anyone is watching," Cedric declares as Titus waves his hand, freezing time again. Cedric drops him to the floor, his hand starting to freeze. When he reaches the ground, Titus transforms into Ambrose.

"An imposter," Cedric hisses, revealing his fangs as his red eyes glows and he charges Ambrose, who disappears and reappears on the other side of the hallway.

"Damn it, Cedric, calm down, old friend," Ambrose says, hands raised, dodging Cedric.

"Old friend? Sir, I have never had the pleasure of meeting you," Cedric snarls, pressing on the handle of his cane and pulling out a sword.

"Cedric, for the love of Virginia, stand down," Ambrose commands, catching the blade as his hands begin to glow.

"How do you know that name?" Cedric inquires, backing up, his eyes narrowing.

"You said it all the time when I was a child growing up. It was not only the passcode you taught us if we were in trouble, but it is the only time I think we ever heard you swear," Ambrose remarks, letting go of the blade as Cedric steps in, grabs his hand, and examines Ambrose for injury.

"The metal glows?" Cedric asks in shock.

"Yes, the metal does not affect me," Ambrose explains.

"Your hands, let me see them!" Cedric demands, grabbing Ambrose's hands and turning them over.

"Looking for something, Cedric?" Ambrose inquires.

"Your hands are not cut? Not even your dueling gloves?" Cedric asks.

"Correct. Vampiric metal does not affect me. It cannot hurt me. It cannot make me bleed. I grew up training with a vampire who taught me how to handle vampiric metals. I also grew up with six older siblings, and nothing phases me," Ambrose explains, spinning his hands as his attire changes, and he is back in his long boots, slacks, tunic, and long coat.

"Your attire is that of an elf. You have pointed ears, and you mention six older siblings? The Ignatius 7!" Cedric declares as Ambrose pauses.

"Wait, you know about us?" Ambrose inquires, smiling.

"It is all I have heard about for the last few days from Elder Yule. He claimed that one of the seven Ignatius descendants was jumping through time and describes exactly how you look right now," Cedric says.

"Interesting," Ambrose remarks, walking toward the archway that looks out over the library.

"What brings you here, Lord…?" Cedric inquires.

"Ambrose," he supplies.

"Well then, Lord Ambrose," Cedric acknowledges.

"No, Cedric. Not Lord anything. I am just Ambrose. I am here because I am looking for someone. But why I am here in this moment...? Who knows why time dumped me here," Ambrose explains.

"Someone?" Cedric asks.

"An elf woman, freaky magic, can control time like me," Ambrose exclaims.

"I have not met or seen anyone like that here. Is she in trouble?" Cedric inquires as Ambrose begins to pace.

"Think, Ambrose. Think. Why would time drop you here? Other than to play its normal bizarre game. Wait. That's it!" Ambrose says.

"What is it?" Cedric inquires.

"Cedric, that is it. It is the book. It has to be. *The Search through Time.* I will get the book, review it, then drop you, Kelvin, Wade, and your pile of books wherever you need to go," Ambrose replies, raising the hood of his long coat. Before Cedric can say a word, Ambrose is gone.

"Oh dear! He left time frozen," Cedric remarks as Ambrose appears at the end of the hallway. Walking toward Cedric, a pedestal materializes, and Ambrose places the book on it. Stopping, Cedric regards the pedestal, placing his monocle over his left eye as Ambrose laughs.

"Please tell me that Lord Dalton Yule did not give you that monocle," Ambrose chuckles, examining the book.

"No, he did not. Fascinating pedestal. Bent metals of gold and silver, vines from the earth, and a clock, but also ancient markings of the Celestials. Very interesting indeed," Cedric remarks, running a finger down the bent metal.

"Yes, Cedric. It is old. Now, can you focus, please?" Ambrose says as Cedric regards him.

"You're an elder?" Cedric inquires.

"I will not answer that. Besides, this book should be interesting to read," Ambrose remarks, his hand running down the cover as the book flies open, and Ambrose and Cedric disappear into the pages.

"I see why this was in the restricted section," Ambrose laughs, examining the place where they land as Cedric helps lift him off the ground, dusting them both off.

"Where are we?" Cedric inquires when he hears a voice.

"Wow! Cedric, you're strong," Wade says as Kelvin stands with his wand drawn.

"Cedric, put me down, please," Ambrose orders as Cedric drops him. "Talk about not having manners."

"Cedric, where are we, and who is he?" Kelvin inquires, poking Ambrose with his wand.

"That young, Master Kelvin, I am trying to determine. Master Wade, please stay near me," Cedric says, annoyed as Wade bolts around, looking at everything.

"Hey, Wade, touch nothing. We do not know what magic it may have or if it is dangerous," Ambrose remarks, pulling his wand.

"Who are you?" Kelvin inquires.

"A wizard from the future," Cedric remarks, looking displeased, knowing what will happen next.

"The future? Time magic? Sweet. I have so many questions for you," Kelvin remarks, pulling out a parchment and quill.

"No," Ambrose replies, examining the space closely.

"But I didn't even get a chance to ask my questions yet," Kelvin complains.

"Master Kelvin, you won't be able to ask any questions. For me to share any information goes against thousands of rules. Besides, I live by the policy of not sharing anything. This way, time will not break anymore," Ambrose explains.

"Seriously, time is already broken. What if I ordered you to tell me?" Kelvin asks.

"I would still deny your Royal Highnesses' request," Ambrose explains, continuing to examine the room.

"Hmm, looks like thirteenth-century craftsmanship," Ambrose remarks, trying to avoid Kelvin.

"It is the fourteenth century. Masters Kelvin and Wade, as your father is not here, I am in charge. Therefore, touch nothing, and I mean nothing," Cedric declares, giving Wade a stern look.

"Oh, does that mean this as well?" Wade says, holding up a tray of food.

"Especially food. Wade Phoenix put that back," Cedric commands, taking the tray and throwing it across the room.

"You're an elf," Kelvin observes, pointing at Ambrose's ears.

"Yes, I am," Ambrose responds, examining the wall.

"Are you related to King Casper Ignatius?" Kelvin asks.

"You know, kid, while I want to answer your questions, I am looking for a way out of here for all of us. Care to help? Or are you going to stand there asking stupid, obvious questions?" Ambrose asks as Kelvin raises his wand.

Liquefacio.
Melt away.

"Problem solved, the wall is no longer there, and I am *not* a kid. I am fourteen," Kelvin notes, stowing his wand and walking past Ambrose.

"Same thing," Ambrose remarks, looking at Kelvin and shaking his head as the four enter a long corridor. When Wade starts running around, looking at everything, Cedric grabs him by the hand and holds onto him tightly. The four walk along the corridor until they reach a giant room at the end.

"Wait! This place…" Ambrose exclaims, his eyes narrowing.

"…is so cool," Wade completes Ambrose's sentence, while trying to pull away from Cedric.

"Cool? It is a room full of rocks and dirt," Kelvin declares, turning up his nose.

"This place is more than that, kid," Ambrose replies.

"I take it you know this place then?" Kelvin inquires.

"Of course, he knows it," a voice declares as the four look around startled.

"Hello?" Ambrose calls as a cloaked figure materializes.

"Hello," the figure says, lowering its hood.

"Minnie, it is good to see you," Ambrose declares, hugging her.

"Lord Ambrose, we have all been worried and looking for you," she responds as she looks carefully at the other three.

"Well, it appears we have Cedric and the young princes, Kelvin and Wade," she remarks, smiling.

"It is a pleasure, ma'am," Kelvin replies, bowing as Cedric keeps his distance.

"Minnie, what brings you here?" Ambrose asks.

"Noble Elder has fallen ill," she replies.

"So, you came to get me?" Ambrose asks.

"Yes, but that is not all of it," Minnie says.

"Minnie, can you explain what is going on then?" Ambrose asks as Minnie points toward the ceiling and fog circles overhead.

"Fascinating," Cedric says, looking up.

"What is that?" Kelvin inquires.

"Minnie, can you get them back to their own time?" Ambrose inquires.

"No can do. They are on this journey with you," Minnie replies as Kelvin rummages through his bag.

"I know it is in here somewhere," he declares, as he continues rummaging through his bag, pulling things out and throwing them on the ground.

"Brother, what are you looking for?" Wade inquires, looking over the side of the bag as Kelvin pulls out a white and purple cloak.

"Master Kelvin, I insist you mustn't do that," Cedric declares, raising his hand as Kelvin drops the cloak on the ground. It rises into the air, transforms to full size, and a young girl appears.

"Kelvin," she says, smiling and hugging him.

"Hi, Nadia. We need some help," he replies as they separate from the hug, and she lowers her hood.

"This place is rather gross. Please tell me this is not ours?" Nadia asks, turning and examining the space. Then, she stops and looks right at Ambrose and Minnie.

"Oh, hello," Nadia says.

"Hello," Ambrose replies, smiling and bowing.

"He bows to you, but not us," Kelvin says, crossing his arms and grumbling.

"My Lady. Master Kelvin thinks you might be able to assist us," Cedric remarks.

"Indeed. Kelvin. Don't you know a cleanup spell?" Nadia jokes as Minnie points up toward the ceiling.

"Oh no. That is more than a cleanup spell. Ha! Cleaning up is not the issue at all. It is dealing with that," Nadia exclaims, walking the length of the cave and examining the ceiling.

"Do you know what it is?" Ambrose inquires.

"Yes, it is a rather simple tear in time," Nadia declares.

"A tear in time? Interesting," Ambrose says, raising his right hand as it starts to glow, and the fog begins to circle into a spiral. The fog picks up speed as the winds kick up the sand in the cave.

Everyone runs toward Ambrose, remaining close to him. The winds pick up even more, and Ambrose's eyes start to glow white as a magic field creates a dome over them.

"What is going on?" Nadia inquires, her arm raised, shielding her face from the wind as Ambrose levitates into the air.

"What is he?" Wade inquires when light flies around the cave.

Minnie stands, arms crossed, tapping her foot. Cedric, Nadia, Wade, and Kelvin watch the light flying around them as they begin to transform. Finally, the light flashes, and there stand the older versions of themselves.

Walking on air, Ambrose lowers down to the floor as he raises his hand, causing lightning to strike it as he projects the lightning into the ceiling, causing the fog to disappear.

"Now, that is an extraordinary feat of magic," Cedric says, leaning on his cane and smiling at Ambrose.

"Old friend," Ambrose greets him with a hug.

"Master Ambrose, it is good to see you," Cedric declares.

Nadia and Kelvin approach, hugging Ambrose.

"It is good to see you," Ambrose says, smiling.

"I see you are back to full power," Nadia says.

"Somehow, and yet in all of this, with my magic, I brought you back to life?" Ambrose inquires.

"Indeed, you have," Nadia replies.

"Some of the most interesting necro magic I think any of us have seen to date," Wade declares, shaking Ambrose's hand.

"Sorry, where are my manners? Everyone, this is Lady Minnie. She is an Elder," Ambrose says but then the room begins to shake.

Examining the area, Kelvin points at an individual who is fading in and out of materializing.

"Ambrose, it is Luciana," Minnie notes, spinning magic around the cave, trying to control the materialization of Luciana.

"She is fading," Nadia declares as she and Kelvin raise their wands and spin them as streams of white magic fly around the space and begin to spiral around Luciana.

An orb zips around the cave as Nadia looks back at Ambrose, who is standing in the center of the cave, his eyes glowing purple, his hand raised as magic flies around him.

Tempus. Meus es mandatum.
Time. You are mine to command.

Thousands of clocks of all shapes and sizes appear, floating in the air as their hands spin rapidly. Then, all freeze and, within seconds, Luciana fully materializes.

Examining herself, she looks somewhat confused. "Is it possible? Am I standing here?" Luciana asks as she notices everyone standing there watching her.

"Father?" she says, running to him, arms open as the two hug.

"Are you okay?" Ambrose asks.

Then, clapping is heard.

"Bravo! Brava! How sweet! Such a beautiful reunion. Such a shame it will not last long," Merlin laughs, suddenly appearing.

"Merlin," Kelvin and Wade say, wands raised, as Cedric pulls his sword, and Nadia stands next to Ambrose, her wand also drawn.

"None of you can stop me. You have not before, and you won't now," Merlin shouts, dismissing them.

"Now, girly, give me the Curpendulum and the watch!" Merlin demands holding out a hand as Ambrose steps in front of Luciana.

"Luciana? I want you to get out of here now," Ambrose says as his eyes turn black.

"I am not leaving," she replies as Merlin raises his hands, and the entire cave goes pitch black as a giant ball of light floats in front of Ambrose.

The orb spins rapidly between Ambrose's hands as rocks fly into the air and planets, stars, and the solar system begin to appear. Nadia, Kelvin, and Wade circle in amazement as Merlin raises his hand, casting streams of black magic against Ambrose. Then, suddenly, everyone disappears.

Seconds later, Merlin finds himself falling from the sky.

"What magic is this?" he asks, spinning his hands, but he lands face-first on the cave's dirt floor. Looking around, he finds Ambrose sitting on a stone throne in the middle of the space, smiling at him and still holding the orb. Angrily, Merlin projects dark magic at Ambrose, but it goes right through him.

"An illusion," Merlin declares, raising his hand and stomping his foot as the illusion disappears, and he finds a sword at his throat.

"Now, Merlin, what were you saying again?" Kelvin asks as Merlin disappears.

"You think you have won. I will have the Curpendulums! I do not care who has them, dead or alive, they will be mine," Merlin's voice echoes through the space, then fades.

Suddenly, two Dark Council members fall from the ceiling. They hit the cave floor dead.

Ambrose approaches, turns one over, and examines them. Pulling back the hood, he finds that the council member has been hexed.

"Hexed? By whom?" Minnie inquires, looking over Ambrose's shoulder. Then, a pop occurs and a weak Noble Elder stumbles, collapsing to the floor.

Chapter 24
Passing

"Noble Elder!" Minnie exclaims as she and Ambrose run toward him.

"Ambrose," a weak Noble Elder acknowledges.

"Sir, you're weak. You must save your strength. Please rest," Ambrose says as Noble Elder takes Ambrose's hand.

"Noel, my lad, the time is upon us," Noble Elder states, placing the necklace in Ambrose's hand as the others look on.

"No! Noble Elder, you must hold on," Minnie says, tears rolling down her face.

"Minnie, it is time," Ambrose replies, looking at her kindly as she wipes the tears from her face and nods. Then, standing up, Minnie backs away as Nadia hugs and comforts her.

"Noble Elder, it is time. I have it from here, old friend. Rest," Ambrose murmurs as multiple beings of light appear.

"The Celestials," Kelvin and Wade say as everyone takes a knee, bowing.

"Our friends, rise," the Celestials say collectively.

"Noel, promise me that you will stop Merlin and protect all magic. The earth needs you. The people need you. The creatures…" Noble Elder says as he closes his eyes and takes his last breath.

Everyone stands quietly in reverence for Noble Elder as Ambrose waves his hand over Noble Elder's body, and it dissolves. Closing his eyes, Ambrose bows, then opens his eyes as he stands up. Holding up the necklace, Ambrose examines it.

"The necklace of Noble Elder," Minnie exclaims as Ambrose smiles at her, and the Celestials watch.

"That it is, Minnie," Ambrose replies, placing the necklace over his head as magic spins around him, levitating him into the air.

"I think we may want to take cover," Nadia says looking at the others.

Magic spins around the cave as lightning strikes the ground repeatedly around Ambrose.

"I have never seen this much magic in one place," Wade remarks as the group ducks behind boulders in the cave, and chunks of the wall cave crack and fly into the air.

"He is bringing the place down," Cedric declares.

"Cedric, you are correct. This is the one time we do not know what to expect with magic," Nadia states as the group ducks as another chunk of the wall flies overhead.

"Look," Luciana points as images appear in the space.

"Nadia, are those the stories of time?" Kelvin inquires.

"They are, my love. Luciana, no! Take cover!" Nadia commands, raising her hand and deflecting the stones that are flying toward Luciana as she wanders out from behind the boulder looking around. Nadia follows.

"Kelvin, protect Minnie," Nadia directs.

"Cedric?"

"Sir, I have the Lady Minnie. You go with Nadia," Cedric states as he grabs Minnie's hand. Minnie quickly pulls away, crossing her arms.

"I will not argue with you. We have to work together. I have to keep you safe," Cedric remarks, looking at Minnie as part of the cave wall crashes into the boulder that they are hiding behind.

"Luciana, we must take cover!" Nadia shouts as lightning hits the ground inches from her.

"You take cover. I will be fine," Luciana declares as she pulls out the pocket watch, and it levitates into the air.

Unaware that Luciana has the watch, Ambrose observes the magic spinning around him, running his hands through the streams of magic.

On the ground, the others watch while continuing to deflect the flying stones around them.

"Nadia, the winds are picking up," Kelvin yells, spinning his wand and redirecting the sand.

☙

Across time at the university, the ground begins to shake.

"Earthquake?" Ms. Tulip asks, flying into the air as several fairies dive from the sky, landing near her.

"Look, Ms. Tulip, magic," the fairy general points.

"General, hold this line. I must get word to the Queens," Ms. Tulip replies, shooting up into the air and soaring along the streams of magic in the sky. Running her hand through the streams of magic, she looks back, noticing that her wings are glowing.

"I have never seen or felt anything like this," she remarks, diving.

"Was that an earthquake?" Chancellor Fae demands.

"My lady, we have no clue," one of the elite fairy guards replies as Ms. Tulip lands.

"Chancellor, earth's magic has grown," Ms. Tulip says, resting her hands on her legs and catching her breath.

"I can see that," Chancellor Fae responds, circling Ms. Tulip and examining her wings.

"Ms. Tulip, your wings…" Prince Phineas says as he approaches.

"From the magic," she replies, pointing toward the sky.

"Phineas, get my cousins immediately," Chancellor Fae declares as multiple pops echo as Rose, Zander, Oliver, Ethan, and Sebastian appear.

"Ms. Tulip," Rose says, approaching, examining her wings.

"A surge of magical power," Zander declares, examining the area.

"This is amazing! I have never felt anything like it, Rose," Ms. Tulip explains as the ground shakes again.

"That is the third earthquake in less than three minutes," Chancellor Fae notes as Queen Amaryllis lands, her wings also glowing.

"Dear Phoenixes and Ignatiuses, the magic of earth trembles. It is growing in power. We have never seen anything like it," Queen Amaryllis declares, very excited.

"She is correct. We have never seen anything like this," Lord Leo roars as he walks up, bowing.

Flapping is heard as the group clears the area, allowing Belinda and Autumn to land.

"Thoughts, Dad?" Oliver inquires as a pop is heard, and Mora arrives. "Mom?"

"Alezander, Belinda," Rose replies regarding both of them and giving them a sideway look.

"Oh. I understand," Zander says.

"What's going on?" Ethan inquires.

"Noel has returned," Zander states.

"Which means that Noble Elder has passed away. Oh dear!" Queen Amaryllis says, shooting magic into the air as the fairies follow, showing their respect for him.

"General, solidify all fields. Oliver, alert the parliament immediately. Merlin may use this to his advantage," Rose directs as magic spins around at the top of the dome.

"Do we need to worry about that?" Ethan asks, pointing at the swirling magic that flies into the field and begins glowing.

"I do not think so," Rose replies as Kells, Peter, and Michael arrive.

"Grandma, Grandpa, please tell us you have answers," Michael says as horns sound.

"Michael, we will be able to answer your questions in a few minutes," Rose replies.

"Leo?" Zander calls as an explosion is heard.

"Merlin is attacking the far lightfield. He has trolls with him," Ari explains, approaching the group.

"Phineas, I think it is time to evacuate the students underground for safety. Although we have vampires and centaurs, trolls will complicate things," Chancellor Fae says, pulling back her hair and summoning her bow and arrow.

"Ari, let your siblings and the armies of elves imbue their arrows with as much magic as possible. Trolls will be dangerous in a fight," Zander directs.

Lightning strikes the field as a column of light explodes, hitting the ground. A being steps out.

"Did I hear you mention trolls?" Rusty asks, walking out of the light column, carrying his staff.

"Father, you are okay," Kells asks, running up to him.

"I am fine. Mom, Noble Elder…" he begins to say when Rose raises her hand.

"We know," she replies.

"He went looking for Noel," Rusty explains.

"Do we know where he is?" Rose inquires.

"No," replies Rusty as Rose throws an orb into the air, and a ghost-like image of Esther appears.

"Grandma, Merlin is on the march. He has trolls, goblins, dark dwarves, elves, and he has packs of werewolves," Esther explains as the group watches her spinning orbs.

"Werewolves? We need to alert the covens. Trolls are bad enough. Werewolves require a different level of weapons and fighting," Chancellor Fae declares.

"Esther, what is the status of magic?" Zander asks.

"Grandpa, it is like nothing we have ever seen. Magic is growing in strength. I have multiple magical reads on Cousin Ambrose. It is weird. It is like he has multiplied," Esther describes as an orb flies around her.

"Esther, what is going on with that orb?" her grandmother asks.

Holding up her hand, she motions for the others to wait.

"Grandma, that was great-grandpa Kelvin. He is with Ambrose, and all hell is breaking loose. He has never seen magic like this," Esther explains, looking concerned.

"Esther, where is he?" Rusty asks.

"Uncle Rusty, he did not say, and I cannot locate him," Esther responds, her hands turning orbs and throwing them out of the way.

"Mom, get to Esther and help her out. It looks like the nexus is working overtime," Zander says as Michael whistles and Sophia, Isabella, and Willow arrive.

"You rang, dear Brother?" Isabella inquires.

"Ambrose is in trouble," Kells notes.

"Where is he?" Willow asks.

"We do not know. Your great-grandpa and I assume Cedric is with him," their grandmother replies as the ground shakes again, knocking everyone off their feet.

"Are these quakes caused by Ambrose?" Chancellor Fae asks.

"Willow, you may need this?" Martha says, approaching and handing Willow her phone.

"Auntie Rose, the darkness is here. We need to help. I think the Ignatius six have this," Martha notes, winking at Willow as part of the field explodes.

"Quickly! Reinforce it," Rose screams.

"Autumn, get me into the air," Zander yells, running and jumping onto her back.

"Go! I will stay with them. I swear nothing will happen," Belinda pledges as she wraps her tail around the six, and they all disappear.

"Willow, any time now," Isabella says as fire flies around them, and they land in a field, far from the university.

"I am working on it. But I do not understand this thing," Willow says as Pete comes up and takes the phone from his sister.

"Allow me," Pete says as a map appears along with a flashing circle.

"Peter, you are a genius," Willow declares, hugging him as all six raise their hands.

"Look at me, you five, we have never done magic like this. Focus! Remember that we don't know what to expect when we arrive, but he needs our help, and we need his help," Isabella remarks as the six form a circle around the map, touching hands.

Belinda wraps herself in a circle around the six Ignatius siblings as streams of magic fly around them.

Accipe nos ad Fratrem Nostrum.

Accipe nos ad Fratrem Nostrum.

Accipe nos ad Fratrem Nostrum.

Take us to our brother.

Isabella spoke the words three times as the streams of magic spin around them and they disappear.

৵

Stones and sand continue to fly around the cave as Kelvin reaches Nadia.

Funis.

Cords.

Cedric and Wade grab the rope and hold it tight, pulling Kelvin and Nadia toward them as the two continue to be lifted off the ground.

"How do we stop this?" Wade inquires as Nadia and Kelvin finally reach the boulder.

"We may not be able to stop it. He is growing in power," Nadia declares.

"It is next to impossible to see in this place," Kelvin remarks when a flash of light appears.

"Nadia, Kelvin, everyone, look," Cedric says, pointing as a second flash of light appears. Flames explode in the sand, turning it to glass, shattering around them.

Everyone takes cover as Belinda appears.

"It seems that the cavalry has arrived," Minnie says as the six Ignatius siblings look around at the cave as part of the wall crashes in on Michael.

"Wow! This is intense," Kells declares as Pete and Sophia create a lightfield that holds the cave walls in place.

"Great-grandma?" Willow inquires, seeing Nadia and the others appear.

"Willow," Nadia replies, hugging her.

"We watched you pass. How is it that you're here?" Michael inquires as Nadia nods her head, motioning for them to look toward the ceiling.

"Holy smokes! He is gaining power and fast," Michael exclaims.

"This is why the earthquakes are happening," Willow says.

"Is all this supposed to happen?" Isabella inquires.

"He gained magic back almost all at once. Remember, magic has rules, but in your brother's case, they don't exist," Nadia notes as the ceiling begins to crumble, until Belinda catches and holds it.

"May I suggest getting out of here?" says Belinda.

"Great-grandma, it is good to see you. Belinda, get them out of here. The six of us have this," Isabella directs, pulling her wand, catching the magic, and spinning it, trying to gain control of it.

"Go, Belinda! We will handle this," Willow says as Kelvin and Cedric help Wade and Nadia up onto Belinda's back.

"Where is Luciana?" Kelvin inquires.

Cedric disappears, then returns quickly, holding Luciana.

"Get her onto Belinda's back. Quickly," Kelvin yells, placing a hand on Isabella's shoulder.

"We will be right behind you," she declares, winking.

"Good luck," he replies as Belinda pushes off, soaring into the air where the dragon repeatedly flaps her wings, fighting against the sheer strength of the wind.

"They will never make it out," Sophia declares as she and Kells catch more of the crumbling ceiling of the cave.

"His magic is going to bring this place down. We have to get them out of here," Michael replies, looking concerned.

"Hey, has anyone seen Pete?" Kells asks as the siblings look around.

Suddenly, Pete is there, on a broom, zipping around the cave.

"Belinda, can you follow me?" Pete asks.

"Child, you will get hurt," Belinda replies, still flapping.

"Trust me, Belinda" Pete shouts as he races into the air.

Following him, Belinda soars, dodging falling stones from the cave ceiling.

Liquefacio.
Melt away.

Pete commands, holding his wand up as the falling rock melts and turns into mud.

"Look out below," he yells telepathically at his siblings as he stops, floating in the air as Belinda blows by him.

"Get them to my grandparents. We will be right behind you," Pete directs, diving on his broom into the cave's center where a giant ball of light is floating.

"I'm sure I will regret doing this, but, hey, I need to help him," Pete declares, pulling up on the broom's handle as his five siblings hold hands, forming a circle on the ground. Then, another earthquake knocks them off their feet.

"Ambrose?" Pete yells as a light shoots past him.

"Isabella, what is going on?" Sophia inquires.

"It appears that the magic is protecting him," Isabella says, reaching into her bag and pulling out a broom. Then, she nods at her siblings as she jumps on the broom and soars into the air next to Pete.

The other four follow, zipping around the cave until they are circling the ball of light in the middle of the cave ceiling.

"Ambrose," the six say in unison as light spins around them.

Suddenly, the light extinguishes, and Ambrose falls unconscious from the air.

"Someone grab him!" Isabella commands as Pete zips past his siblings and catches his brother in midair.

"Come on, Bro, wake up," Pete shouts, landing gently and lowering his brother to the ground as Willow lands and runs toward Ambrose, followed by the others.

"Is he okay?" Sophia asks, as Willow checks Ambrose.

"He is breathing, but he is unconscious," she replies, waving her hand as a giant book appears. Kells raises his hand, levitating the book as Isabella spins her hands, making a pedestal appear.

Kells levitates the book onto the pedestal as the area around them begins spinning, and the seven land in a library with a grimoire lying on the floor next to Ambrose.

Reading the cover, Pete picks it up. *The Search through Time*, he says.

"He is in a vision, inside another vision," Sophia remarks, taking the book from Peter, wrapping it in purple cloth, and sliding it into her bag.

"Okay, so we are in a vision. That does not help us or anyone else. How do we get out of here?" Isabella asks as Michael interrupts.

"Look, guys" he says, pointing.

Ambrose is gone.

"Where did he go now?" Isabella asks when they hear someone clearing their throat from one of the archways.

"I am right here," Ambrose declares, leaning against the archway holding his head.

"You're okay!" Willow declares as she is the first to hug him.

"Yes, but I am a little off balance. The magic has not fully settled in," he replies, leaning on her as Pete and Michael rush up to help.

"Get under his right arm, Michael. I have his left," Peter directs.

"What are you two doing?" demands Ambrose.

"Supporting you," Peter and Michael reply as they walk with Ambrose into the main hall of the giant library and help him to sit down.

"Now what?" Kells asks.

Chapter 25
The Return

"If we are still stuck in a vision, then there is something here that we have to find," Willow explains, examining the library.

"This place is empty," Michael says, walking down a row of tables, picking up books, and examining them.

"I do not understand. Normally, we are teleported out when a vision is over," Sophia says.

"But this is not a normal vision, now, is it?" Ambrose inquires as he regards his siblings.

"You're the Noble Elder. Now, zap us out of here," Michael suggests.

"Oh, it will be a long day if you think my powers work that way," Ambrose replies, holding his head.

"What?" Michael asks.

"We want him to keep his magic, not give it up again," Isabella explains.

"What is it about this place that we need to see or find?" Willow asks as she tilts her head and looks down at the floor.

"Hmm," she says, raising her wand and blasting the tables out of the way.

As they flip, they shrink and disappear.

"Guys," Willow calls to the others, examining the mosaic on the floor closely as Ambrose rises slowly to his feet.

"It appears to be a story and not just any story. It is the seven of us and 1-2-3…15, Curpendulums," Ambrose says as he stumbles.

"Wow! Before you fall down, let me help you," Pete declares as Ambrose looks at him suspiciously.

"Drop me, and I will greatly enjoy hexing you into next century," Ambrose jokes as Pete laughs.

"It is nice to see the two of them getting along," Sophia whispers to Willow, who nods in reply.

With Pete's help, Ambrose examines the story in the circle.

"The story of the seven and the Curpendulums. What are we missing?" Ambrose asks.

"Where is that?" Pete inquires.

"It is a field," Ambrose notes as Kells yawns and leans on the counter.

Suddenly, the floor turns, and a new mosaic appears.

"Wow! What just happened?" Ambrose inquires.

"No one move," Pete says as Ambrose examines the circle.

Getting up from where he was leaning, Kells stands, steps away from the counter, and begins to walk over to examine the floor. The image turns back to the original.

"Kells, Pete said not to move," Willow remarks. Isabella levitates a pile of books onto the spot where Kells had been leaning and the floor rotates back.

"It appears that the old guy is Merlin, and the seven of us are fighting him," Pete states as Ambrose looks at him.

"How many books are there?" Ambrose inquires as Sophia, Peter, and Willow count.

"There are only fourteen floating," they reply.

"Exactly, but there are fifteen if you count the one I am holding in the image with the watch floating above it," Ambrose exclaims.

"Do we know which one it is?" Kells inquires.

"No! We can't make out the titles on any of the books," Sophia responds.

"But we can tell the books apart. Look at the cover on the one pointed towards us," Willow says.

"*Liber Dryadalum Sequere Magicae* has an elf holding a star on it," Isabella remarks.

"Okay, we need to figure out which Curpendulum is which. I want to know about the book I am holding," Ambrose declares.

Together, they take the time they need to identify the different books. Ambrose and the other five stand waiting patiently for Willow to review the parchment on which she has recorded the Curpendulums.

"It is the *Liber Divine* (*The Grimoire of the Divine*) that Ambrose is holding," Willow declares.

"How do you know?" Sophia asks, confused.

"Easy, it has a figure holding a watch on it," Willow explains.

"Do we know are there any other Curpendulums involving time?" Kells inquires.

"Only the *Liber Divine* (*The Grimoire of the Divine*)," Ambrose says.

"The question is, is that the liber that great-great-grandma is supposed to have?" Sophia asks as Ambrose pauses, thinking.

"You know, I believe you're right sis," Ambrose says after a moment.

Then the group hears a crash. They retrieve their wands as they spread out around the library.

Checking carefully, six of them declare the area clear when an elfish arrow whizzes past Willow and sticks into the table just inches from Ambrose.

"Clear? I think not! We have company," Ambrose declares, snapping his arms down. His elfish blades appear as a cloaked figure attacks him. Ambrose spins his arm back, guarding himself as a sword strikes his arm blade.

As Ambrose engages the figure, arrows rain down over the library as Willow appears behind her brother, creating a shield.

"Careful, do not get hit," Ambrose warns, spinning his hands in front of himself as his blades begin to glow. Looking around, Peter taps his staff as a bow and arrow appear, and he suddenly disappears.

"Kells, Michael, Sophia, if any of you get a shot, take it," Isabella orders.

"Some vision," Michael remarks, ducking under a table as the arrows stop raining down on them, and a figure falls from the rafters, screaming as they hit the ground with a thud. Multiple snaps are heard as the figure engaging Ambrose stops and disappears, reappearing next to the dead figure. As the figure begins to raise its wand, they are stopped by an arrow pressed into the back of their head.

"If I release the arrow this close, the sheer speed and impact would be more fatal than a bullet," Peter remarks calmly as the figure raises their hands and Willow grabs their wand, holding it, and kicking the bow away from the dead figure. Kells kneels down and flips the figure over.

"She is an elf."

"The same one from my dream. The one with the poison arrows," Ambrose declares, approaching the other figure, grabbing their hood, and lowering it.

"You're an elf, too," Isabella remarks.

"Who are you?" Willow asks.

"A faction of the elves will never recognize any of you as the true rulers," the elf replies, spitting towards Willow as Ambrose backhands the elf with a closed fist.

"Spit at my sister again, and you will be like your friend, dead on the ground," Ambrose threatens as the elf wipes his nose and starts laughing.

"You think you can stop Merlin or My Lady Raven?" the elf sneers as Ambrose grabs him by his forehead, dropping him to his knees. Astonished the other six siblings look at each other, backing up as Ambrose's eyes turn black.

"Now, where are Raven and Merlin?" Ambrose demands in a deep tone, tightening his hold on the elf.

Grimacing, the elf replies, "Merlin is marching on the university to reach the bunker. Master says that the weapons there will be enough to do away with everyone. My mistress is seeking another Curpendulum."

"Which Curpendulum?" Ambrose barks.

"Like I would ever tell you that," the elf declares, spitting at Ambrose.

Effligo.
Knock Out.

"Ambrose, are you crazy? Eff… is a knock-out spell! Seriously?" Isabella exclaims, kneeling and checking to see if their guest is still breathing.

"Wow! Why did you knock him out?" Michael inquires.

"I know none of you will understand what I do," Ambrose replies, annoyed.

"Brother, look at me. They may not understand, but I will. And I will translate for them if need be," Willow declares, placing her hand on his face.

When he closes his eyes, she understands his intent for knocking out the elf.

"Willow?" Isabella asks.

Willow nods and opens her eyes. "Ambrose knocked him out in order to be able to enter the mind of the elf," Willow explains.

"Ambrose, need I remind you? An elf's mind is next to impossible to enter. Look at the seven of us," Kells remarks.

"Correct, Brother, but not for three particular elves," Willow explains regarding her two sisters.

"Why would you want to enter his mind?" Peter asks.

"Because, if we can draw Merlin away from the bunker, we can buy our family time to protect the university," Ambrose declares, tripping over his words.

"Draw him away?" Michael asks.

"Michael, um, how do I say it. If I can enter the elf's mind, I can locate the whereabouts of the Curpendulums, thereby drawing Merlin to me."

"You do realize that if you are in the elf's mind, and our sisters are out of commission because they have to help you enter, that leaves only Michael, Kells, and me to fight Merlin."

"Pete…" Ambrose begins.

The others freeze, waiting to see what is about to happen.

"You are one of the wisest amongst the elves. You also refuse to use the full potential of your magic. I guess all of us have been guarded with our magic, but remember, your magic can stop Merlin in his tracks. I count on my three older brothers to keep our sisters and me safe."

"Wait! You trust us?" Michael asks.

"I have always trusted my older siblings. I have looked up to all of you, and I apologize that my magic has caused you to be afraid of me. We all have our moments but, then again, what siblings do not. We are on this journey together. I cannot do this alone. We must learn to trust each other," Ambrose declares.

Michael, Kells, and Peter regard Isabella as Willow explains, "Sophia, Izzy, and myself, once we connect Ambrose to the elf's mind, will be out of commission. So, we are all relying on you three to keep us safe."

"We will do what we need to do," Kells comments as a giant hammer appears. Ambrose spins his arm blades down out of his sleeves and hands them to Pete.

"Keep them safe, and please do not scratch them," Ambrose directs, stepping back and spinning his hands, creating a field around him and his three sisters.

"Brothers, you heard our siblings. We have our responsibilities. Kells, take the door. You are the first line of defense. Michael, take the balcony. You are our eyes. I will work to protect the field."

"Willow? Assessment?"

"Ambrose, his mind is complex. It is going to take some work on our part."

"Great! That means more of a challenge."

"Ambrose as your eldest sister, I have to advise strongly against this."

"Isabella, your concerns are noted, but I need to know what he knows about those Curpendulums and where Raven is headed."

"Understood. But, at the sign of trouble, I will give the order for Willow and Sophia to break the connection in order to protect you," Isabella explains.

Ambrose nods as the three sisters spin their hands, touching palm to palm as Isabella touches Ambrose's hand and Willow kneels to touch the elf's forehead with her fingers.

❧

"Hello?"

Stopping and listening, Ambrose stands in the pitch-black, waiting quietly for something to happen. Then, a single ball of light appears. Walking toward it, Ambrose raises his hand as he steps into the vision. Looking around, Ambrose stops to listen again.

"My Lady Raven, how do you plan to find the Curpendulum?" the elf asks.

"General, have you forgotten? My Lady Morgana hunted for the whereabouts of the *Liber Caligo* (*The Grimoire of Dark*) for years. But, by putting the pieces of the puzzle together, I have finally figured out its whereabouts," Raven declares, smiling and running her long, pointed nail down the parchment.

"What about Merlin?" the general asks.

"He will handle those nasty Arcane. When he reaches the bunker and gets the *Liber Lux* (*The Grimoire of Light*), all will bow to him," Raven responds.

"My Lady, what do you wish for my sister and me?" the elf general asks.

"I have a special assignment for you two. Your magic has proven interesting time and time again. Enter the dream state and stop the seven brats, by any means necessary. Then, join me at the gates of Avalon. The Ladies of Avalon will give me the *Liber Caligo* (*The Grimoire of Dark*), or I will rain fire upon Avalon, tearing it apart," Raven declares, smiling as the image spins, and Ambrose lands back in the dark space, where only the orb is glowing.

"Hello," a young voice says again as a child transforms into the elf and attacks Ambrose.

❧

Outside the field of protection, the library begins to darken. A scream is heard as multiple dark creatures phase through the walls and floor. Kells catches one dark creature with the edge of his hammer and slams it into the ground.

"Pete, we have company," Michael yells, spinning his wand and blasting the darkness with light. Placing his hand on the field, Pete's eyes begin to glow as magic spins around the field, strengthening it.

"Isabella, Sophia, Willow, we have company," he warns them telepathically as he spins his wand and catches a blast of dark magic that slams him into the field. Jumping over the balcony, Michael puffs out his cloak as he leaps over the banister, soaring down three floors and landing on the main floor and bolting for the field as the darkness flies toward the ceiling, spinning, and diving on the field.

The three brothers regard one another as the darkness continues to fly toward them until, suddenly, it stops and flies up into the air screaming as Merlin appears.

"Must you bratty children always interrupt what I am doing?" Merlin yells, throwing magic at the three.

"Oh, so now we have your attention," Michael remarks as the darkness flies around the room.

"Pete, this place is getting dark," Kells says as the three hear Merlin laughing.

The darkness lands and starts taking form.

"General, kill them."

Marching towards the field, the area grows even darker with each step that the dark creatures take. Then, the darkness screams as light explodes around them. The field lowers and Willow releases an arrow that flies into one of the dark creatures. As the arrow soars through the air, multiple dark creatures explode. Merlin projected magic toward Michael, but it stops and disappears. Confused, Merlin examines his wand as multiple dark creatures smash into the air and the walls as Ambrose emerges, his eyes glowing white.

"Noble Elder," Merlin sneers with disgust.

"That's Noel to you, Merlin," Noel greets him as he catches multiple blasts of dark magic from Merlin.

"How is it that you are always in the way?"

"Because, Merlin, you're annoying. You lack any plan, and you're just plain grumpy," Noel states as multiple charging dark creatures explode around him. The six stand behind Noel as he flies into the air, magic flying around him.

"General, handle them. I have other things to do," Merlin commands as he begins to fade.

The general pulls his sword as Merlin summons fire around himself, and the darkness begins to attack the six until Noel appears in front of Merlin, lifting him by his throat into the air.

"Willow?" Noel yells

When she appears next to him, he regards her thoughtfully.

"Noel, no! But I do understand," she replies, touching his hand as he hands her a bag.

"You know what to do," he says, disappearing with Merlin.

Reaching into the bag, Willow retrieves an orb, which she throws into the air and a tornado touches down, sucking all the darkness into it as the six siblings scramble toward each other.

"We have to help him," Sophia declares, holding up her arm as papers fly into the tornado.

"No, he will be fine. We have to get to everyone else. We know where the Curpendulum that Merlin and Raven are after is. Noel has his responsibility, and we have ours. We must stop the darkness from advancing. So, hold on," Willow warns, holding up a second orb that flashes, and they all disappear.

❧

Hissing and screaming, the darkness attacks the field of light that is protecting the university. Strike after strike, the field of magic regenerates after each blow. Members of the Dark Council march through the rows of dark creatures as arrows fly through the field, striking down the darkness.

"Hold this line! We cannot let them advance!" Ari yells, lowering his sword as the elf archers release a second wave of arrows, followed immediately by a third, fourth, and fifth wave of arrows.

Looking up, Ari notices that the clouds in the night sky are turning various colors. He raises his wand, sending a spark into the air, drawing everyone's attention to him. Likewise, the dark creatures look, observing the sky changing colors as well. Quickly, the dark creatures turn and start to lower their weapons as the sky opens and a light column explodes, hitting the top of a hill in the distance.

Hissing, the darkness begins running toward the column of light as multiple arrows fly out of the column and vines explode from the ground. Water sprays, striking multiple rows of the darkness and as the light column lifts, there stand six of the Ignatius 7, decked out in armor and peering down the hill at the darkness.

"Do they think they can take us?" Pete asks, holding up his wand.

"How do we do this?" Isabella inquires.

"Together," the other five answer in unison as they summon magic around themselves and strike the dark creatures. The six move down the hill in a synchronized attack. As they advance, horns sound and rows of elf guards charge through the lightfield, engaging the darkness. Emerging through the lightfield, Belinda flaps her wings, bellowing fire down on the darkness as Rose jumps from her back, spinning her wand and blasting multiple creatures backward. When one of the Dark Council members tries to attack her, they all freeze.

Everyone looks around, noticing the darkness standing frozen until, suddenly, they all fly in different directions toward the outer edges of the giant sports field as a cloaked figure materializes. After quickly examining the area, the figure spins its hands, levitating the darkness off their feet. Everything comes to a halt when the figure walks across the field. They raise their arms as time unfreezes, and, in the figure's hand, a staff appears, which they spin, striking multiple dark creatures. The darkness begins to charge the figure, snarling and hissing with weapons in hand, but as the figure spins their staff again, multiple rows of the attackers are taken out. With each strike of the staff, light explodes and spins, dissolving many of the dark shadows on the spot.

The figure throws their staff into the air as they flip over backward into an aerial spin, grabbing the staff. Light flies from the star at its tip as the bright stone is activated. Streams of magic fly around the field, striking the darkness repeatedly as the weapons of the darkness dissolve.

One dark creature charges the figure, but the figure catches the blade between their hands as it starts to glow.

Liquefacio.
Melt away.

The blade melts as the dark creature shuffles backward, trying to escape the figure. Then, the creature flies backward into the air, choking as the figure raises their other hand, slams their hands together, and then, separating them, tears the darkness apart.

Observing what is happening, the remaining darkness bolts toward the figure who raises their hand, the stone in their ring glowing and flashing bright light. The advancing dark creatures hiss and fly into the air. Merging, they create a column of darkness. The cloaked figure holds up a star as it merges with the tip of their staff. He, then, throws back his hood, reaches up, undoes the clasp on his long coat and lets the wind grab it, pulling it off his back and revealing his prominent elvish features. His ears are more prominent, his hair is short and spiked, and he has donned armor with long white robes flowing underneath. It is Noel.

Noel spins his staff, and a crown appears on his head as he sweeps multiple dark creatures off their feet, his staff resting behind him as he lands on one knee, raising his hand and launching his attackers into the air.

Placing his palm on the ground, the field bursts into flames, revealing a giant pentagram.

Magia Terrenum, Prodeunt. Produc Ignem.
Magic of Earth, come forth. Bring forth fire.

Looking up, Noel's eyes glow silver as magic spins around him. As the darkness advances toward him, each section of the pentagram lights and the darkness explodes or dissolves.

Standing again, Noel catches multiple streams of black magic flying toward him as he holds his staff in front of him, spinning it and pulling the dark generals off their feet. When the pentagram is fully lit and begins glowing, Noel slams his hands together. Lightfields explode from the various lines drawn into the grass and the darkness, becoming confused, runs into these fields. Spinning his hands, the lightfield walls move in on the darkness. The walls move, rotating and forming a giant cube that contains and imprisons the darkness. When Noel snaps his fingers, the box grows bright, flashes, and the darkness is gone.

From inside the field of protection, multiple Arcane watch as Noel fights the darkness alone.

"Truly remarkable. None of us have ever seen magic like this," remarks one of the elfish guards as Ari and Theo glance at one another. A pop sounds over the space as Rusty appears, raising his hand as magic allows him to see what is going on. He smiles at the sight of Noel and his power.

Running down the field, Noel slides on the ground, striking down multiple dark creatures. He catches the blade of one of his attackers, flips them into the air, and slams them into the ground face-first, knocking his attacker out before it explodes. Reaching for his wrist, Noel clicks the dial of his watch, and a swarm of nano-bots take off down the field, striking multiple dark creatures in the process. Each explodes when it is struck.

"Sir, more darkness is advancing," one of the guards declares as Rusty raises his hand, motioning for everyone to remain where they are.

Two of the Dark Council members appear, engaging Noel in battle. When they raise their wands, Noel taps his staff on the ground, and the star lights, blinding them and causing them to back up and drop their wands.

Screams are heard echoing around the field as Noel pulls down with his hand and magic swirls around him, lifting the dark creatures off their feet. Then, he releases the magic, causing the darkness to drop to the ground. The shear impact of the fall causes the darkness to dissolve.

"What is happening?" one of the elf guards asks as the group witnesses the dissolving darkness transforming back into Mundane and Arcane.

"We have to help them," Theo orders as the guards run through the barriers, grab the people, helping them up, and running back toward the barrier as the darkness charges after them.

Stopping midway down the field, magic streams fly around the charging darkness as Noel raises his hand and starts pulling them back as if pulling on a rope. A spearhead catches Noel's gauntlet as he raises his free hand, blowing a dark creature backward with a fireball. The darkness continues advancing but Noel alone can stop them.

Running across the field, a significantly large group of dark creatures appears, wave after wave appearing behind them, moving rapidly down the field toward Noel. Looking to his right, then to his left, Noel kneels, placing his fingertips on the ground and speaking,

Expergiscimini Spirituum.
Awaken the Spirits.

As the last part of the spell leaves Noel's mouth, magic explodes from the earth, spinning. Vines wrap around dark creatures as several rows are pulled into the earth through quicksand. The hands of spirits appear rising out of the earth of the field, pulling the darkness down and slamming them face-first into the ground.

Looking up, Noel's eyes glow white as a column of light explodes around him, spinning. Streams of white magic fly around the field, striking down the darkness.

When the last dark creature has disappeared, Noel looks around, then raises his hand, teleporting anyone remaining in the area back into the protection of the field.

"Uncles, please secure the field. That was only the first wave. Merlin will be sending more," Noel declares, walking through the group until he reaches his father. Rusty places a hand on Noel's shoulder and then hugs him.

"Hello, Noel," Rusty says, smiling as everyone around them bow. Rose and Sophia are the first to reach him, hugging him.

Chapter 26
The Curpendulum

"My dear grandson," Rose says, hugging him, then backing up, and holding him at arm's length, looking at him.

"Hi, Grandma," he replies, smiling.

"That was awesome, Brother," Sophia says as Pete pats him on the back.

"Merlin will be ramping up his second wave. All of you need to work together to hold him off. He is after the bunker. I need to get to Avalon to help them stop Raven," Noel explains.

"We are going with you," Pete declares as the other five siblings nod, agreeing.

"No, I need you guys here. The six of you can help hold Merlin and his guards off."

"Noel, you cannot fight Raven alone," Pete replies.

"Brother, I am not alone. I am far from ever being alone, not with the magic I wield," Noel responds, walking away from the group toward the opening.

"Noel," Rose says, bowing.

Noel bows his head in response, raising his hands as lightning strikes down around him, and he disappears.

"Well, what are you six doing standing around? You heard your brother," Rose retorts.

"Yes, Grandma," the six reply in unison as Dalton appears.

"You guys are here. Where is Noel?"

"Raven is attacking Avalon. He went to stop her," Willow responds.

"Alone?"

"Yes. Why?"

"No, no, no! That is how the timeline altered last time. His fighting alone causes chaos and tears time apart. Go after him and help him," Dalton declares, frantically raising his hands to open a portal, but the vortex spins and goes out.

"Is that supposed to happen?" Michael asks.

"That is not good," Pete remarks.

"Grandma, what should we do?"

Rose whistles three times, and a roar is heard as Belinda lands. Mr. Cee jumps down from her back and runs toward Willow.

"You rang, Lady Rose?"

"Yes, Belinda. The six and Lord Yule need a lift to Avalon."

"Hop on and hold on. We will need to ride with the winds. My Lords and Ladies Ignatius, someone buckle that dear sweet cat into a bag. I want no mishaps like last time," Belinda remarks, lowering down as the six climb onto her back, followed by Lord Yule. Belinda pushes off and soars straight into the air. Autumn, Drago, and several other dragons fly next to Belinda.

The portal spins open as Noel steps out at the edge of the beach.

Avalon. Hmm. It is quiet. A little too quiet for my liking, Noel thinks, raising his staff as three stars shoot from the end of it into the air as a white stallion gallops up.

"Lampos," Noel bows as the horse lowers its head, bowing in return.

"We need to get to Avalon and make haste."

The stallion takes off at a gallop as Noel observes magic flying down the beach as he rides. Lampos runs through the streams of magic and Noel runs his hands through it. In the distance, he can see the darkness striking a field of vines and water that is protecting Avalon.

"Haya! Faster! Come on. Faster, Lampos."

The stallion picks up speed as Noel raises his staff and stars fly around the tip as he throws them at the magical field in the distance. As the stars reach the field, they merge with it, strengthening the field as they begin to glow purple. Riding into the field, Lampos phases through as Noel kicks the stallion's side. Lampos gallops up the winding walkway toward the main entrance where the two blow through the gates.

"My ladies. I am here to help," Noel calls as the magical field begins to crumble and the darkness dives into the palace courtyard. Looking up, Noel raises his hand in which he holds an orb. It flashes and begins to glow as the darkness hits a lightfield and flies back up into the air, avoiding the field.

"Lord Noel. There are too many for you to hold back by yourself," Nimuway remarks, running across the courtyard, spinning her hands, and launching multiple dark creatures away from the walkway of the Palace of Avalon.

"They are after the Curpendulum, My Lady," Noel explains, flipping over several of the creatures as he runs to grab the general by the collar, flipping him, and slamming him into the ground.

"Sisters, you must protect the holding," Nimuway orders as she and Noel turn back-to-back.

"How do we do this?" Nimuway inquires.

"With all the magic we can summon," Noel replies as the darkness flies into the air, creating a dark cyclone spinning above them.

As they dive on the two, the center of the cyclone lights up and explodes. Light engulfs the column as Noel's eyes turn white.

"Get out of here," Noel directs as he begins glowing.

"Guys, what is that?" Sophia points from Belinda's back as they see a glowing light in the distance.

"It looks like Noel is going light," Lord Yule remarks as Mr. Cee pokes his head out of Willow's bag, hissing as he climbs out.

"Mr. Cee, no!" Willow cries, trying to grab him as the cat runs down Belinda's neck to her head and sits watching.

"Hold on," Belinda says, diving towards the palace. Pawing at the air, Mr. Cee's eyes begin to glow green as the cat dives from Belinda's head and transforms.

Landing inches from Noel, Mr. Cee is now the size of a panther as he attacks the darkness.

As Belinda soars into the courtyard, the six pull out their wands and magic flies, throwing the darkness back.

Landing, Belinda bellows fire as she swings her tail, taking out multiple advancing dark creatures. The six jump from her back, engaging the darkness in battle.

Looking around, Noel kneels, placing his fingertips on the ground. When he looks up, his eyes are glowing black.

Expergiscimini Spirituum.
Awaken the Spirits.

Magic flies from the ground spinning, around him. Screams echo around the palace as spirits appear, striking the darkness and destroying them.

"Is he doing what I think he is doing?" Pete inquires, catching dark magic and redirecting it.

"Yes, Pete. It is necro magic," Lord Yule replies as he walks through a group of twelve dark creatures, frozen and floating in the air. Then, when he reaches the opposite side, he unfreezes them, causing them to crash into each other.

Rising, Noel's eyes continue to glow black as he walks around, raising his hand and throwing the darkness back as they dissolve. Then, approaching one of the dark generals, Noel raises them off the ground.

"Where is Raven?"

"Not here," the general laughs as Noel slams him into the ground, then picks him back up.

"I will ask you again. Where is Raven?"

Choking, the general answers. "Looking for the Curpendulum."

Noel raises his wand in his other hand, and as he releases the general, the general's spirit leaves his body. Turning, Noel spins his hands and he and Dalton arrive at the holding.

"The door is sealed," Lord Yule notes.

"Of course, it is," Lady Dawn replies, approaching with the other Sisters of Avalon, as the torches in the hallway start going out, one by one.

Noel's eyes narrow as he stops, closes his eyes, takes a deep breath, and grabs the air. When he opens his eyes, Raven appears, choking.

Magic flies down the hallway, hitting Noel as he backs up, dropping Raven as she summons a sword. He catches the blade with his gauntlet, grabs the sword, and the two struggle for it until Raven suddenly freezes.

"I really do not have time for you," Noel says as he grabs the sword, disarming her as Lord Yule fights the other advancing dark creatures in the hallway. The two work together to freeze everyone in the hallway until Noel raises his hand, opens a portal, and, pointing his wand, all of the dark creatures and Raven are sucked from the hallway into the portal, which then disappears.

"That was a little too easy for my liking," Lord Yule remarks as a member of the Dark Council appears behind him, placing his wand to his throat.

"Now, Noel, unless you want him babbling for the rest of his life, I would advise opening the vault and giving me the Curpendulum," the Dark Council member demands as Noel tilts his head, the room darkens, and a scream is heard. When the lights in the hallway turn on again, the Dark Council member is laying on the floor, sucking their thumb, and rocking back and forth.

"I hate when they cross me," Noel remarks as Lord Yule hugs him.

"Okay, I stand corrected. It is not going to be as easy as I thought," he says, looking at Noel.

As the two check out their surroundings, Nimuway appears.

"Open the door," she orders as the Ladies of Avalon raise their hands. They begin to glow and the locks on the door pop open. The door swings inward, revealing a vault holding various artifacts.

"I assume these are the artifacts Merlin never found?" Noel inquires, walking through the door as Lord Yule follows.

"Yes, while your ancestor, Merlin, was hellbent on world domination, some of us did our job and hid these away from him," Nimuway replies as Lord Yule stands examining a set of chimes that are hanging from the ceiling while Noel looks around.

Rummaging through the shelf, Nimuway pulls out a box and hands it to Noel.

"I believe it is time to entrust this with you for safe keeping," Nimuway says as Noel balances the box and opens it. Pulling back the white cloth, Noel reveals a Curpendulum.

"*The Liber Caligo* (*The Grimoire of Dark*)," Noel says, pulling the book from the box and holding it in his hand. The grimoire levitates into the air as light appears to encircle it.

"What is that?" Lord Yule asks.

"My way of reading the entire book quickly," Noel notes, smiling.

"Wait! What? You read the entire Curpendulum?" Nimuway inquires.

"I have, yes," Noel responds as the three hear an explosion.

"That is our cue to return to the courtyard and help them," Lord Yule says as the three disappear.

ȣ

Running across the courtyard, Sophia slides across the walkway into the rain, double blades in hand, slashing the calves of the dark creatures.

"I hate these things!" Pete shouts through gritted teeth, spinning his wand and hitting the dark creatures with light.

"You hate them? We all hate them, Brother," Isabella replies, striking a dark creature with her sword as she throws a dagger into another one.

Dark creatures continue to crawl over the walls in large numbers when a watch appears, floating in the air. The hands spin, causing the darkness to march backward as Lord Yule emerges through the wall, spinning his hands as an energy orb floats between them.

"Guys, it looks like help has arrived," Michael states, smiling as dark creatures fly backward over the wall. As Lord Yule continues to walk across the stone courtyard, holding the orb, the dark creatures stop, freezing in place.

One of the Dark Council members appears, laughing and casting magic against Lord Yule, who blocks it. Strike after strike of dark magic fly toward Lord Yule until a pentagram appears around the council member, turns blood red, and the ground opens under him. Screams ring throughout the courtyard as the dark creatures perched high on the palace walls hiss and hands reach out of the ground toward the Dark Council member.

"Get away from me," he shouts, kicking the hands that are reaching for him. He raises his wand as the dark creatures howl, diving down into the courtyard.

"Ah, Lord Yule, what are we doing?" Pete asks as he and his siblings turn back-to-back with wands and weapons ready as the pentagram begins glowing.

"Is that supposed to be glowing?" Willow asks as dark magic flies around the courtyard and *The Liber Caligo* appears, floating in the air. Everyone stops and watches the Curpendulum floating. Then, the Dark Council member raises his wand, summoning the Curpendulum toward himself. But the magic backfires, throwing him to the ground, the hands reaching for him again.

Suddenly, four demons jump from the pentagram, hissing at Lord Yule and the six Ignatius siblings. Then, they all hear Noel's voice echoing over the space.

Per Viam Tenebrarum Prodeunt Dominos
Tuos ad Infernum Quod Venerunt.
Per Viam Tenebrarum Prodeunt Dominos
Tuos ad Infernum Quod Venerunt.
Per Viam Tenebrarum Prodeunt Dominos
Tuos ad Infernum Quod Venerunt.

Through the way of darkness come forth. Take your masters back to the hell from which they came.

Magic explodes from the pentagram, grabbing the dark creatures and pulling them into an open, glowing, red pit. The Dark Council member rises to his feet as the four demons grab him and pull him into the pit.

Screams echo around the courtyard as magic explodes out of the pit, reaching for the sky.

Within seconds, three dark sage dragons are being pulled toward the pit. When Noel appears, his eyes are solid black. He tilts his head, looking at the pit. Then, he raises his hand, and a light appears around the pentagram, securing it.

Per Virtutem Sigilli, Tenebrosi Lacum Hoc.
Per Virtutem Sigilli, Tenebrosi Lacum Hoc.
Per Virtutem Sigilli, Tenebrosi Lacum Hoc.

By the power of dark, seal this pit.

After the words are spoken, the pit explodes with white light and seals. The courtyard, the palace, everything, falls silent as the six Ignatius siblings regard one another. Willow carefully walks past the floating Curpendulum, pulls her cloak and places it over Noel's shoulders.

Weak, Noel wobbles as he gets up and holds up his wand.

"Noel?" Willow says, placing her hand on his arm.

"Brother, can you hear us?" Peter asks as Noel swings at him as the others back up.

"Pete, his eyes are still black," Michael exclaims, the others carefully approaching him.

Lord Yule walks up and kisses Noel, bringing him back to reality.

"Wow," Noel says, falling into Dalton's arms as Pete and Michael help to hold the two of them up.

"Are you okay?" Dalton asks, smiling as Noel nods, holding his head.

"That type of magic will take time to wear off, Hun. That is why those Curpendulums are never used," Dalton says as Noel raises his hand, and *The Liber Caligo* hits the ground, falling into a puddle of water.

Quickly, Willow runs over, levitates the book up off the ground as Isabella wraps a cloth around it. Nimuway causes the box that normally contains it to appear. Once the Curpendulum is safely inside the box, Nimuway seals the lid with the help of Michael and Pete.

"Please make sure that, once he is to full power, that box is hidden," Nimuway remarks as Willow waves her hand over the box, shrinking it, and carefully sliding it into her bag.

Upon Willow securing the box, time begins to freeze.

"Dalton? What are you doing?" Noel asks.

"It is not me," he replies as the others look around.

"If time is freezing, Merlin must have found a Curpendulum," Nimuway remarks.

"The bunker!" the siblings all say aloud.

A pop is heard, and Noel disappears.

"I hate it when he does that," Dalton declares as he raises his hand, stopping the magic that is freezing time.

"What do we do now?" Kells asks as Lord Yule casts a circle of magic around himself.

Raising his hands, he pushes the edge out.

"Quickly, get inside the circle," Dalton directs as the magical circle glows and the magic freezing time strikes an invisible field. The six siblings and Nimuway stand behind Dalton inside the circle, looking around.

"This is not good, not good at all," Isabella says.

"How do we stop this?" Pete inquires.

"I will stay here and stop magic from freezing completely. First, you will need to find your brother and help him stop Merlin," Dalton says, raising his other hand and holding magic in place.

"We do not even know where to look," Michael grumbles as Nimuway whistles. Dalton throws his arms out, expanding the circle, as Belinda touches down with Autumn.

"Lady Belinda, please get them out of here. You are the only one who can fly against the streams of time magic," Dalton declares, spinning his hands, catching the flying streams of magic, and stopping time from freezing any further.

"Lord Yule, my daughter has trained for this moment. I swore, long ago, when this moment came, I would protect you and keep time balanced," Belinda replies, bowing.

"You heard the Lady Belinda. Quickly, you six get onto Autumn's back," Nimuway directs, shooing them along.

"We cannot leave you," Willow says as she regards Nimuway.

"I will be fine. My place is here. Besides, it is my sworn duty to protect Avalon and the Lord Yule. You six must help your brother," Nimuway explains, hugging Willow as Michael extends his hand to his sister. Turning, Willow grabs Michael's hand as he pulls her up onto Autumn's back.

"Mr. Cee, you know what to do," Isabella directs the cat, still the size of a panther, as he growls and disappears.

"Autumn, my dear child, hear me. You have trained for this. The Noble Elder needs you now. You must succeed. Fly against the winds, soar through the magic, and push with all of your strength against the power of the streams of magic," her mother instructs, wrapping her neck around Autumn and giving her a big dragon hug.

"Autumn, when I open the circle, push straight up and fly as fast as possible," Lord Yule directs as Autumn nods.

"Hold on, Ignatiuses! This may get bumpy," Autumn declares, raising her long neck into the air, getting ready to shove off as Willow puts on her helmet. Then, she motions and puts her head down as two different size lenses lower over her eyes.

"Now," Lord Yule yells, dropping his hands as Belinda wraps her tail around him, breathing fire as Nimuway spins her hands, creating a lightfield as Autumn launches straight into the air, flying against the wind.

Rapidly soaring into the air, the wind pushes against Autumn as she roars.

"Michael? Help her!" Willow shouts as Michael reaches down and places his hand on Autumn's neck.

Her eyes turn green and magic spins around her.

Isabella spins her wand, and a portal opens in the distance. Roaring again, Autumn folds her wings to her sides and shoots through the portal.

Back at the university, darkness strikes the field as screams echo around the area. Elves engage the darkness as Rose spins her wand, flinging the darkness back.

"Where is Matthew?" she asks, looking at Ethan.

"We have lost contact with him," Ethan replies.

"We have trouble," Sebastian says, pointing as a magic portal opens in the air and falls from the sky, spinning around the darkness and the elves, freezing them.

"Merlin found a Curpendulum," Rose states, regarding Ethan and Sebastian with concern as multiple Arcane who are running toward them, freeze like statues. Raising her hand, Rose casts a circle similar to the one Lord Yule cast in Avalon. As the magic of the circle expands, Rose's eyes glow white.

"Get behind me," Rose yells as she pushes out the circle's perimeter.

"A time circle," Sebastian declares as he helps multiple elves into the circle.

"Sis, is there any way to cast the circle larger?" Ethan asks, grabbing her shoulder as both of their eyes turn white and Rose pushes the circle further out. Zander and Oliver arrive, carrying Olivia, Mr. Bruin, and multiple elves. As everyone looks around, Mr. Bruin drops an orb, and Alviss and Bardagul appear.

Chapter 27
The Timekeeper

Holding her hands still, Rose works to steady the magic of the invisible barrier, protecting them, as stream after stream strike it.

"I think I might need to help you with that," Oliver remarks, kissing Olivia and grabbing Rose's shoulder, his eyes glowing as the three hold the magic at bay. Then, a roar explodes overhead as a portal opens in the sky and Autumn blows by with green streams of magic spinning in a helix around her.

"That's Autumn with the grandkids," Zander says as Rose looks over at him, her eyes still glowing.

❧

"Bardagul, me son," Alviss says.

"Yes, Pa."

"Quickly, me lad," Alviss motions, pulling a pocket watch, the hands of which are spinning out of control. He hands the watch to Bardagul.

"Pa, this is the pocket watch of time motion."

"Aye! You take it. Get it to the clock tower. You must install it to stop time. Now, go me son," Alviss says, hugging his son as lightning strikes in front of him, and Gorodra and Luciana step out.

"Quickly, Brother," Gorodra says, holding out her hands.

"Me daughter, protect your brother. Make sure he gets that watch to the tower," Alviss instructs as time streams strike the barrier that Rose, Ethan, and Oliver are holding in place. Zander regards Luciana, who reaches down as Gorodra and Bardagul grab her hands tightly. The area around them spins and, in a mere second, Luciana, Gorodra, and Bardagul land on the floor high up in the clock tower.

"Brother, look at me," Gorodra says as Luciana kneels.

"Yes, Gorodra," he replies, a tear running down his face.

"Master Bardagul, why do you cry?" Luciana inquires, smiling and wiping the tear.

"We are all afraid, my Brother, but moments like this make us stronger," Gorodra explains, as a sinister laugh echoes through the tower, sending chills down their spines.

"Master Bardagul, get going and do not stop, whatever happens," Luciana directs, spinning her hands as her arm blades appear and she blocks the blade of a dark general. Luciana snaps her fingers causing the dark general to explode. Then, she notices Merlin leaning against a pole, clapping his hands. Bardagul takes off running, sliding under the legs of several of the advancing dark creatures as he bolts up the staircase to the clock tower.

"Good evening, Luciana. Must you always be in the way like your pesky fathers?" Merlin inquires with disgust, raising his hand as his eyes turn black and magic flies around his hand.

"Well, Gorodra. Look! It is old and cranky himself," Luciana smiles.

"Give me the watch," Merlin demands, holding out his hand.

"No! We would rather not," Luciana replies as she and Merlin circle one another.

"I will not ask again, elf! The watch, if you please," Merlin snaps.

"Aye, he is snapping," Gorodra remarks as she watches Luciana.

Merlin raises his hand and dark creatures appear, lining the staircase.

"Very well, my pretty creatures. Kill the boy and bring me that watch," Merlin laughs as he casts streams of black magic at Luciana. Catching every blast of black magic, Luciana redirects them to the floor or throws them into the walls. Furious, Merlin points his wand at the rafters above Bardagul's head, spins his hands, and the beams explode, and hurl down toward him. Luciana quickly raises her hands, levitating the falling debris.

"Gorodra, protect your brother. Go! I will handle Merlin," Luciana declares, glaring at Merlin as Gorodra pulls out her sword and spins it, holding the blade to the underside of her arm and running up the stairs, striking the dark creatures as she goes.

"Handle me, child? Handle me?" Merlin laughs as he blasts the floor, stomping down, and launching pieces of wood in the air at Luciana.

As the wood dissolves, *The Liber Lux* (*The Grimoire of Light*) appears.

"*The Liber Lux!* How did he get it?" Luciana wonders aloud. Then, raising her hand, the book flies into the middle of the room as she and Merlin engage in a magical tug of war over the book. Their magic collides with other items in the space and the book levitates into the air swinging back and forth between them.

Various orbs fly around the room, zipping around until one of the orbs begins to glow. Multiple orbs move out of the way as Noel pushes his way through them, walking toward the one that is glowing.

"Luciana," he calls, holding up his hand and capturing the orb, examining it carefully while turning it over in his hand.

You, my dear daughter, should not have to undertake this battle alone. Spinning his hands, Noel bowls the orb in front of him and the tower appears around him as he watches what is occurring. Everyone is suspended, frozen as he circles Merlin. as he walks across the floor, he tilts his head to one side to look at *The Liber Lux* (*The Grimoire of Light*).

"This is not a play toy," Noel remarks aloud, picking up the book and replacing it with a scroll. Then, he holds the book in his hand as an apple appears in his other hand. Taking a bite of the apple, he walks across the floor, reading the open book, then floats into the air and up the stairs, examining the dark creatures until he comes to Bardagul.

"Fascinating. Well, what do we have here?" Noel asks, raising his hand over the watch. It begins to spin in Bardagul's frozen hand.

"This is also not a child's toy," Noel remarks as the watch disappears and a bronze watch appears in its place as a replacement. With a simple wave of his hand, presto!, it looks identical to the original watch.

"Noel, you have outdone yourself. Thank you," he says, laughing as he raises his hand, and reappears back in the room of orbs, holding *The Liber Lux* (*The Grimoire of Light*) and still eating his apple. Time remains frozen as he continues to read. When he finally closes the book, he disappears and reappears in the Sanctuary of Legend and Lore.

"This Curpendulum should remain in a safe place. Besides, Merlin must not be reading this book. It is too advanced for him," Noel says aloud, placing the book on a pedestal.

"What is too advanced?" the voice asks as they place their hand on Noel's shoulder.

Reaching up, Noel places his hand on top of Dalton's. Then, he turns.

"I see you found a Curpendulum," Dalton remarks.

"How do you come to be here? You were protecting time," Noel asks as Dalton reaches up to kiss him, but the image ghosts through Noel.

"You are not here. You are projecting yourself," Noel says.

"Yes, and we do not have much time."

"I am listening."

"Noel, you have to turn back time. Go back in time to find my sister. Tell her that time and magic are going to collide. Explain to her what has happened, and she will help you set things right. Tell her the Timekeeper is broken," Dalton explains as he begins to fade.

"No, Dalton, wait," Noel calls, his hand raised.

"Turning back time is easy for you, Mr. Yule, but not so easy for me. But, OK, here goes nothing."

Turning slowly around and observing the space, Noel begins to spin his wand as a giant clock appears. Spinning his wand again, the hands of the clock begin to spin backward as the library transforms around him. The room remains the same, but the sun and moon are rapidly changing position outside the window until the hands finally stop spinning. Noel looks around, examining the library.

∾

"The Curpendulums are still here. Hmm, did it work?" Raising his hands, he disappears only to reappear on a snow-covered sidewalk of a city street. Looking around, Noel spins his hands, transforming his attire. He flips the collar of his long coat up as he slides the sleeves down, hiding the markings on his gauntlets. Kneeling, Noel clicks the clasps on his boots as he furtively looks around, examining the street.

Find my sister. Dalton said. Easier said than done, my love," Noel thinks, walking down the street as Mundane bustled by.

Are they always in a hurry? Oh no! I sound like any other Arcane when observing the Mundane," Noel laughs to himself, noticing a paperboy on the corner selling newspapers.

"Hey, kid, how much?" Noel asks.

"Twenty-five cents, sir," the kid replies as Noel hands him one hundred dollars.

"Keep the change," Noel says, walking away and reading the paper.

"Thank you, kind sir! Oh, thank you, indeed, kind sir!" the paperboy shouts, jumping up and down.

New York City, November 13th, 1950. Hmmm. Why did time dump me here? Noel wonders, flipping through the paper. Then, he turns back to the front page and begins reading one of the articles.

New York Antique Shop features the Fine Clocks of Ms. Citrine.

"Well, Lady Yule, you have a very different career now," Noel declares, laughing and folding the newspaper. Tucking it under his arm, he walks down the street until he reaches the shop. Several people on the inside approach the door. Noel holds it open for them, allowing them to pass through, and then, he walks into the shop.

"Good morning. Welcome to Citrine Antiques. What can I help you with?" the young clerk greets Noel from behind the counter.

"Morning, ma'am, I hear that you have some of the finest clocks in New York," Noel says.

"Indeed, we do, sir. On the second floor at the back," the clerk smiles as Noel nods and heads for the second floor. The clerk watches him closely, then reaches under the counter, tapping a button.

Noel strolls through the stalls on the first floor, examining different items. Then, he ascends the stairs and begins looking around the second floor. Stopping several times, he observes that the staff members are watching him.

Entering through a grand archway, Noel turns and examines the backroom where clocks line the walls from floor to ceiling.

"Interesting place this is," Noel remarks out loud.

"Do you think so?" a woman's voice asks.

"Yes, ma'am," he replies, nodding his head.

"Fascinating, aren't they? All were designed for the same purpose, but each is different and unique in its own way. Wouldn't you agree?" Citrine asks.

"I would have to agree with you about that," Noel smiles.

"I am very sorry. Where are my manners? I am Citrine, the proprietor of this establishment, and you, sir, are…?" she asks, extending her hand.

Pausing for a moment, Noel thinks, then replies "A pleasure to meet you, Ms. Citrine. I am Russell."

"I see. What brings you in?" Citrine inquires.

"Just looking. I read in the paper that this place has the finest clocks around," Noel replies.

"That I do. But you did not come to just look at the clocks. I can tell by the way you're dressed that you must be here on business. No. I suspect that there is a wonderful lady in your life, and you are looking for an anniversary clock? No, that is too easy. You are looking for a clock for your dear mother," Citrine suggests as she watches Noel closely.

"To answer your question, I am looking for a clock but not for a special lady," Noel replies.

"Go ahead and look around. Let me know if I can be any help, sir," Citrine says, walking past him to greet another customer who has just entered the shop. Noel strolls along the walls looking at the various clocks when, suddenly, a grandfather clock, in the middle of the room, begins to chime. Each time it chimes, more customers become annoyed and leave the area until Noel is the only one left walking among the clocks, unphased by the chime.

"Ma'am, the grandfather clock," one of the workers remarks.

"Yes, I hear it. Tell the staff to lock the doors and clear the store. Unfortunately, we may have a problem on our hands," Citrine directs as she holds her hand down at her side and an energy orb appears. Watching Noel from the other side of the room, Citrine raises her hand, and she launches the energy orb at him. Noel jumps into the air over the orb as the orb strikes the wall, damaging several clocks. Landing, he turns, looking at Citrine.

"What was that for?" Noel demands.

"Arcane!" Citrine yells, launching energy orb after energy orb at him.

Every orb hits Noel and he absorbs the magic from each of them. Furious, Citrine raises her hand again, causing all of the clocks to come to an absolute stand still. As Noel looks at them, his eyes begin glowing blue.

Solvo.

Release.

Streams of magic fly around the space and through each of the clocks as the hands all start spinning rapidly. Citrine covers her ears, doubling over. Noel raises his hand as the hands of the clocks slow to their average pace. Then, he walks over to Citrine and offers her his hand.

"Get away from me," she snaps, pushing his hand away as she stumbles to her feet.

"Are you okay?" Noel asks kindly.

"You could have killed me," Citrine remarks, looking displeased.

"Pfff! Lady Yule, you're a Noble that is impossible. Actually, now that I think about it, there is no way to kill an elder," Noel smirks.

Citrine attempts to slap Noel, but he catches her by the wrist.

"Now, My Lady, stop. Lord Yule sent me," he says.

Watching her facial expression, he lets go of her arm and backs away from her.

"Lord Yule? That is impossible! It has been years. No one has seen or heard from Lord Yule," she declares, looking at Noel with a curious look on her face.

Noel runs his finger over a set of chimes as he examines them.

"I just spoke with him. He mentioned that I should find his sister, that she would be able to help me," Noel replies, smiling at her.

"And what do you need the Lady Yule's help with," Citrine asks, watching as Noel causes two chairs and a table to appear.

"Shall we?" he motions and the two sit down.

"You have magic that seems unusual for an Arcane," Citrine declares.

"That is because I am not a 'normal' Arcane, and that is all I am going to say about that. It may mess up the very fabric of time if I say more," Noel remarks, waving his hand as a tea set appears and the teapot levitates into the air, pouring tea into the cups.

"The fabric of time? Ha! What you did with that spell alone could have disrupted time. You should never accelerate time like that," Citrine explains, accepting a cup and saucer.

"If I remember, Lady Yule, you like cream and three sugar cubes," Noel says, ignoring her comment about him speeding up time.

"You, sir, have not answered my question."

"More like a statement. And, no need, My Lady. I know the rules, but the rules are meant to be broken."

"My good sir, time rules must not be broken. So, what is so pressing that Lord Yule sent you."

"The Timekeeper is broken," Noel states.

"What did you say?" Citrine inquires, her eyes narrowing.

"The Timekeeper is broken. Look, Lady, I do not have time for this. Either you are the Lady Citrine Yule, or you are not. In which case, you are wasting my time. I need to speak with the true Lady Yule. The Lady Yule, after placing three cubes of sugar in her cup, always stirs her tea five times counterclockwise, then taps the spoon against the rim six times before placing the spoon to the right of the cup," Noel states, looking annoyed.

"Why, whatever do you mean?" Citrine inquires.

"Your spoon is still dripping tea and is to the left of the cup, not the right," Noel replies, raising his wand.

"All right, Gloria. No! Stop!" a voice says as the young clerk enters the room.

"Sir, lower your wand, please. I am the true Lady Citrine Yule. Gloria is my decoy. These are dangerous times that we live in," the woman acknowledges.

"Lady Yule," Noel says, bowing and lowering his wand.

"Gloria, thank you. I will take it from here. Please tend to the store."

"My Lady," Gloria notes, standing, bowing and then, walking away.

"I heard you say your name was Russell. May I ask the name of your house?" Lady Yule inquires, sitting in the chair as she pours herself a cup of tea. Noel watches her every move.

"My lady, as I explained to your stand-in, to explain any more would mess with the fabric of time," Noel says as Lady Yule sits back in her chair.

"I see. Have you forgotten that you are sitting with one of the masters of time? But if it would make you feel better…" Lady Yule remarks, snapping her fingers as everything freezes.

"Freezing time, my Lady, is all well and good, but I must still error on the side of caution. Time is bizarre, and we do not need it to be broken," Noel explains.

"Very well, sir. You mention the Timekeeper and that it is broken?" she asks.

"Yes, I was told to tell you that," Noel replies.

"Tell me, what trouble has that dear brother of mine gotten himself into this time?" she inquires.

"It is a long story," Noel replies, standing and pacing the floor.

"You are an elf?" Lady Yule asks, sipping her tea and watching Noel's response.

"I am, but how can you tell? My ears are hidden," Noel remarks, waving his hand as he reveals his actual ears.

"An elf, who can screw with the very essence of time, is not fazed by the chime of my grandfather clock, claiming that he knows Dalton, and talking about the Timekeeper. You must be Noble Elder," Lady Yule concludes, smiling.

"Yes, and may I ask, 'What is the Timekeeper?'" Noel inquires.

"Lost," Lady Yule replies, spinning her hand over the floor as an orb appears, projecting image after image.

"Elder Yule," Noel declares, approaching the image.

"Indeed," Lady Yule responds, continuing to watch Noel.

"He is young in this image. That must be around the time when Merlin stole the first Curpendulum," Noel remarks, looking back over his shoulder at Lady Yule.

The room darkens. The blinds lower over the giant windows and the shop staff appear on the second-floor balcony, leaning on the handrail and listening.

"You know your history. Yes, this is my father a week before Merlin stole the *Liber Mortuus Caelum* (*The Grimoire of the Dead*). At that moment, my father had a vision of what Merlin would do and took steps to make sure that the Timekeeper was secure," Lady Yule explains.

"What is the Timekeeper?" Noel inquires again.

"My father's watch, an arcane artifact so powerful that if Merlin ever got hold of it, he would wreak havoc on time," Lady Yule explains as Noel reaches inside his jacket pocket and pulls out a long chain with a pocket watch dangling from it.

"The Timekeeper," Lady Yule confirms, moving to examine it, but Noel closes his hands around it.

"If this is the Timekeeper, we have nothing to worry about. It has stopped. Merlin won't be able to use it," Noel explains as Lady Yule tilts her head, looking up at him.

"Stopped? Are you from the future then? Tell me, Elder, the time you are from, has Merlin found a Curpendulum?" Lady Yule inquires, tapping her foot impatiently, her arms crossed.

"Yes, he discovered *The Liber Lux* (*The Grimoire of Light*)," Noel replies.

"Gloria? Check the time nexus. Ensure that no disruptions have occurred. Darren, send word to Queen Amaryllis that Merlin has discovered *The Liber Lux*. Angie, go to the forest, locate Lord Leo and tell him of what is occurring," Lady Yule orders as her staff start disappearing, some of them flying into the air as the glass ceiling opens onto the night sky.

"What is all that about? I took the Curpendulum away from him," Noel says.

"Either way, if he found one, he can find them all. My father did not hide them and mess with time to have Merlin get around that magic. Many of the Arcane have been sworn by the Nobles to keep an eye on things. The slightest chatter of Merlin and all of the Arcane will know what is occurring," Lady Yule replies, walking up to Noel and holding out her hand. Reluctantly, he hands the watch to her.

"I take it the watch has something to do with where magic and time meet?" Noel asks.

"Indeed, it does. Noble Elder, you understand that, with time, things are never what they seem. The Timekeeper watch is designed to detect whenever Merlin finds a Curpendulum. The hands stop completely, and the Timekeeper has to be reprogrammed," Lady Yule explains, flipping the watch over, removing the back, and turning the gears.

"Wait! So, the Timekeeper is designed to alert us to Merlin's actions?" Noel inquires.

"Yes, and the Timekeeper will alter time accordingly. In other words, it is a failsafe to protect the Arcane and Mundane from Merlin."

"I understand now why it is that he cannot ever have this."

"Oh, no. Merlin must not get his hands on the Timekeeper. It would spell the destruction of all Arcane and Mundane as we know them."

"Lady Citrine, the tower at the University of Arcane and Mundane Studies, does it still amplify the power of the Timekeeper?"

"It does. It will bring time to a complete halt. No one will be able to move. And, unfortunately, not even my brother would be able to control the time at that point. It is the one fail-safe to stop Merlin altogether. But, tell me, young Noble Elder—I believe you go by Noel—there are other ways to stop Merlin. Aren't there?"

"Yes, my Lady. But, as you said, things are not what they seem," Noel replies, sitting down on a chair.

"All fixed. You are ready to go. Five turns of the dial, and time is yours to control," Lady Citrine Yule remarks, handing the Timekeeper to Noel.

"I don't even know where to begin to fix things," Noel declares.

"That I cannot tell you. But what I will say is, 'Stand up. Take a deep breath. Five turns of the dial, and then, speak the spell. Time will be yours to control. But, Noel, the Timekeeper is designed to listen to you alone," Lady Citrine Yule warns, pulling him out of the chair.

"Why me?"

"Because, Noel, my father saw something in you that no one else has seen," Lady Citrine explains smiling and straightening Noel's collar.

"What is that, My Lady?"

"Your heart," she replies, placing her hand on his chest.

"My heart?" he inquires.

"The one true prophecy known about you amongst the Elders is that your heart, your love for everyone, will fuel the power of your magic and the power of time," Lady Yule explains regarding Noel. Stopping and closing his eyes, Noel sighs, then opens his eyes.

"Thank you, Citrine."

"Any time, my dear future brother-in-law."

What? Citrine wait!

But she is gone.

Okay, Noel, it is time. Let's do this. You have hated magic for years, but now everyone needs you. Magic needs you. Our family needs you. And Dalton needs you.

Holding up the Timekeeper as it floats before him, Noel looks about the space one last time. Then, he claps his hands together and his staff appears, the Elven Star glowing on its end. His attire transforms. His long coat turns black with purple inlay. His long-sleeved tunic is blue, and a diadem headpiece appears upon his head with seven stones.

He clicks the button on his wristwatch as nanobots fly around him, merging with his clothes. Holding up his arms, he examines his sleeves as the nanobots make it appear as if he is wearing chainmail.

My siblings will laugh when they see what I am wearing, he thinks. *Okay, Noel, we have to find the bunker, stop Merlin, save our family, and protect everything. This should be easy.*

Tempus Custodis, Tempus Permittit Fix.
Magicae Temporis Lanuae,

Timekeeper, let's fix time. Magical time teleport.

Spinning the dial of the Timekeeper five times, the watch flies around Noel and the space. Noel watches as time begins changing around him, as the beautiful and vibrant room he has been standing in now appears to be burned, the clocks smashed or missing, and vines growing through the windows. Broken glass lays on the ground, and the floor is covered in dirt and leaves.

"Interesting. Where, and when, have you dropped me, Timekeeper?"

Chapter 28
The Bunker

Wow, I am still in Citrine's shop, but this place needs some work. Well, I see the Timekeeper is working again. I only hope it has fixed things.

Walking through the archway, Noel looks around curiously as he descends the stairs and examines the first floor of the shop.

This place is in shambles. What happened here?

Walking out the door, he steps into the cool evening air where he observes dark creatures running up the sides of the building and chasing Mundane in the street. Two dark creatures stop, snarling at Noel.

"Really?" Noel says, his staff appearing in his hand.

As he raises it, the Elven Star grows bright, flashes, and the dark creatures are gone. Multiple dark creatures stop what they are doing and turn their attention to him, diving from the buildings and circling him.

Screaming, the creatures charge Noel. He spins his staff, taps the tip on the ground, and streams of magic fly out from the Elven Star. Spinning, he strikes the dark creatures with magic. Then, he closes his eyes. Re-opening them, the star lights, causing the darkness to dissolve. The dark creatures turn and begin running toward multiple buildings. Noel raises his staff.

Spirituum Accerso Exetcitum.
I call for the army of the spirits.

The darkness flies into the sky and begins screaming, hissing, and howling as stomping can be heard in the distance. A massive army of spirits come marching down the street, drawing their swords and spears. Twelve spirits rise out of the ground around Noel. Circling him, the twelve regard one another, then turn to face the dark creatures.

Magister Spirituum urbem et populum defendat.
Master Spirits protect the city and the people.

Noel declares as the twelve spirits raises their spears and disappear. Within seconds, the army of the spirits begin rolling over the buildings, taking the dark creatures captive, and forming protective barriers around the Mundane.

Walking through the battle, Noel spins his hands, capturing one of the dark generals. he raises his hands and pulls them apart, tearing the general in two and throwing the dead body parts out of the way.

"I grow tired of you," Noel declares as multiple dark creatures encircle him, snarling.

One dark creature charges Noel, but Noel catches the creature's spear blade between both hands and, quickly turning, strikes the pole with his palm, snapping the weapon in half. The remains of the spear's pole lights and cracks, lightning surging through it as the dark creature dissolves. Three more dark creatures charge toward Noel trying to grab him. He disappears and reappears behind the biggest of the three, grabbing them by their shoulders and slamming them into the ground. A second later, he snaps his right arm down as a dagger appears. He throws the dagger into one of the other dark creatures who doubles over. Noel rolls over the creature's back, raises his wand, and holds it to the creature's chest.

Accendo.

Ignite.

The creature explodes into flames as it dissolves. In the distance, a child stands in the middle of the street crying. When Noel runs toward the child, his wand disappears replaced by his staff, as the darkness that is advancing down the street flies back.

One dark creature dives from the side of the building and grabs the child. Then, the creature drops to the ground, shaking.

Accendo.

Ignite.

A stream of white magic flies around the creature as it explodes into flames and dissolves. Just then, Minnie walks up.

"Clearly, you will never learn," she remarks, smiling and, raising her wand as another creature dissolves. As she reaches the child, several dark creatures begin to circle the two of them. Looking around, Minnie smiles for a second time. Then, she steps in front of the child protecting them.

"The child or the Timekeeper?" the dark general says, holding out his hand as he approaches.

"Neither," Minnie replies, moving across the ground faster than any of them expected. She lifts the dark general off his feet. Then, she sinks her teeth into his neck. His legs shaking, he drops to the ground dead as she licks the blood from her lips.

"So, you're a vampire," Noel declares, smiling and striking two dark creatures that are running toward her.

"Yes, Lord Noel, I swore an oath to protect the line of the Noble Elders," Minnie explains as she walks through one of the dark creatures, turns, and grabs them by the shoulder, slamming them into the ground. Noel carries the child back to her mother as he watches Minnie fight.

"Minnie, I will be back. I left time frozen at the clock tower," Noel explains.

"No, you did not. You are an hour earlier. Time brought you back one hour in time and dumped you here. So, for now, your daughter, Bardagul, and Gorodra are all safe," Minnie exclaims, walking through another of the dark creatures, turning and slamming it into the ground.

"By the way, that is the second time you have done that move. Would you care to explain why you fight like Cedric?" Noel inquires.

"He is my uncle," Minnie replies, simply.

"Your uncle? Are you kidding me?" Noel responds as he strikes a dark creature with his staff, and the creature explodes.

"He is, and he trained me when I was younger," Minnie replies as she and Noel turn back-to-back.

Then, a white and silver phoenix flies in from overhead, lands on the ground and looks up at Noel.

"Well, hello. Aren't you beautiful?" Noel says.

"Sir Fintan, Lord Noel. Lord Noel, Sir Fintan, the phoenix of the Noble Elders'," Minnie introduces them as the phoenix puffs out its wings and bows.

"The phoenix of Noble Elder. This should be fun," Noel says pointing his finger as the phoenix flies into the air and shoots across the sky, pursuing several dark creatures.

"Sir, there are too many of them," Minnie declares.

"Not for them," Noel points as the army of spirits run past them. The spirits form a wall rolling up the street, taking out the dark creatures. Noel's eyes turn white. Raising an orb in his hand, light flashes around him and he flies into the air as the orb grows in size. Holding it between his hands, he launches it into the ground. Light columns explode into the sky, striking and taking out the darkness. Once the area is cleared, Noel lowers back down, walking above the ground on the air.

"Minnie, I leave the army with you. Take them and tend to the Mundane. I must help my family, and I need to deal with Merlin," Noel remarks, holding the Timekeeper as it begins to spin in his hand.

"Sir, hold tight to that. If Merlin gets it, I hate to tell you what will happen. Besides, you will need that when you get to the bunker," Minnie says, looking intently at Noel.

"Thank you, Minnie. Lady Citrine Yule told me about the Timekeeper. Speaking of which…" Noel stops.

Regarding the area, Noel looks at the Timekeeper. Then, he walks back down the street to the door of the ruins of Citrine's Antiques. Holding the Timekeeper in his hand, he places it against the door and closes his eyes.

Restituo.

Restore.

Magic explodes around him as Minnie steps back, watching the building as it begins to be restored. Within seconds, the building stands fully restored. The lights glow in the shop windows as the flower beds sprout tulips and roses. A giant clock appears on the door with a band circling around the outer edge. The band of roman numerals spins in the opposite direction of the clock. Opening his eyes, Noel steps back, examining the shop.

"Get the Mundane and take refuge here. The place is equipped to fight back against the darkness," Noel explains.

"Minnie, do you know where the bunker is? I have to get there before Merlin reaches it," Noel says as Fintan flies down and lands on Noel's shoulder.

"I do not, but he does," Minnie replies, nodding as Noel regards Fintan for a moment, and then, the two disappear.

❧

Appearing in the field next to the university's green houses, Noel looks around until he notices that the night sky is lighting up.

"Well, Fintan, it looks like everyone has their hands full. Now. to find that bunker. Can you show me where it is?"

Flying into the air, Fintan glides over the ground and lands on the fence on the far side of the field. Disappearing from where he had been standing,

Noel reappears, looking at Fintan until he notices a glow of light. Kneeling, he brushes off some boards, pulls back some shrubs and finds himself peering through them into a large room.

"Wow! This reminds me of a New York train station," Noel comments, looking around as he raises his hand, summoning two spinning orbs. The orbs land as two beings of solid white light appear.

"We are the Guardians. What is your emergency?" they say in unison.

"Guardians, please create a protective barrier over this area. If any darkness tries to get in here, light them up," Noel commands, spinning his hands as magic flies around him and Fintan soars overhead. Noel kicks the boards back and jumps into the hole. Landing on his feet, he scans the area.

I would say that was a good four or five-story drop, Noel notes and then, he hears voices. Ducking behind one of the long tables, he watches as two dark guards walk by. His eyes narrow on the blade that is sitting in front of him. Rising, he examines the rows of tables and the weapons on them.

Wow! He did not just take artifacts. He has the entire elfish armory down here, Noel thinks, picking up one of the blades.

Nicely balanced, I would say gilded in the Baroque era. Probably made of elfish steel, which means the blade is indestructible and should light up.

Noel taps the blade, and it begins to glow ruby red.

A fire blade. Merlin definitely should not have this. In fact, he should not have any of this stuff. He could hurt himself with these.

Raising his hands, Noel spins them as the items around him shrink. He snaps his fingers, his bag appears, and he redirects all the items into it for safekeeping. Picking up the bag, Noel spins his hands as his cloak appears. When he raises his hood, he completely disappears from sight. Noel walks through the giant archway onto a balcony, looking around cautiously. Examining the space further, he notices that it is five stories deep. Then, several individuals catch his eye.

So, they have Alviss, Bardagul, Amelia, and Matthew all tied up. Remember what Minnie said. This is an hour before the events at the tower take place, so Bardagul is still here. Ha! But not for long. I think it is time to fix time.

Jumping over the rail, Noel glides down to the ground floor where he makes his bag disappear. Then, he walks up to the chair where Bardagul is restrained. Reaching up and clicking his watch, a nanobot appears. It flies directly to Amelia.

"Well, hello, little guy," Amelia acknowledges as Matthew, whose mouth was covered, looks at her curiously.

"Is that one of your buggy things?" Bardagul asks quietly.

"It is indeed. My dear little friend, did RJ send you?" Amelia asks as the nanobot shakes its head in the affirmative and the ropes holding Bardagul fall to the floor as Noel lowers his hood, reappearing before them.

"Quiet, all of you," Noel whispers as Bardagul hugs him.

Then, Noel slices the ropes binding Amelia and Alviss. When he reaches Matthew, he points his finger and the ropes along with the gag over Matthew's mouth disappear.

"Cousin Matthew, take Amelia, Alviss, and Bardagul and get them out of here," Noel directs as darkness begins screaming at the sight of Noel, flying into the air, and circling the ceiling.

"I want to stay with you," Bardagul cries, holding on to Noel's leg.

"Hey, Bardagul, I need you to go with Amelia, your Pa, and my cousin, Matthew. Get out of here. I have work to do," Noel says as he snaps his arms down, his cloak disappears into his armor, and his elfish arm blades appear.

"Go! Now!" Noel yells, running across the floor as he slides onto his knees, sweeping three dark creatures off their feet. When he comes up again, he strikes another one dead center on its chin and throws it across the room.

Matthew, Amelia, Alviss, and Bardagul run toward the opening as Matthew spins his wand, trying to open a portal.

"We have a problem," Matthew remarks as Noel raises his hand. Fintan dives down from the ceiling, screaming, as sonic waves drive the dark backward.

"Fintan, get them out of here. Now!" Noel orders as he begins to spin streams of fire and water around himself like a whip, fighting the darkness. Swooping down, the great phoenix grabs Matthew and Amelia as they grab Bardagul and Alviss' hands, flying up into the air. The phoenix soars like a rocket through the opening in the ceiling, and the four land in the field. Matthew raises his wand and points it toward the sky as a ghost-like form of a phoenix explodes into the air, soaring into the sky and exploding into a knight in armor, galloping through the sky and disappearing.

"I would recommend standing back and getting ready," Matthew suggests as multiple columns of light explode from the sky. The light beams hit the ground causing the charging darkness to fly across the field and sky, striking the field, and exploding. Emerging from the center column are Oliver, Ethan, Rose, Sebastian, and Zander, their right arms raised, wands in hand, and magic flying around them. Forming a second lightfield, they stop the second wave of darkness in their tracks.

"Matthew," Ari acknowledges.

"Noel is down there," Matthew says, pointing as he approaches his five cousins.

"What do you mean 'Noel is down there'?" Rusty yells.

"Cousin Rusty, you heard me. Noel is going all freaky magic on the darkness," Matthew explains as Rusty runs past him and up to the Guardians as a clear crystal levitates into the air.

"Please state your business," the Guardians inquire, palms touching as a field of magic spins over the opening into the bunker.

"I am High Prince Russell Ambrose Alezander Elderchild Ignatius, Sr. I am the father of Noel. I command you to allow me to pass so I can help him," he declares.

The Guardians glance at one another, bow, and separate allowing Rusty to pass. Reaching the opening, Rusty stands at the edge, raises his hands, listening, and feeling the air. A whistle sounds, and Fintan jumps up, flies into the air, grabs Rusty by the shoulders and dives, carrying him into the bunker. Magic is flying everywhere. Streams of magic circle the ceiling as darkness by the hundreds continue to attack Noel as he fights to hold them back.

Fintan lets go of Rusty, who lands feet first on the ground in a bent position, his right palm resting flat on the ground. When he stands, his attire has transformed. His robes are now identical to Noel's, only in green and brown, and an elfish headband rests on his head, a green emerald glowing in the center. Raising his wand, magic spins around him as he levitates a table off the ground, which explodes into flames as he spins it in the air. Looking around Rusty speaks,

Iacto.

Throw.

The flaming table is launched into a sea of advancing dark creatures. Noel, fighting back the dark creatures sees his father standing there, and then, Rusty throws an orb into the air. When it falls to the ground, it explodes and members of the Houses of Phoenix, Ignatius, and Knight materialize from the shattered pieces.

At the sight of the others appearing, the darkness screams, snarls, and hisses as multiple orbs fly into the air, exploding. Suddenly, fire flies into the air as the flapping of a giant beast approaching can be heard. Arrows soar through the air, striking multiple dark creatures as Pete, Michael, and

Kells dive from Belinda's back, landing on the stone circle, weapons in hand, streams of magic exploding around the stone circle as they touch down.

"Little Brother, are these things troubling you?" Kells inquires as Isabella, Sophia, and Willow appear in the middle of the four brothers.

"It appears they are a problem. Clearly, they have not met us," Isabella remarks as the six siblings join Noel in the circle, ready to fight.

"It is nice to have you six with me," Noel smiles, raising his hand as the circle flies into the air, spinning. Then, reaching up and touching his temple with his index and middle finger, Noel says, "Grandma, Grandpa, Dad, everyone please focus on protecting the artifacts and stopping the darkness from getting any further weapons. We will handle Merlin."

The circle flies through the air as Noel raises his hands, steering the stone circle. Diving into the lower tunnel, the seven fly into a giant chamber as torches light, and they find Merlin sitting on a throne, encircled by water, with a single path leading to it, his head resting on his hand until he looks up.

Noel brings the circle down to land as Merlin begins laughing.

"Are you seriously here? I just want to reign over the Arcane. Why don't you get that?" Merlin yells, rising to his feet.

"Stay close, you six, and watch all corners of the room," Noel says as Merlin jumps up from the throne and starts to walk across the water.

"Oh, so now he thinks he is some sort of god," Isabella quips sarcastically.

"Nasty child! I *am* a god, a god of demons, and you will bow to me," Merlin snaps as he blasts dark magic toward the circle where they are standing. Noel catches the dark magic in his hands and is pushed back. Michael and Pete push against Noel, holding him up.

"How sweet! They are helping him. Enjoy it now because he will turn on the six of you when he does not need you anymore," Merlin remarks, laughing as he causes flames to explode around the chamber and four giant griffin statues come to life, roaring.

"I swear that someone needs to silence him! My dear siblings, do not listen to him. He is trying to psych us out," Isabella declares as she lifts one of the griffins off its feet with her magic and throws it into the flames.

"Stop them, you six. Merlin is mine," Noel declares, disappearing from where he has been standing.

"See? Even now, he runs. Oh, Noel. Why are you running? Are you scared?" Merlin laughs as he launches more dark magic at the lightfield. But the magic stops in the air, halfway across the room as it turns to light.

"What? No!" Merlin yells as Noel appears, holding the arm that Merlin's wand is in. Merlin pulls a dagger, trying to stab Noel. Time freezes around the chamber as the griffins stop in their tracks. The Ignatius siblings look around as Noel's eyes begin to glow. Merlin is still moving slowly when a giant magic dome rises over him and Noel.

"Isabella, what is he doing?" Pete asks, as a pop echoes throughout the space, and Lord Yule appears.

"Protecting time," he explains as Merlin starts moving more rapidly under the dome and appears as if he is going mad. Black magic flies from his mouth as his skin begins to drip from his face. Noel continues to stand there, holding Merlin's arm. Two Dark Council members appear, wands raised, striking the dome with dark magic as Raven appears, doing the same.

Before anyone can respond, a female Dark Council member drops her wand and holds her hand in pain as magic explodes from the dome, protecting itself. Then, a cloaked figure appears. In an attempt to strike the figure, the same Dark Council member is swept off her feet. The cloaked figure raises an alarm clock in their hand.

"Citrine, no!" Lord Yule yells and she lowers her hood.

"Brother, you have forgotten. This is not about my temper," Citrine replies. Then, she smashes the Dark Council member in the face with the clock and the woman freezes, then turns to stone. Walking across the room, Citrine points her wand and a clock appears under the other Dark Council member. They freeze and then appear in a mirror. Walking past the mirror, Citrine taps it with her wand, and it breaks into a thousand pieces. Backing up, Raven laughs, then she multiplies.

"Witch, I have no time for you," Citrine declares, raising her hand as the eleven copies of Raven freeze, leaving only the original moving.

"Got you," Lord Yule remarks as he runs Raven threw with his sword. Holding her stomach, she spits blood as she stumbles backward, and her body dissolves before it hits the water. The two remaining griffins explode at the same time that the dome holding Merlin and Noel also explodes. Suddenly, Merlin grows to be three stories in size.

Backing up, Noel disappears briefly, then reappears in the circle where he lowers his hands. Willow and Isabella take his hands and their eyes started to glow different colors. The others follow suit and as the nine hold hands, they form a circle around Merlin. With magic flying around, Merlin is smashed heavily against the magical barrier that is protecting them.

Illuminare.
Illuminate.

Noel speaks the spell as the magic continues to spin around the circle, and a cyclone forms around Merlin, a lightfield rising around him. Shrinking, Merlin raises his hands over his head, pushing against the barrier as he shrinks until he is smaller than a dwarf. Pushing back against the barrier, Merlin declares,

Magic Obscura Custodi Me.
Dark magic guard me.

The column of light starts to flicker as it turns black. Then, Noel's eyes turn white.

Per Potentias Lucis Illustra.
Illuminate by the Powers of Light.

Streams of white and black magic collide as the column continues to flicker. Noel closes his eyes as the Timekeeper appears, floating in front of him.

"The Timekeeper! Give it to me!" Merlin screams as he reaches for the watch. The area around them all transforms, and they are standing amongst the stars and planets. The Timekeeper floats into the air until Merlin's hand is inches from it. Then, when Noel opens his eyes and blows on the clock, it begins spinning rapidly in the air.

Lady and Lord Yule's eyes narrow, watching, as the Timekeeper spins and time starts to play backward. The group re-emerges in the chamber as Merlin flies back onto his throne and vines rise from the ground to encircle him as Willow raises her hand.

Pete touches the ground, and the throne begins to dissolve under Merlin. Kells and Sophia launch arrows at the ceiling, causing it to crumble around Merlin. Michael summons fire to surround the throne and Isabella causes a pentagram to appear.

The Timekeeper continues to spin as magical barriers of white light explode from the lines of the pentagram. Noel walks rapidly to the outer circle of the pentagram and touches the barrier of light. It flashes, the ceiling dissolves, and the night sky appears. Stars circle overhead and begin flying toward the place where Merlin sits, exploding one after another. Then, Merlin and the throne are gone. All that remains is an orb.

Approaching the orb, Noel taps it with his boot. He then levitates the orb off the ground and throws a white cloth over it. Pete walks up and captures the orb in a wooden box, slamming the lid shut. Willow approaches the box, waves her hands, and vines with thorns wrap themselves around the box. Lord Yule opens a portal in the middle of the circle as Noel takes the box from Pete, walks across the stone floor, and the waters recede. Reaching the portal, Noel raises his hand as four orbs appear, spinning around the box.

Per Potentias Lucis Illustra.
Illuminate by the Powers of Light.

The orbs start glowing as they create a stream of magic to protect the box. Then, Noel lets it go. The box levitates into the air as Noel throws his hands out in front of himself, launching the box into the portal, and the portal spins shut.

Turning, Noel regards his siblings as he hugs Willow.

"Is that the end of Merlin?" Pete asks, patting Noel on the back.

"For now, yes," Lord Yule responds as Noel approaches and kisses him.

"Hi! I love you," Noel says, pulling slightly away from Dalton.

Then, they kiss for a second time.

"Are you two always going to be doing that?" Michael jokes as Isabella and Willow give him a disgusted look and shake their heads.

"What?" Michael asks.

"Leave them be," Isabella responds.

When Noel and Lord Yule stop kissing, Noel backs up and speaks.

"Citrine, I think you might find that there is a particular shop awaiting its keeper. My siblings, our paths will cross again. Lord Yule, be good, be safe, stay out of trouble. I will be back in no time."

With that Noel raises his hand as a book explodes through the wall and circles him.

"Noel, remember that as long as you hold the Timekeeper, my love is with you, and your magic is unstoppable," Dalton declares as the Curpendulum continues to spin around Noel.

"I have work to do. The timelines need to be restored. Time is still broken. And Luciana needs to be returned to her time," Noel says, smiling at them all as he raises his hand and captures the Curpendulum that is flying around him. Fintan lands on his shoulder, and Noel winks and disappears.

Chapter 29
What Comes Next?

"Is he going to be okay?" Pete inquires, concern in his voice.

"Yes, he will be. The journey for the Curpendulums has just begun," Willow explains as Isabella raises her hand, and everyone appears in the field at the University.

The siblings notice that the elfish guards have arrived and are cleaning out the bunker. Artifacts float by as fairies stand at attention around the entry, guarding it. The artifacts are being loaded into chests and boxes by the elves and fairies. Queen Amaryllis is flying up and down the rows checking all of the artifacts as they are loaded. Ms. Tulip flies behind her, holding a clipboard and quill, writing everything down by hand.

Pausing, Lord Yule looks around until he sees several of the dark guards and their general sitting on the ground, with their hands bound, as Luciana walks through the crowd with her wand out.

Approaching her, Dalton smiles. "You succeeded, I see."

"No, Papa. *We* succeeded. Does he have the Curpendulum?" Luciana asks.

"He has *a* Curpendulum and the Timekeeper," Dalton responds as a dark griffin charges the group. Standing with her arms extended, Willow causes vines to explode out of the ground, stopping the griffin in midair as the vines wrap themselves around the legs of the beast. Then, appearing in front of the beast, Kells swings his hammer, uppercutting the creature as Michael appears, dropping from the sky and jamming his sword through the beast's chest, dropping it to the ground, dead.

"Guards, take the creatures away," Zander orders, as he approaches and pats Dalton on the back.

"Papa, time is fixed?"

"For now, yes. We still have many challenges ahead," Dalton replies as Luciana nods in understanding.

"Then, Papa, so shall it be. Time can rest at this point. But the story's outcome remains unclear," Luciana remarks just as Esther appears with Nordika, Elvey, and Alviss, with his family in tow.

"Me Lords and Ladies," Alviss greets them, bowing.

"Master Dwarf," Lord Yule acknowledges him.

Bardagul is holding Amelia's hand as Luciana extends her hand to him.

"Come, my friend. It is time to go home," she says, looking at her cousins and friends.

"Luciana, Noel is waiting for you in the realm of time," Dalton comments, hugging her.

"Allow us," Rose says, raising her hand as a portal flies open.

The group bows, then turns and walks through the portal as it disappears.

"We are not going to see them again, are we?" Willow asks, sadly.

"No. When Noel took back his power, he changed time. As a result, when they return to their timeline and time, Noel will see to it that they cannot return until the time is right," Lord Yule explains.

One of the elf guards approaches.

"Yes, Commander," Vivian, who is standing next to her mother, acknowledges.

"My Ladies," the commander says, bowing.

He holds up a sword offering it to Rose. Picking it up, she turns it over, examining it. Then, she smiles.

"Please take this to my study for protection," Rose says.

"Is that the sword of Grandpa, King Caspar Ignatius?" Rusty inquires.

Peering over Rusty's shoulder, Zander is also observing the sword.

"It is," Rose responds.

"Well, then, that should remain in yours and father's private collection. Noel will come for that sword at some point," Rusty says, leaning on his staff.

"Why would Noel come for it?" Vivian asks, being snarky.

"Because, dear sister, he already controls the Elvan Star. He will want the sword to go with it," Rusty explains, laughing and smiling as Vivian shakes her head.

"What about the other artifacts? Is there a way to process them at the school? We definitely can't leave them in the middle of this field," Isabella remarks.

"Lady Ignatius, I may be of assistance there. It seems I have recently regained my shop," Lady Citrine Yule says, bowing as she approaches the group.

"Absolutely. I trust they will stay protected under your watch. We will deal with each artifact, one by one, once we know what we have. Until then, they are to go to Lady Yule's shop," Rose directs.

A screech is heard in the sky as Fintan appears flying overhead. He drops a package, which Zander catches. Approaching Rose, he holds it up, showing the handwritten address.

Grandmother, Queen Roslynn Sophia Nadia Ignatius
c/o Time, Magic & a Truly Magical Bird

Regarding each other, the siblings quickly move behind their grandmother to observe what is in the package as Rose tears back the paper.

"Zander," Rose says, holding the half-opened package that contains a Curpendulum.

"He found one. Well, this is going to get interesting," Zander declares as Rose spins her hands. Instantly, she, Zander, her children, members of her family, and grandchildren along with Lord and Lady Yule all arrive in the library.

"Mr. Bruin, everyone, quickly! Secure the library!" Rose orders as she summons her staff, taps it three times, and the Lady Mora appears.

"You're all back," she acknowledges. Then, her eyes narrow when she sees the package in Rose's hand. Rose flips the book over, removing the remainder of the wrapping. Examining the grimoire, she finds an envelope hooked on the back cover.

Mora and Zander regard Rose curiously.

My dearest family,

Many greetings on the journey through time. This will take some getting used to. I still dislike magic, but it is growing on me. The journey has just begun for all of us. Please secure this Curpendulum immediately.

As I find others, I will send them for safekeeping. This particular Curpendulum that you now hold should be handled with exceptional care. It is one of the more powerful, but sought after, Curpendulums. The darkness will want this one particularly. The Liber Caecus (The Grimoire of the Arcane) should remain in the battlement for safe holding. The spells of this book alone would frighten anyone.

By the way, I have returned Luciana and our friends to their time. I will be back soon, but I will send word if I need extra help. For now, blessings.

Yours truly throughout time,
~The Noble Elder, Noel

Everyone watches as Rose opens the book, reads the cover page, and closes it.

"Mom?" Vivian and Rusty inquire.

"*Liber Caecus* (*The Grimoire of the Arcane*)," Rose remarks, walking toward the battlement and placing the Curpendulum on a cart as several dwarfs disappear into a tunnel with it.

"Moving forward, we will all need to work together to keep any and all Curpendulums safe," Rose declares, acknowledging everyone with a nod when a pop is heard and a portal flies open. Several dark creatures scramble out, trying to get away from whatever is chasing them. Suddenly, the head of one of the dark generals rolls across the floor. Pete stops it with his boot, gazing down at it.

"Well, buddy, it looks like you had one hell of a time," Pete laughs as Noel emerges, arm blades drawn, blood dripping on the floor from the blades.

"Well, you look like shit," Michael remarks, pointing out a giant scratch running from the side of Noel's left eye down to the corner of his mouth. Noel is holding his bloody right hand in his left, and his leg is torn up.

Before he can completely exit the portal, his siblings surround him, checking him over to make sure he is okay.

"I appreciate the attention, but please back away from me. This is quickly getting annoying, especially if I have to deal with this every time I get injured," Noel exclaims as he pushes his way through the group around him and sits down.

"Are you okay?" Dalton asks, looking concerned and handing him a rag to wipe his face.

"Yes, for the most part. Fintan is here, I see. So, the Curpendulum is safe," Noel says.

"What happened?" Rose asks.

"Merlin, then more Merlin, and, oh yeah, Merlin. He has made copies of himself. I think the one we captured in the bunker was one of his clones," Noel explains.

"Grandmama, how is that possible?" Vivian inquires of Mora.

"Noel, my dear boy, how do you know this?"

"Because, Great-grandma, when I reached for the Curpendulum, so did Merlin. I watched carefully as he used his magic to copy himself. The true Merlin is old, crippled, and dying. He is sick. There is something off about him," Noel explains.

"Sick? That is good, right?" Michael and Pete inquire in unison.

"That would explain the copying spell," Rose says.

"Mom? Is it possible for Merlin to have such magic?" Zander asks, looking at his mother in surprise.

"Zander, I pray it is not so," Mora replies.

"What is going on? Is there something we are missing?" Willow asks.

"They are asking, sister, if Merlin could have utilized one of the Curpendulums to amass his power. If he is dying and copying himself, that type of magic can only be found in the Curpendulums. It could cause some serious issues as he could make unlimited multiples of himself. One thing remains consistent. When the other timelines were created, they each had their own version of Merlin, but the ability to copy himself is unlike anything we expected," Noel states, cringing as Willow works on healing the injury on his leg.

"That is creepy and disturbing," Sophia remarks.

"That is correct. However, I also worry that if Merlin has such power, then it means we have a traitor among the Nobles because one of them must have taught him that spell," Mora declares as Minnie appears.

"Noel," Minnie says, approaching and handing him an orb.

"What is going on?" Willow asks as Noel spins his hand over the orb.

"Thank you, Minnie," Noel says, his eyes fixed on the orb.

Then he stands.

"You are in no condition to go anywhere," Willow protests as Noel holds up the orb and disappears.

"Minnie, where did he go?" Rose asks.

"To the Realm of Time," Minnie replies looking at Lord and Lady Yule.

"Is everything okay?" Lord Yule asks as Minnie nods in the negative.

❧

Landing in the circle, kneeling on one leg, his right hand resting on the ground, Noel scans the area. Luciana stands in the center of the circle, watching the Timekeeper spin.

"Amazing, isn't it?"

"Yes, but it is also annoying how one simple watch can cause so much trouble," Noel declares, standing and waving his hand, causing a throne to appear as he pulls his cloak up and sits down.

"Do you care to tell me why you are here? I thought I was clear when I dropped you off," Noel says, watching Luciana closely.

"You were clear. But then, I began thinking that I should check on the Timekeeper," Luciana explains.

"Luciana, why are you here? The timelines could be disrupted again, and the Timekeeper is working fine," Noel replies, watching her as she taps on the watch's glass face.

"No, it is not that."

"Then, would you care to explain what is going on?"

"Dad, things are not what they seem."

"Luciana, explain, please. What do you mean?"

Spinning her hands, Luciana raises her right hand and the area around the circle grows bright with light. Luciana and Noel appear in a cave.

"Okay. So, this is a cave."

"Dad, look around. Pay attention to what is going on."

Getting up, Noel strolls along the walls, running his hands over the runes inscribed there. Then, he stops.

"The runes tell the story of time, but it is an incomplete story."

"Yes. Exactly! The seers could not finish the story," Luciana explains, leaning against the wall.

"And this concerns you?"

"Yes, Dad, it does."

"Why?"

"As I said, things are not what they seem. Merlin can copy himself. The timelines are acting up. The Timekeeper is still unpredictable. Does none of that concern you?"

"Luciana, that is not an easy question to answer. It does concern me, yes, all of it. But what I have learned is that the things that are not what they seem happen for a reason. Your aunts, uncle, and even your father have taught me that we grow from the things that we learn. Do I want to control everything? Absolutely! But, right now, the story not being complete means that we are writing the story as we go. That is good for us because Merlin cannot see what is to come next"

"You're okay with that?"

"I am because we, and I mean all of us, will stop Merlin together. You have held time together. Now, let me take that burden. In your timeline, I was not there. Now, let me fix that, please."

"Dad?"

"Yes, Luciana."

"Thank you," she replies, hugging him.

"You're welcome, kiddo. Now, time to get you back to your own timeline, and no more time jumping. We cannot risk breaking the Timekeeper," Noel says, looking at Luciana kindly.

"One last question. When you and Papa find all the Curpendulums, what do you plan to do with them?"

"Destroy them. They are too dangerous to be used by anyone on either side. They must not fall into anyone's hands, and I intend to keep it that way."

"I agree," Luciana says, hugging him as she disappears.

"Goodbye," Noel says as he turns and walks along the wall, examining the runes one last time.

"You know, I always knew you would be better at being Noble Elder than I was," a familiar voice declares as Noel turns to face Noble Elder.

"Hello, Noble Elder."

"Please, Noel, call me Elder Illuminary," he replies, sitting down on the throne.

"To what do I owe this visit, sir?"

"The Celestials sent me."

"It must be important if they sent you. What seems to be the issue?"

"Noel, magic is yours to control. But so is time. The Celestials and the Elders made a vow never to interfere with humans, but they are curious,"

Elder Illuminary explains as he holds an orb in his left hand, spinning his right hand over it.

A fog circles the inside of the orb.

"Curious about…?"

"What is to come next, Noel?"

"That, sir, is the greatest mystery," Noel replies, watching the fog continuing to circle inside the orb.

"That it is, my dear boy. A suggestion?"

"I am listening."

"Merlin will never stop. He will continue for as long as the darkness fuels him."

"Then, Elder Illuminary, it is simple. We must stop the darkness."

"But it is not that simple, Noel. First, you would have to strike at the source of that darkness, and that would be no easy feat. The gates of the Incubus realm are protected."

"The Celestials sent you to tell me this, sir?" Noel inquires, an eyebrow raised.

"They did."

"Why? What happened with the rule of them never interfering?"

"Well, this time, they have made an exception to the rules."

"So, they broke the rules?"

"Noel, my boy, they simply overlooked them."

"So, am I to understand that to stop Merlin, I have to strike at the lair of the Incubus?"

"Correct! You are Noel. Therefore, things are not what they seem."

Raising an orb, Noel spins his hand over it and the darkness' lair is revealed.

"That will be easy to find," Noel remarks, disappearing and reappearing in the sky. Looking down, Noel closes his eyes, then he raises his foot and, taking a step, realizes that he is walking on air.

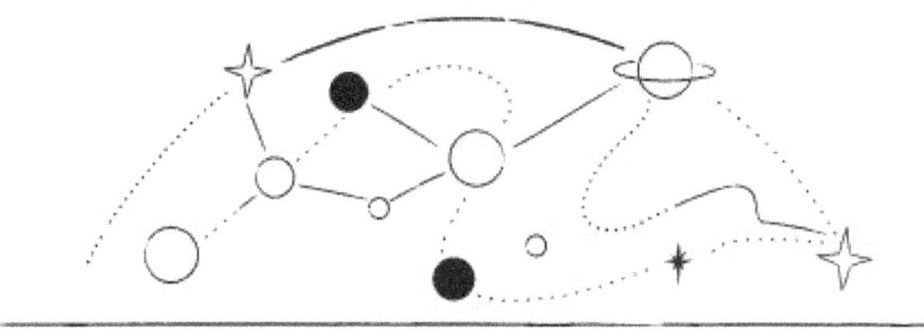

Chapter 30
The Journey Begins

Night after night, on his journey, Noel walks across the sky, the stars spinning around him. From this vantage point, Noel stops and observes the earth, watching the Mundane and Arcane go about their lives. Catching a star, he holds it in his hand, turning it over before letting it go. Pulling his hands apart, a glowing orb appears as rocks and water fly from the earth in a circle around him in the sky. At this point, his magic transcends everything ever seen by any Arcane. For now, as Noel, walking among the stars and the planets in his power, his magic has no limits.

Closing his eyes, he concentrates on the orb that he holds between his hands. The energy spins around his hands, encapsulating them. Standing, he listens, hearing the voices of every Arcane and Mundane on the wind. Magic flies around him as the planets begin to spin. Opening his eyes again, he witnesses the galaxy, planets, and stars under his control. Transcending any magic form, Noel now knows what magic truly is and that it is his to control.

Turning his hand left and right to control the orb in his hand, the rocks, streams of water, and planets spin around, slowing and then speeding up based on the turn of his hand. Knowing what this means, Noel closes his eyes again as he focuses his magic onto the orb.

When he opens his eyes, the orb flies into the air as the stars around him disappear. Noel raises his hand, and the stars spin around him as he lands on an old street of many row homes. The darkness moves against him, but when he raises his hand, revealing light, they all freeze and dissolve. Walking further down the street, Noel regards the area around him, noticing streams of magic flying down the street. Reaching up, he seizes control of one of the streams of magic. Examining the stream of magic, he allows it to run between his fingers. Then, he flips his hand open, and an orb appears. Holding it up, stars appear, flying down the dark street and lighting the way.

"Well, this is different. I guess the stars will serve as my guide."

Walking slowly, he examines the surrounding area as he descends the street. After five minutes, he comes to the city's edge where he raises his hand, and a portal opens. Stepping through, he climbs out into a forest. Strolling among the trees, he comes to an opening. Sitting down on a stump, he listens to the river running by. Then, he reaches into his bag and retrieves his journal.

Dear Journal,

Life has changed forever. Just six months ago I hated magic. That hatred has been present for almost my entire life, and I swore I would never use it again, yet here we are. So, where does one begin to answer the question?

You see, our story has stopped, but then it has re-started. The journey for the Curpendulums has just begun. The hunt for these extraordinary grimoires will be the most significant challenge yet. But, this time, I won't do it alone.

In fact, I know now that I am not alone in any part of this extraordinary journey. Just three months ago, my siblings and I were practicing at the Aelfdene Village when the darkness attacked. Amid the great attack, the Sprite Library was set ablaze, and many of the texts and artifacts of my people were lost. However, because of my siblings and our combined power, we quickly altered time to reverse the destruction, lifting the library and relocating it to protect it from attacks. The darkness, in their attempt, also tried to set our village ablaze. We worked together to stop the darkness.

Unfortunately, the darkness has recently attacked libraries worldwide, setting them ablaze. Great-grandma

Mora and Dalton have said that the blazes remind them of the burning of the great Library of Alexandria. Grandma believes the darkness is targeting the library in the hope of stopping any further Curpendulums from falling under the control of myself and my family.

My siblings are always close by, watching, ready to jump into action when needed. However, each of them has also taken on more significant roles at the school or the university. Pete just graduated and has moved back to Ignatius Manor with Mom and Dad. He is currently traveling, helping Lady Citrine Yule handle and process the artifacts discovered in the bunker. Dalton and I came to learn that they are dating.

Dalton and I graduated from the university. Willow has become Assistant Headmistress under Grandma's supervision at the school. Michael, Kells, and Sophia are working with Dad and Grandpa at the Aelfdene village, and Isabella is busy with my two nephews. I know my biggest challenge will be getting along with my brother, Pete, but I am willing to give it a shot.

The handsome and ever alluring Lord Yule and I are engaged. We will have a simple, yet elegant, wedding. We found it only fitting since he and I are the highest-ranking and most powerful Arcane. So, we decided to keep our wedding simple. Great-grandmother Nadia and Mora will preside over the ceremony accordingly. Although he and I have laughed about it, he will become the new Elder Yule once we are married, about which Dalton is not pleased.

So, he has decided that since I am going by "Noel" these days, he will go by "Lord Yule-Ignatius" or "Lord Elder-Ignatius." Personally, I do not care, but you know how everyone else is about rules and traditions.

Amelia is close by, and, like Pete, she works at Lady Citrine's shop, building new technology for the Arcane and has formed a new Knights of the Round Table based on the same model as Camelot. Her technology is proving invaluable in our continued fight against the darkness.

The seers have always told of the remarkable story of time, foretelling everything that will occur. But, recently, they have fallen silent. They sit, day in and day out, in front of their crystal balls, runes, and divination tools, and everything is quiet. They cannot foresee what is to come, which means I am in control of time.

Stopping and placing his quill on the open book in his lap, Noel raises the pocket watch, looking to see what time it is.

I still have time. Besides, I am the one who sets the time now.

Placing the watch back in his pocket. Noel examines the field from the boulder where he sits. Then he picks up his quill again. He places the quill's tip on the page, but stops for a moment, thinking, allowing ink to bleed all over the page. Then, he continues writing.

We have learned that Merlin, the Council of Dark, and none of their associates know what is to come, as time is now writing the story as it goes along. So much mystery remains with Merlin, but, in the recent weeks, I have noted in your pages, the most exciting and perplexing things about Merlin. All of us joke about that, "Things are not what they seem." In the case of Merlin, this is exceptionally true.

On another note, it is nice to have the help and support of my family. I am sure that there will be many challenging moments to come with them, but I do appreciate their support. Our journey through time to find the Curpendulums has just begun.

For now, the Sanctuary of Legend and Lore is safe under Minnie's care, my family is busy with what they need to do, and Dalton is doing what he does best, keeping time in line. With each passing day, we have discovered that the artifacts from the bunker hold extraordinary power and significance for the Arcane. Still, we have learned that it is never good to have Mr. Cee around as he seems to find some of the strangest artifacts among the piles and causes problems.

Willow wrote to tell me that Mr. Cee found a ball of yarn the other day. Much to everyone's surprise, it was the yarn of life and fates. Athena quickly scooped it up and hid it, saying that things could have gone terribly wrong.

Well, for now, this is where I end. I have work to do, and it is just beginning.

~Noel~

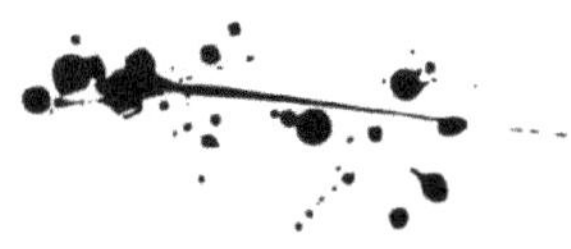

Closing his journal, Noel rises to his feet, then points his staff at the top of the hill where a portal appears. He walks toward the portal and entering it, arrives in a cave with bubbling lava all around him.

"What a charming place! Who is the interior decorator?" Noel laughs out loud as he walks along a stone walkway. Then, approaching a large open area, the darkness, hanging from the ceiling, dives on him as his staff lights, slamming them into the cavern ceiling.

"Your place is right there on the ceiling," Noel declares, smiling.

Approaching the gothic castle carved into the side of a mountain, Gargoyles drop down in front of him, lowering their spears as Noel raises his hands, and they are instantly turned to stone.

"Pathetic," Noel says aloud.

Walking between the frozen gargoyles, he pushes them over. They fall, shattering. Reaching the castle's giant oak and steel doors, Noel looks around cautiously. The ground shakes as he raises his staff, causing the door to crack down the middle. The Elven Star on the staff's tip begins to glow brightly and the doors explode off their hinges. Entering the grand entryway, Noel catches multiple streams of dark magic, which he absorbs into the Elven Star, and it grows brighter, finally exploding and throwing the darkness against the wall. A troll runs up, swinging his club as Noel jumps over his head. The troll swings his club again at Noel's feet, but Noel flips easily over the troll, and strikes him with his staff, throwing him face-first into the ground. The troll flips over and stands, grabbing Noel and squeezing him. Noel raises his hand and freezes the troll. Extracting himself from the troll's grasp, Noel pushes the frozen troll over. As the troll falls, it shrinks down to the size of a dwarf. Noel reaches down, pats the troll on the head, and, turning, walks away. When he reaches another set of doors, an old crone approaches him.

"What is it that you want?" she snaps, pulling a dagger.

"Crone, I advise you to watch your tone. I am here to see your master," Noel states, holding his staff over the crone's head as she hisses and fumbles, pulling out a set of keys. Sliding the skeleton key into the lock, she turns it as the lock clicks. The bearings on the door shift, clicking again as the doors swing open.

"You first," Noel says as he follows the crone.

Incubuses are hissing and climbing the walls up to the dark ceiling.

"I ask for an audience with your king," Noel declares as a large shadowy incubus appears, striking Noel's staff with his sword. The Elven Star grows bright, and the Incubus King is thrown back into his throne.

"Now that I have your attention…" Noel says.

"How dare you?" the king yells, rising to his feet, but Noel holds up his staff, the Elven Star growing bright, blinding the Incubus King.

"Now, as I was saying. Hear me. Call off your guards and provide no further support to Merlin. Remove your troops from earthside, or I will tear every part of your kingdom apart, starting with you," Noel threatens, pointing at the king.

"I take orders from no one," the king snaps, spinning magic around him.

When he hurls it at Noel, Noel catches it with both hands, holding it in front of him.

"Your magic is weak and easy to absorb," Noel declares, smiling as the dark magic dissolves.

"You dare threaten me?" the king yells as his sword blade lights.

Attempting to strike Noel, the king is thrown backward for a second time as Noel, with both hands, slams his staff down in front of him. Noel transforms, on the spot, into a being of solid light as Fintan appears flapping his wings. Reaching up, Noel grasps Fintan's tail, and they fly up into the air together. Multiple incubuses dive on them, but they fall down straight into the lava below as they are blinded by light magic.

Rising, the Incubus King barrels down the walkway toward Fintan and Noel. Peering down, Noel reaches into his cloak pocket and pulls out an orb, which he drops to the ground below him. Light flies around the cave as he and Fintan disappear.

In that very moment, a flash of light occurs, like a shooting star across the sky. Then nothing. Only one Arcane knows the truth about what is yet to come. For you see, things are never what they seem.

Epilogue
Things are Not What They Seem

Shifting, altering, and repeatedly replaying, one timeline after another, is acting up. When fifteen timelines act up all at once, a new, rebellious Noble Elder must calm the chaos and re-establish the balance of time, magic, and everyday life. Noble Elder grows into their new role despite moments of wanting to throw up their hands and walk away. Traveling through time, meeting hiccup after hiccup along the way, Noble Elder collaborates with six headstrong Ignatius siblings, learning to navigate complex and, at times, downright awkward relationships with them.

Working together and, sometimes, against each other, the Ignatius 7 quickly learn that things are not what they seem when they discover a truth that rocks the very core of what they know about magic. Noble Elder, tired of the growing attacks of darkness, seeks the help of Arcane and Mundane alike in a battle between light and dark.

When magic stops working because of time disruptions, RJ, Amelia, Minnie, and Dalton return to support and help, but they must learn to navigate the complex relationships that exist among the Ignatius 7. Will their epic journey to find the Curpendulums, restore time, and bring normalcy to the earth succeed? Or will time break the spirit of Noble Elder and, eventually, stop altogether? Will Noble Elder discover new ways to handle the challenges of life, magic, and darkness?

Chronicles of Phoenix

Words have the power to transform a person's life in many ways and are one of the most transformative art forms known to man.

~Kurt W. Oster

I knew the journey in The House of Phoenix Chronicles, Volume I, *Rise of the Magical Three* was just the beginning. With the growing success of Volume I and a remarkable and truly unique storyline that pushes literary bounds, I understood that I had to keep things going, and ten months after the release of Volume I, it gave me great pleasure to share with all of you, my readers, Volume II, *Secrets Echoed,* of this epic and fantastic series. Volume II continued the story of Rose, her twin older brothers, and their friends and family as they navigated the complexities of family, magic, and time-travel.

Now with two volumes in circulation, and again ten-months later, it gives me a great pleasure to share with you the readers, Volume III, *The Ignatius 7.* The epic journey of seven headstrong siblings, learning to navigate life, and learning what it means to be siblings. With Rose and her twin brothers now grandparents, they embark on an incredible journey of leading the next generation of Arcane and Mundane, alike in the new installment Volume III of the House of Phoenix Chronicles.

As a writer, the journey of developing the storyline, the characters, and the lives becomes an art form in itself. As I noted in the Afterwards of Volume I & II, my writing is very much influenced by my career as a licensed therapist. My experience working with mental health, life coaching, and helping the neurodivergent and LGBTQ+ communities, combined with my love of history, has influenced the story themes, characters, and relationships portrayed in the House of Phoenix Chronicles series.

When asked to summarize the series, I would say this. It is a fantasy love story that includes some exciting characters along the way. One of history's greatest wizards, Merlin is at the forefront of the story but with a bizarre twist that brings magic, time travel, mystical creatures, technology, and the challenges of growing up to life in this epic tale.

As readers and writers, we are aware of many literary themes one of which is the most popular—the *Hero's Journey*. Unfortunately, society has taught us that most of the time, the female heroine is cast as the "damsel in distress" who is saved by colorful companions, usually a man. In Volumes I & II, Rose is the heroine of the story and now in Volume III, moves into the elder sage who assists the new hero on their journey.

As a gay man and as the father of a teenage woman, I feel there are not enough stories with female heroines in the literary world. The House of Phoenix Chronicles explores the life of a young heroine, her two brothers, and their struggles with love and power that will shape their destinies. I hope this series inspires the next generation with a love for reading, our fellow humans, and values that redefine the role and acceptance of all people.

Although I grew up in a family of readers and academic scholars, I hated books with a passion as a young person. It was not until my high school years that I began to enjoy reading and became engrossed in fantasy fiction. In college, I discovered that I am dyslexic, a severe reading disability. Once I had that under control, I began to thrive in my college education far beyond what I could ever have expected. As the late Ruth Bader Ginsburg said:

> Reading is the key that opens doors to many good things in life. Reading shaped my dreams, and more reading helped make my dreams come true.

In developing the House of Phoenix Chronicles series, I live by Ginsburg's words. My goal as an author is to write a series that helps open doors to many good things in life, enjoyment, happiness, amusement, a sense of awe, adventure, and an overall love for reading.

At first, for me, reading was my enemy. Coming to love reading opened the doors for many opportunities in my life, opportunities that I hope others will experience through my writing.

Sincerely Yours,

Kurt W. Oster

Kurt W. Oster

Character List

The Noble House of Phoenix

The House of Phoenix continues to be the pivotal character line of the series. The members of this house share Arcane, Mundane, and magical heritage. Members of the House of Phoenix have married into the Houses of Elder, Ignatius, Knight, and Drake. The Noble House of Phoenix is a critical member of the Arcane community and serves in high-ranking roles of the Arcane. The

members of the House of Phoenix play critical roles to the Arcane and Mundane communities throughout the story.

Queen Phoenix (Royalty, Princess, Mundane)

The Queen of the Land. Mother of Merlin. It is unclear if she is living or deceased. Merlin seeks the Curpendulums because of her sudden disappearance.

Merlin Ambrose Phoenix (Arcane of Mystical and Magical Experience, Dark Sorcerer Warlock)

Merlin is the series' main antagonist. In his early years, he served as King Arthur's court advisor. He is the self-proclaimed King of the Arcane and one of twelve founders of the Arcane realm. Merlin continues to disrupt time with his quest for power as he seeks out the Curpendulums.

The spouse to the Lady Nimuway. He is the father of Titus Phoenix and father-in-law to Flora Aine Phoenix. He is the grandfather to Kelvin, Wade, and Terra Phoenix. He is the great-grandfather of Oliver, Ethan, Bethany, Daemon, Eric, and Roslynn Phoenix. Throughout his life, he was the teacher to Morgana and later to Alezander for several years. He is half incubus (father) and half-human (mother, princess). Upon the disappearance of his mother, he was driven-mad and became consumed with finding her and destroying anyone who stood in his way.

He is the second great-grandfather of Madeline and Gwendolyn Phoenix, Matthew Knight-Phoenix, and Ari, Theo, Hope, Vivian, and Rusty Ignatius. [Appearing in books I-V].

Lady Nimuway Gwendolyn Phoenix (Arcane of Magical Experience, Mystic, Witch, Sister of Avalon)

A mystic with excellent knowledge and understanding of the living earth. She is the great Lady of the Lake who takes on this persona to confuse everyone with whom she interacts. She is the Queen of the Arcane and one of the twelve founders of the Arcane realm. In death, she becomes the Queen of Avalon and serves as its mystical guardian. Nimuway has worked behind Merlin's back to ensure he cannot succeed. Although a virtue of purity and light, many mysteries remain around the great lady. She is the co-leader of the Sisters of Avalon. She is a key historian as it pertains to Noel and holds critical information on the whereabouts of the Curpendulums.

The spouse to Merlin Ambrose Phoenix, she is the mother of Titus Phoenix and mother-in-law to Flora Aine Phoenix. Grandmother to Kelvin, Wade, and Terra Phoenix. She is the great-grandmother of Oliver, Ethan, Bethany, Daemon, Eric, and Roslynn Phoenix. Nimuway is the best friend of the Lady Mora Elder.

She is the second great-grandmother of Madeline and Gwendolyn Phoenix, Matthew Knight-Phoenix, and Ari, Theo, Hope, Vivian, and Rusty Ignatius. [Appearing in books I-V].

Lord Kelvin Chadd Phoenix (Arcane of Magical Experience, Sorcerer, Retired Arcane President)

He was born the high Prince of the Arcane realm and became the Third King of the Arcane realm upon his father's death. He was the first and now the retired President of the Arcane and serves as one of the leading Magical Ambassador of the Arcane to the Mundane. Upon his retirement, he serves as an advisor to his son, Oliver Phoenix, who becomes President after his father. He utilizes a wand or staff, interchangeably, as his primary weapon of choice.

He is the eldest child of the late King Titus and Queen Flora Phoenix. He is the eldest brother of Wade and Terra Phoenix. He is the eldest grandson of Merlin and Nimuway. He is the spouse of Nadia Freya Drake. He is the father of Oliver Phoenix, Ethan Knight-Phoenix, and Roslynn Phoenix Ignatius. He is the uncle of Bethany, Daemon, and Eric Phoenix.

He is the grandfather of Matthew Knight-Phoenix, Madeline and Gwendolyn Phoenix, and Esther, Ari, Theo, Hope, Vivian, and Rusty Ignatius. In addition, he is the great-grandfather of Isabella, Peter, Michael, Kells, Sophia, Willow, and Russell Ignatius. [Appearing in books I-V].

Lady Nadia Freya Phoenix {nee Drake} (Arcane of Magical and Mundane Experience, Diviner, Witch Goddess)

High Princess of the Arcane realm. Member of the House of Drake. Upon Nadia's reunification with her children, she becomes the wise mother who is always there to guide them on their journey. She utilizes a wand or staff, interchangeably, as her primary weapon of choice. However, Nadia has been known not to need a weapon to be able to fight or cast magic.

Eldest sister of Hawke Drake and Emma "Destiny" Drake-Phoenix. Daughter of Fortis and Dawn Drake. Spouse of Kelvin Phoenix. Mother of Oliver, Ethan, and Roslynn Phoenix. Witch Goddess, highest witch of the realm. Child of two realms. Second leader of the Arcane Resistance. She serves as the advisor to her children. She is the grandmother to Matthew Knight-Phoenix, Madeline and Gwendolyn Phoenix, Esther, Ari, Theo, Hope, Vivian, and Rusty Ignatius. In addition, she is the great-grandmother of Isabella, Peter, Michael, Kells, Sophia, Willow, and Russell Ignatius. [Appearing in books I-V].

Oliver Kelvin Cuinn Phoenix (Arcane of Mundane Experience, ArchSorcerer, President)

High Prince of the Arcane when his parents were heir to the throne of the Arcane realm. Currently works in Magical Law Enforcement and serves as an advisor to his father, the President of the Arcane. ArchSorcerer. Member of the Magical Three. He utilizes a wand or staff, interchangeably, as his primary weapon of choice. However, Oliver has been known to fight with a sword.

He is the eldest son of Kelvin and Nadia Phoenix. Grandson of Titus and Flora Phoenix and Fortis and Dawn Drake. Husband of Olivia. Great-grandson to Merlin and Nimuway Phoenix. Twin brother of Ethan Knight-Phoenix and older brother of Roslynn Phoenix Ignatius. Father to Madeline and Gwendolyn Phoenix.

Brother-in-law to Sebastian Knight-Phoenix and to King Alezander Ignatius. Uncle to Matthew Knight-Phoenix, Ari, Theo, Hope, Vivian, and Rusty Ignatius. Great-uncle to Esther, Isabella, Peter, Michael, Kells, Sophia, Willow, and Russell Ignatius. [Appearing in books I-V].

Olivia Madeline Phoenix [nee Pendragon] (Mundane of Arcane and Mystical Heritage, Advisor to the Arcane Parliament)

Is a member of the House of Pendragon. She is a descendant of King Arthur and Queen Guinevere. Non-magical but lives among the Arcane. Loved by the covens. Serves as Mundane Advisor to her father-in-law, President Kelvin Phoenix. She is the wife of Oliver Phoenix. Mother to Madeline and Gwendolyn Phoenix.

Sister-in-law to Ethan and Sebastian Knight-Phoenix and Alezander and Rose Ignatius. Aunt of Matthew Knight-Phoenix and Esther, Ari, Theo, Hope, Vivian, and Rusty Ignatius. Great-aunt to Esther, Isabella, Peter, Michael, Kells, Sophia, Willow, and Russell Ignatius. [Appearing in books I-V].

Madeline Heidi Phoenix (Arcane of Magical and Mundane Experience, Witch)

Works for the Arcane Parliament in magical artifacts. Travels the world with her husband. Daughter of Oliver and Olivia Phoenix. Granddaughter of Kelvin and Nadia Phoenix. Niece of Ethan and Sebastian Knight-Phoenix and Alezander and Rose Ignatius. She utilizes a wand or quill, interchangeably, as her primary weapons of choice. Aunt to Martha Magnus. First cousin of Matthew Knight-Phoenix and Ari, Theo, Hope, Vivian and Rusty Ignatius [Appearing in books II-V].

Gwendolyn Theresa Magnus [nee Phoenix] (Arcane of Magical and Mundane Experience, Witch)

Arcane writer teaching the Arcane about the Mundane. She writes on the history and times of the Arcane. Daughter of Oliver and Olivia Phoenix. Sister of Madeline Heidi Phoenix. Granddaughter of Kelvin and Nadia Phoenix. Niece of Ethan and Sebastian Knight-Phoenix and Alezander and Rose Ignatius. First cousin of Matthew Knight-Phoenix and Ari, Theo, Hope, Vivian and Rusty Ignatius. Widow. Mother to Martha Magnus. Like her sister, she utilizes a wand or quill, interchangeably, as her primary weapons of choice. [Appearing in books II-V]

Martha Magnus [nee Phoenix]. (Arcane of Magical and Mundane Experience, Witch)

Martha is the corky and chipper cousin of the Ignatius seven and Amelia Pendragon. Daughter of Lord Magnus and Gwendolyn Theresa Magnus.

Granddaughter of Oliver and Olivia Phoenix. Niece of Madeline Heidi Phoenix. Great-granddaughter of Kelvin and Nadia Phoenix. Great-niece of Ethan and Sebastian Knight-Phoenix and Alezander and Rose Ignatius. Martha works at Dwarfbrew at the Arcane University and is close to her cousin's Amelia Pendragon and Russell Ignatius, Jr. She utilizes a wand or staff, interchangeably, as her primary weapons of choice. Healer among the Arcane. [Appearing in books III-V].

Ethan Ambrose Kenrick Phoenix [Married name Knight-Phoenix]
(Arcane of Mundane Experience, ArchSorcerer, Professor)

High Prince of the Arcane when his parents were heir to the throne of the Arcane realm. Currently works as the Potions Teacher of the Arcane Academy of Magical Teaching. ArchSorcerer. Member of the Magical Three.

He is the second eldest child of Kelvin and Nadia Phoenix. Grandson of Titus and Flora Phoenix and Fortis and Dawn Drake. Husband of Sebastian Knight-Phoenix. Great-grandson to Merlin and Nimuway Phoenix. Twin brother of Oliver Ignatius and older brother of Roslynn Phoenix Ignatius. He utilizes a wand or staff, interchangeably, as his primary weapon of choice. However, Ethan has been known to fight with a sword.

Brother-in-law to Olivia Phoenix and Alezander Ignatius. He is the father of Matthew Knight-Phoenix. Uncle to Madeline and Gwendolyn Phoenix and Ari, Theo, Hope, Vivian, and Rusty Ignatius. Great-uncle to Amelia and Martha Pendragon and Esther, Isabella, Peter, Michael, Kells, Sophia, Willow, and Russell Ignatius. [Appearing in books I-V].

Sebastian Nolan Quid Knight [married name Knight-Phoenix]
(Arcane of Magical Experience, Sorcerer, Necromancer)

Sorcerer and Necromancer. He is the head of the Arcane Magical Law Enforcement division. He utilizes a wand or staff, interchangeably, as his primary weapons of choice but he is skilled in various weapons in combat.

Son of Aden and Divinity Knight. Older brother of Liam Knight. He is the husband of Ethan Knight-Phoenix. He is the father of Matthew Knight-Phoenix.

Brother-in-law to Oliver and Olivia Phoenix and Alezander and Rose Ignatius. Uncle to Madeline and Gwendolyn Phoenix and Ari, Theo, Hope, Vivian, and Rusty Ignatius. Great-uncle to Amelia and Martha Pendragon, Esther, Isabella, Peter, Michael, Kells, Sophia, Willow, and Russell Ignatius. [Appearing in books I-V].

Matthew Nolan Kenrick Knight-Phoenix (Arcane of Mundane Experience, Sorcerer, Necromancer)

Sorcerer who serves the Arcane Parliament in an undisclosed position only known by his father Sebastian and his uncle, Oliver. He was discovered during the Mundane Realm Siege. He is a necromancer and utilizes a wand as his primary weapon of choice. He has had multiple love interests throughout his life, both male and female.

He is the son of Ethan and Sebastian Knight-Phoenix. In addition, he is the grandson of Aden and Divinity Knight and Kelvin and Nadia Phoenix. He is the nephew of Oliver and Olivia Phoenix and Alezander and Rose Ignatius. He is first cousins to Madeline and Gwendolyn Phoenix, and Esther, Ari, Theo, Hope, Vivian, and Rusty Ignatius. [Appearing in books I-V].

Wade Brennon Phoenix (Arcane of Magical Experience, Wizard, Member of Arcane Council)

He was born the Prince of the Arcane realm and was the second heir to the throne of the Arcane realm behind his brother until the birth of his nephews and niece. He works for the Arcane Parliament and serves as an advisor to his brother Kelvin when he is President of the Arcane. He utilizes a wand or staff, interchangeably, as his primary weapon of choice.

He is the second child of the late King Titus and Queen Flora Phoenix. He is the younger brother of Kelvin Phoenix and the older brother of Terra Phoenix. He is the second eldest grandson of Merlin and Nimuway. He is the spouse of Lady Bethany Phoenix. He is the father of Bethany Minerva Phoenix Fae. He is remarried to Emma "Destiny" Drake. He is brother-in-law to Nadia Phoenix. He is the uncle of Oliver, Ethan, Rose, Daemon, and Eric Phoenix. [Appearing in books I-V].

Lady Emma Destiny Phoenix [nee Drake] (Arcane of Magical & Mundane Experience, Witch, Historian)

She is the Magical Three's protector who resides in the Mundane realm. She was a high school teacher to Mundane students and later took a post as the Head of History education for the Arcane Academy of Magical Teaching. She is the leading living Arthurian historian among the Arcane and Mundane. She is the daughter of Fortis and Dawn Drake. She is one of the three heads of the Arcane Council. In addition, she serves as an advisor to her sister Nadia and her niece Roslynn. She is the second spouse of Wade Phoenix. She is the stepmother to Bethany Phoenix Fae. She is the sister-in-law of Kelvin Phoenix. She is a friend of

Mora Elder Ignatius and Alezander Ignatius. She utilizes a wand or staff, interchangeably, as her primary weapon of choice.

She is the younger sister of Nadia and Hawke. She is the aunt of Oliver, Ethan, and Rose. She is the great-aunt to Madaline, Gwendolyn Phoenix and Matthew Knight-Phoenix, and Ari, Theo, Hope, Vivian, and Rusty Ignatius. [Appearing in books I-V].

Deceased Members of the House of Phoenix

Titus Marvin Phoenix (Arcane of Magical Experience, Wizard)

Second King of the Arcane. Spouse of Flora Phoenix. Son of Merlin and Nimuway. Father of Kelvin, Wade, and Terra Phoenix. He is the grandfather of Oliver, Ethan, Rose, Bethany, Daemon, and Erik Phoenix. (Deceased). [Prequel].

Flora Aine Phoenix (Arcane of Magical Experience, Witch)

Second Queen of the Arcane. Spouse of Titus Phoenix. Mother of Kelvin, Wade, and Terra Phoenix. She is the grandmother of Oliver, Ethan, Rose, Bethany, Daemon, and Erik Phoenix. (Deceased). [Prequel].

Terra Discordia Phoenix (Arcane of Magical Experience, Witch)

Late Princess of the Arcane Realm. Daughter of Titus and Flora. Granddaughter of Merlin and Nimuway Phoenix. Sister of Kelvin and Wade Phoenix. Mother of Daemon and Eric Phoenix. Aunt of Oliver, Ethan, Roslyn, and Bethany Phoenix. Member of the Dark Guard. Killed by Cedric. (Deceased). [Book I].

Daemon Merlin Phoenix (Arcane of Magical Experience, Conjurer)

Baron of the Arcane realm. Son of Terra Phoenix. Grandson of Titus and Flora Phoenix. Great-grandson to Merlin and Nimuway Phoenix. Member of the Dark Guard. Brother of Eric Phoenix. (Deceased). [Book I].

Eric Marvin Phoenix (Arcane of Magical Experience, Conjurer)

Baron of the Arcane Realm. Son of Terra Phoenix. Grandson of Titus and Flora Phoenix. Great-grandson to Merlin and Nimuway Phoenix. Member of the Dark Guard. Brother of Daemon Phoenix. (Deceased). [Book I].

ॐ

The Mysterious House of Drake

The mysterious House of Drake is an Arcane family of vast power and serves as the protectors of the ancient Arcane village. Academy of Magical Teaching, which was founded initially by the Lady Mora Elder. Members of the House of Drake have married into the House of Phoenix and other notable Arcane families. The members of the House of Drake are all of Arcane and Mundane Experience as the Drake Family remained behind in the Mundane realm when Merlin created the Arcane realm. Members of the House of Drake have exceptional magical power, with the origins of their magic still a great mystery to date.

Dawn Rhiannon Drake (Arcane of Magical Experience, Witch, Sister of Avalon)

Spouse of Fortis Drake. Mother of Nadia and Hawke Drake. Grandmother of Oliver, Ethan, and Roslynn Phoenix. Is a member of the Sisters of Avalon. Turned back to the side of the light. Assists Lady Nimuway and Noel throughout the story. [Appearing in books I-V]

Deceased Member of the House of Drake or Whereabouts Unkown

Fortis Mael Drake (Arcane of Magical Experience, Knight, Wizard)

Knight of the Court. Chief of the Guards of Light the Ancient City. Spouse of Dawn Drake. Father of Nadia and Hawke Drake. Grandfather of Oliver, Ethan, and Roslynn Phoenix. (Deceased). [Prequel].

Hawke Adie Drake (Arcane of Magical Experience, Wizard)

Son of Fortis and Dawn Drake. Uncle of Oliver, Ethan, and Roslynn Phoenix. Brother of Nadia Drake Phoenix. Member of the Dark Guard. [Whereabouts unknown].

ॐ

The Dark House of Knight

The dark House of Knight is an Arcane family of magical experiences. A long-standing house of the Arcane community. After it was discovered that Lord Aden was in league with Merlin, Morgana, and the Dark Council, the House of Knight took on the mantle of the dark house and because of the actions of Lord Aden, the Lady Divinity divorced her husband to live among the Arcane people. A powerful Sibyl, she is considered the supreme mistress of divination among the Arcane. The Members of the House of Knight are Arcane of Magical Experience.

Divinity Macha Knight (Arcane of Magical and Mystical Experience, Mystic, Sibyl, Sorceress)

Sorceress. Head of the Arcane Council of Light, one of twelve founders of the Arcane realm. Head Sibyl. Mother of Sebastian and Liam Knight. The ex-spouse of Aden Knight. Friend of Kelvin and Nadia Phoenix. Current teacher of Arcane. [Appearing in books I-V]

Liam Tarlock Knight (Arcane of Magical Experience, Summoner, Warlock)

Warlock. Summoner of Darkness. Second Head of the Dark Guard. Son of Aden and Divinity Knight. The younger brother of Sebastian Knight.

Whereabouts of the Members of the House of Knight Unknown

Aden Duncan Knight (Arcane of Magical Experience, Summoner, Warlock)

Warlock. Summoner of Darkness. Head of the Dark Guard. Father of Sebastian and Liam Knight. The ex-spouse of Divinity Knight. Whereabouts at this time are unknown. [Whereabouts unknown].

∾

The Extraordinary House of Ignatius

Considered to be the eldest and largest of the Arcane Houses, The Extraordinary House of Ignatius is an Arcane House and the Royal Family of the elves. The Extraordinary House of Ignatius has been the ruling family over the Aelfdene village for centuries. A family known for their beauty and grace, all the members of the House are known as incredible wielders of elemental magic, archery, weapons, and healing abilities. The Extraordinary House of Ignatius has married into the other notable Arcane Houses, including the Houses of Elder and Phoenix.

Lady Mora Ignatius {nee Elder} (Arcane of Magical and Mystical Experience, Elder, Witch Goddess)

Dowager Queen of the elves. Headmistress of the Arcane Academy of Magical Teaching until her retirement. Mother of Alezander Elderchild Ignatius. Spouse of the late King Caspar Ignatius. Grandmother of Ari, Theo, Hope, Vivian, and Russell Ignatius. Great-grandmother to Esther, Isabella, Peter, Michael, Kells, Sophia, Willow, and Russell Ignatius. Witch goddess and sorceress. The eldest living Elder, she became the only living original Elder upon the passing of Noble Elder. She utilizes a wand or staff, interchangeably, as her primary weapon of choice. However, Mora has been known not to need a weapon to be able to fight or cast magic. [Appearing in books I-V].

High-King Alezander Elderchild Ignatius (Arcane of Magical Experience, Elder, Elf, ArchSorcerer)

Reigning king (upon father's death) of the elves. Former student of Merlin. Second youngest member of the Council of Elders. Spouse of Roslynn Phoenix. Brother-in-law of Oliver and Olivia Phoenix and Ethan and Sebastian Knight-Phoenix. Uncle to Madeline and Gwendolyn Phoenix and Matthew Knight-Phoenix. Father of Ari, Theo, Hope, Vivian, and Russell. Grandfather of Esther, Isabella, Peter, Michael, Sophia, Kells, Willow, and Russell Ambrose Ignatius. Teacher at the Arcane School of Magical Teaching. Member of the elf royal family. Cousin of Avery, Maria, Alvina, and Lukas Ignatius. Nephew of Otta Ignatius. Weapons Master of the elves. Known for his skill with the long sword and his superior intellectual ability. He utilizes a wand or staff, interchangeably, as his primary weapon of choice, however, in combat will fight with Elfish Long Blade. [Appearing in books I-V].

High Queen Roslynn (Rose) Sophia Nadia Ignatius {nee Phoenix} (Arcane of Mundane Experience, Arch Sorceress, ArchSeer)

Former High Princess of the Arcane realm. She became the queen of the elves upon her marriage to her husband, King Alezander. ArchSorceress. Member of the Magical Three. Headmistress, and Head Librarian of the Arcane Academy of Magical Teaching. Daughter of Kelvin and Nadia Phoenix. Granddaughter of Titus and Flora Phoenix and Fortis and Dawn Drake. Great-granddaughter to Merlin and Nimuway Phoenix. Sister of Oliver and Ethan Phoenix. Aunt to Madeline and Gwendolyn Phoenix and Matthew Knight-Phoenix. Mother of Ari, Theo, Hope, Vivian, and Russell Ignatius. Grandmother to Esther, Isabella, Peter, Michael, Sophia, Kells, Willow, and Russell Ambrose Ignatius. ArchSeer and Time Cycler. Sage who helps Noel throughout his Journey.

She utilizes a wand or staff, interchangeably, as her primary weapon of choice. However, Rose has been known not to need a weapon to be able to fight or cast magic. [Appearing in books I-V]

Ari Torion Ignatius (Arcane of Magical Experience, Elf, Wizard)

Eldest son of King Alezander and Queen Roslynn Ignatius. Spouse of Amber Detlar Ignatius. Father of Esther Ignatius. Nephew of Oliver and Ethan Phoenix. Grandson of Kelvin and Nadia Phoenix and Caspar and Mora Ignatius. Uncle of the Ignatius Seven. Cousin of Madeline and Gwendolyn Phoenix and Matthew Knight-Phoenix. He utilizes a wand or staff, interchangeably, as his primary weapon of choice. Time Traveler. Leader of the Elfish Guard. Member of the Elf Royal Family. [Appearing in books I-V].

Amber Ignatius {nee Detlar} Arcane of Magical Experience, Elf, Witch, Seer)

Wife of Ari Ignatius. Mother of Esther Ignatius. Daughter-in-law of King Alezander and Queen Roslynn Ignatius. Elf Seer. Member of the Elf Royal Family. She utilizes a wand or crystal ball, interchangeably, as her primary weapon of choice. [Appearing in books I-V].

Esther Ardulriina Ignatius (Arcane of Magical Experience, Elf, Grand ArchSeer, Witch)

Elf Witch. Daughter of Ari and Amber Ignatius. Niece of Theo, Hope, Vivian, Rusty and Meredith Ignatius. Granddaughter of King Alezander and Queen Roslynn Ignatius. Great-granddaughter of Mora and Caspar Ignatius and Kelvin and Nadia Phoenix. Cousin to the Ignatius Seven. GrandSeer. Member of the Elf Royal Family. Head Lady of the Magical Nexus. She utilizes a wand, staff, orbs or her marble guards, interchangeably, as her primary weapon of choice. He utilizes a wand or staff, interchangeably, as his primary weapon of choice. [Appearing in books I-V].

Theo Merlion Ignatius (Arcane f Magical Experience, Elf, Wizard)

Second eldest son of King Alezander and Queen Roslynn Ignatius. Nephew of Oliver and Ethan Phoenix. Grandson of Kelvin and Nadia Phoenix and Caspar and Mora Ignatius. Uncle of Ester Ignatius and the Ignatius Seven. Cousin of Madeline and Gwendolyn Phoenix and Matthew Knight-Phoenix. Time Traveler. Second Leader of the Elfish Guard. Member of the Elf Royal Family. He utilizes a wand or staff, interchangeably, as his primary weapon of choice. [Appearing in books I-V].

Hope Fenmenor Ignatius (Arcane of Magical Experience, Elf, Healer, Witch)

Third child and eldest daughter of King Alezander and Queen Roslynn Ignatius. Niece of Oliver and Ethan Phoenix. Granddaughter of Kelvin and Nadia Phoenix and Caspar and Mora Ignatius. Aunt of Esther Ignatius and the Ignatius Seven. Cousin of Madeline and Gwendolyn Phoenix and Matthew Knight-Phoenix. Time Traveler. Leader of the Elfish Guard. She is an an elf healer. Member of the Elf Royal Family. She utilizes a wand or staff, interchangeably, as her primary weapon of choice. [Appearing in books I-V].

Vivian Shazorwyn Ignatius (Arcane of Magical Experience, Elf, Priestess and Warrior, Witch)

Fourth child and second eldest daughter of King Alezander and Queen Roslynn Ignatius. Niece of Oliver and Ethan Phoenix. Spouse of Bridgett Agarvran. Granddaughter of Kelvin and Nadia Phoenix and Caspar and Mora Ignatius. Aunt of Esther Ignatius and the Ignatius Seven. Cousin of Madeline and Gwendolyn Phoenix and Matthew Knight-Phoenix. Time Traveler. Leader of the Elfish Guard. She is a elf priestess and warrior. She utilizes a wand or staff, interchangeably, as her primary weapons of choice but is trained to use various other elfish weapons but her first choice is the elfish arm blades. Member of the Elf Royal Family. [Appearing in books I-V].

Russell (Rusty) Ambrose Alezander Elderchild Ignatius (Arcane of Magical Experience, Elf, Heir to the Aelfdene Throne, Grand Sorcerer)

Fifth child and second eldest son of King Alezander and Queen Roslynn Ignatius. Nephew of Oliver and Ethan Phoenix. Grandson of Kelvin and Nadia Phoenix and Caspar and Mora Ignatius. Uncle of Ester Ignatius and the Ignatius Seven. Cousin of Madeline and Gwendolyn Phoenix and Matthew Knight-Phoenix. Spouse of Meredith Amser Elder. Father of Isabella, Peter, Michael, Sophia, Kells, Willow, and Russell Ignatius. Time Traveler. Grand Leader of the Elfish Guard. Member of the Elf Royal Family. Heir apparent to the Aelfdene Thrne. Grand Sorcerer. Aid to Noel. He utilizes a wand or staff, interchangeably, as his primary weapon of choice. [Appearing in books I-V].

Meredith Amser Ignatius (High Arcane, Celestial, Immortal, Sorceress)

Wife of Russell Ambrose Alezander Elderchild Ignatius. Mother of the Ignatius 7. The extent of her magical power is still unclear, foretold to be the Successor of Lady Anwara. She is the daughter of the Lady Anwina, "Anwina, the Luminous," and the older sister of Sloan, the Nature Warrior. [Appearing in Books II-V].

The Ignatius 7

The extraordinary seven siblings who shape the story of time. The seven are exceptionally gifted sorcerers and sorceresses whose magic is the strongest of all Arcane. The seven are the allies of Noel and Lord Dalton Time Yule. The seven are the children of Russell and Meredith Ignatius and grandchildren of King Alezander and Queen Roslynn Ignatius. The seven have the gift of time travel and jump in and out of the various timelines, influencing the outcome of the story.

Isabella Roslynn Ignatius (Arcane of Magical Experience, Elf, Elemental ArchSorceress, Arch Seer, Immrtal)

Acrh Sorceress. Elf Princess. ArchSeer with the ability to read minds. The eldest daughter of Russell and Meredith Ignatius. She is the second granddaughter of High King Alezander and Queen Roslynn. Niece of Ari, and Amber, Theo,

Hope, and Vivian Ignatius. Cousin to Esther Ignatius. Great-granddaughter of Mora and Caspar Ignatius and Kelvin and Nadia Phoenix. Descendent of Merlin and Nimuway. Member of the Royal Aelfdene Family. Sibling of Michael Peter, Kells, Sophia, Willow, and Russell. Wife of Bradley. Mother of Bradley, Jr. and Edwin. She utilizes a wand or staff, interchangeably, as her primary weapon of choice. [Appearing in books II-V].

Michael Cunnings Ignatius (Arcane of Magical Experience, Elf, Elemental ArchSorcerer, Immortal)

The eldest son of and second eldest child of Russell and Meredith Ignatius. He is the third grandchild of High King Alezander, and Queen Rosylnn. Nephew of Ari, and Amber, Theo, Hope, and Vivian Ignatius. Cousin to Esther Ignatius. Great-grandson of Mora and Caspar Ignatius and Kelvin and Nadia Phoenix. Descendent of Merlin and Nimuway. Administrator of Aelfdene. Member of the Royal Aelfdene Family. Sibling of Isabella, Peter, Kells, Sophia, Willow, and Rusell Ambrose, Jr. Weapons Master, resides at the Aelfdene Village, works for the Arcane Parliment forging partnerships with the Mundane. He utilizes a wand or bow and arrow, interchangeably, as his primary weapon of choice. [Appearing in books II-V]

Peter Kelvin Ignatius (Arcane of Magical Experience, Elf, Elemental ArchSorcerer, Immortal)

The second eldest son of and third eldest child of Russell and Meredith Ignatius. He is the fourth grandchild of High King Alezander, and Queen Rosylnn. Nephew of Ari, and Amber, Theo, Hope, and Vivian Ignatius. Cousin to Esther Ignatius. Great-grandson of Mora and Caspar Ignatius and Kelvin and Nadia Phoenix. Descendent of Merlin and Nimuway. Member of the Royal Aelfdene Family. Sibling of Isabella, Michael, Kells, Sophia, Willow, and Rusell Ambrose, Jr. Sorcerer of Elemental Magic, exceptional fighter, historian of ancient artifacts. Troublemaker. Grandfather of Elvey Peter Ignatius, Nordika Destiny Ignatius. He utilizes a wand or staff, interchangeably, as his primary weapon of choice. Boyfriend to Citrine "Time" Yule. [Appearing in books II-V].

Kells Ingálvur Ignatius (Arcane of Magical Experience, Elf, Elemental ArchSorcerer, Immortal)

The third eldest son of and fourth eldest child of Russell and Meredith Ignatius. He is the fifth grandchild of High King Alezander, and Queen Rosylnn. Nephew of Ari, and Amber, Theo, Hope, and Vivian Ignatius. Cousin to Esther Ignatius. Great-grandson of Mora and Caspar Ignatius and Kelvin and Nadia

Phoenix. Descendent of Merlin and Nimuway. Member of the Royal Aelfdene Family. Older twin brother of Sophia. Sibling of Isabella, Michael, Peter, Willow, and Rusell Ambrose, Jr. Member of the Council of the Elfish Priory, Trainer of Elf Monks. Master of Weapon and Non-weapons combat although he utilizes a wand or giant mace, interchangeably, as his primary weapon of choice. Second tallest of the Ignatius Seven. [Appearing in books II-V].

Sophia llivhrae lgnatius (Arcane of Magical Experience, Elf, Elemental ArchSorceress, lmortal)

The second eldest daughter of and fifth eldest child of Russell and Meredith Ignatius. She is the six grandchild of High King Alezander, and Queen Rosylnn. Niece of Ari, and Amber, Theo, Hope, and Vivian Ignatius. Cousin to Esther Ignatius. Great-granddaughter of Mora and Caspar Ignatius and Kelvin and Nadia Phoenix. Descendent of Merlin and Nimuway. Member of the Royal Aelfdene Family. Younger twin sister of Kells. Sibling of Isabella, Michael, Peter, Willow, and Rusell Ambrose, Jr. Member of the Council of the Elfish Priory, Trainer of Elf Monks and Priestesses. Master of Weapon and Non-weapons combat although she utilizes a wand or elfish arm blades, interchangeably, as her primary weapon of choice. Elf Seer, mind reader, and telepath. Has the ability to animate texts, and art works making them come to life, mentee of Lady Marybelle. [Appearing in books II-V].

Willow Lillian Cemno lgnatius (Arcane of Magical Experience, Elf, Elemental ArchSorceress, lmmortal)

The third and youngest daughter of and sixth eldest child of Russell and Meredith Ignatius. She is the seventh grandchild of High King Alezander, and Queen Rosylnn. Niece of Ari, and Amber, Theo, Hope, and Vivian Ignatius. Cousin to Esther Ignatius. Great-granddaughter of Mora and Caspar Ignatius and Kelvin and Nadia Phoenix. Descendent of Merlin and Nimuway. Member of the Royal Aelfdene Family.

Sibling of Isabella, Michael, Peter, Kells, Sophia, and Rusell Ambrose, Jr. Assistant Headmistress under her Grandmother, the Headmistress Roslynn Ignatius. Master Herbalist and trainer of Elemental Magic. Summoner of Earth Magic. Master Archer. She utilizes a wand or bow and arrow, interchangeably, as her primary weapon of choice. However, she has been known not to need a weapon to be able to fight or cast magic. Master of magic technology and develops her own weapons and gadgets. Elf Seer, mind reader, and telepath. Love interest in Barrett Lane an unusual gentleman [Appearing in books II-V].

The Master of the Curpendulums and Time

Russell Ambrose Alezander Elderchild Ignatius, Jr. "RJ" aka Noel (High Arcane, Mundane of Arcane Experience, Elder, Grand ArchSorcerer and Necro Sorcerer, Immortal, Master of the Curpendulums and Time)

Successor of Noble Elder. Grand ArchSorcerer, Immortal. Unable to be killed. Elemental ArchSorcerer. Known as the Master of the Curpendulums and Time.

Born Russell Ambrose Alexander Elderchild Ignatius, Jr. he grew up going by Ambrose. He is the youngest child of Lord Russell (Rusty) and Lady Meredith Ignatius. He is the eighth grandchild of High King Alezander, and Queen Rosylnn. Nephew of Ari, and Amber, Theo, Hope, and Vivian Ignatius. Cousin to Esther Ignatius. Great-grandson of Mora and Caspar Ignatius and Kelvin and Nadia Phoenix. Descendent of Merlin and Nimuway. Member of the Royal Aelfdene Family.

He grew up loving books and hating magic. He had a very difficult childhood as his magic was "unusual." Of his six siblings, he was the closet to the youngest of his sisters, Willow. The only Arcane who uses nanofairies in battle, although he utilizes a wand, staff, bow, or timekeeper interchangeably, as his primary weapons of choice. However, he has been known not to need a weapon to be able to fight or cast magic. Spouse of Lord Dalton "Time" Yule. Father of Luciana Roslynn "Time" Yule-Ignatius. Ally to the Houses of Phoenix, Ignatius and Elder. Best friend of Cedric, Minnie, Lord Dalton Time Yule, and Amelia Pendragon. [Appearing in books I & II as Noble Elder, books III-V as Noel].

Lord Dalton Time Yule (High Arcane, Arcane of Magical & Mystical Experience, Elder, Grand ArchSorcerer, Master of Time)

Successor of Elder Yule. Upon his father's death became the Master of Time. Spouse of Noel. Papa of Luciana Roslynn "Time" Yule-Ignatius. Younger brother of Lady Citrine Time Yule. He utilizes a wand, staff, or the timekeeper interchangeably, as his primary weapons of choice. However, he has been known not to need a weapon to be able to fight or cast magic. Is noted to be thousands of years old. Master of Time and Time Turner. [Appearing in books II-V].

Luciana Roslynn Time Yule-Ignatius (High Arcane, Arcane of Magical & Mystical Experience, Elder, Grand ArchSorceress, Master of the Curpendulums & Time)

Successor of Noel. Upon her father's death became the Master of the Curpendulums and Time. Daughter of Noel and Lord Dalton Time Yule. See utilizes a wand, staff, or the timekeeper interchangeably, as his primary weapons of choice. However, she has been known not to need a weapon to be able to fight or cast magic. Master of Time and Timeturner. [Appearing in books III-V].

Mr. Cee (Arcane of Magical and Mystical Experience, Familar)

Cat of Russell Ambrose Elderchild Ignatius, Jr. Is an shapeshifting animagius. All black cat. His right eye is blue and his left eye is green. Serves as the protector of Noel in panther form [Appearing in books II-V].

Fintan (Arcane of Magical and Mystical Experience, Familar)

Phoenix of the Noble Elder, passes from one Noble Elder to the next. Multi-colored Phoenix based off magic use or affect. [Appearing in books III-V].

Lampos (Arcane of Magical and Mystical Experience, Familar)

Mystic Stallon of Avalon, will aid those in greatest need. Protector of Avalon, white in color, immuned to magic. Assists Noel when needed. [Appearing in books III-V].

Aelfdene Village House of Ignatius

Archduke Elvey Peter Ignatius (Mundane of Arcane Experience, Member of the Aelfdene Royal Court)

Elf,

Serves as the overseer, Archduke, and head of the Aelfdene village from another timeline. One of the last remaining Member of the Royal Aelfdene Family. Non-magical. Grandson of the Late Peter Kelvin Ignatius. [Appearing in book III].

Duchess Nordika Destiney Ignatius (Mundane of Arcane Experience, Elf, Member of the Aelfdene Royal Court)

Serves with her brother as the overseer, Duchess, and head of the Aelfdene village from another timeline. One of the last remaining Member of the Royal Aelfdene Family. Non-magical. Granddaughter of the Late Peter Kelvin Ignatius. [Appearing in book III].

Archduke Lucas Ignatius of the Glen Sheldon (Arcane of Magical Experience, Elf, Member of the Aelfdene Royal Court, Sorcerer)

Serves as the overseer, Archduke, and head of the Aelfdene village. From the elfin tribe of Sheldon. Succeeded his father as regent of his family's glen. Appointed by King Alezander Ignatius to oversee the Aelfdene village. Cousin to the King through the paternal line. Lukas' father is one of the younger brothers of King Casper Ignatius. Cousin to Alvina, Maria and Avery. Nephew of the Lady Otta Ignatius [Appearing in books I-V].

Countess Alvina Ignatius of Glen Sprite (Arcane of Magical Experience, Elf, Member of the Aelfdene Royal Court, ArchSorceress)

Member of the Ignatius Royal Family at the level of Baroness. Serves as an overseer to the Aelfdene village. From the elfin tribe of Sprite. Head of the Sprite Library. Sister of Maria and Avery. Daughter of Otta Ignatius. Cousin of Lucas Ignatius and King Alezander Ignatius [Appearing in books II-V].

Countess Maria Ignatius of Glen (Arcane of Magical Experience, Elf, Member of the Aelfdene Royal Court, ArchSorceress)

Member of the Ignatius Royal Family at the level of Baroness. From the elfin tribe of Sprite. Serves as an overseer to the Aelfdene village. Sister of Alvina and Avery. Daughter of Otta Ignatius. Cousin of Lucas Ignatius and King Alezander Ignatius [Appearing in books II-V].

Duke Avery Ignatius of Glen Sprite {aka Duke Sprite} (Arcane of Magical Experience, Elf, General, Member of the Aelfdene Royal Court, Sorcerer)

Serves as the second overseer when the Archduke Ignatius is not present. From the elfin tribe of Sprite. Member of the Ignatius Royal Family. Succeeded his father as regent of his family's glen. Appointed by King Alezander Ignatius to help oversee the Aelfdene village. Cousin to the King through the paternal line. Avery's father is the second eldest brother of King Casper Ignatius. Youngest child of Duke Ignatius and Lady Otta Ignatius. Younger cousin to Alvina and Maria. Master horseman. Highest ranking elf Archer Commander [Appearing in books II-V].

Lady Otta Ignatius (Arcane of Magical & Mystical Experience, Elf, Seer of Aelfdene)

The seer of the Aelfdene village. Is a member of the Ignatius Royal Family. Wife to the Duke. Mother of Alvina, Maria, and Avery. Stripped of her powers by Lord Time Yule. Concerns around prophecies and loyalty. Sister-in-law to King Caspar and Dowger Queen Mora Ignatius [Appearing in books II-V].

Deceased Members of the House of Ignatius

King Caspar Ignatius (Arcane, Elf, Wizard)

Deceased King of the Elves. Father of Alezander, Raven and (Brother) Ignatius. Spouse of Mora Elder. Grandfather of Ari, Theo, Hope, Vivian, and Russell Ignatius. (Deceased). [Prequel].

The Divine House of Noble

The living house of the Elders also known among the Arcane as the "Nobles." The Nobles are an extraordinarily gifted group of Arcane appointed by the Celestials to serve as the leaders of the Arcane. Formed the first council of Arcane. Govern the rules of magic. The Nobles are thousands of years old and live among the Arcane. The Nobles are comprised of the Elders, The Celestials, and the Elegent House of Yule.

The Elders of the House of Noble

Noble Elder (High Arcane, . Succeeded by Russell Ambrose Alexander Elderchild Ignatius, Jr. Arcane of Magical & Mystical Experience, Elder, Grand ArchSorcerer)

Member of the Arcane Council of Light. Most powerful living magical being. Father of Elder Light. Grandfather of the Lady of White [Appearing in books I-V].

Elder Illiminuary (High Arcane, Arcane of Magical & Mystical Experience, Elder, ArchSorcerer)

Member of the Arcane Council of Light, later became the Head of the Arcane Council and was succeed by the Noble Elder. He is an Elder. Died mysteriously without explantation. Best Friend to Queen Phoenix. Held the only known magical cure against the darkness. Is equal to Anwara, Noble Elder and Elder Yule in power. [Appearing in book III].

Elder Light Noble (Arcane of Magical & Mystical Experience, Elder, Wizard)

Member of the Arcane Council of Light. Grandfather of Mora Elder. Son of Noble Elder. Husband of Lady Elder Noble. Father to the Lady of White Noble [Appearing in book I].

Lady Elder Noble (Arcane of Magical & Mystical Experience, Elder, Witch)

Member of the Arcane Council of Light. Grandmother of Mora Elder. Daughter-in-law of Noble Elder. Wife of Elder Light Noble. Mother to the Lady of White Noble [Appearing in book I].

Lady of White Noble (Arcane of Magical & Mystical Experience, Elder, Witch)

Mother of Mora Ignatius. Daughter of Elder Light Noble and Lady Elder Noble. Grandmother to King Alezander Ignatius [Appearing in book I].

Lord Count Vladimar Dracula (Arcane of Mystical Experience, Vampire)

The first vampire. Member of the Council of Light. Possesses magical power. Father of the vampires. Ally of Noble Elder and Elder Yule [Appearing in books II-V].

Lady Minnie (Arcane of Mystical Experience, Elder Animagus Vampire)

The vampire animagus assistant to Noble Elder. She serves as the guardian of the Sancutary of Legend and Lore and the Noble Elder. Much of her back origin is unknown until Noel discovered she is the niece of Cedric. Protector of the line of

Noble Elders. Holds the various secrets of the post of Noble Elder. Youngest of the Elders. [Appearing in books II-V].

The Celestials

Lady Anwina, "Anwina, the Luminous" (High Arcane, Immortal)

Celestial whose powers are unknown. Is an immortal being. Known amongst the magical texts and teaching as "Anwina, the Luminous Being of Light," she is known by her friends and family as the Lady Anwara. She is the mother of Meredith Amser and Sloan. Grandmother of the Ignatius Seven. Mother in-law to Russell Ambrose Alexander Elderchild Ignatius, Sr. She is mysterious, her magic is complex, and many times misunderstood or feared among the Arcane. [Appearing in books II-V].

Sloan, the Nature Warrior (High Arcane, Immortal)

Celestial whose powers are unknown. Is immortal. Known as the Nature Warrior. Son of the Lady Anwara, "Anwina, the Luminous Being. Younger brother of Meredith Amser. Brother-in-law to Russell Ambrose Elderchild Ignatius, Sr. Uncle of the Ignatius Seven [Appearing in books II-V].

<u>*The Elegent House of Yule*</u>

Elder Yule (High Arcane, Arcane of Magical & Mystical Experience, Elder, ArchSorcerer)

The Master of Time. The origins of Elder Yule are unknown. One day, he just showed up, appointed by the Celestials to the Council of Light. Controls and manipulates the power of time. Creator of the Timekeeper [Appearing in books II-V].

Lady Nova Astria Yule (Arcane of Magical & Mystical Experience, Elder, ArchSorceress, Sister of Avalon)

Wife of Elder Yule. Mother of Lady Citrine Time Yule and Lord Dalton Time Yule. Is considered one of the most powerful seers. She is the co-leader of the Sisters of Avalon. Foretold many of the prophecies of the Arcane and Mundane alike. Parents and lineage are unknown [Appearing in books II-V].

Lady Citrine Time Yule (Arcane of Magical & Mystical Experience, Elder, ArchSorceress, Master of Time)

Keeper and store owner of Citrine's Antique. Master of Time. Tinker of clocks and is known for her exceptional skills in rebuilding clocks. Older sister of Lord Dalton Time Yule. Sister-in-law of Noel. Aunt of Luciana Ignatius. [Appearing in books II-V].

❧

The House of Brewer

Mr. Bruno Brewer (Arcane of Mystical Experience, Dwarf)

Member of the Dwarf High Council. Owner of Dwarfbrew. Father of Alviss Brewer. Father-in-law of Chalia. Grandfather of Goodra and Bardagul. Brother of Mr. Bruin. Wealthy. Worked for King and Queen Ignatius. [Appearing in books III-V].

Mr. Bruin Brewer (Arcane of Mystical Experience, Dwarf)

Second in charge of the Academy Library. Dwarf Warrior. Best friend of Mr. Giggles. Brother of Mr. Brewer. Uncle of Alviss Brewer. Queen Roslynn's right-hand assistant in the library [Appearing in books II-V].

Alviss Brewer (Arcane of Mystical Experience, Dwarf)

Member of the Dwarf High Council. Father of Goodra and Bardagul Brewer. Spouse of Chalia. Son of Mr. Brewer and nephew of Mr. Bruin. Wealthy. Dwarf Warrior. Best Friend of Noel. Protected in alternative timeline by King and Queen Ignatius. [Appearing in books III-V].

Chalia Brewer (Arcane of Mystical Experience, Dwarf)

One of three female Members of the Dwarf High Council. Mother of Goodra and Bardagul Brewer. Spouse of Alviss Brewer. Dwarf Warrior. Best Friend of Noel. Protected in alternative timeline by King and Queen Ignatius. [Appearing in books III-V].

Gorodra Brewer (Arcane of Mystical Experience, Dwarf)

Daughter of Alviss and Chilia Brewer. Granddaughter of Mr. Brewer and older sister of Bardagul. Dwarf Warrior. Protected in alternative timeline by King and Queen Ignatius. [Appearing in books III-V].

Bardagul Brewer (Arcane of Mystical Experience, Dwarf)

Son of Alviss and Chilia Brewer. Grandson of Mr. Brewer and Younger Brother of Gorodra. Dwarf Warrior. Protected in alternative timeline by King and Queen Ignatius. Godson of Noel. [Appearing in books III-V].

<u>House of Dragonne—The Dragon Guard</u>

Dione (Arcane of Magical & Mystical Experience, Dragon)

The original beauty and danger. Dione was the only living dragon for centuries and worked closely with the Elders. She had one child , the great Queen Belinda. She is known as the first and the one to whom all dragons came. Ally to the Houses of Phoenix, Ignatius, and Elder [Appearing in books III-V].

King Drago (Arcane of Magical & Mystical Experience, Dragon)

Second eldest dragon, Father of all dragons, King of all Arcane beasts. Spouse of Belinda. Ally to the Houses of Phoenix, Ignatius, and Elder [Appearing in books I-V].

Queen Belinda (Arcane of Magical & Mystical Experience, Mother Dragon)

Eldest dragon. Mother of all dragons, Queen of all Arcane beasts. Spouse of Drago. Ally to the Houses of Phoenix, Ignatius, and Elder [Appearing in books I-V].

Autumn (Arcane of Magical & Mystical Experience, Familiar)

Princess dragon. Child of the king and queen dragon. Ally to the Houses of Phoenix, Ignatius, and Elder [Appearing in books I-V].

House of Fae

Queen Amaryllis Fae (Arcane of Magical & Mystical Experience, Fairy)

Queen of the Fairies. Mother of Phineas Fae. Friend of the House of Phoenix. One of twelve original founders of the Arcane realm. Serves as the guardian of Oak Glen. Head of the Fairy Council and Army [Appearing in books I-V].

Prince Phineas Fae (Arcane of Magical & Mystical Experience, Fairy)

Prince of the Fairies. Son of Queen Amaryllis. Second of the Fairy Nation. Husband to Lady Bethany Phoenix. Professor of Agriculture at the Arcane University [Appearing in books I-V].

Lady Bethany Minerva Fae {Nee: Phoenix} (Arcane of Magical Experience, Witch)

Princess of the Arcane. She is the cousin of Oliver, Ethan, Daemon, Eric, and Roslynn Phoenix. She is the best friend of Sebastian and grew up in the Arcane realm. She is the spouse of Prince Phineas Fae. She is a Professor of Arcane Studies and becomes the Chancellor of the University. She is the daughter of Wade and Bethany Phoenix. She is the granddaughter of Titus and Flora Phoenix and the great-granddaughter to Merlin and Nimuway Phoenix. She is a member of the Arcane Council [Appearing in books I-V].

Fayette of Glen Willow (Arcane of Magical & Mystical Experience, Fairy)

Fairy student at the Arcane University. Assistant to Professor Fae. Come from the Glen Willow Tribe of Fairies. Garden Fairy with magical abilities in teleportation, earth magic, and herbology.

Marigold of Glen Oak (Arcane of Magical & Mystical Experience, Fairy)

Serves as a earth fairy tending to the flowers. Was the fairy to discover the rise of the Dark Army and alerted the queen.

The House of Pendragon

King Arthur Pendragon (Mundane, King)

King of Camelot. Head of the Knights of the Round Table. Spouse of Gwenivere. Friend of High Kind Alezander Ignatius. Ancestor of Olivia Pendragon Phoenix [Appearing in books I-V].

Queen Gwenivere Pendragon (Mundane, Queen)

Queen of Camelot. Spouse of Arthur Pendragon. Ancestor of Olivia Pendragon Phoenix [Appearing in books I-V].

Brooke Pendragon (Mundane)

Descendent of King Arther and Queen Gwenivere Pendragon. Is the sister of Olivia Pendragon Phoenix. Sister-in-law to Oliver Phoenix. Grandmother of Amelia Pendragon. [Appearing in books I-V].

Amelia Pendragon (Mundane)

Descendent of King Arther and Queen Gwenivere Pendragon. Is the granddaughter of Brooke Pendragon. Grear Niece to Oliver and Olivia Phoenix. Cousin of Martha Magnus. Best Friend of Russell Ambrose Alexander Elderchild Ignatius, Jr. She is a master of technology, exceptional fighters, non-magical but has exceptional knowledge of the Arcane. Created the new knights of the round table. [Appearing in books II-V].

Arcane of Mystical Heritage

Lord Count Conrad, The Second Dracula. (Arcane of Mystical Experience, Vampire)

Son of Vlad Dracula. The second Lord Count Dracula. The head of the Vampire covens. Prisoner in the Priory of Dark. Good friend to Lord Dalton Time Yule. Ally of the House of Ignatius and the Magical Three. Sworn enemy of Merlin [Appearing in books II-V].

Conway (Arcane Mystical Experience, Vampire)

Second of the vampire conven. Prisoner in the Priory of Dark [Appearing in books II-V].

Cedric (Arcane Mystical Experience, Vampire)

Vampire. Butler to the House of Phoenix. Protector of the family. Age is unknown. Feared by Merlin. Friend to the Houses of Phoenix and Ignatius. Keeper of many of the secrets of the Houses of Phoenix and Ignatius. Protector of the Ignatius children. Uncle of Minnie. [Appearing in books I-V].

Leo (Arcane of Mystical Experience, King, Creature)

The king of the forest. Lion. Spouse of Lucy and one of twelve original founders of the Arcane realm. Member of the Arcane Council [Appearing in books I-V].

Lucy (Arcane of Mystical Experience, Queen, Creature)

The queen of the forest. Lion. Spouse of Leo and one of twelve original founders of the Arcane realm. Member of the Arcane Council [Appearing in books I-V].

Leaf (Arcane of Mystical Experience, Wizard)

Animagus. Friend to the Magical Three. Member of the Arcane Council [Appering in books I-V].

Athena (Goddess, Greek Mythology, Immortal)

The great goddess of all knowledge, warfare, and strategy. Serves as advisor to Queen Roslynn Ignatius and the Lady Mora Ignatius. Keeper of the Library of Knowledge [Appearing in books II-V].

Gloria (Arcane, Witch)

Is a clerk in the store of Citrine's Antiques. Works as the decoy of the Lady Citrine Time Yule in the shop. [Appearing in books III-V].

Ms. Claria (Arcane, Witch)

News reporter with Arcane Tribune. Is the Arcane Gossip Columnist reporting on all the happenings in the Arcane Community. Not liked by the House of Phoenix, Ignatius, Drake and Knight. [Appearing in books III-V].

The Faculty

Lady Marybelle (Arcane of Magical Experience, Sorceress)

Teaches reading at the Arcane Academy. Has the ability to animate texts and make them come to life. Head of Arts and the Humanities [Appearing in books II-V].

Professor Giggle (Arcane of Mystical Experience, Dwarf)

Eldest living dwarf. Teaches Economic Education. Has a temper. Best friend of Mr. Bruin [Appearing in books II-V].

Mr. Wolf (Arcane and Mundane of Mystical Experience, ½ Vampire)

Teacher of Physical Education at Arcane Academy. Co-chair of Physical Education [Appearing in books II-V].

Mr. Terran (Arcane of Mystical Experience, Centaur)

6'8" Centaur. Teacher of Physical Education at Arcane Academy. Co-chair of Physical Education [Appearing in books II-V].

Ms. Hoot (Shapeshifter, Arcane of Magical & Mystical Experience, Sorceress)

Teacher of mystical creatures. Creatures Mistress. Shapeshifter from human to owl. Taught Lord Leaf when he was a child [Appearing in books II-V].

Ms. Adwin (Arcane of Magical Experience, Sorceress)

Teacher of Art and Choral. Known as the Art and Choral Mistress. Has the ability to animate paintings and works of art. World-renowned artist. Type of Arcane is unknown [Appearing in books II-V].

Ms. Tulip (Arcane of Magical & Mystical Experience, Fairy)

Garden Fairy of earth and environmental magic. One of several fairies who can take full size and walk among the Arcane and Mundane. Teacher of Elemental Magic for Arcane Academy [Appearing in books II-V].

Lady O (Arcane of Magical Experience, Witch)

Assists around the Arcane Academy. Oversees nourishments for the students of the Arcane Academy [Appearing in books II-V].

~

Other Characters

Morgana (Dark Arcane, Sorceress)

Dark Arcane Sorceress. Self-declared Queen of the Arcane. Continues to be brought back to life by the Council of the Dark. Seeks the Curpendulums. Enemy of Merlin and the House of Phoenix [Appearing in books I-V].

Lady Raven Helegella Ignatius (Dark Arcane, Summoner, Witch)

Dark Witch. Assumed the role of second in command of the dark armies upon her teacher, Morgana's death. She is a Summoner of Darkness. General f the Dark Army. Love interest of Liam Knight. Younger sister of High King Alezander Ignatius. High Princess of the Elves. [Appearing in books I-V].

Lord Balimore Oblivion (Arcane of Magical Experience, Warlock, Head of Dark Council, True Origins are Unknown)

Serves as the head of the Dark Council. Sworn enemy of the Houses of Noble, Phoenix, Yule, and Ignatius. Servant of the Incubus King. Acts of a teacher and mentor to Merlin. His true origins are unknown but is believed to be as old as Anwina, "Anwina the Luminous." Adopted father figure to Merlin. [Appearing in books II-V].

Father Francisco (Arcane of Mystical Experience, Spiritual Leader)

Serves as the head of the Priories of the Arcane. Is the keeper of certain texts and Arcane artifacts. Spiritual advisor of the Arcane communities. Head of the covens. Serves as an intermediary between the Arcane and Mundane communities. Member of the Arcane Council. [Appearing in books I-V].

Key Groups

Sisters of Avalon (Arcane of Magical & Mystical Experience, Mystics, Seers)

Sisters of Avalon are a magical and mystical group of Arcane women whose duty is to protect all earthly magic and the knowledge of the Nobles and the Celestials. The Sisters serve as advisors to the Noble Elder, Elder Yule, and Arcane of Light. The Sisters are protectors of mystical artifacts held in Avalon. Mystic Healers. The Queen Nimuway serves as one of the two co-leaders of the Sisters of Avalon. The other co-leader of the Sisters of Avalon is the Lady Nova Yule. When Arcane women pass or ascend many of them become Sisters of Avalon swearing an oath to continue to protect magic, the Arcane, and the Mundane. Immortal upon becoming a Sister of Avalon. [Appearing in books II-V].

Council of Light {aka Arcane Council} (Arcane of Magical & Mystical Experience)

The Council of Light (aka the Arcane Council) is the governing body of all magic associated with the light. The Arcane Council has a love of life, Arcane and Mundane alike, earth. Work to protect all life. The term Council of Light if used to define the members of the ancient times the Nobles, and Elders appointed by the Celestials to guard and oversee magic. The use of Arcane Council was adopted by the new Council and serves as the current governing body of the Arcane. [Appearing in books I-V].

Council of Dark (Dark Arcane of Magical & Mystical Experience)

The Council of Dark is composed of Dark Arcane who left the Council of Light or are Dark Arcane who seek to control the Curpendulums. The head of the Council is Lord Balimore Oblivion. [Appearing in books I-V].

Vampire Coven (Arcane of Mystical Experience)

The Vampire Coven is the last remaining coven of pure vampires. Over the centuries, Merlin turned many of the vampires to his side. Angry, Merlin locked the Vampire Coven away in the Priory of Dark, as it is known by the Dark Arcane, or the Lost Priory, as it is known by all other Arcane. The Vampire Coven aids the Sisters of Avalon and anyone seeking to protect the Curpendulums. [Appearing in books I-V].

The Necro-Army (Arcane & Mundane)

The Necro-Army is the most powerful army in existence. Controlled by Noel. The Army is comprised of the souls of Arcane and Mundane who have died.

Fairy Council (Arcane of Mystical Experience)

The Fairy Council is comprised of the heads of each Fairy Tribe. The members of the Fairy Council serve as regents and advisors to Queen Amaryllis Fae.

Elemental Council (Arcane of Mystical Experience)

The Elemental Council is the five deities of the elements believed by the Arcane to be where all elemental magic descends from. An ancient council of magical and immortal beings, very little is known about them among the Arcane. The Elf scholars of Aelfdene preserved the knowledge and teaching of the Elemental Council and its five members in the pages of the Grimoire of Historia Terra.

The Noble Elder is the only known Arcane able to commune with the Council. The council is made of Lady Terra Nova the Lady of Earth, Lord Pyro Ablaze, the Lord of Fire, the Liege Adira Gali, the Liege of Water, the Liege Skye Coro, the Liege of Wind, and the Lord O'Ryan, the Lord and Master of Spirits and Ether.

❧

About the Author

Kurt W. Oster, LICSW, LCSW, MAT, RPT™ is a gay author, clinical social worker, and educator who advocates for the needs of children through his practice as a clinical social worker and as a Registered Play Therapist™.

His writing is devoted to encouraging the transformation of children with attention deficits, autism spectrum disorder, anxiety, OCD, ODD, learning challenges, and coming out issues. He explores these traditionally unspoken topics and brings awareness to neglected groups via his literary works and bibliotherapy that features neurodivergent and LGBTQ characters.

Kurt obtained his Bachelor of Arts (BA) from Rutgers University, a Master's in Social Work (MSW) from the University of Pennsylvania, and Master of Arts in Teaching (MAT) in Elementary Education from the University of Southern California.

Through his writing, Kurt aims to demonstrate that anything can be achieved while making storytelling enjoyable and changing how it is done.

Other Publications from Perceptions Press

Now Available from
All Genders Press
A division of Perceptions Press
Publishing LGBTQ+fiction and non-fiction
https://allgenderspress.ca/

Rise of the Magical Three (2021, revised 2023)
House of Phoenix Chronicles, Book 1
Kurt W. Oster
Raised by a mysterious grandmother and believing their parents to be dead, Roslynn and her older identical twin brothers, Oliver and Ethan, had only read of magical beings and creatures. But, transitioning into young adulthood, the three embark on an incredible journey as they are introduced to the riddles of their family's past that will forever change who they are and are yet to become.

As the three siblings discover the ways of the magical arts, they quickly learn that they are not alone in their quest. Finding help when and where they least expect, the three develop friendships, confront the darkness, work together to save their family from an ancient curse, and learn of a mysterious and ancient bloodline that will forever shape the fabric of time and love.

Their fight becomes more significant than even they had anticipated and forces them to make decisions about whether they can effectively save the world, the multiple realms, and magic as they know it. Learning that magic is driven by passion, knowledge, bloodline, and time, will they be the ones to save time, or will they become mere echoes of time? (https://allgenderspress.ca/echoes-of-time/)

Secrets Echoed (2022, revised 2023)
House of Phoenix Chronicles Book II
Kurt W. Oster, LICSW, LCSW, MAT, RPT™

Ten years after the events that changed the very fabric of the Arcane and Mundane communities and set a new era of peace in motion, the incredible journey of Rose, Ethan, and Oliver continues. The Noble House of Phoenix, the most ancient of all Arcane bloodlines, must now forge and navigate new allegiances while living among the Mundane.

As the darkness claims control, the three siblings are, once again, thrust into the heat of battle. When multiple disappearances rock the Arcane community, the three siblings put aside their careers, differences, the spaces that separate them, parenthood, and time to join forces, working together again to save their families, friends, and the world as they know it.

In this battle of good and evil, the Magical Three learn of the Curpendulums, a most advanced form of magic. Will the Curpendulums provide the answer to their struggles against the darkness? Or will they prove to be the very weapon that the darkness needs to destroy all Arcane bloodlines and enslave the world? Will magic be lost forever? Lines are drawn, sides are taken, and new secrets are revealed, leaving all to wonder if the echoes of a dark past will remain or be forever changed.

(https://allgenderspress.ca/secrets-echoed/)

Mystical Way of Time (2023)
Kurt W. Oster, LCSW, RPT™
(A children's book)

In a moment of boredom, young Lord Time stops, thinks for a moment, then gets out his paintbrushes and starts creating.

What emerges is a beautiful village, with many people, all different but living and working together in harmony.

Take a magical journey with Lord Time and his sister, Citrine, as they stroll along the Mystical Way.

Here everyone is welcome, all are accepted, and each person celebrates the ways in which each one is unique.

When a new library opens, Lord Time and Citrine help create a memorable moment of acceptance for the new librarian in town.

(https://allgenderspress.ca/mystical-way-of-time/)

Bibi The Happy Trans Girl (2023)
Karla May-Strange
Bibi is a vibrant young transgender 7 year old who love everyone, especially herself. Perfectly Trans.
(https://allgenderspress.ca/bibi/)

Eli The Happy Trans Boy Takes Testosterone (2023)
Karla May-Strange
Eli is a tween, a transgender boy tween. He is just starting out on his journey to become a young adult.
(https://allgenderspress.ca/eli-the-happy-trans-boy/)

Norm As I Am! (2023)
Cy Nelson
Late spring brings larvae to the garden. Some are pink and some are blue. However, Norm does not conform to these expectations. Follow the journey to find Norm's rare and beautiful authentic self.
Available in French **Norm Comme Je Suis!**
Available in Spanish **Norm Como Soy!**
Available in Chinese **Norm Jiu Shi Wo!**
(https://allgenderspress.ca/norm-as-i-am/)

PUBLICATION EXPECTED IN 2021
The Gospel of a Witch
Diana Bishop

The 200 angels who procreated with human women and fathered the Nephilim were cast out of Heaven. Their Nephilim children were ordered by God to be destroyed because of their destructive and corruptive behavior on Earth, but not before they fathered children of their own. These children of Nephilim came to be the witches, vampires, and werewolves of lore. It was generally believed by these supernatural beings that God disapproved of them, although they were three-fourths human and were left untouched by the purge. Lena's parents were such Nephilim offspring. They suffered under the same assumption until they met Jesus when he was physically among humankind. They became a part of his discipleship and Lena was born in his presence. They, and, in turn, Lena, were charged by Jesus with the mission of spreading the message among the Nephilim decedents that they were loved by God and were welcome in Heaven upon their death, contingent on the life they had lived. *The Gospel of a Witch* is a part of Lena's story as she endeavors to complete her mission.
(https://allgenderspress.ca/the-gospel-of-a-witch/)

Coming soon from
All Genders Press
https://allgenderspress.ca/

PUBLICATION EXPECTED IN 2024
Things are Not What They Seem
House of Phoenix Chronicles Book IV
Kurt W. Oster, LICSW, LCSW, MAT, RPT™

Shifting, altering, and replaying over and over, one timeline after another is acting up. When fifteen timelines act up all at once, a new, rebellious Noble Elder must calm the chaos and re-establish the balance of time, magic, and everyday life. Noble Elder grows into their new role despite moments of wanting to throw up their hands and walk away. Traveling through time and meeting hiccup after hiccup along the way, Noble Elder collaborates with six, headstrong Ignatius siblings, learning to navigate complex and, at times, downright awkward relationships with them.

Working together and, sometimes, against each other, the Ignatius 7 quickly learn that things are not what they seem when they discover a truth that rocks the very core of what they know about magic. Noble Elder, tired of the growing attacks of darkness, seeks the help of Arcane and Mundane alike in a battle between light and dark.

When magic stops working because of time disruptions, RJ, Amelia, Minnie, and Dalton return to help and must learn to navigate complex friendship with the Ignatius 7. Will their epic journey to find the Curpendulums, restore time, and bring normalcy to the earth succeed? Will time break the spirit of Noble Elder, and stop time altogether? Or will Noble Elder discover new ways to handle the challenges of life, magic, and darkness?
(https://allgenderspress.ca/things-are-not-what-they-seem/)

PUBLICATION EXPECTED IN 2025
The Curpendulums
House of Phoenix Chronicles Book V
Kurt W. Oster, LICSW, LCSW, MAT, RPT™
(https://allgenderspress.ca/the-curpendulums/)

The **House of Phoenix Chronicles** *is planned as a series of books filled with wizards, witches, fairies, elves, dwarfs, centaurs, mermaids, and dragons in the fight of their lives to protect their ways of life, their families, and the earth. The Phoenix siblings, Roslynn and her older identical twin brothers, Oliver and Ethan, embark on a remarkable journey of friendship, romance, hatred, and mystery as truths are revealed, challenges faced, and battles with ancient darkness fought. Bending magic to their will, Roslynn, Ethan and Oliver, step in and out of time, breaking the rules at every stage of their remarkable journey. Along their way, they meet friends from the past, present, and future, and discover an ancient secret that could forever change the fabric of history, including our understanding of Medieval times and the Knights of the Round Table: a curse sent by darkness to unravel time as it is known. One minute, magic was at its height, the center of life and the community. In the next, cities and villages lay in ruins, a mere echo of a time that was. Can the three siblings channel their family's magic, one of the most powerful magical bloodlines ever to live, for good? Or will their efforts backfire, leading to the destruction of all magical beings? Will they be able to break the curse that affects their family? Can they save their bloodline and the ways of magic? Will they help bring magic back to earth, or will they become the continuation of the curse?*

PUBLICATIONS EXPECTED IN 2025
The Two Princes
Masters of the Curpendulum Book I
Kurt W. Oster, LICSW, LCSW, MAT, RPT™

PUBLICATIONS EXPECTED IN 2024
Holidays at the Mystical Way of Time
Kurt W. Oster, LCSW, RPT™
(A children's book)

Following his moment of boredom when he created a beautiful, magical village (see Mystical Way of Time), Lord Time and his sister, Citrine, continue to welcome villagers from diverse places to the Mystical Way. As a result, the village is bustling and ever-changing. But one shop remains empty. Suddenly, a unique-looking tree appears, and, like magic, snow begins to fall. Curious villagers turn to Lord Time and Citrine to sort out what is happening.

While exploring the situation, Lord Time and Citrine meet a new neighbor who has just moved to the Mystical Way. The villagers soon discover that their new neighbor is rather "odd," leading some of them to become concerned.

Lord Time, with the help of Citrine and Biblia, the librarian, find creative ways to promote acceptance and welcome their new neighbor while, at the same time, dealing with the ever-changing nature of time in the village. https://allgenderspress.ca/holidays-at-the-mystical-way/)

PUBLICATION EXPECTED IN 2024
Dancing Dylan is a Happy Non-binary Child
Karla May-Strange
(A children's book)
Dancing Dylan is a self confident, non-binary teenager. They/Them, Dylan, is enjoying the freedom of being genderqueer and learning how to experience life with an open heart.
(https://allgenderspress.ca/dancing-dylan/)

Publications from Other Divisions of Perceptions Press:

Perceptions Press www.perceptionspress.ca
Stephanie Castle Publications www.stephaniecastle.ca
TransGender Publishing www.transgenderpublishing.ca
Castle Carrington Publishing www.castlecarringtonpublishing.ca